Wingless

a novel

Wingless

a novel

Anuradha Muralidharan

BLUEJAY BOOKS

An imprint of Srishti Publishers & Distributors
New Delhi & Calcutta

BLUEJAY BOOKS
An imprint of Srishti Publishers & Distributors
64-A, Adhchini
Sri Aurobindo Marg
New Delhi 110 017

First published in paper back by *BLUEJAY BOOKS* 2004
Copyright © Anuradha Muralidharan, 2004

ISBN 81-88575-38-0

Typeset in AGaramond 11pt. by Suresh Kumar Sharma at Srishti

Cover design by Sandip Sinha
40/223, C R Park
New Delhi - 110 019
Email: sundeepsinha@yahoo.co.in

All rights reserved. No part of this publication may be reproduced, stored in a retrieval system, or transmitted, in any form or by any means, electronic, mechanical, photocopying, recording or otherwise, without the prior written permission of the Publishers.

They call me mad
but I know I'm not,
for what is madness
but sanity turned inside out.
They go along their
busy paths
seeking name and fame,
guts and glory
and I hide behind
the shadows
of my own self.

(stanza from the poem 'The Mendicant' – a collection of metaphysical poetry called ***The Garland*** *by Amara Bavani Ramdev)*

Contents

PROLOGUE

ONE SUMMER NIGHT

When Prabhu woke up that night, he didn't know whether it was to the sound of voices within or outside his head, which had disturbed his sleep. His dreams were always cluttered by frenzied activity. Unknown faces smiling and disappearing, people walking and him running behind them. Sometimes they smiled, other times they walked away. After these dreams he always woke up feeling tired, as though all the activity had drained his muscles of their power. It was ironic that many of those faces he saw in his dreams were nameless masks, which fell away like wasted skin in the morning. Once in a way, visions of his father and mother were there, smiling benevolently. He wanted them to hold him but they were smiling only at each other in a secretive manner. It was his father and mother that he wanted to hold, but he was always holding a faceless woman in a sexual position. These dreams were not about girls but about female bodies – sexual beings, and sometimes he tossed around in his sleep, caught in the throes of a pleasurable sensation. But in the mornings, these dreams also assumed an insignificance that belied their importance of the night before.

Whenever he awoke in the middle of a dream, he believed somehow that dream and reality were intertwined. The dark shadows of the night always aided that feeling. However, if he woke up in the morning, the dreams of the night before were barely there, like silhouettes of shadowed strangers walking down a dark corridor. If he tried to focus, they only walked away faster and receded to the chambers of his mind. So, he never bothered about them. The sexual dreams he believed to be a natural part of his manhood. He was in his late thirties and it was only natural that his body craved for a physical relationship. But his aim in life was not to dilute his focus with meaningless sexual encounters. Sex had a lot of power. If you allowed it to control you, then everything else would lose its importance. Not for him the surrender of control. Other men – and there were many in the village, could spend their nights and days in pursuit of sex, for him it was his land, the people on the land and the monsoons which brought him real happiness.

As he tossed tonight restlessly, he wondered if it was a dream or it was a noise outside that woke him up. In the dream he had been trying to kiss a woman – a faceless mask with a smile as secretive as the curves of her body and that was when he had heard the noise. He woke up with a suddenness, which sent the maiden of his dream scurrying into the corner of his mind. That was how life was. When illusion took over, it seemed so real. An interlude with a fantasy always assumed so much more than involvement of the senses and yet, with just one stroke, reality could wipe away all the sensations of a fantasy.

The dream was gone. In its place there was only noise. But it was a noise so delicate that it disturbed him in its faintness. Opening the window slightly, Prabhu peeped into the darkness. Outside, the moonless night cast dark shadows and the swaying trees seemed to take on strange and eerie shapes.

"Who is it?" he called out into the stillness.

Except for the slight rustling of leaves, as the wind blew through them, adding a ghostly sound to the quietness, there was a silence to the night. And then he heard the soft crunch of footsteps. There was no doubt that someone was creeping around outside!

"Who is it?" he shouted again.

His eyes strained to cut into the cloak of darkness surrounding the hut. And then he saw him, for just a second, before the person crashed into the bushes, disappearing into the night.

Prabhu tried to shut the window but the latch was broken and it swung open again. He went back to his cot. In the soft light of night, the room seemed cozy and cheerful. The small wick lamp played with the darkness, as dark shadows interspersed with pockets of light. He stared at the door, knowing that a slight heave would push it open. Why was that mad fellow walking around at this hour? But perhaps, that was what made a mad person different.

The slight disturbance had woken him up completely and as he lay in his cot, his eyes flitting around the little room, his thoughts wandered to Raju. Why had he been walking around in the middle of the night? It looked like he was searching for something or somebody, the way he was rushing into the bushes.

Prabhu tried to recall the dream again. Why was he dreaming about sexual encounters in the night when a real relationship with a woman seemed so unimportant in the daytime? He knew the answer – it was all there in his head. His past would not let go of him. He was forced to ignore the wants of his body as long as he could.

He watched a shaft of moonlight slanting its silvery rays into the room and in its soft beam of brightness he saw the photograph hanging on the wall. In the photo, his father boasted a bushy mustache that hinted at toughness, which Prabhu knew, was not really true of him. He took in his father's eyes and the slight frown on the forehead. The determined look in his eyes. This was the face of a man who had lived life with a purposeful goal. A man who knew his mind. Sometimes tough but at most times kind. There had been so much to this person but all that remained of him now was a photograph. All human beings became mere wall decorations after their lives had ended. But was that true? He questioned himself. These were not just photographs. They were actually memory catchers. The kind of memories they invoked in people who saw them was actually their touchstone to immortality.

From photographs to memories to life, Prabhu's mind revolved around a spectrum of images till he slowly felt his body succumbing to sleep. A soft breeze blew in through the open window, kissing the hairs on his forehead like a soft lullaby. In that state of consciousness which people experience when they are neither asleep nor awake, Prabhu's mind once again drifted around memories which came back to him sharp and clear. His grandfather had served the *maharaja*. It was a thought that pushed the others to the background and stood out prominently! He really had no idea as to why he suddenly remembered this fact. But he lay there allowing his thoughts to flow freely.

His little village, Karipumedu, flanked by the western *ghats*, had been the home of his great grandparents who had lived there long before the Britishers decided to come to India. In those days, the little village belonged to king Dharma Varma.

As he lay there with the rustling sound of the leaves whispering a soft tune in his ears, Prabhu imagined how life would have been then. Definitely the vessels were gleaming silver (he had one souvenir in his trunk under the bed) and the bed covers were pure silk. The cot he slept on now was nothing more presumptuous than a badly woven jute cot, but his grandfather had slept on a cot made of solid teakwood. The banisters were carved like lion's heads with their mouth hanging open in toothy smiles. Staring dreamily into the darkness, Prabhu felt he was back in that period of time. He searched for incidents stored in his subconscious, for little pieces of information that would help him in this memory journey.

His grandfather had been fond of hunting, his father often said proudly, and the bare walls used to be covered with the heads of bison and elephants, bearing testimony to that fact.

"Do you know that the elephant's heads would have their ivory tusks intact? My father had no use for the ivory. According to him it was better to leave it on the elephant's head to indicate how old and strong it was," Prabhu's father's fingers would play with his mustache as he recounted that particular tale while Prabhu sat at his father's feet, watching the inward growing toe nail on the third toe of his father's right foot.

"Those days we ate out of gold plates," he would whisper

softly as Prabhu wondered where the gold had gone. His mother wore a pair of plain gold earrings and Prabhu knew what gold was. He also knew that gold was very expensive, because his mother never took off her earrings even at bath times.

As though answering his thoughts his father had said, "Land is our gold Prabhu, and the paddy which grows on it, is equivalent to gold grains. Gold cannot feed an empty stomach but rice can, and I have bought all this land for you!"

Suddenly, like a breeze sweeping away a dead leaf, he lost touch with the glorious and transient life of his grandfather. The thought of land brought with it memories of his childhood. He saw himself as a little boy with his father. This was his life and hence the memories were more real. They caused strange feelings in the pit of his stomach and the region of his heart. Like shards of glass lying in sunlight, each memory evoked a matching emotion. He wished he could go back to thinking about his grandfather whose memories cloaked him like a warm shawl. But that had passed. He tried to sleep and keep his mind still but the memories continued to flood him like a sea in high tide.

His father too had lived on memories but that had not stopped him from joining the freedom movement. Prabhu remembered watching his father and a group of villagers huddling at night, talking softly. Somehow the memory of that incident drew a small film of sweat on his forehead, even now. When the police came, dressed in their tall headgear and khaki uniforms, he thought he would faint with fear and hid inside the kitchen.

But they had not beaten his father. They stood respectfully – the Indian police – doing a job they were secretly ashamed of. It was a strange charade where the accused held his head high and the accusers stood shameful and unhappy. They had walked behind his father like a king's bodyguards as he was led away. He never really knew why they had taken away his father but his mother mentioned proudly to all who would stop by that his father had hit a white man, a *vellaikaran!* This memory brought with it strong emotions. And now Prabhu did not feel that he wanted to shut them out.

How long ago all this had happened. In his own preoccupations he had never ever spent time thinking or recollecting these memories. He felt glad that he was able to do it now.

Another distinct memory was already crowding out the last one. His father had thrown away Prabhu's only silk dress, bought when he was a little baby, into a fire shouting 'Jai Hind!' Prabhu's eyes had watered a little from the smoke, but mostly from watching his silk shirt burning. The sharp feeling of losing something precious made Prabhu close his hands into fists even now. So strong was the emotion. That was one memory he did not relish. Why did his father have to be different? His grandfather would surely not have thrown away a silk shirt! It was the only time he resented his father's actions.

As the memories coagulated into those from his own life, it was as though his father had gone to reside in a photo frame on the window shelf along with his grandfather.

The memories came fast and furious – of his mother lovingly guiding him through school and childhood. Holding his little hand to help him frame words on the slate. His fingers would move helplessly, only finding direction when guided by his mother's. She would keep the slate like a precious possession till his father came back home. Then she would say excitedly, "See this. See what our little Prabhu wrote today." If it were a word in Tamil, his father would swing him high up in the air. But if it was a word in English he would scowl and say, "We don't need their language! We don't need them!"

His mother stood quietly, her face hidden in shadows. Her patriotism did not extend to moulding a son of the soil. She knew that it was only if he learned the foreign language that he would get a good job, perhaps a highly placed government one. Otherwise he would be nothing better than a peon. Torn between the two, Prabhu learnt to write in both languages. She never spoke aloud her feelings but he knew in his heart that she wanted him to learn English. So be it! *Amma* for mother. *Appa* for father. *Vellaikaran* – Englishman. Cotton – Khaki.

It was not only in the languages that he saw two different worlds. The little *beedi* shop (the only one in his village) sold *beedis* wrapped clumsily in flimsy paper, fighting for space with the exotic looking packets selling cigarettes. Prabhu knew what cigarettes were because he had watched carefully as men tore the cellophane packing, opened the packet and drew out the milky–white, chalk like stick. He watched as they put this between their lips and lit it. There was absorption in his gaze as they drew from it and blew out smoke.

In the dark, his hands searched for his cigarette packet. He only smoked a brand called *Scissors*, made in India. As he lit the cigarette, lying there in the enveloping darkness, he remembered the first time he had smoked. It was the day his father had been beaten by an Englishman sitting on a huge horse.

The horse rider had been trampling their paddy fields so his father shouted in English, "Do you know what that is you are trampling? It is our food! Without this we cannot live!" Anger had changed his father's face into a tightly drawn mask of skin and bones. As he watched his father's wrathful face, with a shock Prabhu realized that his father could speak English. He had never known this. Before he could register this shock he heard the sharp crack of a whip, which swept his father down to the ground with a thud!

When the man swung the whip Prabhu felt a pain. A pain in his heart, his mind and his limbs. So he ran. He ran towards the little shop and pulling out some change, gave it to the shopkeeper for a cigarette. Seeing the six-year-old boy, the shopkeeper had refused to sell one until Prabhu promised that the cigarette was for his uncle who had come from another town. It was Prabhu's first cigarette. He lit it carefully and dragged on it the way he had seen the men do.

The need to be Indian was never felt as strongly before! For his father, maybe it was easy because he was not so exposed to the advantages of the British Empire. He had shut his mind, but for Prabhu everything had a question attached to it and yet he also knew that to be loyal to his father meant that he had to follow in his father's footsteps. And so he never bought an attractively packed chocolate with the 'Made in Switzerland' mark though he could afford to. Instead he bought sweets made out of groundnut bound together with cane sugar or jaggery.

When he could read, and books on travel and the world in exotic color schemes began to be available in his school, he deliberately brought home badly printed and bound Tamil books. In every incident he knew clearly what he had to do, but the questions had persisted. Prabhu never knew whether his father was aware of the doubts in his mind but he did not wish to hurt him so he took special care to make sure he never knew.

He realized that his mother might have known because on those days when his father would be away, she mixed some strange powder in a kettle of water and gave it to him to drink. It tasted of meat and tomato and made him feel like a different person. It is soup she would say pronouncing the word as 'sooppu'. Whatever it was, it was something that the villagers did not drink. But when he drank it he was no more a villager's son. He felt that he could hold his own amongst any *vellaikaran*!

When he saw his father's hair turning grey, he knew that just like the fighting spirit was ebbing in his father's blood, similar feelings were being echoed by the British Empire.

When the English went away, he firmly believed that they did not see the possibility of being able to control this group of villagers. As Prabhu had never been out of his village he thought that all of India was a big village. Indians did not wear shirts.

They wore their dhotis like loincloths. They hated the English; in fact, they hated all fair skinned people. So why on earth should the English people stick around in this country?

But the fragile, old, loin cloth clad man who had made it his life's mission to send the Britishers away – did he know that he had also played a major role in Prabhu's life?

Prabhu remembered standing in a row along with other villagers. His father, now frail and old, was leaning against a tree, his head lolling on his shoulder like a tired limb. Prabhu had stayed with his father till the urge to roam had made him move away and mingle with the crowds.

"Mahatma is coming, Mahatma is coming!" the cry went up.

He knew what *mahatma* meant – a man with an extraordinary soul! Would he come in a golden chariot like the one his grandfather used to travel in? Or would he come on a big black horse? Prabhu waited and watched. When finally the Mahatma came, the skies had turned a curious purple colour, the clouds full of water that would burst any moment. But for once the villagers who loved the rains prayed loudly that it would not choose to come now. Was this Mahatma then more important than the rains too? For eight-year-old Prabhu this conflicting behaviour was tough to understand.

As the dust rose from the earth and people who stood in rows facing each other, shouted, 'Jai Hind', he saw the Mahatma coming. Old and thin but with spunky strides, holding onto a walking stick and yet using it only as a propeller to guide him, his feet hardly touching the ground, he raced across it.

The sweet he held in his hands dropped to the ground as an awestricken Prabhu raised his voice and shouted, 'Jai Hind'. He saw the Mahatma pause briefly near his father. Their hands touched and he saw tears flowing from his father's eyes. His own eyes clouded over as his father said something to the Mahatma and both turned in his direction. Mahatma smiled. A smile that reminded him of the rain soaked earth. Fertile and cherished. Smiling back, he shouted as loud as he could, 'Jai Hind'. As the Mahatma neared him, Prabhu tried to clean his grubby hands on the seat of his knickers all the time shouting like a maniac, 'Jai Hind'.

Gandhiji came to him and said, "When you grow up, look after the land and the people who live here. It is your duty."

Overcome, Prabhu bowed his head. When he looked up he saw that the old man had moved away.

The change in his life happened immediately and drastically. He no longer coveted the Swiss chocolates, the foreign cigarettes or even the books. He read the *Ramayana* and the *Mahabharata* written in Tamil. He read *Bharadhiyar* and he read *Thiruvalluvar*. His mind enriched with patriotism, he imbibed an understanding of his land, something he never thought had existed in him.

In the early morning light, he could see the calendar swinging softly. It was the year 1977. He was in his late thirties. The last few years had been almost monotonous in their similarity. Waiting for the rains, paddy cultivation, tending to his goats and cows. Alone, having lost both his parents and yet strangely disinterested in changing his single status, he focused his energies on making his little village one of his priorities.

When his father died, it was with a pleased smile on his face because he had lived to see India gain her independence. Sometimes, in moments like this, Prabhu almost envied his father his patriotism. That strong emotion had over ridden everything else, making every incident that happened a landmark in his life. Prabhu could barely remember any such incidents in his own life, which he could chalk up and say confidently that it had been a turning point or a milestone.

He had heeded the Mahatma's words and made the land and the people living in it his life's duty. It was a life filled with contentment and yet, there were moments when he felt that he was merely suspended in time. Neither moving forward, nor backward. He lived. He existed. Nothing exciting. At the same time, nothing dramatically sad. Suddenly he remembered the reason for having woken up. He had seen Raju creeping around in the darkness! He wondered what the boy had been up to.

When his eyes finally closed in sleep the first shafts of sunlight were slanting through the window into his room.

ONE Chapter

The villagers gathered around the dead body. It was a warm morning indicating that this summer would be a hot one. The heat was already playing havoc with the body. Prabhu pushed the crowd aside and looked at the face. Mariamma's dead face looked cold and yellow, like a slab of rotten fish. She smelled like one too. Crinkling his nose, Prabhu looked at the wound on the left side of her chest. A knife wound, which had pierced the thin cotton sari, had struck the loose blouse that clung to her shrivelled breasts and pierced the bony cage inside. A mound of caked blood marked the place where the knife had plunged into her body. Some flies were flitting around, unsure whether to land on the blood or not. Greying hair hung in dirty strands around her face. She looked a miserable sight when alive and if possible, looks even worse dead. The thought passed through Prabhu's mind as his eyes absorbed the details.

His mind roaming around, his thoughts shifted to Mariamma. He recalled her dirty face, with its deep wrinkles. The sun had burnt her skin and turned it into a leathery mask where the only expression was one of constant worry. How could she become like that? And yet, at one point in time she had been an attractive young girl, with black hair and dark secretive eyes. Was it lack of food that had turned her face into a leathery mask? Or was it her thoughts? Thoughts that had turned her son dumb and made her into an ugly old woman.

Standing near a tree he heard a mynah letting out a call to its lover. The sound distracted him, like a harsh reminder of the exotic world. To the dead it meant nothing, but standing here, near the dead body, knowing that the body could neither hear nor see nor experience, Prabhu felt a strange excitement. He was alive and he could enjoy the mynah's call. Just like in the nights he enjoyed the sexual fantasies he shared with his secret dreams. The human body could pleasure itself and it was an ultimate joy to know that you did not have to look outside for pleasure. He wondered slightly if it was fear of a relationship or fear of becoming unfocussed which had prevented him from getting married. Maybe a bit of both, he thought and wondered why suddenly the thought of marriage was haunting him when he was standing here near a dead body. Could it be that a dead body always brought home the fact that life was short? He didn't know the answers.

His eyes observed Mariamma's tangled hair. She looked mad! With a mother like that it was no wonder that Raju behaved the way he did, refusing to talk to anybody. Refusing to talk? Why had he stopped talking? His thoughts flitted round and round.

How old would Raju be? Eighteen, nineteen? Not more than that. Not only had the boy stopped talking, he walked in a strange fashion, shuffling his feet. The village children teased him about his ungainly appearance and he ran away when he saw grownups.

In an effort to shut out the stench and the scene, Prabhu moved away. He gazed at the sky – a clear, crisp blue, with soft, cotton wool clouds. He looked around him at the group of men. Each one of them had a name, a trait, an occupation and a wife. Some had more than one and some of the women standing around definitely had more than one husband. *Of course no one ever talked about that*! Prabhu looked beyond the men into the vista far away. In the distance, a train choo-chooed quietly like a toy and heads of paddy nodded softly to the billowing clouds. A few gooseberry trees, with their shady leaves and sour fruit, dotted the place. All around them palm trees grew, like tall sentinels guarding the scenic beauty.

He looked once again at the dead woman. Someone was calling for Gokulan and Prabhu saw him walk brusquely to the front.

Standing a little away from the body, Gokulan cleared his throat and said stiffly, "This is murder!"

Prabhu noticed the way Gokulan said the words, holding his breath as though the smell of the body would interfere with his words.

Though theirs was a small village, Prabhu realized that there were a lot of people about whose lives he knew next to nothing.

Come to think of it, he knew hardly anything about Gokulan himself! They had grown up together in the same village but while Prabhu was far richer than Gokulan, it was Gokulan's family who had always been the *panchayat* leaders. He tried to recall incidents about Gokulan. Yes! He had been a bit of a ladies man – even as an adolescent, he was constantly getting into trouble because of his escapades. Prabhu felt a smile playing with the corners of his mouth as he watched Gokulan now. He himself had never felt the need to find a woman. Life and land had much more to offer than any woman could, that's what he believed. Not that there weren't any attractive belles in the village. He knew that he would get married someday. But not now.

Gokulan's young wife, Rani, stood a little away from the crowds. She was nearly half his age! Prabhu watched Rani's dark and beautiful face. How did the man manage to find himself such a young wife? He really was a conqueror of hearts. He admitted to himself that women or not, Gokulan made a good leader for their village. Some of his solutions were not ones he himself would have decided – like the time he had allowed toddy to be brewed in a place close to the village. Till then their village had not had toddy or raw whisky, as it was called, and the effort of walking a few miles to get their quota had been a deterrent to avid drinkers. But now toddy was being brewed close by and Prabhu knew that several men spent their evenings there. With limited incomes and families to support, money spent on drinking was not a good idea. Prabhu felt that Gokulan had made a wrong decision about that one. There were other small incidents – incidents that the villagers did not notice but Prabhu had noticed. Like the time he had separated a couple because they belonged to different castes. The caste system was still rife in the village and Prabhu knew that many of the lower caste people did not even walk along the same paths, which he and Gokulan frequented.

Someone in the crowd made a noise – a mix of a gulp and a sob.

"This is murder!" Gokulan's eyes swept over the gathered crowd and came to rest on Samudi's tall frame.

Samudi quickly averted his eyes.

Once again his eyes swept over the crowd and he said loudly, "Hey Samudi, go and bring that Raju over here!"

"Raju?" asked Chinnadurai, an elderly man with a frail frame, leaning on a crooked walking stick. "What can that mad idiot do? He has not spoken to this lady, his mother, for so many years. Do you expect him to carry the body and light the pyre?"

"Don't I know that he is mad?" asked Gokulan, his voice indicating his displeasure at being questioned. "Of course! We all know that he is mad. But that is not important right now! The dead woman is his mother and someone needs to inform him. Go Samudi. Go and bring that fool here."

Samudi looked at the crowd and then ran in the direction of the lake. They all knew that Raju spent his time sitting on the banks of the dark lake, which supported the village with water when the rains forgot to arrive.

The villagers were silent as they waited for Raju to come. The only movement and noise came from the flies buzzing around.

Gokulan looked around for a place to sit. A little away stood a tall tree. He strode across and sat down on its protruding roots. As if on cue, the villagers took off the folded cloth hanging on their shoulders. Called *thundus*, the cloth varied in colour, texture and price, each indicating the status of the man on whose shoulder it hung like a soldier's stripes. Gokulan was the *panchayat* head and if Gokulan sat under a tree, the villagers knew that he was ready to take on his role as the village head.

Shutting his eyes, Gokulan folded his arms across his body. It pleased him to see that even with a dead body close by, the villagers never forgot to pay homage to him. A feeling of pride welled up but it was quelled by dismay as he tried to think of the best way to handle the problem. Unfortunately, all that his mind could conjure up were graphic pictures of the dead woman's face. Opening his eyes, he looked at the pitiable figure, now a distance away.

The crowds sat around him in a semi-circle and waited patiently for him to speak. Twirling his mustache, a habit he indulged in whenever he was thinking, Gokulan said, "Nambi, can you see if you can find out when the old lady died?'" His words were directed at a tall youth.

Nambi walked up and rubbed his hands against her upturned feet. They were like cold jelly. Moving to the front, he lifted her eyelids and looked into her eyes. Even sitting a distance away, Prabhu felt a shiver passing down his spine.

"She must have died around twelve in the night, Nambi said authoritatively.

The crowd's collective groans sounded like the distant breaking of thunder. Gokulan closed his eyes. Of course! Yesterday was the new moon night, a*mavasae*! It was the 12th of February 1977! He loved to remember dates along with the year. It somehow made him feel educated. How did he forget that it was a*mavasae*? This was an added complication. He sighed audibly and closed his eyes for a second. When he opened them, he saw that Nambi was waiting expectantly for further orders.

Looking hard at him, Gokulan asked, "Are you sure that she died at twelve in the night?"

Nambi nodded his head humbly.

"In that case," Gokulan sighed again before continuing, "we have to appease the gods. Murder on an amavasae night! This will bring us a lot of bad luck."

Murder on a new moon night at twelve meant that evil spirits had claimed the woman's soul. It would bring bad luck and disaster unless a sacrificial *pooja* was carried out at the Muneeshwara temple in the village. All the villagers knew this and they worried about missed rains and forgone meals.

One of the women piped up, "If the rains don't come this

time, we are done for."

"We shall bury Mariamma before noon today," Gokulan said, adding as an afterthought, "since Raju is not normal, would anybody else perform her last rites?" His eyes, half-closed in thought, swept over the assembled crowd.

Prabhu stepped forward and looked at Gokulan. "I will," he said in a whisper.

It was a day for surprises, thought Gokulan. First the time of the woman's death and now, Prabhu wanting to perform her last rites.

He got up slowly and walked towards the body. A few of the village woman had brought garlands of wild flowers, which they placed on her chest. A soft yellow sunflower covered the murky, red gash.

"Don't we need to inform the town police?" asked Prabhu, looking at Gokulan.

"What for?" asked Gokulan grimly. "Do you think they will try to solve the murder? They will only take some of us to the station and beat us up. We all know who did it, don't we?"

The crowd looked fearfully at him.

With his mustache trembling in the breeze and the hair on his forehead fluttering like windswept paddy stalks, Gokulan said in a stiff voice, "He cannot help it. He is mad. Let us not harm him by reporting to the police. They will beat him to pulp and turn him into a dog."

With that, he had pronounced the murderer, solved the death

ritual issues, and handled problems related to supernatural powers. All within a few minutes. That was Gokulan's power, thought Prabhu. It was this quick ability to make decisions and pronounce judgment that made him the *panchayat* head. Suddenly, out of the blue, like a blow to the head, he remembered the face peering at him in the darkness. So that was what Raju had been up to. Could madness push someone to murder his own mother? He tried to remove the word madness from his mind and think of Raju as a normal adolescent. A voice whispered that something was wrong, but the thought was elusive and only confused him all the more.

As the crowd waited for Raju to turn up, some of the older women sat in a circle around the body. One of them blew her nose loudly on her sari *pallu* and cleared her throat. A sad lyric of bygone years and dreams, of winds sweeping away the dust from the feet of human beings and burying them under the dirt of their deeds, burst out of her throat in a strong tune. The other women sang along and the sound of their moaning voices cast a spell of gloom over the men. They waited and watched, their eyes as clear as the morning sun, men whose women wept.

Suddenly, breaking through the noise, they heard the wail of an animal. A terrible wail that chilled the bones of the villagers and stopped the singing immediately. He came running through the crowd. The sound of a wail rose from his stomach hit his throat and was spat out harshly. Springing to action, some of the villagers held Raju as he stared at the body of his mother.

This is no murderer. This is the voice of a man gone insane with pain. A voice said inside Prabhu's brain.

Watching the mad boy, his mouth open, letting out inhuman wails, Prabhu felt a choking feeling in his throat. He cleared it, but it would not go away. A few tears crept down his face. Averting his eyes from Raju, Prabhu wiped his tears and looked around to see if anyone had noticed. All the men were crying quietly, tears rolling gently from their eyes like the falling of the first summer showers on a parched piece of land.

Prabhu went down to the lake and after a brisk scrub and bath, wore a white *thundu* around his waist. The village barber was sitting under a tree, waiting for him. The reverberating sound of the conch shell hit him as he began to feel the razor. As his hair fell off in chunks he wondered why he had volunteered to perform Mariamma's last rites. Why did he care? It was his duty to care for the people in the village. He provided them with land to stay on and employment on his paddy fields. But today he had gone a step further. He was involving himself in the life of an adolescent. Was this what duty meant?

As his thoughts fluttered around, his eyes focused on the activities happening around him and he saw Deva unsteadily cutting a few palm leaves. Deva's hands were shaking from the effects of the fresh palm toddy he had gulped down a little earlier, as he wove a green mat which would carry Mariamma's body, from the spot where she was found, to a clearing near the lake, where she would be burnt on a heap of wood and dried cow dung cakes. As his fingers knit the leaves together, Deva sang a song, from a film he had seen recently in the local tent. The song had a captivating tune but it was sung harshly and loudly. A few small boys gathered to watch Deva work and one of the boys began to tap his feet rhythmically. As though that was a signal, a man picked up a conch shell and blew it. Another man picked up a drum made from goatskin and beat his palm on it. The sound of the conch shell and the beating drum carried the message of death. It hit the tall palm trees from which birds flew out, disturbed from idle chatter. An unperturbed Deva lowered his voice and continued to hum the lyric. The sound of the mournful background music fell heavily on Mariamma's body.

Prabhu closed his eyes and listened to the noises around him – the sharp click of the barber's scissors, Deva's song, and the conch shell. Could someone stuff that conch shell with cotton wool, he felt like asking. But that would be construed as disrespect for the dead. Ironically, the dead cannot hear and this noise can kill the living. Despite the situation, Prabhu felt a smile breaking out on his face.

As the sun climbed up the eastern sky, Prabhu led a small procession to the clearing where bodies were burnt. His bald head smelt faintly of sandalwood and lake water and he carried a small pot from which wafted the smell of burning charcoal. A group of young boys in torn shorts swung their arms and legs and danced to the beat of the goatskin drum. Their bony knees and thin legs moved freely in the loose khaki shorts they wore. One boy beat his chest the way he had seen his mother do when she was close to a dead body but his actions were at odds with his mouth which laughed with glee at the freedom of his limbs.

Gokulan, Pandiyan and Nambudri followed this group. The fourth person was Raju whose body was doddering under the weight of his mother's left foot. To help him along, Rani, Gokulan's wife walked beside him, supporting his body weight on her young frame. As they walked, she covertly looked at his face more than once but all that she could perceive was a silence. A heavy silence. No tears, no anger, just silence, which covered her heart like a dark robe. She saw that his eyes were half closed and his shoulders seemed to bend under the weight of the body. Somehow that bothered her. Why could he not walk straight? Why did he have to bend so? Why did she feel guilty about the way he walked?

Wasn't she able to walk straight in spite of all that she had been through? Life hadn't been easy for her so far. Her mind drifted to her marriage to Gokulan that had happened under the most extraordinary circumstances. Her father had borrowed heavily from Gokulan when the monsoons failed. She had been a little girl of fifteen, with dark eyes and long black hair. Often, she would hear her father and Gokulan talking loudly. Whenever Gokulan came by, her father would quickly usher all of them into the little hut and shut the door. She would peep from the keyhole, where a little ray of sunshine penetrated. Once when she heard her father's voice raised in anger, she had stepped out. It was a bright morning and the sun's rays got into her eyes, after the dimly lit interiors of the hut. As she blinked and stood there, her young figure outlined against the green hut, she didn't realize that Gokulan's eyes had fallen on her. She didn't realize that at that very moment, Gokulan had found a way to get his money back from her father. She didn't realize any of this. All that she did realize was that her father was suddenly looking at her with scared eyes. He seemed to look at her and then again at Gokulan. His eyes seemed to dance between the two of them. Finally when her eyes had adjusted to the light, she heard Gokulan asking her father, "Is this your daughter?"

She never waited to hear what her father said as she ran back into the hut.

The next time Gokulan came by, it was a year later and the month was September. The time of year when the rains are spent and cooler days are on their way. This time his voice was soft and her father's was angry. She wondered when the roles between them had switched, but these were thoughts that she did not discuss with anybody. She watched with interest when her father brought Gokulan into the house. He ensured that she was outside this time. But there was a definite advantage in being outside rather than inside, because she stood just near the door and listened to what they talked. She could also sprint away if they caught her listening. Her mother, standing beside her father, was crying softly. Rani noted with interest the way Gokulan pressed a laden tray into her father's hands. But when he opened the door suddenly and asked her to come in and wear the red sari, she felt a strange fear passing through her heart. The only times she had seen this happening was when one of the girls in the village was getting married. But she was too young and Gokulan did not have any sons. His three children from his first wife were younger than her, but not by too many years.

She wanted to ask her father what the matter was but the look in his eyes bothered her and she had dumbly changed into the sari. Her mother had marched her into the little room, where Gokulan sat in a corner on a small stool. His hands were playing with his mustache but he was watching her intently. She wanted to meet his eyes, but her feet seemed so clumsy with the weight of the sari dragging her down. She had walked slowly, careful not to trip.

That night, as she lay awake outside the hut, watching the stars, her mother had crept up to her softly.

"Amma, why did you make me wear that sari and walk in front of that old man, Gokulan?" The question was matter of fact.

"Hush!" her mother's fingers shut her mouth as she said softly, "he is not an old man. He is barely forty years old."

"Forty! And not old?"

How could that be? She was only sixteen. He was more than double her age!

"Rani, do you believe that your father has done a lot for you?"

She tried to think of instances that meant her father had done a lot for her. Yes, he had given her two meals a day (which was more than some families had). He had stopped her from going to school (because it was too far and her feet would hurt, he had said). He had made her work in the fields for Rs.15 a day (which I will save for you, he had said). Yes, he had done a lot for her.

Her young heart had felt a strange guilt stir in it.

"Do you know that you now have a chance to repay him?" Her mother's words were like a soft whisper. Without pausing, she added, "Gokulan wants to marry you and if you do, he promises to forget all the money your father owes him."

Her heart stopped beating and then it raced like a storm torn sea. She wished that she could shut out the words but there was no way she could. She watched her mother's face, wondering why her mother was crying. After all it could not be all that bad if her father's loans were cleared! She remembered listening in fear to her parents' discussions. We have to live in the outskirts - inside caves. She had been so terrified. Those dark caves with no sunlight and the roof hanging low over your head. The only time she had gone inside one, she had felt faint as though the breath was being crushed out of her body. The roof of heavy stones looked like they were hanging there precariously, waiting for a chance to fall on her. She had run out and promptly vomited!

She felt a strange contentment now. She could show her father that he need not worry.

"Why are you crying Amma? I don't mind marrying him. He is a little old but I am sure he will look after me like you and Appa do."

Her words only made her mother cry all the more and the tears seemed to roll on and on all through the wedding ceremony and after.

Once the decision was made, with the suppleness of youth to support her, Rani quickly adjusted herself to her role as Gokulan's wife. She tended to his first wife's children, playing the role of mother, when she was barely a few years older than them. She spent the nights in Gokulan's arms, wondering why he did all that he did to her body. When she asked him, he had laughed and said that she would soon have a little baby of her own.

"But why do I need a baby, we have so many already," she had replied, trying to twist her body out of his grip when she felt the stinging slap. After that, she knew better than to talk at night time and learnt to accept the atrocities to her body.

As she walked now supporting Mariamma's body, her eyes swept over Raju. He would be only around her age and yet, she felt so much older than him. Marriage did that to one. Maybe if Raju got married he would be all right. She should suggest this to Gokulan.

Rani was not the only one whose mind wandered. As the pallbearers walked, each one was preoccupied with his thoughts and fears. Gokulan walked quietly but his thoughts were not quiet. They never were. In fact, in the nights after he had sated his desires on his young wife, he lay awake staring at the darkness. Many a night he was sure that there was someone creeping around outside, waiting for a chance to come in and stab him. But in the daytime, when the sun shone brightly, he managed to stall the fears and focus on his role as *panchayat* head.

As they walked, he saw a procession of black beetles on their own busy journey, transporting food. As was his habit, he brought his foot down on them heavily, crushing them. In his anxiety to ensure that they were dead he rotated his left foot over them, till he felt the other pallbearers staring at him. They were not moving in unison!

Prabhu walked quietly in the front, the burning charcoal in a little pot, bearing testimony to the fact that it would soon be setting fire to a body. This role was not new to him. In fact he could even say that he was experienced at this. When he was barely five, he had walked with his father to burn his grandfather's body. Then he had walked alone to burn his father's body and a year later his mother's.

Strangely death did not bother him. After all, he had seen his father die a happy man and he remembered his father's last words, "Son, don't cry for me when I die, as I die a happy man. Instead, concentrate on doing everything you want to do in this lifetime. Because then, when you die, it will be a happy death. Don't waste even a single day."

As he remembered his father's words, the same listlessness of spirit attacked him. What was he doing with his life? He was nearly forty years old. There was not a single incident, which he could chalk up as a milestone. He just seemed to exist like the stars, the mountains, the earth and the sun. The same continuity! Nothing new. Nothing different.

A few women and children tagged along. Two of the women were loudly discussing Mariamma's earrings. Apparently, the gold studs were missing. So was the finger ring – a gold one with a ruby studded in its centre. One woman was sure that the murderer had benefited, but the other woman felt that the jewelry must be hidden somewhere in her hut. Both silently decided that they would pay Mariamma's house a visit later in the night.

The ceremony did not take more than an hour. If there was any delay, it was because the damp firewood took a long time to light up. The burning smell of dry cow dung, charcoal and firewood swept the place, its acrid smell burning the villagers' nostrils. A few of the village drunks were dancing rhythmically to the beat of the goatskin drum. One persistent old lady insisted on telling Mariamma's tale in a loud, wailing tone. She often referred to Mariamma's mad son who had the devil in him, who had caused his mother untold pain, and finally, death.

If Raju heard her, his face revealed nothing as he stood, leaning crookedly on a nearby tree. His eyes seemed focused on two sparrows, sitting on a branch. Prabhu, who was watching Raju, followed his gaze and saw the sparrows. In their fluttering hurry to get on with life, the sparrow's tiny claw kicked an egg. As Prabhu and Raju watched, the egg fell down and crashed. The two birds flew around the broken egg, their wings whispering their sorrow. Huge tears rolled down Raju's cheeks and wet his shirt. Prabhu ran across to the boy, but hearing the footsteps, Raju turned and ran off.

Someone who cried at the distress of sparrows! Was this the behaviour of a murderer? Worry gnawing his insides, Prabhu wished he could drink toddy and stop thinking, losing his mind to intoxication, like Deva. But somehow he had never got into that habit. Automatically, his hand reached for the familiar cigarette packet when he realized that he did not have his shirt on. Wiping his sweating face, Prabhu cursed softly under his breath. It was turning out to be a hot day. He looked around for Gokulan. He needed to go home and find his cigarettes. In the sharp afternoon light, the lake shone green and clear. Gokulan was washing his hairy body. Prabhu walked up to him and sat down on the bank, his feet resting in the water.

"What kind of ceremony did you have in mind?" he asked.

"Not ceremony. Pooja to appease the gods. Goat sacrifice. What else?" replied Gokulan, concentrating on removing a small boil on his upper arm. As he pinched the boil, he wondered how much the *pooja* would cost. A goat alone would cost two thousand rupees.

"How do we raise the money for the pooja?" Gokulan's tone indicated that he was only half concentrating on the *pooja*. But as suddenly as he was pinching the boil, he stopped and looked up.

Slowly he said, "Why does that mad idiot need a house now? Anyway he spends all his time here, near the lake. Should we put it up for sale?"

By now, a few of the villagers had gathered around. Some of them were calculating the cost of the small hut with its acre of land. It could easily fetch ten thousand rupees.

Prabhu turned and looked for Raju but he had disappeared.

"I don't think we can decide that without asking Raju," he said softly.

Gokulan sniggered. "What's happened to you? It looks like the sun has got you. Do you expect that mad boy to take decisions? He is too young to know what is good for him. Don't forget that he is mad." Chuckling, he added, "We will need to spend about five thousand for the pooja and the remaining money, we could keep it safely for him."

Ha! That's a joke! Prabhu felt like saying. Keep it for him? As if these people would!

Instead, he said, "I still think it is his decision and we need to check with him."

Gokulan squeezed the boil on his hand and turned to look at Prabhu. An expression of irritation flitted across his face.

"Listen! The pooja must happen within the next week. Before that, we have to get the money together. If you want to talk to Raju, go ahead. But make sure that by tomorrow evening you let me know how the money will be raised for the pooja. Otherwise, I have decided that the house will be sold."

He turned his attention to another small pimple on his belly. As he tortured the pimple, he felt a pair of eyes watching him. Turning around, he saw Raju watching him from behind a *Neem* tree.

TWO

Chapter

Prabhu caught the gooseberry tree and shook it. A rush of green berries fell like emeralds all around him. He shook the tree again, and yet again. Crouching on the ground on his haunches, he gathered the fruit in a basket. He had only a few hours time in which to find Raju and talk to him. The idea of selling Raju's property seemed a terrible one. Frowning in concentration, Prabhu wondered if he could give one of his own goats for the sacrifice. But what about the money for the lunch? The slaughtered goat would have to be cooked in juicy gravy. A few kilos of rice would also have to be cooked. This could cost another thousand, and the money would have to be raised by Mariamma's family, otherwise the benefits of the *pooja* would be lost.

Hearing a soft patter, he turned around, to see Raju standing a little away watching him. He observed that the mad boy of the village looked even worse after his mother's death. The shirt he wore was brown and dirty. Half knickers hung baggily around his waist. On his feet was a pair of broken slippers.

"You want a berry?" Prabhu asked impulsively.

Raju continued to stand and stare.

"What are you looking at me like that for? I had to burn your mother's body. After all, someone had to do it...and I knew her quite well. If you had been okay you could have done it. God only knows what is wrong with you. Why don't you ever talk? I know that you are not dumb. Mariamma told me that you used to talk a lot as a small boy. You even told her stories. Why don't you speak any more?"

As he talked, he kept picking up the berries, wiping them clean and putting them in the basket. Most of the berries were a tender green while a few were fat and yellow. He popped the fat ones, scarred from their fall, into his mouth.

Raju still stared at him.

"I must be a fool trying to talk to you. But I wonder whether I am a fool or whether you are trying to make a fool of all of us. I am glad I saw you now, there is something I need to talk to you about. Your mother died at midnight and that means we need to perform a pooja to save her soul from the devils."

Prabhu wondered where these devils were who had put in their appearance suddenly to mess up their lives. But he did believe in *karma* and rebirth. He had read the *Mahabharata* and sometimes, when the night was bright enough for him to sit outside, he had read the *Bhagavat Gita*. It was true that everyone's life had a predetermined pattern, a path that was carved by their own actions, carried over, lifetime after lifetime. Poor Mariamma had led a wretched life. If they could do something, anything to make her soul peaceful, why not? As he talked, and chewed on the berries, his mind ran over some of the passages in the *Gita*.

"I sometimes feel you don't like any of us and that is why you don't want to talk. If you are really as smart as I think you are, tell me where to look for the money for your mother's pooja."

Lifting his eyes, he looked towards the spot were Raju was standing a few minutes ago only to find that he was not there now. Surprised, Prabhu looked around, but Raju had disappeared.

Where had he run off? Shaking his head in exasperation, Prabhu looked around when his eyes alighted on a shining object on the ground. Picking it up he saw that it was a gold ring with a red ruby in the centre. That was the place where Raju had been standing a few seconds earlier. He must have dropped it. Where had he seen this ring Prabhu wondered. Suddenly he remembered. He had seen the ring on Mariamma's finger once or twice when she had come to the temple. It was probably valuable. Why had Raju dropped it here? Prabhu twisted the ring around. The ruby shone with an inner gleam as though it held secrets in its heart that could not be fathomed. It was obviously worth a lot of money. Well, well! The cost of the *pooja* was now taken care of. He smiled.

It was only later as he walked back to his hut, carrying the basket of berries on his head that he realized that Raju must have specifically brought the ring as a gift for him. Prabhu brushed off a small fly humming around his face. He felt a lump building up in his throat and as he cleared it, he saw that the eastern sky looked sullen and overcast. A storm was definitely in the offing.

As far as the eye could see, the fields were covered with tender paddy saplings planted in watery earth. They would, if the right amount of water and sunshine were available, grow into a good harvest this season. But if the rains came too soon, the saplings would be washed away and the land would become too marshy for any other harvest. As Prabhu gazed worriedly at the sky, a few of the villagers, gathered around Gokulan, were equally preoccupied. A bad harvest would plunge them into loans. Maybe, even famine.

"Is the goddess already angry with us?" a soft male voice asked. The voice belonged to Maieelan. Maieelan harboured several guilty secrets in his heart and a fear of the wrath of the gods constantly tormented him. It was therefore natural that he should ask the question that was on everyone's minds. Gokulan's right hand played with his wiry mustache, twisting and twirling and torturing it. He wondered if he believed in spirits. The answer was a big yes!

After all, how had he managed to break his hand the very day he had raised it at his wife in the morning. It was true that she had nagged him about his nocturnal habits and she had well deserved that slap, but soon after that he had walked past Kaliamma's temple, flexing his arm muscles, when a bull had run straight into him. As they had rushed him to the hospital, he had wondered if his traitorous thoughts outside the temple had caused the hurt. Since then, he had been careful as to what he thought about when it came to matters regarding god.

If the skies were clouding over, it meant rain. If it were a light rainfall, the crops would be saved. Anyway, as the village headman, he had to speed up the *pooja* matter or the villagers might hold him responsible if things went wrong. From experience he knew that these same people who hung around him reverently, would not hesitate to throw him to the wolves. With hardly two meals a day and hard labour, it was their belief in the supernatural that sustained them through their hardships. Even if he acted funny with the gods and the gods forgave him, these human beings wouldn't! Gokulan realized the moment the thought had passed through his mind that the gods, if they had heard him, wouldn't like to be referred to so carelessly.

Hurriedly, he looked around and whispered, "Sorry".

A dog, that had till then been lying down quietly, got up and snarled at him.

"Okay, okay, I am sorry," he repeated, just as the first roar of thunder sounded.

"Shall I go and bring Prabhu here?" Maieelan asked.

A gruff voice replied, "That won't be necessary."

Standing a distance away from Gokulan, Prabhu looked at the crowd of ten to fifteen villagers. He knew they were worried about the rains. He also knew that by volunteering to help out with Mariamma's funeral he had got himself into a situation that he could neither understand nor resolve. A feeling of frustration mingled with uncertainty and Prabhu felt a slight shiver pass through his body.

Gokulan's eyes were focused on the dog, which stood near Prabhu's legs. It wagged its tail quietly.

Heaving a sigh of relief that the matter between him and god had been sorted out, Gokulan asked Prabhu authoritatively, "Where is the money for the pooja?"

They had always shared an amicable relationship. Now, Prabhu felt vaguely uneasy about Gokulan. A discernible distance had settled between the two.

Reaching into his shirt pocket, Prabhu pulled out the ring. Sticking his hand out, he asked softly, "Will this take care of the expenses?"

Gokulan got up from the stone where he sat and came up to Prabhu, his eyes focused on the ring. The villagers also came closer, like vultures circling a dead body.

Clearing his throat, Gokulan asked, "Whose ring is this?"

"It is Mariamma's," Maieelan replied.

"How did you get it?" asked Gokulan, his eyes fixed on a spot above Prabhu's eyes.

Why doesn't he look directly at me anymore? The question ran through Prabhu's mind as he told them the story of Raju's visit to his gooseberry grove.

Gokulan took the ring and quickly slipped it onto his little finger. He flexed the finger and gazed at the red ruby, admiring his newly acquired treasure. It was definitely valuable, worth a lot more than the cost of the pooja, but if that dull headed son of the dead woman wanted to part with it, then who was he to question god's wishes? There was a small spattering noise and he put his hand to his head. For god's sake - bird droppings! He cursed under his breath and bent down to pick up a leaf.

With the threat of rain looming over them like god's verdict, Gokulan decided that the next day would be ideal for the *pooja*. Soon the news sped around the village. An air of festivity shed its warm glow, and for the time being, the villagers forgot about the threat of rain. Some of the men went to the temple to clean it.

The temple was an open space with a large towering statue of Muneeshwara, garbed in angry, bright-coloured clothing. In his four hands, he grasped different weapons. His eyebrows raised and mouth open in a snarl, he stood there, unmoved by nature. None of the villagers had ever climbed to the top. One man had tried once to do so, boasting that he would be able to reach Muneeshwara's head. He had climbed slowly and steadily and the villagers watched quietly while he placed a foot on one lap and the other on Muneeshwara's hand. From the hand to the head was a good two feet distance. As he sat there poised to climb up, he had looked at Muneeshwara's face. From this proximity, the teeth gleamed bright and white – a shining, dazzling white that blinded his eyes. With a huge scream he had fallen down, impaling his body on a spear pointing upwards. What had happened for him to lose his balance and fall down?

The crowds had prayed and screamed and cried but since then, though over ten years had lapsed, none had tried climbing the statue. They stood on the ground and shut their eyes and prayed. More often than not, the older members of the village remembered the crazed grin on that fellow's face, as his body hung on the sword.

Today they rushed around, washing Muneeshwara's feet and wiping it clean. A group of women sat in a corner, plaiting flowers into colourful garlands. Jasmines and roses fought for space, while *vetive*r and *sampangi* flowers spread a mesmerizing fragrance around the temple.

In a bustle of activity, the villagers were getting the sacrificial goat ready for the *pooja*. Succulent tender shoots of green grass were piled up in front of the goat. As it chewed steadily, a few boys ran around the goat, singing songs and clapping their hands together. If the goat suspected its fate, it would surely have run away towards the hills. But it continued to stand there steadily chewing on the grass, oblivious about its future.

Prabhu went around the temple, ensuring that everything was being taken care of. He noticed that Gokulan was not scrimping over the expenses for the *pooja*. Huge bundles of firewood were being brought to the cooking place. One man was going around cutting off green plantain leaves on which the food would be served. The older women sat in a corner peeling garlic and onions.

Except for an occasional rumble, the skies seemed to have sobered down. A cool breeze blew around the temple, as the villagers spent the night in preparation for the morning *pooja*.

As the first rays of the sun shafted across the sky, the villagers headed towards the lake for a ritual bath. With a cold, wet, loincloth tied around each waist, they came back and stood around the statue. The musky smell of incense sticks mixed with the morning dew, and the temple took on the appearance of a celestial abode.

The *poojari* – a tall, thin man with a small plait, tied like a hangman's noose at the back of his bald head, came forward. Softly chanting *mantras*, he walked towards the statue. Bowing slightly, Gokulan handed over the tray with the *pooja* material on it.

Prabhu dragged the sacrificial goat to the front. Someone had placed a garland of fresh yellow *samandhi* flowers around its neck and a huge red *sindhoor* adorned its forehead like a bullet wound. It stood around waiting patiently, unperturbed by the excitement.

And then someone rang the bell. The *pooja* had started.

Deva stood quietly in the corner. Along with playing the role of the village undertaker, he was also called upon to behead sacrificial animals. If he was indifferent to the dead, the same was not true about his feelings for the animals he would slaughter. A good dose of toddy intoxicatingly shifted his focus from the goat's head to Muneeshwara's face. The white teeth gleamed in a huge grin. The warm feeling he had savoured till then seeped out as if Muneeshwara had emptied a bucket of cold water on his head. Cursing softly, he hurriedly averted his glance.

Prabhu looked around the crowd, searching for Raju. Where was he? Would he not be there for the *pooja*? Prabhu touched his stomach gingerly. Whenever he thought of Raju, he felt his stomach muscles tightening. Was Raju really dumb or had life, circumstances and unspeakable sorrows made him speechless? Were all these silly villagers with their customs adding to the load in Raju's heart? He walked around, ill at ease and worried.

He tried to recall memories of Raju. But there were very few. One was of little Raju running away from the school and a bunch of small children following him laughing and shouting. He had intervened and held Raju's body close to his own, the pattering sound of Raju's heart beat, hitting his thigh like a drum, his mouth opening and closing silently. On seeing Prabhu the children had gone back and a minute later Raju had escaped out of his hands and run away towards the lake.

Another memory was of Mariamma beating the boy. Her open palm landed resoundingly on the little boy's cheek. On seeing Prabhu, she had stopped beating the boy but had instead started beating her own head. He had tried to talk to her but she wouldn't listen. Hysterically crying and beating herself she had pulled her son towards her and hugged his body close.

These memories saddened Prabhu and his eyes fell on the goat a distance away. Silence could be abused. Why wouldn't the boy speak?

It was at ten in the morning that the *pooja* reached its final stage. By then, the goat had wandered off to the side to graze on a grassy patch. Deva was feeling slightly dizzy and sick. Gokulan was idly twisting the ruby ring around his finger. Prabhu felt inadequate. No matter how much he wanted to, he could not utter a single prayer. Undaunted, the *poojari* kept chanting the *mantras* in his singsong voice.

Deva pulled out the hatchet. It was time for the sacrifice. The villagers gathered closer even as the women tried to shoo the children away. The stronger and braver men came forward to hold the goat's body. Closing his eyes, Deva lifted the knife high above his head and brought it crashing down on the goat's neck. With surprise in its eyes, the animal's head rolled onto the ground as the body twitched and jumped. Someone put a vessel near the neck to catch the blood that gushed out. Congealed blood would be used for the cooking.

It was over! Prabhu heaved a sigh of relief. The goat's body had stopped twitching and the men whisked the carcass to the backyard. Carrying the head, Gokulan placed it delicately between the feet of the statue.

The crowds roared and shouted maniacally, "We are sinners and at the mercy of god. Please forgive us! Do not bring heavy rains, which will destroy our crops and kill our families."

They were still praying when suddenly the first drops of rain fell like pebbles on their heads.

The huge drops enveloped them. Prabhu squinted up at the sky. The clouds of the night before had been swept away; this seemed more like a summer shower. Exactly what the crops needed – a light rainfall.

"God has forgiven us," shouted Gokulan in a loud booming voice.

"Yes, yes, yes," yelled the crowd, breaking into clapping and rigorous dancing.

The raindrops washed Muneeshwara's statue and dripped onto the goat's head, pink rivulets flowing down like a rainbow hued offering.

While the women started the cooking process, vendors began setting up stalls to sell their wares. A bangle seller spread out a piece of cloth and displayed different coloured bangles on it. Some were a bright red, a few leafy green. The aquamarine bangles had gold veins running through them. Small girls with plaited hair and colourful ribbons fluttered around the bangle seller.

"Colourpuul bangles for young lady hands," the bangle seller was proud of his knowledge of a few English words and never missed an opportunity to throw them at the villagers.

Prabhu wondered how the fellow would react if he had decided to say something to him in English. Not many knew that Prabhu could speak English.

Another man was pouring tea from a huge kettle and the men flocked to him like bees attracted by the smell of nectar. Lighting up their *beedis*, they gulped down the hot tea.

Somewhere in the distance, the smell of pure sugarcane wafted out as the sugarcane juice man cut sugarcane stalks in anticipation of a hot and humid afternoon.

Prabhu walked towards the lake. He crossed a clump of trees

and saw a few goats grazing quietly in the distant meadows. There was a melancholic peace in watching their quiet grazing. As he watched the goats, he suddenly spotted Raju standing some distance away. In his arms was a small goat, black in colour, with eyes like melted butter. He was cuddling and hugging it.

"Hey Raju!" Prabhu shouted.

At the sound of the voice, Raju dropped the baby goat and shuffled away.

The small goat stood unsteadily on doddering feet making a soft bleating sound. Prabhu looked around for the mother goat. He knew from experience that ewes didn't take too kindly to strangers handling their little ones. All the goats were placidly chewing on the wet grass, the small bells tied around their necks swinging rhythmically. And then he realized with a feeling of sorrow that the goat that had just been sacrificed was the little one's mother. He nuzzled his face close to the baby goat, a tear staining the down on its neck. He felt its tiny body shivering and he held it close. Shrugging slightly to shake off the questions in his mind, he walked determinedly to his hut. His flock would embrace the little one.

When Prabhu returned to the temple it was the smell of spicy, aromatic gravy that first hit him. With a start, he realized that he had not drunk his morning *kanji*.

As he walked towards the statue, he heard a soft footfall, which fell in line with his own. Turning around, he saw that it was Kuyili.

"So, what do you think about all this?" she asked him in a voice well suited to her name.

He wondered how her mother had realized that her daughter's voice would be like the lyric of a bird when she named her. As the thought passed through his mind, he realized with a start that she was hardly a baby anymore. He was seeing her after a long time and he noted with surprise the change in her appearance. He remembered her as a tall, lanky, dark-skinned girl who would peep at him, from behind her mother's sari. He remembered enquiring about Kuyili around a year ago from her mother, who said that she had finished her SSLC and was now at home.

He stole a glance at her. Draped in a bright yellow sari, she had stuck a yellow rose in her hair.

"Looks like you are all dressed up for the pooja?" he teased, waiting to see her blush. He noticed the way her figure had blossomed into beautiful curves and how her neck arched long and slim towards a pretty face.

Many of the village girls blushed when he talked to them but he was used to that. They also grew tongue-tied and shy. Whether they really found him awesome, or whether their mothers told them to act coy with him just because he was a well off bachelor, he did not know.

"What about you? You are also looking grand with your bald head." She giggled loudly.

Embarrassed, he touched his shaved head. Tiny hairs, like thin wires, were already casting a grey shadow on his head. He had not even thought about how this would affect his appearance.

Blushing lightly now, he replied, "This is no joking matter. When a mother dies, her son must remove the hair on his head."

As he said these words, he realized that in the last few days, he had almost started feeling like Mariamma's son.

"Who do you think murdered her?" Kuyili asked.

Once again, he marvelled at the way she had grown up. She had studied in a town school close by, and maybe that was where she had acquired her confidence. His eyes roamed over her slender figure.

It was a question with which he too was preoccupied. Who had murdered the lady and for what?

"Who do you think murdered her?" He threw the question back.

"Do you know that you always send a question back when you do not have an answer?" she asked, looking at him.

"Do I? I didn't know that." Curious, he continued, "But how do you know that? I don't think you have even spoken one full sentence to me."

She grinned at that and said, "But I have heard you talking to my mother and to the villagers."

"Have you?" That surprised him. Girls were definitely more observant than men.

Around the temple the merchants were spreading out colourful pieces of cloth and displaying their wares on it. One man who was selling toys, combs, small mirrors and purses, announced that any item could be picked up for five rupees.

A little away sat his competition selling the same goods for four rupees.

Not to be outdone, the first vendor was shouting that his goods were made of very good quality and would last longer.

And so it continued, each vendor trying to outdo his neighbour. As they walked on, Kuyili looking at all the things and Prabhu pondering about Mariamma's death, they neared the bangle seller. Yellow bangles brashly advertised their presence as the sky blue ones relaxed in the background. Most of the younger girls were buying bright pink bangles.

Prabhu saw the bangle seller watching him and asked impulsively, "Can I buy you some bangles?" He surprised himself with the question.

It seemed to make her blush. A soft colour rose up her face. Her soft lips opened and hovered between a yes and a no.

Smelling a customer, the bangle seller called out loudly, "These bangles will match your sari very well."

She wondered if Prabhu knew the significance of buying bangles for a woman. Watching his calm face, she realized that he didn't. For a second there was a feeling of disappointment that he was buying her bangles without any significance attached to it.

As she felt the rough work worn hands of the bangle seller pushing the bangles around her wrist, she looked again at Prabhu. What she saw was a handsome man with strong arms and shoulders. She observed his gentle eyes and firm jaw. She felt a never felt before sensation in her stomach.

"Food is ready, food is ready." A small boy, whose khaki shorts were almost falling off, ran around shouting gleefully.

In the temple backyard, the rice had been cooked. Mutton gravy simmered in huge cauldrons. As the women blew on the flames, kindling and sparking them with renewed energy, the men brought more logs of firewood. Little children stood in groups, waiting for food.

Kuyili and the younger girls spread long mats and placed green plantain leaves in rows. Gokulan sat in a prominent place, along with Prabhu and the other important men from the village. The younger girls now served the food. Kuyili piled Prabhu's plate with rice and gravy. She searched around in the serving vessel for succulent pieces of meat. This too she heaped on his plate.

"Why don't you sit down with me and eat?" he asked.

Once again she stole a glance at him, wondering whether he felt a little of what she had begun feeling for him. But there was no change in his visage at all.

An old lady with dangling ear lobes and three nose studs said loudly, "What hopes! First we elders need to fix the date for the marriage and then, after that, both of you can sit next to each other and eat."

"Marriage? Who is talking about marriage?" asked Prabhu with a startled look.

"As if I want to marry you!" Kuyili retorted and angrily walked away.

"Hey, hey, Kuyili! Wait!"

Suddenly, Prabhu saw that all the villagers had stopped eating and were watching him. One of the men, sitting opposite, twirled his mustache in a macho way. This was a man thing.

After the last villager had eaten, and stray dogs were picking at the bones, Prabhu walked towards the temple. The goat's head was still there, between Muneeshwara's heavy legs. He turned around and saw that Gokulan was standing next to him. He had a pleased look on his face.

"Everything went off well, right?" he asked Prabhu.

"Yes, it has gone off well. The gods also seem to be appeased."

Both of them looked at the sky. Though still grey at places, the sky was now clear and bright. The short rainfall had been just enough to wet the tender paddy shoots and cool the wild flowers.

"Was the money you got from the ring enough for the pooja?" Prabhu asked, looking at Gokulan.

Without missing a beat, Gokulan said, "Yes! It was just about enough."

As an afterthought, he added, "The ring is apparently not as expensive as it seemed."

The words flowed easily. Actually the ring had a very valuable ruby and must have been around for a long time, is what the town goldsmith had told him. As he lied fluently, Gokulan's eyes fell on the goat's head, caught between the two legs. As he watched, the goat opened its eyes and closed one eye softly in a wink. Suddenly, the goat's face was like his own.

"Rubbish!" he said loudly, alarmed at his fancy.

"Yes, this is all rubbish. Why do we have to kill a goat to appease the gods? If we are god's creatures, then are the goats, which are better than many of us, the devil's creatures? If this is true, then who is god and who is the devil?" questioned Prabhu.

Horrified, Gokulan looked sharply at Prabhu and said, "I did not say 'rubbish' because I did not like the pooja. We have to do more poojas like this, more and more."

As he repeated the words, he shut his eyes tight and tried to block out the face of the goat with the wicked grin.

Giving him a disbelieving look, Prabhu walked back home, tired.

THREE

Chapter

As the sun broke free on the eastern horizon, all the strong men and women walked determinedly towards the paddy fields. The next two months was a busy time for them, as they tended to the paddy and ensured that there was enough water for the saplings. The women carried small tiffin boxes that would invariably contain boiled rice and pickles. The cool rice *kanji* would wet their parched throats and cool their stomachs as the noon heat hit them and the pickles would tickle their taste buds into believing that the food was exotic.

Prabhu walked his goats to a distant pasture behind the hills. The path to the pasture was overgrown with thorny bushes, but there was a small path for him to walk on. His forty goats went ahead of him, idly stopping to sample the grass. Outlined against the gold of the morning sky, the hills looked brown and strong. Finding a convenient patch of shade under a large tree, Prabhu spread a mat and sat down. It was quiet and peaceful. The only sounds he heard were the rustle of the wind blowing through the leaves, the humming of bees and an occasional distant car horn. It reminded him that just a little away, on the outskirts of the village, was a town where many people lived, where the houses were different. They were stone buildings and some of the structures even had two floors. On a morning like this, young boys and girls in ill-fitting uniforms and slates in their hands would be running to school. The shopkeepers would be sweeping the ground outside their shops. The post office and bank, never in a hurry to start work, would open later.

Prabhu had once visited a friend who lived in a small house in the town. The stone walls looked clean and whitewashed and the man actually had two chairs in the hall. As Prabhu sat down on one, the man called out to his wife to bring some coffee. In a few moments, the woman brought two glasses of coffee.

"We have a kerosene stove, you know," the man had said.

As he remembered this, he also told himself that when he got married he would buy his wife a stove. None of the firewood and smoke for her!

Maybe he should get married, but as the person who had performed Mariamma's last rites, he would be in mourning for a year. The sun had risen in the sky and in the nectar fresh morning, the sun's glow lit up a yellow butterfly, flitting around. The colour reminded him of Kuyili's sari and bangles. She would make a strong wife as she walked to the fields with him, her head held high. This was the first time he had seriously contemplated marriage. The thought brought with it an embarrassed smile.

Suddenly, breaking through the silence, he heard a muffled

noise, which sent a chill down his spine. He remembered the villagers telling him that wild dogs sometimes came by to catch goats. Hurriedly he looked at his goats. All of them were chewing on the tender grass. Were any of them wounded? He got up and looked around when he heard the cry again. Running in the direction of the cry he suddenly knew what it was even before he saw the crouched body near the tree.

Raju's face was sunk in his lap.

Prabhu walked up to him and asked softly, "Raju, what is wrong?"

The tears were flowing freely from Raju's eyes, drawing a screen over the expression in them. It was not sorrow, fear, or even hurt. Prabhu felt a strange constriction in his throat.

At a loss for comforting words, he bent his head and said, "Raju, stop crying. I am here to help you. What is worrying you, my son?"

Hearing a slight noise, Prabhu turned in the direction of his goats. Two of them were flashing their horns threateningly at each other. When he turned back, Raju had run away, to become a fading figure in the distant horizon.

He probably hasn't got over Mariamma's death. Feeling disturbed and unnerved, he moved towards his goats when he saw a shining object lying in the grass. He sat down on his haunches. Lying there, hidden by the grass, was a knife. Prabhu picked it up and looked at it. It had dried blood spots on it. Was this the knife, which was used to murder Mariamma? If so, how had Raju got it? Unless. Yes! Unless Raju had murdered his mother. A feeling of disquiet in his heart, Prabhu carried the knife and placed it on the mat next to the tree.

Murders, rituals, fights were not unknown in his village. In fact several years ago, human sacrifice had also been prevalent. Now the tamed villagers appeased their sacrificial nature by beheading a goat or a cock or two. Fights, especially drunken brawls, happened and people were wounded. But in the morning, they woke up and went to work in the fields. Murder.... it was not uncommon, but this was the first time he was directly involved. And try as he may, he could not see Raju in the role of a murderer.

Who was the diabolic person who had murdered Mariamma? Why would that individual want to murder an old woman? It just did not make sense. It was easier to blame the mad son and yet the mad son did not behave like a murderer. He wondered if he should take the knife to the police station. But that would complicate matters if there were an enquiry. Gokulan would not like his decision overruled. He decided that he would talk to Gokulan, and then to Raju, before he pursued any course of action.

At the time, Prabhu had no idea that his decision would meet with an unexpected delay. In fact nobody foresaw how the events of the next few days would throw the harmonious life of the villagers totally out of gear.

It happened the very next morning. As Prabhu lay in bed, dreaming of goats and goddesses, he heard the insistent beat of a drum. Opening his eyes, he flinched at the light and realized that it was morning already. Opening the door of the hut, he heard the drumbeater announcing loudly, "Panchayat meeting at 10 am. All should be there."

Wondering what the matter was, Prabhu walked towards the lake. The path to the lake was covered in green grass soaked with morning dew. He picked his way through the thorny path, avoiding the sharp stones. Reaching the lake, he saw a group of men standing around talking. He got into the lake and the cold water hit his body, waking up his nerve ends and skin. Closing his eyes, he breathed in the smell of the mossy water.

After his bath, he cut clumps of grass around the lake and making a bundle, carried it to his farm. A hungry calf mooed plaintively. He cut some hay to feed the cows, and then went towards his hencoop. The hencoop was a big basket. From inside the basket came the muffled sound of hens in a heated discussion. The moment he lifted the basket, the mother hen stalked out, followed by her chicks, indignant at being cooped up for so long. Standing on thin twiggy feet, the chicks, with soft downy bodies, rushed around her feet, trying to shelter themselves under her stomach.

His cows were in the huge cow shed near the barn where he stored grains, groundnuts, root vegetables and green bananas. He had two young men to look after the cows and he could hear them in the distance, talking and laughing as they milked the animals.

He then walked across to his small vegetable patch. The carrots were sprouting leaves. He would probably uproot a few and make some gravy to go with his rice.

When he headed towards the temple for the *panchayat* meeting, he saw that quite a few people were already there. Seated on the raised stone flooring were Satvarlal Sait – the town goldsmith, another man in a shirt and pant and Gokulan, dressed in a white shirt and white cotton *dhoti*.

Around ten, when most of the villagers were assembled, Gokulan cleared his throat and proclaimed loudly, "This young man is an engineer and he is from Madras."

The man pushed his glasses up his nose in embarrassment.

"You may be wondering what this meeting is about." There was a deliberate pause.

"Well, this man, whose name is Prakaas (he pronounced the name thus though the name was Prakash) is a representative of a very large building company."

Without pausing now, the words hurriedly poured out of his mouth. "His company is interested in putting up a factory in our village."

Prabhu felt a wave of shock course through his body.

One of the older men of the village asked in a shaky voice, "Why our village?"

"Ours is the only village with a lake that rarely dries up. Their factory needs water."

Satvarlal Sait, the town goldsmith, added in a booming voice, "So many of you have mortgaged your things with me. This is the right opportunity to get your things back."

Prakash, the man in the shirt and pant, cleared his throat. He pushed his thick glasses up his nose and stared at the crowd. The sun glinted and reflected on the glass and Prabhu, who stood a little away from the crowd, could not see the man's eyes. Strangely, this bothered him.

"Friends," said Prakash softly. His voice sounded funny as if he was chewing on betel nuts and talking simultaneously.

"Your chief or thalaiver as you call him," here he paused to smile at Gokulan, "only talked about the reason we are building a factory here. He did not tell you of the immense benefits awaiting you once our esteemed factory opens. For one, many of you will be employed on a monthly salary." There was a pause.

"Oooohh!" A wave of happy murmurs floated from the villagers.

"You will never have to worry about the rains, famine or failed crops. You will all have money. Once our factory is put up here, the government will also build roads. These roads will lead to the town, where your children can study. You can all enjoy the benefits of working and earning money. You can build better houses than the ones you now have. Your wives can go to the town showrooms to buy lovely saris. Why, you people can even dress like me!"

Prabhu had an irrational urge to pick up a stone lying near his feet and throw it at Prakash, the stony eyed man.

He looked around at the faces of the villagers. Some of the older men and women were standing without a change of expression on their faces, but the younger crowd was clearly impressed with Prakash.

An old man, with a wart on his nose, demanded of Prakash in a quavering voice, "Who do you think you are? Coming here with this kind of news? Do you want to leave the village in one piece or do you want to be packed in a box and sent to your blessed factory manager in a factory bus?"

The crowd made loud noises. Some of the men were folding up their *dhotis* and a few others were looking around for stones.

Chandran, a local toddy seller, was calculating the way his own financial position would improve if a factory started in the village. His business would boom. He intervened.

"I know that many of you now come to me for arrack and toddy. Once the factory is here you can actually drink bottled drinks from the town."

Deva, the village drunk, licked his chops. This sounded too good for words!

Gokulan looked at the crowd. Definitely, there were two schools of thought here. One, the younger crowd, who were all for it, and the other, the older crowd who were suspicious of this. He needed to work on this, but it was not the right time.

In a very loud voice Gokulan said, "This is only an idea. Nothing concrete has happened. But someone from here has already agreed to sell his property to be used for the factory. I suggest you all go home and think about it. We'll meet again in a week's time."

"Just a minute," interjected Prabhu. "Who is the person who has agreed to sell his property?" The question was directed at Gokulan but his eyes swept over the villagers.

"The name cannot be revealed now. But I will give you all details next week." With this, Gokulan got up from his seat and came down to join the crowds.

Prakash followed him and Satvarlal Sait tried his best to get up without looking fat and ungainly, a rather difficult feat.

Walking out from the meeting, Prabhu thought of the morning's events. He knew that though Gokulan had dismissed the meeting, he would stick to the idea of building a factory. What factory would it be? And who had agreed to give his or her property for this?

He carried on with his day's work, feeding the chicks and the cows. He checked his paddy fields. He was one of the few in the village who hired workers to work on his land. They were already there, men and women, with colourful pieces of cloth around their heads, protecting their scalps from the steadily rising sun. One woman was singing a song and the others were answering in a chorus. Her song was a series of questions from a mother to her child. She sang in a low husky voice.

"Will you have long black hair when you grow up?" she asked and the other ladies responded, "Yessss, my mother, yes amma."

"Will you, my child, get married and go away, when your hair grows long?"

"Yes amma, yes amma."

"Will your husband comb your hair for you?"

The chorus had a mixture of giggles as the women sang, "Yes amma, yes amma."

One of the younger men flirtatiously said, "Who will comb your hair? And who will marry you? I will marry a young lady from the city."

"And she will make you cook for her," replied a cheeky little girl with huge eyes and cherry lips. The young man came running towards her and she ran and hid behind her mother.

Prabhu smiled as he watched from a distance. He looked up and saw that the sky looked a deep blue. No sign of clouds. Unless they had rain now the crops would suffer.

Turning away from the path that led to his house, he crossed a small clearing and came to a tiny path covered with dew stained grass. Small stones tickled his heels and he lifted his white *dhoti*, to prevent it getting stained by the green of the wet grass. He saw the temple, looking clean and tended to. Even now, the *poojari* was decorating the statue with wild flowers and jasmines – flowers that grew in the garden around the temple. Sitting on the balcony, a few women were busy stringing the flowers into garlands. Nowhere else could a temple hint at so much peace thought Prabhu to himself, as he stepped in for a moment, to pray.

After the stop at the temple, he passed by a huge well, where boys and men fooled around, pretending to be bathing. To strangers, the well could look frightening, like a yawning big drop, filled with dark water, but for the villagers it was a water hole to cool their sweating bodies when summer's hot rays hit the earth.

Worried by the unexpected developments, Prabhu set out for Gokulan's house. He remembered the happy faces of the workers. Would all this change once the factory was started?

Gokulan was playing with his little daughter outside his house. The girl was trying to comb his hair and he was sitting there, a willing slave. Prabhu wondered at the difference a child could make to a person. Tough Gokulan was sitting there, grinning like an ape.

"Appa, you have boochies in your hair," said the little girl, searching through her father's hair fervently.

Seeing Prabhu coming, Gokulan pushed her gently, a bit embarrassed. "Go on now and play some other game. Ask your mother for some butter milk for me and Prabhu maama."

The child ran into the house.

As he sat down next to Gokulan, Prabhu felt strangely disturbed. This feeling had started just after he volunteered to perform Mariamma's funeral. Before that, he couldn't ever remember feeling this way.

"What do you think of the factory idea?" Gokulan opened the topic Prabhu was waiting to initiate.

"What factory do they have in mind?"

"Fireworks. Not the kind we use for our ceremonies. Good ones in nice boxes which will be sold in Chennai and Madurai."

The idea of something produced in his village and being sold in cities seemed to please Gokulan. The satisfaction rang in his voice.

"Fireworks!" He would never have guessed that one.

As Prabhu forced his mind to think, Gokulan was continuing.

"The factory will be a small unit. It will provide employment for some of our property less villagers. Their children also can work in it."

"Children? And their studies? That Prakaas was saying that with the money we earned we could send our children to town schools, and now you are talking about them working in the factory?"

Quickly shaking his head, Gokulan replied, "No, no. I too think children should study. But what about those parents who do not send their children to study? Those brats spend the days running around the village like a bunch of wild dogs. They could work in the factory."

"And why do they need water for a fireworks factory?"

Gokulan laughed, looking slightly sheepish. "I had to say something to these people to convince them about my project. Prabhu, remember this." He bent his head in a conspiratorial way and said, "If you want something from a person, praise him. He will do whatever you want. By telling these foolish people that our village was chosen because of the water available here they are very happy. They think their village is the chosen one." He laughed loudly.

Prabhu sat silently watching a cow grazing in the distance.

His heart was beating faster than usual. His mind was sending warning signals but he could not think of anything to say to Gokulan. He just felt that this whole idea would tear their peaceful village apart. Things would never be the same again.

Gokulan placed a palm on Prabhu's thigh. His voice softer, he said, "Prabhu, I know this decision is worrying you. You are not for this change; I can see that. But that is a natural feeling. Change is not easy. Any kind of change will mean a period of adjustment. But you will see that this is a good change. After all, so many of us are poor, depending on the whimsical monsoons. Now we will have an alternate source of income. After all money is important, right?"

'Look after the village'. An old man in a loincloth, who loved this land with its hills and valleys, its harsh summers and wet monsoons, had said. He remembered the old man now. The old man had given Prabhu a tough task. How could he prevent money from entering the hearts of the villagers? He could do it himself not for these people. He didn't know how to handle this situation.

Prabhu stared at Gokulan. How could he explain to him that money was important only upto a certain point? Yes, they were poor but they had their own way of running their lives. They stood by each other and there was never a time when a family went hungry. Yes, there were imbalances. Some were richer and some poorer but that existed in towns too. A factory of fireworks would disrupt the harmony of their lives. He knew it!

Once again he tried to present his fears to Gokulan but his

mind would not frame in words his thoughts. He watched Gokulan's pretty wife walking towards them with a glass of buttermilk in her hands.

She gave him a curious look and asked, "What do you think about Kuyili?"

Startled, Prabhu replied, "Kuyili? What is there to think of her?"

Smiling slyly at him, she said, "I wonder who bought her those yellow bangles?"

Gokulan, who knew nothing about this, asked, "What are you blabbering about?"

Suddenly it hit him. He looked at Prabhu with a grin. "Well, well, so you are a ladies man, eh? Buying bangles and all."

Prabhu felt his face turning red. "What is the big deal about buying a woman bangles? I would buy for you, too."

"Not for me, I am already married to this old elephant."

She ran away towards her house as Gokulan shouted coarsely, "Old elephant, eh? Wait till the night and I will show you what old elephants do."

Prabhu burst out laughing. He felt his mood lightening. Things could not be that bad, after all.

He got up. Flexing his arms, he waved to Gokulan and walked towards the town. He crossed a few green paddy fields and saw small patches of vegetables. Green leafy plants told him that the carrots beneath the ground were ready to be plucked. He walked on past the village temple where a few women were standing around chatting. He saw the village *Banyan* tree, where most of the older citizens sat, talking and smoking endless *beedis*. The Banyan tree's roots hung like long snakes and as the men sat under the tree on the bench and smoked, the roots swung softly around them. One of the men, sitting on the round bench, called out to Prabhu. He was a wizened old man, who had lost his teeth to betel leaves and tobacco. But he was fond of telling little children that he had lost them in a bullfight.

"Hey Prabhu! Since when is our village a business town?" His toothless mouth added a funny intonation to his words, making them sound strange.

Prabhu smiled at the sarcasm in the old man's voice and said, "What are you worried about? You will have enough firecrackers to burst for your granddaughter's wedding."

"Oh yes! I will have enough fireworks and some of it will fall on my paddy fields too," replied the old man, not to be outdone.

Prabhu looked at the old man seriously and asked, "Who, by the way, is giving his property for the factory construction?"

The old man drew on his *beedi*, a small line of smoke drifted from its burning end. He breathed deeply and said, "Gokulan is planning to use Mariamma's land."

"What?" Shock seeped into Prabhu's body. "How can that be possible? That land belongs to Raju. Has Raju given his consent?"

"Who do you think has asked Raju? Don't you know that they all treat him like a mad man? But I, for one, know that he is not mad."

Prabhu sat down next to the old man and lit a cigarette himself. His brand called *Scissors*, was only available in the town shops.

His memories of Raju came back, like a detached rice grain from its husk. He had not paid too much attention to the boy. In fact, until the day of Mariamma's death, he could not remember ever having worried about him. With a chill, he recalled the heartrending cry that had emanated from the boy when he had seen his mother's body. Somebody had willfully killed the woman and that person was hiding behind the fact that the blame would fall on Raju. There were some moments in his life when he trusted his gut feelings and he had seldom been wrong. In this case, he felt almost sure that Raju knew nothing about Mariamma's murder.

With a start he realized that he had been lost in his thoughts. The old man was watching him intently. Would this man know a little more about Raju?

Dragging on his cigarette, he once again glanced at the old man. There wouldn't be any harm in asking a few questions.

Looking directly at him he asked quietly, "What is wrong with Raju? Is he really mad?"

That made the old man laugh.

"Yes he is mad, if you and I are mad." He stopped to drag on his *beedi.* "He was a lovely boy once, who would run around the village singing songs and laughing. But that was only on the days when his father was not around. On other days, he would sit quietly near the lake, out of the way of his father." The old man's voice was tinged with sadness.

"Why? What would his father do to him?" Prabhu's words came out of his mouth in a strange way. They seemed to bring with them tightness in the throat and a breathless feeling in his heart.

"Do to him? He would beat him and box his ears. He would put out his burning *beedis* on the boy's thighs and arms. He once poured boiling hot water on the boy's feet." The old man threw the *beedi* he was smoking onto the ground and ground his slipper on it. "Haven't you noticed the way he shuffles his feet when he walks? One foot was badly burnt."

Prabhu flicked his cigarette and a tiny piece of burning tobacco fell on his foot. Starting with pain, he stared at his foot. If one tiny piece could burn so much, how that little boy would have suffered! His mind drew pictures – pictures his heart wanted to shut out but couldn't. He dragged his mind back to the old man next to him. To distract himself, Prabhu watched a group of young girls walking past with pots on their hips. They would have their baths in the well close by and come back with water for cooking.

"Why?" he asked softly.

"I am not sure, but it is said that he suspected that Raju was not his own son. He had once caught Mariamma with another man and he was never sure whether Raju was his son or not."

A terrible feeling of sadness welled up in Prabhu's chest.

"Why has Raju stopped talking?" he asked.

"That's a very sad story Prabhu. It will make the trees and the birds cry to hear that story."

Prabhu watched one of the softly swaying roots of the *Banyan* tree. It looked like a lost maiden's plaited hair, which had turned brown with age and uncaring. Somehow, watching the root reminded him of Mariamma's sad dead face.

The old man's fingers searched in his pocket clumsily. Lighting another *beedi,* he took a huge drag on it. Breathing out smoke through his nostrils, he said softly, "Every time he got a beating he would run away to the lake and sit there till the pain and the tears stopped. The rest of the time he would run around merrily. But one day he came back home to find his father's wrath turned upon his mother. He was beating her with an iron rod and she was bleeding from a cut on her forehead. Was it the wound and the shock of seeing his mother bleeding? Was it the words the father spat out at the mother? Was it a combination of both? Who knows? All we know is that, since that day he has not opened his mouth to speak a single word."

Prabhu felt tears stinging the back of his eyes. His own childhood had been a happy one and memories of his mother and father always made him feel pleasantly happy. Both of them had died when he was in his twenties and he could let go of them because he knew they did not suffer in their death. His father had died of a heart attack and his mother passed away soon after, having given up her will to live. A fever, which the doctors could not diagnose, had extinguished her life like a wick lamp flickering in the breeze. But now, as he listened to the old man, he could visualize Raju's torment. He could see the dreadful scene. Mariamma cowering from her attacker while he beat her steadily. He could see little Raju trying to pull the man away but only falling down helplessly on the ground. He could see all this and more. He could see Raju's little heart heaving with pain and some part of his brain shutting a door. He wished he could hug Raju and stroke the pain away. Turning away, he tried to hide the tears that were flowing out of his eyes.

Feeling terrible, Prabhu got up slowly from the seat. As he walked away, he asked the old man, "Who was the man Mariamma was caught with?"

He was looking at a distant cloud in the sky when he heard the old man's voice saying, "Everyone in the village knows that it was Gokulan."

FOUR
Chapter

As he walked towards the town, Prabhu felt a strange tightness in his chest. He tried to sort out his thoughts but the images were blurred. He saw Mariamma's body and the knife that had killed her. He remembered the way Raju had carried the body, hardly able to support the weight. He remembered the way Gokulan had taken over the matter and now finally he was even going to take over Mariamma's land!

Turning away from the main road, he crossed to a thickly overgrown path that would lead to the lake. He reached the lake just as the morning sun reached its zenith. It was close to lunchtime.

Standing under a tree, he shouted, "Raju, Raju, come here. I want to talk to you."

He heard a small sound nearby and turning his head sharply saw Raju crouching near a tree.

"Come here! I want to talk to you."

Raju crept up slowly. His feet dragged. Prabhu saw that the

khaki shorts he wore were torn in three different places. His hair was a mess and his face looked as though he had slept in the mud. Prabhu felt the strange tightness returning to his chest.

Gently he reached out a hand and said, "Come here. I won't harm you."

He spoke as he would to one of his lambs. The tiny newborns that shivered if even a light breeze touched their bodies.

Raju stood in front of him, a good two feet away. His eyes were downcast and his mouth turned down at the corners.

What suffering this boy must have undergone to become like this, a voice inside Prabhu said.

Clearing his throat to get rid of the lump in it, Prabhu asked, "Have you given permission for your land to be used for the factory?"

Jerking his head up, he looked at Prabhu and laughed. A loud laugh. An insane laugh, which curdled Prabhu's blood and made his feet turn cold. The sound echoed harshly on the nearby lake.

"Stop it!" said Prabhu, putting his hands to his ears. "I cannot bear your laugh. Are you not bothered that your land is going to be used for putting up a factory? Open your mouth and tell me what you feel and I will ensure that nobody sets foot on your land."

Raju stopped laughing as suddenly as he had started a few minutes ago. He once again looked downwards.

"Please Raju. Talk to me. Only when you start talking, will

all these people stop treating you as if you were mad. Please say something."

There was a strange stillness in the way Raju stood. Just as suddenly as he had broken into laughter, his body shook with silent sobs. His chest and arms heaved.

Prabhu took a step towards him, but Raju stuck a hand out as if to say, 'Stop! Don't come closer.'

Prabhu stopped in his tracks and watched the frail body shake and shudder with the overwhelming flood of tears. He waited till the sobs tapered down to a whimpering sound.

Looking once again at Raju, he said quietly, "If you do not talk, nobody can help you. Gokulan will not listen to me. Come to me and we can both solve this problem. I will even get you married."

At the word married, Raju gave a terrified look and jumping up, ran away towards the distant brown hills.

Frustrated, Prabhu sighed and decided to carry on to the town. He had to buy some cigarettes.

Crossing a narrow path, his mind and heart heavy with the morning's happenings, Prabhu saw Kuyili leaning on a fence, chewing a piece of sugarcane. When she saw him coming her way, she put her hand to her mouth, wiping it clean. He saw a faint blush on her cheeks.

"You look very worried today?" she asked, peeping at him from the corner of her eyes.

"Is it that obvious?" he replied, scratching his head.

The hair was growing back and he knew that his head looked funny. Suddenly, he felt self-conscious. If she noticed his embarrassment she did not show it.

Instead, she asked him with a serious look on her face, "What do you think about this factory business?"

Suddenly he wanted to know what she felt about it. "It's going to be a fireworks factory. What do you think about it?" He watched her keenly for her reaction.

"Here you go sending my question back to me. Okay, if you want my opinion, I hate the idea of having a dirty factory here." She spat out a piece of well-chewed sugarcane.

Why was his heart suddenly feeling so light and happy? He would definitely marry her. Not right now, but soon. He gave her a long look.

She smiled at him and said, "Want a bite?"

"Bite of what?" he asked startled.

"Sugarcane, what else?" she giggled.

"No, no. I don't want that." Giving her a smile, he walked on towards the town.

It took him an hour to reach the place, and by then the sun was sweltering. He stopped at the first shop that sold *beedis*, sodas, colours and *burfis*. Seeing the sweat on Prabhu's face, the shopkeeper opened a soda bottle and poured the liquid into a glass. He squeezed a juicy lemon into it and added sugar. Finally, he broke a piece of ice and threw it in. Prabhu felt his mouth watering. As he sipped the drink, he noticed that the shopkeeper had a small cut on his forehead.

As was the tradition in the village where everyone called everybody else *anna*, which meant brother, Prabhu asked the shopkeeper, "Anna, what happened to your forehead?"

With a shrug, the shopkeeper replied, "Satvarlal Sait's men hit me because I did not repay a loan."

"Sait does that kind of thing too, eh?"

"Of course, he only brought that Prakaas from the city to meet Gokulan. You should be careful."

Prabhu realized that he was right in feeling worried. There was something dreadfully wrong about this whole thing. Finishing the lemonade, he slipped some change into the shopkeeper's hands and walked towards Sait's shop. He passed narrow streets with small stone buildings on either side. A few pigs walked around sniffing the open drains. He saw the small theatre with a group of sweating youngsters standing outside the gate. Whether there was anything else that interested the villagers or not, the townspeople definitely saw every film which came to the theatre.

One of the younger boys yelled out to Prabhu, "Maama, come and watch this film with us. It is supposed to be a good film. Our Vaadhiyar has acted in it."

Prabhu smiled at the youth and said, "Come to my village, I will show you better scenes."

He walked on past a crowded street where business was brisk even at this hour. Toddy selling was a thriving business and a few drunkards were lolling around on the street. He knew that at least one dead body was found every week outside the shop but if it bothered anybody, it did not seem to affect the toddy seller's business in any way.

In a narrow turning off the main road, stood Satvarlal Sait's house and pawn shop. The house was comparatively big and it had an iron gate. His shop had a shutter with four locks. Prabhu saw that the shop was open and Sait was sitting on a low-slung white pillow. When he saw Prabhu coming towards him, Sait did a quick mental check of his loaner list. No! Prabhu had not borrowed from him. Maybe he would now.

Licking his thick red lips, he put on an ingratiating smile on his face. "Come in, come in, saab! What brings you to this humble shop?"

Snorting aloud, Prabhu said, "Humble shop? What Sait? We all know that you can buy this town with the money in the safe there." He grinned when he saw Sait hurriedly looking at the safe.

"No, don't worry. I am not too fond of money and I will therefore never rob your safe," he said, sitting down opposite Sait on some pillows.

Wiping the sweat that flowed down his face, he asked, "So, who is this Prakaas, Sait? People are saying that it was you who brought him to our village."

He was quick to notice Sait's discomfort but it was only for a split second.

Quickly composing himself, Sait said, "Prakaas? Vo badaa

aadmi. He is a very rich man. You and your village are very lucky to have Prakaas build his factory there. You will surely become very rich."

"Ha, ha, ha!" Prabhu laughed and getting up, walked out of the shop.

As he was leaving, he saw Kalliyappa stealing in slowly. Seeing Prabhu, he bowed his head respectfully and waited till Prabhu had gone down the road before he went into the shop.

Sait scowled at Prabhu's back. He could not understand what he had said that was so funny that that fellow had to laugh so heartily. Seeing the reverent look on Kalliyappa's face, he said, "Hey Kalliyappa! Who is that fellow? He is from the village, that much I know, but who is he?"

"Who is he? You don't know that? He owns 300 acres of land – fertile land. Some of it is used for paddy cultivation, some for grazing and a large portion is occupied by labourers who work on his land. He lets them live there free of cost. If he wants to, he can sell his land to the villagers and become very rich." With a malicious look on his face, he added, "Richer than you."

"Then why don't you go and borrow from that saint? When you need to borrow, you all come to me."

Kalliyappa pulled out a HMT watch dangling on a black leather strap. "Are you sure you don't want this?"

Sait's beady eyes snapped greedily. He knew better than to ask questions. "This watch is not very expensive. I can give you twenty-five rupees for it."

Kaliyappa was contused. He had picked this watch off a bus traveller and he wasn't sure about its cost, but surely not just twenty-five?

"If you give me fifty you can take the watch," he said.

"Thirty-five, and not a paisa more."

As Kaliyappa counted the money, Sait pocketed the watch and stroked his chin thoughtfully. Prakash had promised him a decent sum of money if the deal for putting up a fireworks factory in the village came through. Also free supplies of fireworks for all the marriages and functions in his family. He imagined Holi festival and how, while he sat in a corner and guzzled *bhang*, that intoxicating drink which looked like innocent milk, his children would play with endless firecrackers. Nothing like burning other people's money!

When Prabhu reached the village, twilight was stealing in and a few silvery stars were winging their way out. A crescent moon hung dolefully in a corner like a dimly lit bulb as several grey clouds were masking its brightness. He went to his hut. Opening the door, he switched on the light, thankful that his village now had electric supply. But the little lamps in the corner bore a testimony to the fact that power cuts for many hours, especially in the nights, was not uncommon.

He went to the right hand corner where there were a few utensils. He opened one and the smell of fresh curry assailed his nostrils. He opened another and there was tender freshly cooked rice in it. In another, an aromatic vegetable fry. He looked around surprised. Had someone cooked in his kitchen?

Apparently not, because the firewood stove was cold and emberless. Who could have brought food for him? Could it be Kuyili? The thought brought with it a pleasurable feeling. But why should she? Too hungry to speculate, Prabhu picked up a plate and sat down to eat. As he ate his food, the wind outside blew gustily. The coconut trees outside his hut shivered and shook under the weight of the wind. All of a sudden, a heavy downpour began.

He heard a light tapping on his door and shouted, "Come in."

Kuyili came in and sat down timidly.

"Hey, hey! What do you mean coming here in the night?" he asked, not really angry though his voice sounded stern.

"Why? I cannot come but my food can, eh?" she smiled, watching the way he was eating, enjoying his food.

Suddenly the rain came crashing down, even heavier.

Prabhu gave Kuyili a worried look. "How will you go back now? Does your mother know that you are out here?"

"My mother has gone to the town. Moreover, I came to talk to you." Sitting cross-legged on the ground, she said, "Prabhu, will you marry me?"

He ran his left hand through his hair, a habit he subconsciously indulged in when he was nervous. Weighing his words carefully, he said, "Before I answer that question, can I ask you something?"

"Yes," she murmured softly.

"What happened?"

She looked up at him and he saw the troubled look on her face. "It's my uncle, my mother's younger brother – the one who drinks a lot. He has been troubling my mother to get me married to him. My mother is holding him off, but today, when she had gone to the town he came home and tried to…" The words stumbled over each other.

He saw a few drops falling down from a small crack in the roof and watched its steady fall in rhythmic drops. Plop, plop, plop. He continued to eat his food.

Outside, the sound of rain competed with the beating of her heart. But she sat still, not wanting to disturb his decision in any way.

After a pause, which seemed as long as eternity, he said, "Yes Kuyili. I want to marry you, too. But are you willing to wait? I cannot marry you before the end of the year as I have performed Mariamma's death rites."

The words were said in a matter of fact tone, but they carried the promise of a lifetime of togetherness. It was the way he said them, without any tinge of ardency that convinced her that her decision was the right one.

She felt a huge butterfly lift its head and flutter around her heart. Its shining spots spun golden dreams in her mind. She felt a strange tightness in her throat. Lowering her head, she stared at a tiny ant crawling along the ground. When she lifted her head, she saw that he was standing near an old trunk, rummaging in its contents. She saw him fishing out something and then he came to her. She stood up and looked at him. He caught her right hand and slipped a ring onto it. In the soft light of the 60-watt bulb she saw that it was a thin gold band. He smiled at her, his face breathtakingly handsome. She watched him mesmerized as he continued to smile at her.

"Can you take care of yourself for a year?" he asked softly.

Lifting her head and holding it high, she said, "I will cut off his hand if he even touches a hair on my head. From this moment onwards I am your wife."

She opened the door and raced out like a golden deer into the rain.

The next morning, the announcer went around yelling out that there would be a *panchayat* meeting. It would be a day for decisions, felt Prabhu, as he walked on the wet grass. The smell of wet mud hung heavily in the air as he walked towards the temple, where the meeting was to be held.

The rains had watered the paddy fields and the muddy roads were difficult to walk on. When he reached the temple, he saw that Satvarlal Sait, Prakash and Gokulan were already there. So were a few villagers. None of the villagers could sit down because of the wet ground. They stood around and watched Gokulan and Prakash talking in whispers.

After a few minutes, Gokulan cleared his throat loudly and said, "Fellowmen, Prakaas has approved of our village as the right place for the fireworks factory. It is indeed a lucky break for us." He beamed at the crowd, which stared back suspiciously at him.

His smile changing into a frown, Gokulan said, "We have decided to use Mariamma's land for the factory. After all, she cared a lot about the village and her soul will rest in peace if she knows that her land is being used to develop the village."

There! It was out in the open. Prabhu looked around at the crowd to see their reaction. The old man who had told him about Gokulan and Mariamma was looking at Gokulan with a funny expression. The others were not reacting.

Even my goats have more emotions than these people, thought Prabhu.

Gokulan continued, "To start with, Prakaas here needs some of us to help with the factory construction. He ...."

Prakash interrupted. "I will pay you per day wages. I would not *advice* those who are working in paddy fields to give up their jobs to help me but the others can."

Immediately, Prabhu knew that half his workers would now follow Prakash. That one sentence clearly spelt out the fact that he would pay more money than they earned working in the paddy fields. Diabolic and intelligent!

"Once the factory is ready, your village will be the centre of trade and commerce. You will all have big houses to live in."

Prabhu lifted his hand up and said, "Enough! You don't have to give us this sales pitch. You already have the land and you have now bought yourself the workers. Not all of us are so crazy about money that we will risk the lives of our loved ones by encouraging the building of a fireworks factory. Tell me what are the steps you will be taking to ensure that the chemicals do not affect our paddy fields and if there is a fire, what are the steps you are taking to ensure that no lives will be lost?"

All eyes turned to him. The older members were bowing their heads in respect. The three men of the *panchayat* were sending killer looks his way.

This man spelt trouble but Prakash had his own means of getting rid of troublesome men. In another village he had started a quarrel between the villagers and in the end, the entire group of people who lived there were fighting with each other. It had been easy for him to finish off the unwanted specimens. He closed his eyes in satisfaction. He would enjoy finishing off this troublesome man.

"Prabhu," he said, in a voice a mother would use to her naughty child. "Prabhu, I care more for you and the village than you can imagine. I was born in a village too." He took off his glasses and cleaning the lenses on his shirtsleeves, added, "We will take all precautions to ensure that life continues smoothly for the rest of you. Do not worry."

One of the older men asked, "What are you paying Raju for this?"

Gokulan gave an angry look and said, "Why do you ask? Are you his father?"

Prabhu felt a surge of anger.

The old man, glaring at Gokulan, was murmuring under his breath, "I am not as hard up as you are."

If Gokulan heard, he pretended he hadn't and lifting his hands again, said authoritatively, "How many of you feel that we should ask Raju for his permission? Remember that he cannot talk and asking him will be futile."

Prabhu lifted his hand and saw a few more hands going up. The majority of the crowd simply watched.

"Well, that's decided then. I cannot change the decision of the entire village in favour of a few." He laughed contemptuously.

"We will build a hut for Raju to sleep in, a little away from the factory. It will be a different sight for him to see. He watches the lake the whole day otherwise," Gokulan said, before bringing the meeting to an end.

When he got up to go, Prakash turned and gave Prabhu a look. Behind the lenses, his eyes gleamed.

Prabhu walked up to him and said softly, "Don't pull any stunts on me. I will not hesitate to cut off your head and offer it to Muneeshwara."

Prakash felt his glasses slip off his nose.

"What do you mean by talking to me like that?" he asked in a squeaky voice.

"If you don't like being talked to like this then stop gaping at me and feeding poison to the villagers. One more grin from your sordid face and I will cut off your right hand and leg. Then you will be limping Prakaas instead of stony-eyed Prakaas." He laughed loudly.

Prakash scuttled away, his ears ringing with the sound of

Prabhu's laughter.

Prabhu felt a small tap on his back and turned to see the old man who had told him about Raju. The old man was smiling and the smile was playing with the crevices on his face, lighting it up.

"That's the way to handle that rat." The old man laughed. His toothless mouth opened in a series of short sounds and mixed with Prabhu's manly laugh.

The two of them walked towards the lake, lighting up their *beedi* and cigarette.

FIVE Chapter

For the next two weeks, life in the village remained unruffled as the villagers went about their daily work. The paddy was growing well and now the rains would only add value to the fields. But the sky looked cloudless and clear. On most mornings, Prabhu supervised the paddy workers but on special days, when he wanted to be alone, he took his goats to graze in the hills.

As he watched his herd of cows waiting patiently for their morning hay, he wondered if there was a way by which the milk could be sold for a better price. He knew that in neighbouring villages the local people sold their milk to the Milk Federation Society. Selling the milk in the village had its drawbacks. People received less per litre of milk and the money earned was just about enough to pay the milkman. Maybe, if he could get a better rate then he could increase the number of cows or better still, all the cows in the village could be brought together under one dairy farm. His land could be used for this purpose. It seemed idyllic and it would probably be a long time before it worked out. But he would explore the possibilities. After all, if the villagers were looking for a substitute income and nobody could blame them *for that,* then this should surely work out.

Preoccupied with his thoughts, he gave the tiny brown calf a rub down. Its huge eyes stared trustingly at him. He hugged its head to his body and watched the mother carelessly chewing on some grass. It was a sign that she trusted him too. If she didn't, by now she would have been staring menacingly at him. Suddenly, he saw a little egg lying on the hay. He picked it up and looked up at the tree from where it could have fallen down. It had not broken because it had landed on the hay. He saw a small nest on top of the tree. Determinedly, he pocketed the egg and sprung up the tree. Holding on to its sturdy branches, he climbed higher and higher and finally he saw the little nest, resting cozily between two branches. Softly, he placed the egg in it and sat back on a branch. The tree was really tall and he could see the entire village spread out around him. There was the temple and the *Banyan* tree. A little further away was the lake, a crisp blue colour. He saw small huts with smoke floating out of their chimneys. A couple of birds cawed in his ears. Otherwise there was no sound. Absolutely no sound, except for that of the wind rustling the leaves softly and the sound of insects screeching somewhere.

He stared at this village he loved so dearly. There were people who suggested to him that he could sell his land and move to a city, but that was not what he wanted. He had once travelled to

Madras, and his first sight of city life shocked him. The station was dark and dirty, the walls soot covered, and hundreds of people rushing around in a mad hurry. No one cared for anyone else. They simply focused on their next destination. He saw a man spitting on the railings and saw another sleeping very close to the toilet. He had hated the sight of the dirty station.

The city did not seem very different from the station. People were walking around in the sweltering hot sun, sweating profusely, talcum powder mixing with sweat and dust. One woman had *sindhoor* flowing down her face in red rivulets. The pavements were crowded. The buses were crowded. Even the beach was crowded. Everywhere he went, he only saw crowds and crowds of people.

He had wondered then if the city had been this way when the Britishers were here. Had there been more order? Some of the buildings he passed on the road looked different, not a bit like the clumsy little newer houses. The roads had names that had a distinct British cast to them – Poes Road, Besant Nagar, Mount Road, Thousand Lights. The Britishers had gone and left behind them a population, which was trying hard to be different. India was an agricultural country with its countless lakes, rivers and climate. It was a land where kings who were great warriors and amazing human beings had ruled, where rice grains and gold grains were of the same size. A land with a cultural heritage, with temples dating back thousands of years. A land of pomp and splendour. This land had a glorious past and yet standing on one of the roads, watching the red buses swishing past, he knew that India had already moved onto the map as an industrial, densely populated, underdeveloped country. It would not be left behind. But there was a vague feeling of loss when he thought that India was now just another country and that too one which was trying hard to catch up with the more economically sound countries. It was not the India with a golden past. Who cared about its past? Not any of these people who waited in bus stands or walked hurriedly towards their offices.

As he walked and contemplated all this, his eyes took in the slums. He didn't know about their existence till he actually came to Madras. The squalor and poverty hit him like a physical pain. Little children playing near the garbage. Women with dirty uncombed hair standing silently in queues waiting for water, which dribbled out of an ancient tap. Dirt, dust, heat and poverty. Is this the new India? Or would the stage of change always bring about disruption? He remembered a verse from Bharadhiyar's poem, 'If there is no food for a single man, we will destroy the entire Universe.' Did Bharadhiyar see the beggars lining the streets?

He knew that he had looked at the city with jaundiced eyes. After the vast open spaces of serenity his village spelt to him, the city was like a huge dirty market place and yet he admired the cars, the vehicles, the tall buildings and the tarred roads. Civilization had ensured that they could commute, move around and achieve. Achieve – the word brought a strange feeling of disquiet in his heart. The old man had not talked about achievement to him. He had only told him to look after his village. But standing on Mount Road, he felt like a tiny speck that could be blown away by a slight breeze.

Shaking his head he moved on and passed the tall buildings and then he witnessed an accident. A speeding bus hit a man rushing madly across the street. The file that the man was carrying in his hands had flown in the air and landed close to where Prabhu stood, watching horrified. As the man lay in the pool of blood, he saw another young man creeping up to him. Bending his head down as though to hear his heart beat, Prabhu saw the man quietly taking off the injured man's watch. Another was furtively picking up the slippers, which had flown off when he was hit and another was quickly going through the dropped file. Prabhu picked up a paper that had flown near his legs. It was a university degree certificate and it said that Ganesh Manohar was a Bachelor of Arts. It had a date and a university stamp. Prabhu stared at the certificate for a moment. Then his eyes focused on the dying man wondering what kind of life this man had lived; what kind of dreams and hopes and promises had he nurtured for himself and his loved ones. But would he, if he had lived longer and achieved all this, have been as contented as Prabhu was with his life in the little village? No answers. Just a dead body.

As he sat now on the tree, he compared the scene that met his eyes with the one he had seen in the city. Sitting here, surrounded by nature, he knew there was no comparison. This was beautiful and this is where he would live and die and his body would be burnt. His ashes would float in the air, touching the trees he loved and fall on his goats and cows. Some of it would land in his paddy fields, and some of it would mix with the honeydew. Even after death, he would linger here for eternity.

He jumped down from the tree and wandered towards his house. He had not seen Kuyili after the night she had come to his place but he often thought about her. Her face, with its wide mouth and pretty nose. Her arched neck and young body. He wondered what was special about her. There were others in the village that were prettier, smarter. And then it came to him. His relationship with Kuyili was also a part of the universe's plans for him, their lives were interwoven in the same way as his ashes would rest on the trees.

It was a month later that the roaring sound of a truck disturbed the calm village. Children and elders ran out of their houses to see who was coming. The truck was huge and nobody could see what was inside. It drove slowly through the narrow mud roads and stopped closed to Raju's house.

Prabhu watched Prakash getting down and running his fingers through his wind tousled hair. He did not look as meek and timid as he had during the first *panchayat* meeting. On the other hand, he stared at the group of villagers who stood around and with a twist of his arm, asked them to move away. That was when Prabhu realized that this was not merely a truck. It was a huge tractor-like vehicle that would flatten the earth and make it smooth for construction. Looking around, Prabhu spotted Raju standing behind a bush and watching the happenings.

Prakash and the truck driver went into Mariamma's house. A few seconds later, a vessel flew out, followed by another and yet another. Prabhu felt a rage building up within him. He looked around at the villagers. They were all standing silently waiting to see what would happen.

A few minutes later Prakash poked his head out of the hut and shouted, "Hey, there is a trunk here with clothes and other stuff. Who will give it to the mad fellow?"

Prabhu walked, slowly and deliberately, to the front and picked up the trunk, his eyes steadily watching Prakash. He placed the trunk in a corner and quickly started arranging the vessels in a row outside the hut. He called out to a couple of young men who worked on his land. In a soft undertone, he gave them a series of instructions to which the two men nodded their heads vigorously. He then went into the hut.

After the bright sun outside, the hut was dark and it took a few seconds for his eyes to adjust to the dimness inside. Then he saw Prakash, his hands rummaging in another trunk. "Get your hands out of that trunk," he said angrily.

"Sure, sure. Just making sure there is nothing valuable inside. After all, if I throw something valuable outside, the villagers might rob it."

Prabhu spat on the ground. Lifting his fist threateningly, he said softly, "One more word out of your dirty mouth and you will have to swallow your teeth."

He picked up the trunk, and saw Mariamma's photo stuck on the wall. It showed a young Mariamma standing shyly in front of the camera. Behind her was a colourful screen depicting a tiger and a goddess.

Prabhu put the photo in his pocket and turning to a subdued Prakash, asked, "Where are you putting up the house for Raju? And how dare you come here to demolish his house without ensuring that he has a roof over his head?"

A stubborn look flashed on the stony eyed man's face. "You go and ask your *panchayat* head all these questions. I was instructed to start construction today, that's all."

"In that case, take the help of the villagers and put up a hut for him, immediately."

"And if I don't?"

Prabhu smiled mirthlessly at him.

Prakash shrugged his bony shoulders and walked out. He called a few of the men standing around and gave them instructions to put up a hut in a little clearing in a corner of the property. Prabhu saw him pull out a wad of notes that he passed around.

As the day progressed, two sets of activities happened jointly. One – Mariamma's house and the land around it were flattened by the road roller, and on the other side, a group of men put up a small green hut. It was nearly evening when the little hut was ready and Prabhu, who had waited and helped the workers, arranged to bring the utensils and trunks into the house. He took Mariamma's photo out of his pocket and pasted it on the wall. A log and dried grass structure, the walls were erected by firmly planting green bamboo trunks, held together with thick rope. The door was made of coconut leaves woven together like a mat. And a pyramid of dried grass formed the roof of the hut. In the gap between the logs, sunlight arched in, in neat arrows and drew crazy patterns of light and shade.

As he moved around the little hut, putting it in order, Prabhu saw Raju peeping in.

"Come in, Raju. See if you like your new house," he said, smiling.

Raju's eyes darted around the little hut, taking in the vessels and Mariamma's photo stuck on the wall. Walking closer to the photo, he stopped. Prabhu watched him from the doorway. Raju was lifting up his tattered shirt and wiping the photo clean.

As he walked out, he cursed loudly, wondering at the ways of men. Once again he felt a frustrated anger seeping into his veins. How could any human being cause so much suffering for Raju? Returning to the hut, Prabhu tapped Raju softly on his shoulders and then walked out into the enveloping darkness.

For the next two months, there was constant noise in the village - of huge lorries driving in, raking up white dust, of men yelling out to each other and other noises. Noises that disrupted the atmosphere of the village.

Prabhu spent his time as far away from the construction area as possible. He spent more time taking his goats to the hills for grazing. The paddy was nearly ready to be harvested and Prabhu wondered if his workers would come back to help in the harvest. He paid them wages and they stayed on his land, but he knew that Prakash was paying a lot of money to these people. As he stood and gazed at the golden paddy nodding to the rhythm of the breeze, he saw Kuyili walking towards his hut.

It was a long time since he had seen her. As he watched her, he felt a strange sensation in his chest. His heart was beating differently. It seemed to match her steps as she walked towards him, her red sari draping her body beautifully. He saw that she had a red *sindhoor* on her forehead, and red flowers in her plaited hair. She had also tied a red ribbon at the end of her long plait. She smiled at him and he felt the strange feeling in his chest increasing.

"Don't worry about your harvest. Some of the women have talked to their men and the harvest will happen on schedule."

How could she know he would be worried about that? He chewed on his lower lip and stared at her.

She suddenly grinned and said, "One of the men told his wife that Prakaas was paying him lots of money, so she picked up the broom and beat him with it. I heard her yelling, Prakaas gives more money, eh? And who has given you a piece of land to settle your dried up backside on?"

She laughed at the memory and he joined in the laughter. Whenever she was around him, he felt his fears and worries vanishing. Impulsively he asked, "Will you cook for me today?"

They walked back to the hut together. She went in and he strolled to the small vegetable garden at the back from where he pulled out a few onion shoots and plucked some ripe tomatoes. From the ground he uprooted potatoes and carrots. Finally, he picked some beans.

When he went into the hut, he saw that she had already lit the firewood. Logs of wood were burning with a crackling sound. Two vessels sat perched on the mud platform. She worked neatly and deftly and he sat down to watch her.

As the vessels hummed on the fire, her eyes swept around the little hut. She saw a few books piled up in a heap.

"You like to read?" she asked him and he saw that she was surprised.

"Why? Did you think I didn't even know the alphabet?" he asked her teasingly.

"I didn't mean that. I mean I knew you had gone to a school, too." Seeing his surprised look, she added, "I asked my mother and she told me."

"Is it important to you that I should not be an illiterate bum?" he asked her.

"Even if you were, I would still marry you," she replied.

He got up from where he sat and went to her. She watched him tensely as he held out a firm hand. She bent her head and felt a burning sensation in her cheeks. And then she felt his arms lifting her up. He held her at arm's length and drunk in her beauty, her cheeks flushed with the heat from the fire. Stray ash clung to her hair. He brushed it off and his fingers lingered on her hair. From her hair to her face seemed like many miles of beautiful countryside as his fingers moved towards her face. He touched her eyes. He touched her nose and her mouth.

He kissed her hand and then her cheek. As he moved his lips across her face she leaned towards him and breathed in his masculine sweat smell. It intoxicated her and she closed her eyes. They stood interwoven for a long time. It was only when a log on the fire crackled indignantly that they broke off.

As afternoon stole up on them, they ate their food sitting together. And in the light of the early evening she went away.

Prabhu felt a strong sensation in his heart. It was like nothing he had felt for anybody else. As he stood there watching her walk away, he saw Kuyili's uncle walking towards him. He saw it coming but could not stop the punch to his face. As he rubbed his fast bruising chin, he saw the man walking away, whispering obscenities.

A strange fear for Kuyili stole up on Prabhu. She had told him about this uncle who wanted to marry her. Nobody had ever dared raise his hands on him and yet this man had punched him! Maybe he should talk to Kuyili to move out of the village till he was ready to marry her.

As he stood there near the door, watching night descend on his little village, Prabhu thought of the number of changes that had happened in a brief period of time. After many years of mere existence, he felt that his life was changing. It was like an earthquake, which he had felt one night as he lay in bed. His bed rocked and he thought he would be thrown off. It was a feeling of having absolutely no control. It was frightening and yet exciting! When he had rushed out of his hut a moment later, he saw that many of the villagers were standing around. The goats and cows were raising a huge ruckus and the wild dogs were howling fearfully. The same feeling assailed him now. On one side he felt a strange happiness. He rubbed his lips and stared at the darkness. Her soft lips, her tender skin – a feeling of excitement welled up in him but along with it he remembered Raju's face. A boy whose existence he had barely acknowledged a few months ago was suddenly becoming an important part of his life. He felt strange sensations in the pit of his stomach every time he thought of the boy. There were some lessons he would be learning just by being associated with the boy. Lessons which neither the lands nor the weather had taught him. And then he thought of the unexpected happenings in his village. It was not existence any more. It was unexpectedness. Every day brought with it new happenings and while they scared him, he knew that these would be a real test for him. He had no room for boredom, listlessness or even just existence! He had to be alert. Alert all the time!

He remembered the night before Mariamma's body was found. The night when he thought of his boring life. And yet barely two months later his world was changing. Strange were the ways of god. The thought of god reminded him that the *poojari* in the temple would be completing the last *pooja* for the day. As he thought of the temple, he heard the gong of temple bells and he felt his feet moving in the direction of the sound. As he walked he saw the canopy of stars hanging low over his head and a soft moon drifting aimlessly. Whoever had created this world had a specific plan for each of us. He knew now that he had a preordained role to play in this lifetime and yet the fact that he could not see it clearly now was in itself the lesson he would learn out of this role. He walked on into the gathering dusk, carefully winding his way through the bushes. Snakes abounded in the village and he knew that no man could survive a cobra's bite.

As he turned the corner of the mud road, he saw the temple standing there like a sentinel, guarding and protecting this little village. The fragrant smell of jasmines and roses, mingled with the smell of night queen and *vetiver*. Inside the temple the *poojari* stood near the idol, his Sanskrit *mantras* making rhythmic music rather than actual sense to Prabhu's ears. He listened hard. The words made no sense, but they helped to keep his eyes on the idol. He prayed softly for his village, for Raju and for the way their lives would change. When he finally returned to his house, he felt lighter, as though he had left behind a bundle from his heart in the temple.

SIX

Chapter

The harvest season began. The village wore a garb of excitement. A good harvest always had that effect on the villagers and they were ready to start the cutting of the paddy stalks in August. Some of the men were not there but to make up for this, most of the women were.

They worked hard and long, chopping the paddy with U-shaped knives. The harvest would take a week and after that would come the process of separating the rice from its husk. Finally, the rice would be cleaned and packed in gunny bags to be sold.

Throughout this period, the fireworks factory continued to rise. The construction workers were putting up a huge walled in room. The entire construction would be of concrete, with whitewashed walls. Rows and rows of platforms were built for workers to sit on and assemble the crackers. Prakash now stayed in the village, and slept inside the building. Most of the work was nearly complete and he planned to have an official opening of the factory in a couple of weeks' time. He would invite the local MP. Maybe one of the ministers would chair the function. After all, putting up a factory in a village meant a focus on small-scale industries.

The way it worked was really simple. Prakash would pay a sum of money to Gokulan and Satvarlal Sait for their initiative. All the raw materials for making crackers would come from Sivakasi. This factory would be an assembling unit where, after the crackers were wrapped up and pasted, they would be packed in cartons and kept ready for Deepavalli, the festival of lights. The Goddess Lakshmi, it was believed, visited any house, which had lamps shining in it, and the whole country went wild on this night burning fireworks. The labour would continue all through the year for the festival, which happened only once a year. A lot of work was involved as the labels had to be pasted, boxes sealed and packed in cartons. All this had to be done manually since, with fireworks, it was difficult to bring in any machinery, as a small electric spark would set off a spectacular fireworks show!

Prakash knew several ways of making money, just like he had already made a tidy sum in the construction itself. With the constant flux in the real estate market, he realized that it was time to move into a steady job and that is where the fireworks factory would come in useful. He would be appointed as the factory manager and from there it was a simple step to making money by taking cuts from the wages of the workers, a cut from the material – you name it. This was one reason why he had never got married. A wife would always be an impediment, dictating and demanding. But he did have his urges. And that was planned into his personal expenses.

As he sat one night, outside his factory, he felt a strange sensation. Since moving over, he had not had sex and it was a long time. He relaxed on his haunches and thought of all the attractive women he had met and a picture of a girl in a red sari with red ribbons on her hair drifted into his mind. She had a sexy figure and he wished right now that he could buy her. But he dared not; he knew that Prabhu was soft on her and that man was one obnoxious human being. He shivered when he remembered the way he had been manhandled when he was pulling down Raju's hut. Desire dissipating, he cursed softly under his breath.

The same evening, as Prakash sat outside his factory dreaming of women and money, Prabhu walked back home with the goats. Suddenly, he remembered the knife. He had wrapped it carefully and hidden it in his hut. Because of the recent happenings in the village, he had totally forgotten the knife and its relation to Mariamma's death, except for mentioning it to Gokulan once. He reached his house just as the first stars were showing up in the sky. Going inside, he switched on the light and peeped under his cot. In the dim light of the bulb, he saw that the knife was not there. A cold chill ran down his spine. Had he kept it somewhere else? He looked around the hut. No! He had not put it anywhere else, he remembered clearly. Maybe Kuyili had put it somewhere the day she had come over to cook for him. He decided to ask her and walked rapidly towards her hut. As he walked, a crescent moon hung low on the sky and a few fireflies flitted around like tiny torches. He picked his way through the night insects and frogs. The small bulb outside her hut was shining like a beacon.

Reaching his destination, he shouted loudly, "Kuyili!"

She poked her head out and then opened the door when she saw who it was. Wiping her wet hands on her sari she said, "Come inside."

He could see she was flustered. He had not come looking for her to her house before.

Her mother sat in a corner rolling *beedis*. The mother looked young, more like Kuyili's elder sister rather than her mother. Her husband had died tragically in a bullock race, or *jalli kattu,* as it was more popularly known. The woman, since then, had dedicated her life to bringing up her daughter.

When she saw Prabhu, she hurriedly got up and, bending her head in respect, asked him to sit down.

He looked around the tidy hut with its pots and pans. A cot stood in a corner and on top of it was a few magazines. Kuyili's red sari hung on a clothesline in the corner. He sat down on the mat, wondering how he could ask her about the knife in front of her mother. He was sure the mother did not know about Kuyili's visit to his hut. She would be aghast if she knew. Young maidens did not visit bachelor's homes. He waited and maybe Kuyili guessed his thoughts because, after a minute, she told her mother to go across and bring a tender coconut for the visitor. Her mother picked up a sickle and walked out into the darkness.

Hurriedly he asked her, "Kuyili, did you pick up a bundle which was under my cot and put it anywhere else?"

Eyebrows knotted, she pondered for a moment and then shook her head slowly, "No. I don't think so. I don't remember seeing a bundle under your cot at all."

A cold hand clasped his heart and squeezed it. He wondered who would have taken it. Suddenly he remembered Raju. Had he come by and quietly taken the knife away? If Raju had stolen it and it was more than likely that it was he, then he would definitely not tell Prabhu anything. For the first time, Prabhu felt a flicker of a doubt crossing his mind. Was Raju really innocent?

"Oh! You came here only for that."

He heard the disappointment in her voice. He also remembered the stinging slap that her uncle had given him. Maybe he could use this opportunity to talk to Kuyili's mother.

He smiled at her.

When the old lady came back inside with the tender coconut, he said softly, "Amma, I would like to marry your daughter and I would like your permission for the same."

She lifted her head and looked at him. A look of pride and joy, of happiness and thankfulness flitted across her face. She lifted her hands and placing them together, bowed her head. She tried to say something but her tongue was stuck to the roof of her mouth. In a flash, she recalled the last few years and how difficult it had been for her to put Kuyili through her studies. She looked at her soiled fingers. The *beedis* she rolled incessantly had given her a permanent backache.

Finally, she found her voice. "I am so happy, my son." Her voice was quivering, like a leaf on a windy morning.

He smiled at her and she saw her daughter's future husband. He would make her daughter happy, her heart whispered. She ran to a small sill on top of which was perched a black and white photograph of a man. He had red *sindhoor* on his forehead. She rubbed her fingers on the *sindhoor* till the red powder stuck to her fingers. Coming up to Prabhu, she put the *sindhoor* on his forehead. Tears were rolling down her eyes. Brushing them away, she brought out a plate with a coconut and some betel leaves on it. These she pressed into his hands.

As he walked out, he felt a soft tap on his shoulder. He turned around and saw that it was a flower that had hit him and fallen to the ground. It was a yellow *samandhi.* He saw Kuyili laughing at him. He picked up the flower and put it into his pocket. He looked at her for a long moment, and then moved away slowly.

As he walked back, he forgot all his worries and carelessly walked on the thorny path. The moon was hidden behind a few clouds and he had to slow down a bit. It was really dark. He tried to remember the way, but this was not a route he was very familiar with. He walked slowly and steadily, straining his eyes to see the path ahead.

As he crossed a dark shrub, which looked like a crouching man, he heard soft footsteps behind him.

Stopping, he called out, "Who is it?"

His heart was beating faster. He strained to hear a sound but there was nothing. Whoever had been following him had also stopped.

"Who is it?" he asked in a louder voice.

He suddenly felt exposed; standing there unprotected with no idea what or who was ahead or behind him. He turned around and started walking brusquely but this time he was sure of it. A pair of footsteps was following him. Suddenly he felt it. A sharp pain shot up his hand. He blocked the steely blade of the knife with his open hand and felt warm liquid oozing out. Unmindful of the pain, he brought his other hand down with a crushing blow on the man's jaw. He heard the soft crunch of bones breaking. He lifted his hand and brought it down on the man's nose. Suddenly, the man turned around and fled into the darkness. Prabhu debated chasing him, but the pain in his hand was increasing with every second and he was bleeding profusely. As he ran towards the main road, an image of a sharp whip hitting a man's back came to his mind. The man was on a horse and his father, old and frail stood bent with age. How much pain his father would have gone through and for what? Not for himself, not for his family or his son. For the dream of a free country?

The wound didn't hurt anymore as he quickly ran towards the main road. He reached it a few minutes later. By now the blood flow had slowed down but he knew that he needed some stitches. Just as he reached the road he saw the bright lights of a lorry heading his way. He waved his hand and the lorry stopped.

The driver, a young man with a pockmarked face, opened the passenger door for him. He got in with difficulty using his unhurt hand to heave himself into the high seat of the lorry. As he sat down, he saw that the lorry driver was one of the men he had seen near the factory construction site. The man had a horrified look on his face and Prabhu realized that the blood from his wound had dribbled onto his shirt and *dhoti* and he looked a sight.

"As you can see, I am hurt. Can you drop me off at the town nursing home?" He said this with a smile to mask the seriousness of the situation.

The driver, Muthu, started the vehicle with a jolt and they sped into the night. When the lorry reached the town hospital, Prabhu got down and walked in slowly. He felt a bit faint and a soft throbbing pain had begun in his temples.

The hospital looked worn out and dirty. Even at this hour, there were crying babies and mothers, a few very sick looking older people and a couple of men. As soon as the women saw him, they hurriedly walked up to him. Some of the women started crying, and the men came up and stood beside him. One of them was the town's ironmonger, Velayutham.

"Who did this to you, Saami?" he asked humbly. "Tell us his name and I will bring you his right hand."

Prabhu pondered for a second and then said, "No, No. Nobody did this to me. I hurt myself. I was trying to chop down some wood and I cut myself."

Disbelieving looks flitted across the faces but they did not ask him anything further. Instead, they led him into the hospital where a tired nurse was standing.

As he felt the sharp sting of the antiseptic lotion, he wondered who could have wanted to hurt him. If he had not stopped the knife with his hand, it would have pierced his chest. A shiver ran down his spine. The day had been a bad one. First of all, he had carelessly lost the knife that was used to murder Mariamma and now he was knifed. Could the same person who murdered Mariamma want him dead, too?

Tired after the blood loss, he went home quietly and lay down on his bed. As he slept that night, he dreamt of lonely children and wasted mothers. He dreamt of yellow flowers falling on blood. He dreamt of men with terrible masks and gleaming knives. He also dreamt of his father.

Next morning, Prabhu woke up to the sound of someone knocking on his door urgently. He opened his eyes and rubbing them awake, opened his door. His hand felt heavy and painful and it was with an effort that he undid the latch.

Gokulan came in with an anxious look on his face. "How are you, Prabhu? The whole village is talking about how you were attacked last night."

Surprised at this news, Prabhu washed his face outside his hut and then came back inside. "I am all right. It is just a small cut."

"What happened?" Gokulan asked in a surprised tone.

"Nothing much. I was walking back home from Kuyili's house when I felt that I was being followed. I called out loudly to whoever it was but no one answered and then he attacked me. But the moment the sound of the footsteps came closer I turned around and put my hands in front of me. Since it was very dark, the attacker could not see where he was stabbing me."

Suddenly he remembered. "I hurt the man. I gave him two blows to his face."

Excited now, he said, "If we can find out who went to the hospital here or in Kuppam we will know who the attacker is."

Gokulan frowned as he concentrated. Then he said, "Okay, don't worry. I'll take care of that. You just lie down and relax."

As the day progressed, several visitors came to see him. Most of them were labourers who worked in his fields. Kuyili came by but stood in the shadows where he could not see her face. If she was crying, he could not make out and he laughed a lot and behaved more flippantly about the wound, not wanting to make her worried.

The wound took its time to heal and during this time, Prabhu walked his goats to their grazing land near the hills. Little flowers of varying hues covered the slopes like nature's carpets and the goats merrily feasted on grass tinged with dew and flowers soaked in nectar. He used this time to introspect and it bothered him that though he knew that someone was behind Mariamma's murder, he was not acting on it. But then thoughts of Mariamma's murder always brought with them thoughts about Raju and he realized that he was not really sure about Raju. Who else could have taken the knife from under his cot and why? If the murderer was Raju then it was clear that he was mentally unstable and would need treatment. But if it were a diabolic person hiding in the village and benefiting from this then it would be better to keep quiet till he revealed his hand.

Were these excuses he created to avoid confrontation? If this was true then he was a worse person than Prakash. He often wished that his father was here to guide him and then he realized that the answer to almost everything lay with Raju and yet, because he refused to talk, nobody could help or solve anything. So then his first task was to work on Raju, to comfort him and love him. He was sure that if he did that, Raju would talk and then the truth would be known.

Prabhu woke up the next day, his mind resolved on spending time with Raju. When he went to the little green hut looking for him, he saw that the boy had pasted little pictures on the walls of the hut. Pictures of little children, animals and mountains. The mud stove in the corner had a small vessel on it. Prabhu opened the dish and saw some overcooked rice inside. Strange feelings interfered with his breathing and hating himself and all those people who had caused Raju trouble, he walked towards the lake. There, he saw the boy, sitting on a slightly raised stone, throwing pebbles into the water. As the pebble fell in and broke the water into countless ripples the boy's mouth would twist into a distorted smile. He watched the boy and then walked away. He was not strong enough to deal with the boy's broken heart. He was too attached, too involved. He knew that the last thing the boy needed right now was his sympathy. It would only make him feel more abused and sorry for himself.

He would return when his heart was stronger. Not when his eyes clouded over and his voice broke with sorrow when he saw the boy.

One of the village women had a boy who was not normal. He could neither walk nor talk properly. His limbs and his mind were disconnected and his body refused to obey his mind. He had seen the boy's mother look after the boy and the two of them continued to live in harmony, the boy now over sixteen years of age and his mother barely forty but with the wrinkles of a sixty year old. Prabhu had one day asked her how she managed her life.

Her answer had been clear. Even now, her words rang in his ears. "Everything used to hurt me and make me sad. If I saw children playing and my own son lying unmoving on the cot, I would cry. When I went past the school and saw little children there I would cry. I would cry every time I bathed and cleaned my son. When he saw my grief, he became so sad and I realized that it was in my eyes that he was seeing an abnormal self. If I treated him like a normal boy he would begin to react like one. And then I realized that to help him, I needed to detach myself from him. I could neither take away my son's pain or suffering. We both have our own destiny – his to be god's preferred child and mine to care for him like an idol in the temple. Since then, I have no time to feel sorry for myself. I just move on and keep pushing myself to help him."

Her words had reminded Prabhu about the lines in the *Bhagawat Gita* where Lord Krishna tells Arjuna, 'The life we're living now is not our only one. We've been through many. The spark of awareness within us – the self, or soul, or whatever you want to call it, has no beginning and no end. No knife can cut it, no fire can burn it, no wind can blow it away. But that spark of life keeps moving on from one body to the next. At one time you have the body of a child. Then you move on to a young person's body. Then to a middle-aged body and then to the body of an old person. Yet, in all those bodies you feel yourself to be the same you. Because you are the same you. Only your body has changed. Your body changes but you're always the same. So you and your body are different. You are not your body. You can neither destroy nor create life.'

He was not yet ready to help Raju. There was clarity in this thought. Even though this acceptance brought pain with it, Prabhu knew that it was only a matter of time before he took Raju under his wing.

being now is not our only one. We've been through many. The spark of awareness within us—the self or soul, or whatever you want to call it—has no beginning and no end. No knife can cut it, no fire can burn it, no wind can blow it away. But that spark of life keeps moving on from one body to the next. At one time we take the body of a child. Then we move on to a young person's body. Then to a middle-aged body, and then to the body of an old person. Yet in all these bodies you feel yourself to be the same person. Because you are the same person. Only your body has changed. Your body changes, but you always stay the same. So you are. Your body is different. You are not your body. You can [illegible] create life.'

He was accepting life for Raja. There was clarity in the surrender. Even though, this acceptance brought pain with it. [illegible] knew that it was only a matter of time before he took command of his ways.

SEVEN

Chapter

It was a month later, that the villagers began their plans for an event that caused excitement and anticipation. The annual fair or *thiruvizha*, as it was called, was centred round the Samundeeshwari goddess temple. The fair was a thanksgiving to the goddess for the year gone by. It usually happened over a couple of weeks with several different kinds of events happening around the temple. Samundeeshwari was an avatar of Parvati in a serene mood. Her mood sprang from contentment and the villagers nurtured this feeling by thanking her every year for her benevolence and kindness.

With a fortnight left for the Samundeeshwari *thiruvizha*, the villagers went around cleaning and sprucing up their huts. Some of them brought buckets of lime whitewash and painted the walls with rough brushes.

In the temple, the *poojari* and the important people of the village gathered to discuss details for the *thiruvizha*. It was an event that the whole village waited for all year and plans started well in advance.

The temple committee, which consisted of Gokulan, Prabhu, the *poojari* and a few others, met on a sunny morning. They decided to invite a dance troupe from a neighboring village. They also decided that the temple would have story recital or *kalakshebam,* as it was popularly known, when stories of valour and fame from the *Ramayana* and *Mahabharata* would be told over a Public Announcing System. The man who was famous for his singsong voice was Pattuvanar Ramaswamy. He could narrate the stories with all the correct intonations. When he described scenes of love his voice would flow smooth like melted butter but when he described a war scene, his voice would tremble like the angry chords of a violin. All the older people in this, and the neighbouring villages, looked forward to this event. They would sit around in groups and listen to Pattuvanar Ramaswamy and his accompanying drummers.

"What if it rains?" asked Paniyar, who sold vegetables in a stall in the town. "It did rain last year."

The much-awaited rains always came when it was unnecessary and no villager could watch it falling on concrete ground without feeling a tinge of sadness. Rain was meant only for the lakes, rivers and their precious paddy fields.

Suddenly, Gokulan said, "If the factory is ready by then, we can get some fireworks. Colourful rockets can soar into the sky, telling the whole world that we are celebrating Samundeeshwari thiruvizha." His chest expanded with pride.

Prabhu looked doubtful. Once again the thought of crackers made him feel that the harmony of the village would be disrupted.

Softly, he asked, "Won't it interfere with the kalakshebam?"

"So what? Let it. After all, we have all heard that Pattuvanar many times before."

"And yet, the old people look forward to it year after year."

"Let's see. I am not saying that we should have crackers all through the function. We'll see how it goes."

And so the discussions continued, even as some of the younger men swept and cleaned the temple grounds. A group of *poojaris* chanted *mantras* as they washed the temple floors and cleaned the pictures of gods and goddesses, which lined the wall around a platform meant for sitting. At any time a hundred people could sit on this platform.

As the days for the *thiruvizha* neared, vendors set up rows and rows of colourful wares in the market place. This was called *sandhe* and the women flocked to buy ribbons and hair clips. Some of them bought bangles and flirted with the man who sold blouses. Most of them bought new clothes.

Walking around watching the stalls, Prabhu felt an urge to buy a sari for Kuyili. The first shop he went to had different coloured saris spread out on a cushioned mattress. There was simply no way he could decide which was nice and which was not. He recalled that Kuyili liked bright colours – he had seen her in canary yellow and bright red. Maybe he should buy her a blue sari. The blue of a clear summer sky would suit her. He looked at the saris spread out before him but there were none in the particular shade that he wanted. Patiently, he went from shop to shop, till finally, he found what he was looking for. It was the exact blue he had in mind and it had small sunflowers painted on it. The sari reminded him of a sunflower field overlooked by a bright blue sky. He bought it knowing that the man was charging him too much, but he seldom bargained with these people. They earned so little that denying them of any money seemed very unfair to him. These were poor people who tried hard to sell and yet, went home empty handed on several days. He did not feel any satisfaction when he bargained with them.

After buying the sari, he bought himself a comb. His hair had grown back and he had looked for his old comb when he realized that it was lost somewhere. He bought a no nonsense comb made of thick white plastic and ran it through his hair, feeling its blunt teeth massaging his scalp. He paid a rupee for it and turned back home. Hearing a light sound, he saw that Gokulan's wife was walking beside him. She was hiding a smile and he knew that she had seen him buy the sari.

Blushing slightly, he enquired, "How is your daughter?"

"Humph!" she snorted and said, "She is okay but his other wife's children trouble her."

Prabhu wondered who actually troubled whom. Gokulan's first wife had died leaving behind four children and all of them were still young enough to want a mother.

"Buying bangles, and now saris," she said, the words tripping out of her mouth and mingling with a chuckle.

"Not saris, just one sari," he said indignantly.

She laughed then and said, "If you buy a woman a sari you

must also buy her a blouse."

"Why?" he asked simply.

"It is only for widows that we give saris without blouses. For unmarried or married women you must give a blouse along with a sari."

This bothered him. Buying a sari was easy, but asking for a blouse? He could envisage the blouse seller's face, grinning mockingly at him.

As though she could read his thoughts, she said, "Come along. I will buy it for you. Here, give me the packet."

He followed her as she walked quickly to the popular blouse seller's shop. As usual, the blouse (*choli*) seller, a debonair looking young man with a colourful scarf tied rakishly around his neck like a Tamil actor of old, stood flirting with the young women who came to buy *cholis*.

"This colour will suit you. It is the exact shade of your skin," he was telling a dark young girl, showing her a blue blouse.

It won't suit you a bit, Prabhu felt tempted to say, but he watched the way the *choli* seller's eyes were resting pointedly on the girl's breasts. Flustered and vaguely happy, the girl was clasping the blouse piece to her chest like a treasure.

The *choli* seller was now looking at a huge middle-aged woman. His eyes told her believable lies and she felt the years and the extra flesh melting away under his seductive eyes. She too was holding on to several *choli* pieces.

Gokulan's wife said in a business like voice, "Hello hero, can you give me a blouse to match this sari?"

He tried to win her with a sexy smile, but when she lowered her eyes, he became all business-like and instead pulled out a cherry pink *choli* piece.

"Are you colour blind?" she asked him angrily.

Smiling slightly, he said, "No, I will give a blue blouse for the blue sari but this is to match the colour of your cheeks."

Prabhu sighed inwardly and turned his head away. The man was irrepressible. But he admired his knack of attracting women customers.

The *choli* seller was now lighting a *beedi* with a match by rubbing the matchstick on a stone. He put the flame to his *beedi*, and smiled at the impressed women who stood around.

After the blouse was paid for and wrapped up in newspaper, Prabhu walked back home, smiling to himself. He remembered the ease with which the *choli* seller had lit the matchstick. He should embark on an acting career. It would take him places!

As he walked back home, he also remembered Gokulan's wife telling him to hand over the *choli* material early so that Kuyili would have time to get it stitched. He decided to visit her house.

As he crossed the road and walked on the thorny path that led to her house, he passed Raju's house. Without pausing to think, he stopped and peeped inside. In a dark corner, he saw Raju sitting on a mat.

"Hey Raju," he said and entered the house.

When Raju saw him, he quickly hid the pictures but not before

Prabhu caught a glimpse of it. They were pictures of little children, neatly cut out from magazines and newspapers.

He stepped into the hut and looked around. It looked just the way it had, the day he had moved in Mariamma's things into the newly constructed hut. He looked at Mariamma's photo on the wall. Raju had got up from where he sat in the corner and was running his fingers over the scar on Prabhu's hand. This was the first time that Raju had come so close to him and was actually touching him. His instinct told him to stay still, lest he frighten Raju away and so he stood as Raju ran his fingers over and over again on the scar. Suddenly, he lifted his bent head and looked at Prabhu. His eyes were filled with questions.

Prabhu smiled and said, "No, it doesn't hurt so much now. And yes, I gave double what I got. I punched him on his nose." Prabhu made an action with his hands, beating the air, and Raju watched him steadily.

Prabhu looked at the boy. What would make him smile? He felt a cold hand grip his heart and turning his head, he walked out of the shady hut with its green shadows and pictures of little children.

Something had changed, his heart whispered. Raju had not only come close to him but had even looked at him enquiringly. Less than a month ago he had refused to come anywhere close to Prabhu. A small feeling of victory spread its glow within Prabhu's heart. He was entering Raju's lonely world and it was now only a matter of time before the boy actually accepted him. Once again he felt tears stinging the back of his eyes. He cursed under his breath. Till he was absolutely sure that Raju would not see the sadness in his face, he would stay away. The last thing the boy needed was someone reaching out to him from sympathy.

When he reached Kuyili's house, he saw that the uncle who had beaten him was pottering around outside. Seeing Prabhu approaching, he turned and ran away.

Prabhu stood outside the hut and called out loudly, "Kuyili, Kuyili."

His voice, carried by the summer breeze, travelled into the hut and out through the back door where she sat cleaning raw rice. She dropped the plate, scattering the rice and ran towards the sound of his voice. She felt her heart beating in the strange way that it always did at the sound of his voice. Nothing, she told herself, could change the beat. She ran out and stopped when she saw him standing there, his hair neatly combed, with a packet in his hands.

"Kuyili, I bought a sari for you, for the thiruvizha," he said, handing the packet to her.

She held the packet in her hand and looked at his face with its neatly combed hair and clear eyes.

When she smiled, his throat constricted. He swallowed to clear the feeling but it wouldn't go away. As she turned and walked towards her house, he watched her swaying hips. It reminded him of lotus flowers swaying softly on a clear lake.

As he walked back home, with a start, he realized that Kuyili's uncle•fs face was uninjured. Somehow he had believed in his heart that that was the man who had attacked him at night. The thought brought with it several doubts and fears he did not want to acknowledge.

If it was not Kuyili's uncle, then who was it?

The next few days saw hectic activity, as people got ready for the *thiruvizha*. Especially around the temple, the villagers worked day and night to put up platforms. Folk dancers, singers and musicians flocked around the temple looking for facilities and fixing the timings. Gokulan spent most of his time in the temple, ordering people around and ensuring that things were going smoothly. He was at his best when things were going his way. He basked in the attention, which the local talent bestowed upon him. Today it was a group of dancers who were haggling the rates with him. The main dancer and his partner would get the maximum money; the remaining would be divided between the musicians.

Garagatum was a complicated dance in which the dancer would have a conical shaped object, done up in flowers, on his head. The entire dance centred around his ability to dance while balancing the object on his head. It demanded grace, poise and perfect timing. There would also be a singer and the songs would generally be a kind of a duet between the two dancers. This group, which came from a neighbouring village, was there, year after year. And every year, the same bargaining over price, took place. It was almost as though they secretly enjoyed it.

The main dancer, Patwarda, was now waiting for Gokulan to

okay the rates. In the meantime, a soda seller hustled around, pushing soda bottles into the hands of the dancers. It was a ritual, standing under the hot sun, and guzzling sodas.

Prabhu stopped by and watched the proceedings.

Patwarda belched softly and said, "Thaliver, this year we are doing a very special dance. One which none of your villagers would have seen. The theme is taken from the Ramayana, when Rama lifts the bow, shoots an arrow and wins Sita's hand in marriage."

"Sure. And that's what you said you would do last year, but you ended up doing the same dance you do every year," Gokulan snorted.

"That's not true. We did plan to do this dance, but unfortunately my partner hurt her ankle and I had to make do with a substitute."

The partner, Ragini, as she was called, fluttered her eyelashes. If you scrubbed away the makeup and dressed her differently she would actually be pretty, thought Prabhu looking at her. Catching him watching her, she gave him a seductive smile, startling him. The smile was a clear invitation.

Well, well.

Conversation continued along the same lines, with the dancer selling his concept and Gokulan acting the cynical village head.

But beyond the haggling and the sarcasm, an air of excitement hung over the village. There were just two days more for the *thiruvizha* and the villagers gathered in groups, talking and laughing. A group of women strung long rows of mango leaves that would run around the temple like a tall fence suspended in the air. Wild flowers and jasmines were plucked and brought in baskets, in anticipation of the *pooja*.

Prabhu looked around for Kuyili. He hadn't seen her for sometime now. Not after he had given her the sari. Somehow, a day without seeing her seemed so incomplete. He wondered if this was the way the hero in a film he had seen, in a tent long ago, had felt. He had watched that movie one night when sleep eluded him. Also he had wanted to see what attracted the crowds. It was funny, sitting inside a hot tent, on hard wooden benches. Myriad smells invaded his nostrils: fading flowers, *arrack* and *beedis*. And then the film had started. The crowds made so much noise, whistling and clapping their hands that he could barely hear the dialogues. The film had been a love story and the hero was ardently pursuing a willowy lady who took great pleasure in tormenting the poor man. The hero danced around trees and sung sad songs in the rain and Prabhu had found the whole thing incredibly amusing. And yet, now he wondered if this was the way the hero had felt when he had made an ass of himself. Smiling, he looked around and saw that the *garagatum* dancer was watching him. When he looked at her, she closed one eye in a deliberate wink. Seeing his startled face, she broke out into a husky laugh and turned her face away. He felt colour stinging his cheeks and looking up he saw that she was enjoying herself. He felt his own eye shut in a deliberate wink and before she could react, he turned around and walked to the back yard, where logs of firewood were being neatly arranged.

As he watched the men working, he once again remembered the knife and the night attack. The *thiruvizha* would give him the opportunity to see who had hurt him. After all, the man must surely have a crooked mouth after the jaw-breaking blow he had received.

The *thiruvizha* started in the evening, just as the sky lit up with stars. Conch shells and drums mingled with the excited noise of the crowds. Acoustic instruments like *nadhaswarams* and *mridhangams* kept in tune, speeding up the heartbeats of the audience. Groups of people, dressed in all their finery, flocked to the temple. A full moon hung low in the sky and a faint breeze was blowing, carrying with it the smell of flowers and sandalwood.

Prabhu had worn a silk *dhoti* and a silk shirt for the festival. He had also remembered to put on a gold chain, which he tucked inside his shirt collar. His hair had grown back now and he looked handsome as he walked around issuing instructions and ensuring that everything was all right.

Gokulan, too, was dressed in silk, but he also had a silk scarf neatly folded and placed on one shoulder. It indicated that he was an important man.

The *thiruvizha* began with the sound of the musical instruments, followed by a burst of crackers. The villagers looked at the beautiful display of colourful fireworks, which speckled the dark sky with gold, silver and the colours of the rainbow. Prabhu watched in amazement. He had not realized that Gokulan had actually carried out his plan of having a fireworks display. People were clapping their hands and little children were jumping around with happiness. A young boy now set off a long row of small fireworks that burst with a splatter. The deafening noise continued without a gap for about five minutes. Little children cowered in fear and old men and women were retreating to the safety of the temple. And then it stopped as suddenly as it had started. As the crowds waited, in a moment, which was like an anticlimax, Gokulan brought both his palms together in a loud clap. Soon all the villagers were clapping and the musicians, relieved to have the stage back, started the programme.

EIGHT Chapter

The *thiruvizha* would go on for seven days, and on each of these days there would be a special programme. Today, being the first day, was reserved only for the musicians, because the sounds they produced should not interfere with the nightlong *pooja*, which would go on in the sanctum sanctorum. Groups of women walked into the temple and stood around looking at the extravagant *pooja*, where four *poojaris* uttered *mantras* simultaneously. The men gathered in little groups as they waited for their wives to come out.

Around ten at night, the crowds drifted towards the back of the temple where food was being served. Sitting outside, surrounded by a night sky and cool breeze, with the sound of musical instruments, Prabhu felt lighthearted. This was so special. There was nothing to match the gaiety and joy that the *thiruvizha* brought with it. He sat down to eat beside Gokulan.

And then he saw Kuyili. Dressed in the blue sari, she looked unusual in the night, like a peacock that had lost its way in the forest and found itself in the midst of people. He felt a funny feeling somewhere at the back of his throat. As she heaped the plantain leaf with food, he noticed the blue bangles on her hand and the way they jingled. Bent over his leaf, she lifted her eyes to his, her mouth an inch away from his and both were transported to a part of the universe that was uninhabited, save for the two of them. The Milky Way and the solar system spun a crazy pattern around the two and they stood poised in the centre of the universe.

Feeling a soft nudge, Prabhu started and looked around. Gokulan was watching him with a grin on his face. Their earlier antagonism had melted with the summer rains and they were both almost friends now. A soft laugh escaped Gokulan as he watched Prabhu's embarrassment.

"When are you getting married, Prabhu?" he asked with a smile.

"Another six months to go," replied Prabhu, trying to compose his feelings.

"Tch, tch," Gokulan clucked and said, "that's too long to wait. Nevertheless, waiting can enhance the longing – so enjoy this feeling. Believe me, it doesn't last after the wedding." He added in a conspiratorial tone, "After the wedding, they will drive you crazy. They won't allow you to skip a bath; they won't allow you to wear dirty clothes. The whole time they will be issuing instructions and to add to that, they will also compare you with a local stud. It is a losing game, you know."

Prabhu laughed. He could imagine Gokulan's wife saying, "Look at you – dirty clothes and all. Have you seen Prabhu and the way he takes care of himself?"

As they laughed and ate, the *poojaris* inside were going berserk, chanting in a loud rush. And so the night continued, till the tired crowd headed homewards, just as the eastern sky was breaking into a dull orange colour.

The next day the dancers came. The crowds came from neighbouring villages to watch this exciting event.

In the morning, Prabhu went about his usual work – feeding the cows and taking the goats out to graze. The paddy harvest was over and the rice was in gunny bags, ready to be sold. He had more than three hundred bags of rice, which would bring him quite a bit of money. He would use the money stringently, to clear the land for the next harvest, pay the workers and also keep some aside in case the monsoons failed the next year.

In the evening, dressed in a silk *dhoti* and shirt, Prabhu went to the temple. The courtyard was decorated with little coloured bulbs and the entire area was like a fairytale land. On the stage, the musicians were practicing on their instruments. Two drummers were lightly tapping their drums and a man was fiddling with the chords of his violin. The courtyard was thronging with people.

Gokulan stood a distance away, his forehead beaded with sweat. Lifting up the loudspeaker, he said, "All of you sit down quietly. The programme will begin now."

And then the *garagatum* started. What a beautiful sight! The exotically dressed dancers swung around, the conical shaped objects balanced on their heads. Prabhu held his breath. Would the pyramid fall off the dancers' heads? But no. They knew how to balance and to keep to the rhythm. Patwardha looked as fine as a prince as he brandished a bow and arrow, with the pyramid or *garagam* as it was called, poised precariously on his head all the time. And then Ragini came, dressed as Sita. Her pancake covered face glistened with beads of sweat, and she wove a little bit of seduction into her song. Prabhu smiled as he heard the men whistling enthusiastically. She had obviously not read up or even bothered to check details about the original Sita. She strutted around the stage like a vain bird and Patwarda followed her around, in a strange remake of a modern day rural Rama. When the dance ended, Ragini's face was lit up with a huge smile and Patwarda lowered his *garagam* onto the ground. Thunderous clapping echoed around the courtyard as enraged owls and bats flew out of their nests in the tall trees.

Tired and hungry, Prabhu headed back home. The night was dark, and very few stars were visible. As he wound his way through the crowds, he felt a cool breeze blowing through the branches. He looked up at the sky. Suddenly, his thoughts went to Raju. He had not seen him at the *thiruvizha* on both days, but that was not surprising. Some of the little children teased him and even stoned him when they saw him anywhere. He remembered what the old man had said about Raju's childhood. Loneliness all the time even when in the midst of people – was that what life had given Raju?

Impulsively, he turned towards Raju's little green hut. A dim light was burning inside. As he neared the hut a strange feeling overtook him. It was as though a warning bell was ringing somewhere in his mind.

Hurriedly he shouted, "Raju? Are you there?"

No answer and yet Prabhu felt sure that Raju was inside the hut. Running now, he reached the door and flung it open. Raju was lying huddled in a corner. His entire body was curled up in a tight semi-circle. When he saw Prabhu, the look in his eyes changed from terror to calmness. Prabhu felt a sense of shock. The boy's posture so clearly indicated that he was terrified of something. What could it be?

He walked into the hut and coming close to Raju's mat, sat down. A tender night breeze blew in through the open door and then he heard a small sound outside. Immediately, Raju once again tightened his body and his eyes filled with terror.

What was frightening the boy to this extent?

Prabhu listened. The sound was clearly that of someone creeping away. Who could it be? Hanging around Raju's hut in the night. Why was the boy so terrified?

He moved closer to the boy and gently placed his hand on the boy's head. The shivering stopped and the boy shut his eyes. As he sat there, running his hands over the boy's forehead, the boy's eyes slowly relaxed and he fell asleep.

Prabhu waited till he was sure Raju was fast asleep and then got up softly and went out.

In the distance stood the almost completed fireworks factory. A small pinpoint of light indicated that there was someone sitting outside smoking. Disquieted by the night's happenings, Prabhu walked towards the light. As he neared it, he saw that it was Prakash, the stony eyed man. Dressed in a black shirt and black pant with the glinting glasses, he reminded Prabhu of a terrible snake he had once seen in the hills. In a flash, it had killed one of his goats and terrified the others.

"Looks like you came to check on our little friend," he said, eyeing Prabhu mockingly.

"How do you know I came here for that? Unless you were snooping around outside the hut," said Prabhu, the hairs on the back of his neck bristling.

"Sort of," he replied insolently. Pulling out a packet of cigarettes, he offered Prabhu one.

Prabhu waved it away, but took one out of his own pocket and lit it.

"You smoke Scissors, right?"

"Looks like you know quite a lot about all of us." Prabhu blew smoke into the air.

Why was Raju so frightened? Who, or what, had frightened him?

Watching him intently, Prakash said, "You are a lucky man. Though you are not yet married, you at least have a woman. I am stuck here so far away from civilization, where I cannot find a single girl who would like to earn herself some money."

Prabhu felt his ears turning red with anger. His nostrils flared, but he waited to see what else the stony eyed snake would say.

Enjoying his moment of recollection, Prakash said, "In the

city, you can find scores and scores of them – tall and short, thin or fat, costly or cheap." He laughed gustily.

An uneasy fear hit Prabhu's stomach. Stamping down on his anger he said, "So, how do you manage here?"

"Oh, I have my own ways of relieving myself," he laughed. And, as though it was the funniest thought ever, he continued to laugh.

His laughter rang in the night like the howling of a pack of hyenas. The sound reverberated through the trees and fell heavily on Prabhu's ears.

Prabhu cleared his throat and said softly, "Looks like you have not understood the people of the village very well. If something happens here, we don't put an offender through some milk and water routine. Here, we will cut off his tongue and hang it on a tree. If he is a troublesome menace we will cut some other part and hang it up." It was now Prabhu's turn to laugh.

Prakash threw this cigarette down and crushed it. His body was shaking slightly.

"Beware Prakaas. I have a feeling you are up to something. I will keep an eye on you and if I ever catch you doing anything, I will burn your body on a funeral pyre of fireworks." He brought his foot down heavily on Prakash's toe, grinding his foot on it.

"Ouch," shouted Prakash, tears of pain coming to his eyes.

"This is my last warning," said Prabhu and turning away, he walked towards his house.

Sleep took a long time in coming. A desolate feeling was

gnawing his insides. When he finally fell asleep, the first rays of the morning sun were slanting their silver arrows on the earth.

The next morning saw a light rainfall, and the *garagatam* dancers were thankful that the rains were a day late. Packing up their things, they headed out just as the men were clearing a field and fencing it. The third day of the *thiruvizha* was one for which every young man in the village waited. It would be a day to test their strength and skills.

The event was a very macho one, where huge bullocks with curling horns would be set free and the owner of the bullock would have to stop it, either by climbing on its back or by pulling the rope which dangled around its neck. You would have more than fifty bullocks running wildly. Accidents were not uncommon and the year before last, a man had lost his life. However, it was not one of the men who were trying to stop a bullock who died, but a man in the audience. Since the path was narrow and the fence just a make shift one, the danger for the audience was always there. But that year, one of the bullocks had tossed its head angrily and butted a man with its horns. He had fallen down and when it ran over his body, he died within a few minutes.

This year, the path for the running bullocks was slightly wider and the fence a wee bit stronger. Young men were arriving in flocks from the nearby villages. In one shady spot, a high platform was being put up. On this platform, Gokulan, Prabhu and some of the others would sit and watch, far away from the menacing horns. Women rarely participated in this event, though they stood some distance away and watched their men take part in the competition. Women loved to see their men performing daredevil acts, thought Prabhu, as he watched a lazy sun creeping up the sky. It would be a hot day and that was important. He personally loved to watch this event. He had participated in it once or twice when he was younger, but now he felt that it was the younger men who needed a chance. As he gazed at the frenzied activities of the villagers, he saw Kuyili walking towards him.

Her smile reminded him of a shaft of moonlight falling gently on his face. He too smiled at her and their smiles spoke volumes to each other. It was a way of communicating their pleasure. It spoke of the times they hadn't met and it spoke of the longing in their hearts to be together. It spoke of the sudden spark of happiness, just seeing each other made them feel good. She had neared him and was looking at his face. He had shaved that morning. A local barber came by his house thrice a week and as he sat under a tree, the barber would shave the hair off his face, trim his moustache and massage his body with herbal oil. Now his skin glowed and it seemed to captivate her.

"Are you participating in the competition?" she asked him, slightly breathless.

"The younger men need a chance to win too, right?" he queried, a smile playing at the corners of his mouth.

"Oh! Does that mean that if you participate, you will win the race?" she asked seriously.

"Of course! Why? Did you even doubt that?" The smile was

widening into a grin.

She was running her eyes over him and his body responded with a pleasurable feeling flowing within his veins. He understood at that moment, why men liked to boast to women about their strength and victories, albeit made up.

They walked back together and he saw that she was wearing the ring he had put on her finger. As they passed a shady tree, she stopped for a moment and pulled out a small packet. Pressing it into his hand, she quickly moved away.

"Hey Kuyili, what is this?" he called out but either she didn't hear or she didn't want to answer.

The packet was small. He tore it open. Inside was a beautiful comb, very different from the ones you could buy either in the village or in the town close by. He ran its teeth through his hair experimentally. It felt good – not too poky and not too soft. Smiling, he put it in his shirt pocket.

As the afternoon sun rose up in the sky, the assembled crowds waited expectantly for the race to begin. The men had put small white *thundus* on their heads for protection from the heat. Prabhu climbed on top of the little tower and sat there. A few minutes later, Gokulan came, with Prakash in tow. When Prakash saw Prabhu, he did a double take. Prabhu gave him a wry smile. As soon as Gokulan settled down, a little boy brought three coloured colas on a tray. Sipping the chilled cola, Prabhu relaxed back in his chair. A few moments later, Gokulan took the *thundu* that was resting on his right shoulder and waved it like a flag.

The race had begun!

Prabhu first saw a cloud of dust rushing towards him like a gust of wind was curdling it and then he saw them – the huge bullocks and the men trying to control the animals. The first two were definitely losing as the bullocks ran relentlessly, as if possessed by an evil spirit. The crowd watched with fear and excitement.

The third participant was standing in a corner. His bullock was tied to a tree. The fourth man was trying to climb onto the back of the running animal. But it was the fifth who had not only managed to climb onto the bullock's back, but was also steering it by holding its horns, in the same way as a man would maneuver his car.

The sixth contestant fell onto the ground with a thud and the crowds hurriedly pulled him to the side. A second's delay and he would have been trampled to death. The uncontrollable bullocks sped down the racecourse and then dashed away into the nearby fields. They would return when the anger had seeped out of their bodies.

The race continued for another hour and more than fifty bullocks and the same number of men participated. But none of them came anywhere close to winning the race except for the young man who had climbed onto his bullock's back.

Finally, the race was over and the crowds cheered the young man who proudly walked down the racetrack with his bullock. The younger men were cheering him, their voices frenzied. A few of the maidens came closer to take a look at him and as he walked down the path, he was the victor, marching in triumph.

Prabhu, Gokulan and Prakash climbed down. Gokulan thumped the young man on his back and garlanded him. Prabhu gave him an envelope that contained the prize money of ten thousand rupees. Someone was announcing on a crackling loudspeaker that Arjuna from Kuppam had won the race. The announcer was saying that Arjuna had always been a brave man and, as a child, had killed a snake single-handedly.

A few older men came and spoke to Arjuna. Some of them presented gifts to him. The gifts varied in both size and variety – a gunny bag of rice grain, a basket of tamarind, an indignant hen whose legs were tied up, a sunflower from one of the girls and a few young boys were giving him marbles, sweets and rusty blades.

When Kuyili standing a little away turned around, she caught Gokulan and Arjuna exchanging glances. It spoke of a secret comradeship. But the gesture was so quick that she wondered if she had imagined it.

The last event of the *thiruvizha* was *kalakshebams* or *hari katha*, and this lasted for three whole nights. However, now the atmosphere changed as the young people made way for the old and it was the elder members of the villages who came by and settled themselves in comfortable positions to listen to discourses. Narrated lyrically, the dialogues were inundated by umpteen variations in the tempo accompanied by the beating of drums. Stories of valour were narrated side by side with stories of terrible wickedness. When stories of victories were told, with the rolling of drums, the crowd nodded their heads in agreement. When tales of wickedness were narrated, they bowed their heads like stalks of sugarcane bent under the weight of the wind. When tales of love were narrated, they looked around wistfully, remembering their own youth and its heady pleasures. Old age was not complicated in villages. The older men sat under the *Banyan* tree, smoking *beedis* and chatting. The older women stayed at home looking after their little grandchildren. They enjoyed the annual *thiruvizha*, which was their only source of entertainment.

Arjuna stalked around this group of old people, looking for the girl he had seen yesterday.

And then he saw her, standing a distance away, leaning on a temple pillar. Strolling up to her, he felt his heart beating faster. She had not expected to see him and when she did, her eyes widened with surprise and then recognition.

Slowly she smiled at him and said, "You won the race yesterday, right?"

"Yes," he replied, his voice sounding strange to his ears.

"Do you live here?" As he asked the question, he felt like a fool. Of course she lived here.

"No. I don't. Only god lives here, in the temple. My house is down the road, near the field."

He grinned at this and watched her face. She was not prettier than the girls in his village, but there was something about the way she carried herself – an air of confidence and strength. He knew this was his chance to tell this girl, whose name he still did not know, that he wanted to marry her. He felt his cheeks reddening and the man who could control a wild bullock stood helplessly, unable to control his racing heart.

"My name is Kuyili," she said, watching him with a mischievous look in her eyes. Suddenly she remembered the glance he had exchanged with Gokulan and wondered what was going on between the two of them.

And still he stared at her, unable to put in words his feelings. He saw her eyes then, move from him to something behind him and then like a mirror held in front of his face he saw his own feelings on her face. With a sudden sickening wave the thought ran through his mind that he was not the one who was making her heart beat faster.

Turning his head slowly, he saw a group of men standing in the distance. His gut knew who the man was – the one with the neatly combed hair! That was the man he had met in the *jalli kattu*. But he had also seen this man when he and his friend were sent to attack him. His friend got his jaw broken but he had escaped without a scratch. He thought of the money he had been paid for it. A good amount to realize his dreams of owning a tractor.

She smiled when he looked again at her and he heard her say softly, "That is the man I am going to marry."

There was nothing for him to say and he turned away. Suddenly everything bright and beautiful was wiped out and the world looked grey and dreary. The prize money, still in his pocket, held no charm now and reminded him of the moment when victory and defeat came hand in hand into his young life.

Nodding her head, she turned and ran. He wanted to stop her, and ask more questions but he saw her sprinting towards a group of people who stood a distance away.

NINE

Chapter

After the harvest followed a period of quiet. A pause in the daily hectic activities, to breathe and savour the fruits of their hard work. The festivities that were a part of the celebration also ended and soon the villagers would start making preparations for the next paddy cultivation.

The muddy fields would be ploughed till the land was like a patch of brown clay. Some of the villagers had tractors and these would go around the fields making a noise similar to the droning of an aeroplane. Slowly the next harvest cycle would begin.

It was on a similar morning, when Prabhu went to the fields that he felt he saw something different. The fireworks factory was almost ready. A group of painters were painting the walls. Peeping inside, he saw that the huge, dark room had rows and rows of benches made out of stone. Long rows of tables ran down between two rows of benches. The sight of the nearly completed factory made Prabhu's blood turn cold in his veins. Life would not be the same again in the village, his heart whispered. So soon after the gaiety of the *thiruvizha*, even before they had all recovered from the fun, it was obvious that life was beginning to change around them. The realization brought a gust of pain to his stomach. Why could things not remain the same way? Why did life have to change? But he knew that he had no control over it.

He was also being swept along with the others towards a different stage, a different spectrum. He could not understand why he felt this uneasiness, why did he worry so? When people like Gokulan were so positive about the change why was he alone feeling so terrible about it? He did not know and yet suddenly, out of the blue, he remembered the night he had gone to visit Raju.

There was something strange, which he could not put his fingers on. He had a helpless feeling like a newborn baby lying naked in a stranger's hands. A feeling of vulnerability; he was exposed to a chain of events which he would not be able to control. Try as he might, he could not ignore the event's which worried him: Mariamma's murder, Raju's land being taken over, Raju's strange behaviour the night he visited his hut, Prakash's easy access to their village. No. He was only seeing half the picture – the picture that somebody wanted him to see. There was more to it! But without information, without concrete evidence, there was no way he could stop the chain of events.

Turning away from the factory, he looked at Raju's green hut. Walking brusquely towards the hut, he opened the door and peeped in. There was no sign of Raju and the room looked forlorn and sad. He had not met Raju after that night and he cursed himself for not looking out for him. It was because of the *thiruvizha*. It had occurred to him that Raju would not be there and yet he felt like kicking himself for not checking in more often on Raju.

He walked towards the lake just as the sky was shedding a warm evening glow on the earth. Shafts of bright orange light lit up the western sky and the sun looked like a huge orange ball. The path to the lake was thicker with overgrowth after the abundant rainfall, and he picked his way carefully through the path, avoiding the thorns and sharp stones.

The orange sunlight had turned the lake into an orange colour and green moss added its own shade of variety. The effect was a stunning uniqueness to the colour of the lake. Marvelling at the beauty of nature all around him, Prabhu called out to Raju. Suddenly, he heard a shuffling noise and the scurrying sound of feet running. He strained his eyes in the direction of the sounds and saw a man scuttling away.

"Hey! Who is that?" he shouted and had started running behind him when he suddenly saw Raju coming out of the bushes.

The boy looked thin. As Prabhu stared at him, he felt as though someone had punched him in his chest. The boy looked so different. If he had looked sad on the day Mariamma died, he now looked so much sadder. Prabhu eyes took in his disarrayed, torn clothes and dirty face. As he watched, he saw

Raju's face crumpling up and tears flowed down freely like two streams.

Walking up to him, he caught the boy and shook him slightly. He did not want to react with anger, but this feeling of helplessness and frustration was so difficult to control. Why couldn't the boy speak up and say what was wrong? Why was he looking so frightened? As he shook him, he saw the marks on the boy's face. Scratch marks, with dried blood on it. The marks were on his neck and on his hands too.

"Raju, what's wrong with you?" he asked, his hands shaking the boy.

A look of fear came into his eyes as he pointed in the direction of the overgrowth.

"Who is frightening you? Tell me. Only then can I help you," said Prabhu.

Something about the marks on the boy's face bothered him but he could not understand what it was. Making a decision at that moment, Prabhu asked Raju quietly, "Is someone hurting you? If so, tell me who it is and I will kill the person."

Once again Raju pointed towards the bushes.

"Was it the person who ran away when he saw me here?" asked Prabhu. That person had run away too fast and he had not even caught a glimpse of him.

Raju nodded.

Tenderly he asked, "Why is that person hurting you, Raju?"

A mournful wail rose from Raju's throat and jerked out of

his body. The sound chilled Prabhu's bones and fell harshly on the lake. Again and again he wailed, the sound loud and terrible. Prabhu covered his ears with both his hands and yet the sound penetrated and fell on his heart like a cold clamp. As Raju wailed, he sat down on the ground and rocked his body – to and fro, in a strange manner, like he was trying to rock his memories away with the physical movement of his body. He was not crying anymore, but his eyes stared blankly ahead. Prabhu shook him roughly but he did not seem to even feel it. Prabhu felt a fear for the boy's state of mind. Was he losing his control over his body and mind? What events were actually pushing Raju to the brink of insanity?

"Stop it, Raju. I cannot bear this noise," he said, but the boy continued to wail.

When the first stars came out and filled the sky with little twinkling points of light, Prabhu led Raju home. When they reached the hut, a few fireflies were flitting around like lost stars. Raju seemed to neither see nor hear anything as they stepped into the little green hut.

Prabhu opened the vessel in the corner and saw that it had some cooked rice. Heaping it onto a plate, he fried an egg on the wooden stove and put the plate in front of Raju. Sitting a little away, he watched as the boy ate his food. When he finished eating, he cleared the plate and then pulled out the mat for him. Pushing the boy onto the mat, he sat with him till he felt the boy's body relaxing in sleep.

As he walked back to his house, he wondered if he should

move the boy to his house. Raju needed a doctor's help. How did he get so many scratch marks on his face and hands? Did he run through the thorny overgrowth, unheeding the bushes with their hidden thorns?

When would Raju talk? If only he would! Prabhu lay on his bed and watched a moth fluttering around his hut. A large lizard clung to the stone wall and though its eyes were not watching the moth, Prabhu could see that it was waiting. A few moments of hectic flying and then a moment of floundering and the lizard had caught its dinner. Prabhu grimaced in the darkness. Someone or something had to die to feed another's stomach. The paddy grew with richness only to feel the sickle chopping it down. The sugar cane fields grew tall only to be cut down. Sheep were slaughtered to feed the villager's stomachs and hens lost their embryos. From thoughts on death, his mind moved to the changes, which age and experience brought with it.

The old Prabhu was already dead – the one who just lived his life softly like a dewdrop on a lotus leaf. The new Prabhu felt like a wounded animal. There was a constant pain in his body. It was his heart which troubled him the most – beating erratically when he saw Kuyili, to becoming a dead heavy weight when he saw Raju and a clamped closed one when he was with Prakash. All these emotions were strange to him and he wished that he knew how best to handle them. Did his father experience all these emotions the day he felt the whip slamming his body?

As he lay there, quietly, he thought of a moment in his life, which always made him smile. His father and he had gone to the temple and were returning with the goats at sundown when he had spotted a glittering object lying on the ground. Bending down he saw that it was a coin. Picking it up, he had hurriedly passed it on to his father. His father, he remembered, had a soft smile on his face when he had asked, "Prabhu, you gave me the coin because I was there with you. What would you have done with it if you had been alone?"

"Appa, I would have looked around for the person who had lost it. I would have waited here till the person had come back looking for it. That's what I would have done." The words were said with childlike simplicity and his father had stopped on the road to carry him and swing him in his arms.

Some people called it honesty but he had never been dishonest to know the difference. To therefore fathom the terrible happenings covered in deception was difficult. He cursed under his breath and shut his eyes. Somewhere in the distance a lone dog let out a miserable howl. With the sound echoing in his ears, Prabhu fell asleep.

The next morning, when the grass was still wet with morning dew, Prabhu walked around his farm, taking in the land, with its fields, the grassy paths, the wild flowers and the coconut trees. About ten acres of his land had coconut trees. They were just two years old. In a few years time he would get a tidy sum from these trees. He crossed the coconut grove and saw his banana cultivation. A small piece of land had about fifty banana trees in it. It's big leaves providing a green shady canvas to the heavy fruits, which hung from it. As he looked around, Pandu and

Veeran, who lived on the land, came with sickles and baskets. With ease they cut down the banana-laden stalks. Each stalk had around fifty green bananas. After being cut down, these would be kept in a cool, shady place till they ripened. Leaving them on the trees to ripen was out of the question as birds and monkeys would feast on them and there would be nothing left for human beings.

They carried the load back to Prabhu's house, where there was a barn for storing rice grains, vegetables, groundnuts and fruits. The bananas were heaped in a corner. One of the local townsmen would buy the fruits from him.

As he waited for the man from the town to come over, the thought occurred to him that he had enough money to make some of his dreams a reality.

It was another two hours before he finished dealing with the wholesale fruit dealer. He then walked towards the village school. As he neared the building, he could hear the voices of children singing the national anthem in a singsong voice. Though it was nearly noon, this was the time schools started in villages. Teachers sometimes had to travel from neighbouring towns and it took an hour or two for them to reach the villages. They wound up the day by three in the afternoon so that the teachers could go back to their houses before it became dark.

As he climbed down the steps, he saw that the building looked old and broken down. The walls were dirty and cracking in several places. The three classrooms were absolutely filthy and the children sat on the cold ground with black slates and pieces of chalk in their hands. While two of the classrooms were busy, one was empty and as he stood uncertainly, the teacher Vadhiyar Raman came towards him. His name was only Raman, but taking on the name of his profession as his first name, he preferred being called Vadhiyar Raman. He was a young man who had, by choice, decided to work in a village school. Since the government supported the school, he automatically became a government employee and earned around five thousand rupees per month, but there were times when he did not get his salary on time. Seeing Prabhu, he put his palms together and bowed his head. Prabhu smiled at the young teacher. He liked this man with his unruly hair and ill-fitting clothes.

"What brings you here?" asked Vadhiyar in a deep voice.

"I was passing by and stopped to see you," said Prabhu, peeping into the empty classroom.

"The teacher did not come today – so no class for the children who sit in this classroom," he said, his face a little sad.

Very often, the teachers did not come to school. As government employees, they got their salaries, whether they came to work or not and, more often than not, they stayed away.

"This happens quite regularly, no?" asked Prabhu, shaking his head.

"Yes sir. It happens more often than we can afford to have it happen. Once the continuity of school life is broken, it takes some time for children to adjust to school life again."

"But it looks like quite a few children do come to school?" asked Prabhu.

"Yes sir. But that is because of the free midday meal that we give them. Parents pack off their children to school. One less mouth to feed."

As they talked, they walked towards the backyard where a lot of activity was in progress. Three stout men stood in front of firewood stoves, cooking. One young boy sat on a stool, shelling eggs.

"Twice a week we give them an egg with their lunch." Vadhiyar smiled proudly.

Prabhu peeped into the cooking vessels. The rice was good quality and the *sambhar* looked very tasty. In a third vessel, golden potatoes were cooking in gravy.

"Please have lunch with us today," said Vadhiyar humbly.

"Sure," replied Prabhu, a thoughtful look on his face. He looked at the building once again. It looked old and drab. If it rained heavily, the water would seep into the classrooms, from the large windows and the cracks in the roof.

They walked back to a little room where four chairs stood around a wooden table. On the table were books and pens. Pulling up a chair, Prabhu sat down and looked at the pictures hanging on the walls. They were crayon paintings done by the children. One was a depiction of a scene in a jungle. A huge peacock sat on a branch and next to it was a little green parrot. A curious shaped animal fed on grass and the sky was raining huge blobs of broken crayon pieces.

There was another painting of a cow and a man, standing next to each other.

And one painting was of a little boy, holding the hand of a woman.

"Who has painted this?" asked Prabhu.

"Oh, that one! That was done by six-year-old Ganesha. His mother has run away and his father has remarried. If we talk about his mother he starts crying."

Prabhu felt a sinking tug where his heart was. Why did such things happen? But it was not uncommon in the village for a woman who had borne three children to go away with another man. Nor was it uncommon for a man to have two wives living in the same house. But when the actions of grownups affected little children, it was so terrible.

"He is a very bright boy and studies well. If only his father's second wife wouldn't beat him so often." Vadhiyar's eyes, behind his spectacles looked cloudy.

Suddenly, Prabhu thought of Raju. When Mariamma had been around, the boy had not been so disturbed. After her death, he seemed so much more affected. A feeling of frustration suddenly hit Prabhu and along with the feeling came a thought.

He said softly, "Vadhiyar, do you know Raju?"

"Raju? Mariamma's son?"

"Yes."

"I do know him though I haven't seen too much of him since his mother passed away."

"Vadhiyar, I see him very often and I am unhappy to say that his condition is not very good. Every time I meet him, he is crying." Prabhu's voice was sad.

He added, "It would be good if he could be surrounded by people. Can you find some work for him, here, in the school?"

Vadhiyar said with a surprised look, "Of course. If you think it will make him happy. We always have a need for people to help us. But isn't he mad?"

"As mad as you and me," replied Prabhu. "He won't talk though. But he will, I am sure, over time, be okay."

"Can you bring him then?" asked Vadhiyar, a small twist at the corners of his mouth.

Coming back with a start to the little room with its colourful paintings, Prabhu said, "I didn't come here to talk about that, but seeing this room with its paintings makes me feel you can help him."

Not waiting for a reply, he added, "I would like to improve the facilities in this building. I have some money put aside and I would first of all like to repair the existing building and then add two more classrooms to this building."

Tears rolled down Vadhiyar's eyes as he looked at Prabhu. After a moment, he said, "It would be the greatest thing you could do in your life."

Prabhu shrugged embarrassedly and said, "Let us start by getting an engineer to look at the building and tell us how much money and time it would take to make the changes."

Getting up to leave, he said, "Vadhiyar, will you allow Raju to sleep in the school building? He is very scared to sleep in his house."

"Sure, sure, no problem," replied Vadhiyar.

"In that case, you will have to give me and Raju lunch," said Prabhu, with a smile.

Walking down the road, he saw Vadhiyar watching him from the building gate.

Here was a man who could help the school, was the thought in the teacher's mind as he watched the tall, sturdy frame walk towards the lake.

Turning down the overgrown path, which led to the lake, Prabhu saw Raju bathing. He was trying to scrub off the caked mud on his feet. Seeing Prabhu, he smiled shyly at him. The smile lit up his face and Prabhu realized, with a start, that he had never before seen Raju smiling. Treading on the wet mud, he stopped to lean on an old tree. In the afternoon light, the lake looked like a large sapphire, set in green gold. The land around the lake looked lush and soft and green.

"Hey Raju, hurry up with the bath, we are going somewhere for lunch."

A look of fear crossed his eyes, but only for a second. Smiling again, he dived into the lake to wash off the soapsuds.

As they walked towards the school, Prabhu said softly, "Raju, I don't like the way you sit around alone. Vadhiyar from the school wants you to help him with some work. Would you like to do that?"

Seeing the questioning look in his eyes he said, "Nothing very difficult. Just cleaning the vegetables, lighting the firewood and small jobs like that."

Once again, Raju smiled and the smile reflected on the greenery around them like a shaft of golden light.

As they walked, small drops of silver water flowed down Raju's jet-black hair onto his shirt. Though the shirt and pant were shabby, Raju looked like a little lost boy, thought Prabhu, watching him from the corners of his eyes. Suddenly Raju stopped near a tree and peeped inside a little hole in the heart of the tree. Prabhu came up behind him. The tiny cubicle, carved by nature had a little squirrel inside, resting on a mound of soft grass, Prabhu saw that its foot was a little crooked. He turned his head questioningly at Raju, who nodded his head several times and pointed to the top of the tree.

"Oh! It fell of the tree, did it? Is that what you are trying to tell me?" asked Prabhu.

Once again, Raju nodded his head vigorously. He also pointed to his chest and then to the squirrel.

"Okay. You found him and made this home for him?•h asked Prabhu.

Raju reached his hand gently into the hole and picked up the squirrel in his hands. The little squirrel nuzzled into the curves of his palms as he held it tenderly. Prabhu could not help but look at Raju and wonder at the people who had branded him a murderer.

The smell of gravy floated down the lane as they entered the school. Groups of children sat and ate from aluminium plates – rice and gravy with a boiled egg floating in it. When they saw Prabhu, they stopped eating and gaped at him. When they saw Raju, some of them giggled. Prabhu felt Raju's body growing tense next to him and he casually put his arm around Raju's shoulder. Immediately, the giggling stopped.

Vadhiyar was waiting for them near the door to his office and when he saw Raju he said, "Hello Raju! Do come in! You are looking nice and fresh."

A small boy came in with two plates heaped with rice and gravy. And a little girl brought one more plate for Vadhiyar. As they ate their lunch, Prabhu eating small mouthfuls and Raju shovelling in huge ones, the bell rang.

"Raju, after lunch, let us go and tend to the little vegetable garden at the back of the school," said Vadhiyar.

When Prabhu left the room, the last thing he heard was Vadhiyar saying in his soft voice, "Raju, we want someone to sleep in the school to safeguard it. Will you sleep here, please?"

Suddenly he realized an important truth, one more piece in the bigger puzzle. Nobody had actually bothered with Raju before! Now that he was taking care of him, he realized that Raju was quite willing to adapt himself. You throw an infant out and then blame it for not being able to feed or look after itself. With a little love and caring, Raju was changing-slowly. As Prabhu left the building, he felt as though a huge weight was lifted from his heart and he felt almost like singing with happiness.

He knew now that Raju would be safe. The only worry was how would Raju react if the children teased him. Would he run away to the lake or would he stay around. Only time would tell.

TEN

Chapter

Prabhu decided to pay Gokulan a visit and walked towards his house. On the way, he saw that the fields were ploughed and ready for the next harvest. In a few days time he would be caught up with that activity. When he reached Gokulan's house, he saw him chopping firewood in the courtyard. When he saw Prabhu, he dropped the axe and wiped his sweating palms on his white *dhoti*, leaving greasy brown patches on it.

He came towards Prabhu, with a broad smile on his face. "So how are things? Looks like you are all set for the next harvest?" he said.

"Yes! Aren't you?" asked Prabhu with a smile.

"Of course. I only hope that the rains don't stay away."

Both of them looked up at the sky, which was a clear aquamarine blue. A flock of swans were flying in unison in the sky. They made a curious pattern, with one leading and the others following in rows of ten. None of the villagers hunted actively but they all had air guns with pellets. One of the young men,

Kumaresan, did a lot of hunting and he could shoot a bird sitting on a branch, with ease. In Kumaresan's house, the women had to cook these birds for the men. None of them minded eating these birds as long as Kumaresan cleaned them by plucking off the feathers and removing its bile bag.

He spent a quiet morning, strolling through the paddy fields with Gokulan and felt a subtle difference in the villagers' behaviour when he was with Gokulan. They all respectfully bent their heads but when he walked alone, along with the respect he sensed a genuine liking.

Why was Gokulan not a likeable person? He realized with a start that he had never pondered on whether he himself liked Gokulan or not. Come to think of it, Gokulan did not work at making himself likeable. He was too brusque and commanding. He could also be rude, but he was a leader. Prabhu wondered for the first time whether he could be a leader. Never before had he thought of it. But then he realized that in the last few months, people with power were controlling the lives of the villagers. If he became a leader, he would never compromise on the safety of the lives of these people. Maybe he would become the next *panchayat* head. If not for anything, at least to ensure that his people were taken good care of. Did this mean that he suspected Gokulan of compromising on the safety and happiness of the villagers? As this thought crossed his mind, Prabhu glanced at Gokulan guiltily. What if Gokulan could read his mind now? But Gokulan seemed a bit lost in his own thoughts and Prabhu let his own mind run free.

Yes, he did blame Gokulan for the changes in the village. Nobody else could have sold Raju's land to Prakash. Nobody had the guts to do that. Didn't that automatically mean that Gokulan had stood to gain from this transaction? If gain had been the motive, would he shy away from murder? Was he also benefiting from the factory?

While Gokulan was not really poor, Prabhu realized that he had a large family to support. Could temptation do this to a person?

With the sole intention of probing, Prabhu said quietly, "Gokulan, I am planning to invest some money in the school building."

He felt Gokulan turn his head sharply in his direction, but he kept his own eyes focused on the distant horizon. All around them wild flowers grew abundantly, their dew-covered petals letting off heady fragrances and their exotic colours mingling with the blue of the sky. Summer brought with it heat but it also brought with it life. They walked slowly, inhaling and watching the flowers.

"What exactly are you planning to do?"

The words sounded casual and yet Prabhu felt they were not.

"Oh, put up another room or two. Do some repairs to the existing rooms."

"That Vadhiyar is a stupid fellow. Don't trust the money with him to do all this. I have an idea...." Excitedly, he stopped in his tracks and looking at Prabhu said, "How about talking to that Prakaas. He might have some material left over after completing the factory. I am sure if you give him the money he will do a good job." His voice rang with excitement.

Prabhu looked away, unable to hide his thoughts. He watched a brown cow nuzzling her calf as he tried to calm his mind. There was no doubt that Gokulan and Prakash shared something. Obviously they were working together.

How should he handle this? He heard Gokulan's voice interrupting his thoughts as he said, "Shall we go and meet Prakaas now?"

He was already planning to pull out the money from him! He needed to be left alone to sort out his thoughts.

"No! I have some work. The rice mill owner from Kuppam is coming to see the rice I have for sale."

Not waiting for anything more to be said, Prabhu quickly moved away. Sprinting into a slow jog, he ran towards his rice barns. There was no doubt that they had a corrupt leader who was willing to sacrifice their safety for his personal gains. The man was suspected of being Raju's father. Had he then murdered his mistress? Was he aware of the damage to Raju's sanity? Did he not realize that a small spark to the fireworks in the factory could burn down their village?

His mind confused and disturbed, Prabhu walked back from the barns, his pocket bulging with money. Should he talk to the villagers? Or should he confront Gokulan?

When Prabhu returned home, the first stars were bursting in the sky, their twinkling light trying to establish an identity in the slowly enveloping darkness. The setting sun was still there in the western sky, fighting for last minute attention. As he stood outside his house, his eyes swept over the orange sky, to the little stars and from there, to the distant mountains, which were taking on strange shapes in the descending darkness. And then he saw her running towards him like a strange white deer. Her white veil or *davani* flowed behind her and her white skirt billowed out as she ran towards him.

He smiled and watched the way her eyes wandered towards his feet. He saw a faint red glow staining her cheeks as though she had caught a part of the orange sky in her body. He caught her chin and lifted her face, but her eyes remained lowered. He would have kissed her then, but pushing him away she ran into his house. He followed her and watched as she poured a glass of water from the mud pot in the corner. As she drank, small drops of water flowed from the sides of her mouth, down her chin, down her arched neck and stained her blouse into transparent patches. One tantalizing drop swiftly flowed down between her breasts. As he watched her, he felt a strange sensation in his body. He caught her then and pulled her roughly into his arms. The glass fell down with a loud clamour. In the soft darkness, she saw his eyes and the look in them made her heart beat faster. She averted her face not wanting him to see the same in her eyes. But he did not wait to watch. His eyes closed as his lips roamed over her face, licking away the little drops of water. He traced the same path with his tongue.

That night, both of them savoured, tasted and feasted on each other.

There, in the darkness, with only the sounds of the crickets and owls, Kuyili looked at the love of her life, sleeping next to her. A small ant was crawling on his chest. She caught it tenderly and threw it away. Bending her head she kissed him where the ant had been walking around. He pulled her closer and she lay there listening to the sound of his steady breathing.

It was much later that he walked her home. Her head rested lightly on his shoulder and his arm went around her waist in a possessive grasp. They walked in silence, only to stop every few yards to kiss each other. Around them, the still darkness of the night cast weird and frightening shadows. A sinister owl watched them unblinkingly as they went past it. But beyond all the nightlife around them, it was the sky, which watched over them, like a dark velvet canopy studded with diamonds.

When he reached her house, he stopped and said, "Kuyili, for all purposes we are a married couple. In another three months we will be formally married. What happened today was not planned. I saw you and I don't know what happened to me. I am sorry!"

As she walked away, she turned to smile at him and said from the distance, "Yes, but it was I who came to your place today."

"Hey, come back here," he shouted. But laughing lightly, she ran away.

Suddenly the harvest season caught up with Prabhu and his love for his land blocked out all other problems. His beloved land needed him and he focused his attention on it.

It was during the harvest season, when the paddy was ready

to be cut again, that the fireworks factory was ready and the first load of raw materials arrived by lorry. A few men dressed in trousers, clearly belonging to a town and not a village, got down from the lorry and began unloading the materials. Prakash watched the work from a distance. It was time now to begin recruiting people for the factory. A few young men, small boys and little girls would be ideal. But first of all, he would have to kindle the interest of the villagers. In the early afternoon, standing outside the factory, Prakash squinted in concentration and then smiled. He knew where to begin. He called one of the young men who had come along with the truck. They spoke in soft whispers. The man nodded his head several times and accepted the money Prakash pressed into his hands.

It was nearing evening when the man came back, his pockets bulging with the whisky bottles he had bought from the town. Prakash quickly slipped the bottles into his pocket and, shutting the door of the factory behind him, walked towards the paddy fields. A little distance away from the paddy fields stood the tall palm trees. It was from these trees that the villagers got their supply of fresh toddy, a milky white intoxicating liquid. But compared to the good quality in his pocket, he knew that the toddy didn't stand a chance.

As he neared the palm grove, he heard Deva talking. As usual, Deva was slightly drunk and was singing a rhythmic light-hearted tune. Whistling, Prakash walked towards him. Sitting beside the tree were Kumaresan, the village hunter, and Pandu, one of the young men who worked on Prabhu's lands. When they saw

Prakash, they stopped talking. Slowly and dramatically, Prakash pulled out a bottle from his pocket. Making a big show of opening the cap, he watched the crowd covertly. Deva was licking his lips. Kumaresan was watching him with a shrewd look in his eyes and Pandu's jaw hung open in astonishment. Opening the bottle, he put it close to his nose and inhaled. The sound of the air being sucked into his lungs sounded like the hum of angry bees. Licking his lips, he brought the bottle to his lips and took a sip. He felt a fiery flush building up in his throat and spreading towards his stomach. Wherever the liquid flowed, a golden fire followed and his insides glowed with a sense of well being. Puffing out his chest, he stood with his legs slightly apart as he continued to drink.

Slowly, Deva got up from where he sat under the tree, and crept up to Prakash. In a soft tone he said, "Machaan (a colloquial term meaning sister's husband), can I taste that? You can have some fresh toddy in exchange."

"Your fresh toddy, as you call it, will burn my stomach and make my head ache."

The other two came up and the three men stood close around him, inhaling the smell of alcohol. As though his legs were aching, Prakash dropped down onto the wet grass. The others dropped down beside him. Deliberately, taking his time, Prakash passed the bottle to Kumaresan, who gave him a big smile and took a large swig. Deva grabbed the bottle from Kumaresan and drank greedily from it. Finally, when the bottle was nearly empty, Pandu emptied the last few sips into his mouth.

They sat in a circle, allowing the liquid to circulate softly in their veins. A feeling of lightness made Deva sing loudly. The others clapped their hands. Slowly, Prakash put his arm around Pandu's shoulder. He watched Pandu's well-formed shoulders. The bones indicated a fine structure. He leaned his body slightly on Pandu. Pandu's body could not be compared to the other one, but since he was not around, he had to make do with anyone else he could find. A girl would have been preferable but he knew better than to try making a pass at any of the village belles. That would be the end of the factory and everything else.

He blew softly on Pandu's face and watched Pandu turning his head away. A little more whisky might do the trick. He pulled the other bottle out of his pocket. This time none of them waited for him to offer. Deva grabbed the bottle out of his hands and drank thirstily. Pandu sipped slowly, allowing the liquid to trickle down his throat and Kumaresan gulped down what he could.

As he watched, Prakash saw Pandu's eyes closing slightly. Without attracting the attention of the others, he shifted his body till his arm was resting lightly on Pandu's thigh. As he watched Pandu drinking, he moved his hand upwards, till it was resting on Pandu's groin.

"W...w...what arrre yyyou doing?" The words tumbled out of Pandu's mouth, in a jumble.

The dark night was shielding his actions. Prakash knew the others couldn't see him.

"Give him the bottle please," he said, pulling the bottle away from Deva.

He saw that this bottle was also almost empty. He only had one more bottle. Cursing himself for being stingy, he thought he should have bought at least five bottles. These people were used to drinking toddy and they would be able to drink a lot of whisky. But he would not open the bottle now. That was for Pandu.

Clearing his throat, he asked, "Deva, how much money do you earn as an undertaker?"

Deva laughed dryly and said, "Earn? Money? They give me the dead man's *dhoti* and a coconut. If they gave me a palm tree, I would be happy, but coconut? What can I do with a coconut?" He laughed loudly at his own joke.

"Would you like to earn some money then?"

Deva looked at Prakash suspiciously and asked, "Why? Do you have a job for me? What is it?"

"Just answer me," said Prakash, all businesslike in his manner now. "Would you like to work and earn some money?"

"Wouldn't I?" replied Deva, sighing and then belching loudly.

"In that case, come to the factory tomorrow morning. And by the way Deva, you have two children, am I right?"

"Yes! One girl – cursed creature, and a boy just like me."

"Bring them along and I will pay all of you a salary."

Through the fog enveloping his brains, Deva remembered Prabhu warning them about the dangers of working in a fireworks factory. But it was not clear and all that he now wanted to do was sleep. Lying down, he closed his eyes and soon the sound of his snores filled the night with its sound.

Kumaresan was still quite alert. Cursing softly, Prakash opened the third bottle but this time Pandu drank steadily and then handed it over to Kumaresan, who shoved the bottle into his shirt pocket and headed homewards. He would finish off the bottle after he had spent some time with his young wife Devayani. A little alcohol set his senses on fire. As he walked away, he completely forgot about Pandu sleeping on the grass.

As the crescent moon swept across the dark sky and strange insects crept on the grass, Prakash slowly unbuttoned his trousers.

When the early morning dew settled on his face, Pandu opened his eyes. With every passing second he felt as though someone was beating his head with a hammer. He groaned and shut his eyes, trying to recall what had happened in the night. He remembered Prakash coming with bottles of whisky and him and Deva grabbing and drinking. He vaguely recalled some talk about money and work. He shut his eyes. There was something he could not remember. He tried to concentrate, when he felt a wet plop on his legs. Startled, he opened his eyes and saw that he was naked waist down and his dirty *dhoti* was lying in the distance. Why had he taken off his clothes? His head beat to a steady pounding. Getting up unsteadily, he put on the *dhoti*. If any of the villagers had seen him in this state, he would have been the laughing stock of the village. He tried to remember what had happened, but it was vague and hazy. Suddenly, he vomited and brought out yellow bile on the grass. He looked at his body with distaste. Why had he drunk so much? It scared him that he could not remember how his *dhoti* had come off. Had he removed it? His old father, who sat at home and rolled *beedis* all day long, would have loved to see this sight! Never again would he drink like this. His head drooping on his shoulders like an overburdened *Ashoka* tree, he walked home.

Prakash finished his bath outside the factory in the little makeshift bathroom the workers had put together for him. He rubbed his body with Hamam soap and washed away the smell of semen, whisky and urine. He scrubbed his skin so hard that it seemed as though a layer would come away.

After his bath, he ate some rice with pickles and waited for word to spread that he was looking for workers. If he knew Deva well, the man would not only bring his children but a whole pack of villagers.

He was right. As he watched, he saw a few men and women walking towards him. Some of them had little children with them. A few young men were also there. He looked to see if he could spot Pandu, but he was not around.

As they came close, some of them gaped at the building.

"Welcome!" he smiled at the crowd. They stared back stoically.

"I see that you are all looking for work! Am I right?"

Some of the men nodded their heads.

"You will not earn daily wages here like you do when you work in the fields." After a pause, he continued, "But you will get a good monthly salary!"

The crowd watched.

"The children will also get a monthly salary." He picked up one of the small girls.

"What do you mean monthly salary?" asked Rani, Deva's wife. She was calculating the difficulties of keeping the money away from her husband. Once a month now, he would beat her up and take her money away.

"How do we manage for a full month, till we get our first salary?" she added.

"Good question. I know that all of you have no other income and I will pay you all an advance of 500 rupees each for the grownups and 250 rupees for the children. This will be subtracted from your first salary."

"How much will you pay us?" asked Deva, his eyes snapping greedily.

Okay, here it comes. This should have been their first question. Smiling widely, he said, "The owner of this factory will be coming here. He himself will tell all of you what your salaries will be. The reason I asked you to come is to help clean up the building and make it look like a real factory. I also need all of you to help me with a small celebration for the owner and his friends."

Pausing dramatically, he said, "Who do you think the owner's friends are? Not Prabhu or one of your old village idiots. My owner's friends are the police commissioner and MPs. Okay, what will you fellows know about MPs. MPs means ministers. Aah! I can see that you understand better now. Come on then all of you, let's get to work."

The words were spoken loudly, with a touch of arrogance. It had the right effect and the crowds clapped.

"Okay then, come inside and let us start clearing the place. And," he paused threateningly, "if any of you decide to act smart, by taking the advance and not coming for work, believe me, I have my own ways of dealing with you."

It was the next morning, when Prabhu went to his fields that he saw that a lot of workers were not there. A sinking feeling told him where they could be. He spotted Giri, one of the older men and asked him softly, "Where are all the villagers?"

Giri refused to meet his eyes as he replied, "Don't you know? The fireworks factory has opened. They have all joined there as workers."

Once again, the feeling of not being able to control the chain of events invaded Prabhu's insides, turning his muscles into pulp. Without attention and care, the harvest would be a disaster. With a brusque nod he instructed the few labourers to continue with their work and he walked towards the green pastureland beyond his house. The clean open spaces, the panoramic view, the bold colours of nature – the brown, green and blue hues, cleared his mind and with a start he realized that his problems were miniscule in the larger picture of the world. This was just another challenge that he should manage. It was a crisis but not one where lives would be lost, battles fought or kingdoms forsaken. His mind clearer, he walked back and knew what he had to do. There was no point wasting time waiting for the workers to come back. He would have to act now.

After a hurried bath, he instructed Giri, and the few others who were available, to carry on with their work. He then cut across a large expanse of open land. Beyond the land was a large hill. If he crossed the hill he would be in Karupumedu, a small village like his own. He had visited this village a few times and knew the headman. Karupumedu was on the wrong side of the mountains and, more often than not, they lost the rains. Drought and famine were common and the villagers lived on roots and nuts. It would be an opportunity for them to find work here. There was always something good that could come out of a bad situation. Prabhu felt his heart lightening as he watched the soft clouds roaming in a blue sky.

As he crossed over, he saw that the morning was bright and sunny. He walked on and saw groups of women, sitting near a stream washing clothes. Wrapped in colourful saris, they chattered like a flock of birds as they washed and rinsed their clothes. He saw a little boy, almost naked, standing near the stream's bank, screaming for attention. He was so tiny, just about as big as one of the short plants that grew there. Prabhu paused to pick up the baby boy in his hands.

As he smiled at the boy, his mother came running towards him, "Saami, Vannakam!" she said, bowing her head.

"Vanakam," he replied. Smiling, he handed her the boy.

"Why are you crying so much? Can't you see that I am busy washing clothes over there?" she scolded the child.

As he walked away, he heard the child making soft crooning noises.

When he reached the hill, he saw that the morning sun was high in the sky. Climbing the hill, he wished that this entire fireworks factory business had never started. If a monthly salary was attractive, most of the landless workers would go there and the fields would have nobody to tend to them.

Small thorny plants were scattered on the small hill and he carefully wove his way around them. When he reached the top, he paused for a moment. On the other side lay the small village, with tiny huts and smoke swirling out of chimneys. The huts were interspersed with thick vegetation and tall trees lent their shade to the huts.

Climbing down was much easier and he felt energized as he finally reached the bottom. He walked towards the village headman's house and saw that the sun had reached the top of the sky. It had taken him two hours to reach here.

The headman was very different from Gokulan. He was a wizened old man with sparkling eyes and a long white beard. He seldom wore a shirt and his thin chest, sparsely covered with grey hair, could not hide his bony, thin body and wrinkled skin. When he saw Gokulan, he squinted for a moment and then grinned toothlessly.

"Come on, come on in. What brings you to our little village?"

As he spoke, he led Prabhu into a little hut with whitewashed walls and a straw roof. Inside, the hut was cool and as he sat down, Kaveri, the headman's wife, brought some cool buttermilk for him. She too smiled. He remembered seeing her at their village *thiruvizha*.

Outside the hut, on the hot sand, a group of little children were playing with a mangy dog. All the children were semi-clothed and their skins were sunburnt. When he averted his eyes from them and looked at Mahadevan, the village headman, his eyes could not easily adjust to the darkness inside. It was a moment later that he saw that Mahadevan was sitting in a chair, watching him.

"I hear that there is a factory being started in your village?" he asked softly.

"Yes and that is why I have come looking for you."

The old man lit a *beedi* and drew on it strongly.

"I guess all the workers have gone to work in the factory?"

"Yes," replied Prabhu, a sick feeling in the pit of his stomach.

"Well, it happens. It's happened in other villages and it was only a matter of time before yours or my village went through this."

Watching the old man talking, Prabhu felt a calm feeling descending on him. The old man's reactions meant that unforeseen things could happen to anyone at any time. He needed to be able to cope and overcome it. Once again, he did not feel so bad anymore.

"I have come to ask you to lend me some workers. They can stay on my land and I will pay them wages."

The old man was silent for a moment and then he said, "We are much poorer here than all of you."

Prabhu knew that. This village did not have a lake or a stream flowing through and it was only when the rains came that they saw a harvest.

"What is bad news for all of you will be good news for us," he smiled once again and his toothless face took on strange shapes.

"Take them," he added, continuing to smile. "How many men do you need?"

"Around twenty. They can bring their families along."

"I shall send you twenty men in the morning. Now you must go or it will be dark before you reach your village and the hill is not safe in the dark. We have spotted a few wild dogs and hyenas there."

Prabhu did something he had never done before. He bent down and touched the old man's feet.

Dusk was falling slowly on his village by the time he returned in the evening. He saw that in his fields, work had progressed very slowly. Today had been an exceptionally warm day and if the same kind of weather continued, it would rain by the end of the week. This meant that tomorrow and the day after, work would have to progress very fast.

As he went into his house, in the semi-darkness, he saw that Kuyili had cooked some food for him. Looking around, he saw that she was tending to the vegetables in the garden behind. As he looked at her, the ache in his calf muscles disappeared and the heavy feeling in his heart dissolved, like the earth after the first summer showers. Slowly, he walked out and stood beside her.

Looking up at him, she blushed and then smiled. "You went to Karupumedu?" she asked softly.

"Yes. We will be getting twenty new workers by tomorrow."

That seemed to make her happy and she smiled at him, her shyness disappearing with every passing second.

"You have put Raju in the school. I saw him there today. He seemed very happy. Not a bit like the sad, crying Raju who would sit near the lake."

Once again, he felt a summer's breeze blow through his heart. He had not gone to the school to see Raju but this news meant that he had made a good move. Hopefully, getting workers from the neighbouring village would also prove to be a good move.

Seeing the expressions flitting on his face, she said, "Getting other workers cannot be that bad. Paddy cultivation needs to continue. God knows how long this fireworks factory will last and if something happens, then these people won't have anything to turn to."

It was then that he told her about his secret dreams of converting the land into a dairy farm and supplying the milk to the milk federation. He also told her about the money he would invest in repairing the school building. As he talked, she sat quietly and heaped his plate with food. In the near darkness, she watched his shining eyes and firm shoulders. He really cared about the village and loved the people who lived here. She felt a terrible anger at the way Prakash had turned the village almost upside down. But this could not last long.

Over time things would change and like the *Banyan* tree that continued to lend its shadow to every weary traveller, Prabhu would be there for the others.

ELEVEN Chapter

The next morning, Prabhu woke up to the sound of commotion outside. Startled, he got up and opened the door. Outside stood a group of men, women and little children. Some of them carried bags; others bundles on their heads. Amazed, he realized that they must have left their village really early to reach here so fast.

Running his fingers through his hair, he smiled and said, "First of all, all of you please go ahead putting up your huts. You can use the land over there."

His fingers pointed towards a clump of trees, where the land had not been used for cultivation.

"After that, you can use the lake for washing and we will meet here in a few hours time."

One of the younger women, a short lady, came forward and said, "Ayyah, we are very happy about this chance you are giving us. We will work very hard and make you proud of us."

If he had reached down, he could have carried her like a baby, but her words fell on his ears like the beating of a drum.

He cleared his throat and said, "Go on now. No time to waste."

Before they came back and he got busy with the actual work, he walked towards Gokulan's house. Nearing it, he saw that some of Gokulan's workers were missing too. How was Gokulan going to manage?

He then saw Gokulan, sitting under the shade of a large tree.

When he saw Prabhu, he smiled and said, "Have you seen the fireworks factory? Lots of work is going on there."

Suddenly it was clear to Prabhu. Gokulan was not depending on a harvest for his money anymore. He was also on Prakash's payroll!

Gokulan asked him sympathetically, "You must be badly hit by this. Your workers have all deserted you or what?"

"Yes. They have. But in their place I have found others."

"Others? Who others?"

"From Karupumedu."

"Oh. I see!"

Prabhu could see that Gokulan had not expected this. What did he expect? That just because there were no workers, he would give away his land?

"Be careful that these fellows also don't go away to join the factory," Gokulan said, idly picking his nose.

There was no need to say anything. Time would tell.

Prabhu watched Gokulan's children playing in the distance. These children were well clothed and they looked healthy. There was no sign of starvation, as there was in Karupumedu. Maybe starvation was God's way of making man realize all that he stopped thinking about when things were going fine. He knew that Gokulan's children would never go near the factory and yet, if it was true that Raju was his son, he didn't seem to care a bit for that boy.

Prabhu realized that though his reactions to his worries were not quick, he had at least taken care of two major issues – Raju's safety and the harvest. He would also find a way to end this factory mess but not right now. His interference would not be encouraged. People would say that he was acting out of malice because he had lost his workers. He might even lose the trust of the villagers. He knew that Prakash had it in him to twist any story to suit his convenience. He would do what was best for them – to be there when they finally realized that they had made a mistake and needed help. With these thoughts to comfort him, he returned to supervise the workers.

By noon, small green huts speckled the land like green pyramids and grey smoke curled out of the small chimneys. Voices of little children splashing in water could be heard. And the men were already in the fields, turbans tied around their heads to protect their scalps from the noonday heat.

Prabhu taught them the work and watched as the marshy land had little saplings planted in it. The sky still seemed an angry blue and Prabhu hoped that the rains would not fail. Once again he realized that depending on the monsoons was not the solution. They needed wells and pumps for irrigation. Not just one well and one pump, but a series of them, spread over the thousand acres of his village. His land was three hundred acres but only twenty-five acres was being used for paddy cultivation. The large expanse of open spaces, unfenced, belonged to him and he had done nothing to change the utility of the land. His idle mind conjured pictures of a flourishing dairy farm, windswept paddy fields and smiling villagers dressed in finery.

Could he accomplish all this in his lifetime? Was that what Mahatma had meant when he said 'It is your duty to care for the people'? How then had he never thought about this before? Was it only because of the calamity of Prakash opening the factory that his mind was working? Was a crisis situation an opportunity or was it the dead end? He didn't know the answers to the questions, but accepted that it was after Prakash had come in that he had actually started thinking.

His mind flew back to that night when he had been in his little hut, worrying about the state of boredom and yet all around him there had been opportunities. Opportunities he had never seen before. For the first time in the last few months, he wondered if Prakash's factory was in god's bigger plan. Smiling at his disarrayed thoughts, he tied his *dhoti* firmly around his midriff and bent down to work on the land.

Over the next month, work progressed on Prabhu's land. Everywhere else, the land took on a barren look as it lay untended. Small patches of vegetables were the only signs of cultivation. Men, women and children spent their time at the fireworks factory. The first lot of chemicals, wrapping paper and packaging material arrived and along with it, on a cool, misty day, the fireworks factory was formally inaugurated.

Chettiar, the owner, had invited two local MPs and the police commissioner. For the first time, the village saw a fleet of large cars, sweeping up the dust as it drove on their mud roads towards the factory. The villagers gazed in wonder at the cars and the mysterious men who sat behind wound up black windows. They stood a distance away and watched as the men got out. Chettiar was dressed like the rest of them in a white *dhoti* and shirt, but around his neck and wrist, he wore chunky gold chains and bracelets. On his fingers were huge gold finger rings studded with shining stones. The police commissioner was dressed in a black suit and the two MPs were dressed in *dhotis* and shirts.

Along with the other villagers, Prabhu stood in a corner and watched the visitors. Prakash had arranged for some garlands. Now, rushing forward, he garlanded the visitors. All of them immediately took off their garlands and held it in their hands. The white jasmines and yellow *samandhis* hung loosely in their hands like forgotten stories. The police officer was trying to brush away the yellow dust of pollen that had fallen on his suit.

Prakash had also arranged a microphone system and he passed a mike to Chettiar.

"Vanakkam!" Chettiar's voice was loud and harsh.

"I have come here to see that all of you are happy with my plans of providing an alternate employment opportunity for all of you." He paused, waiting for applause.

Prakash clapped furiously and watching him, some of the villagers clapped half-heartedly.

"I want this factory to be the best in Tamil Nadu." Once again, there was a deliberate pause.

"I have several factories, most of them in Sivakasi and its surrounding areas. But this is the first time I have ventured out from that area."

"I see that your village is very beautiful."

The people were watching unblinkingly. A little unnerved by their stoic silence, he said, "I realize that all of you have been working on an advance of five hundred rupees." A pause. "Children will be paid thousand henceforth." Seeing the astonished look on the faces of the villagers, he smiled. "Didn't Prakash here tell you that it is children we want to employ in the factory?"

Prabhu felt a sick feeling start somewhere in the pit of his stomach. Children? What would this herd of people do? He looked around. There were some who looked disappointed, and others who looked shocked.

This was a bit of shock, even to him.

One of the younger men said, "Why did Prakash then say that we had jobs available here? We were working in the fields, now we don't even have that." His voice shook a bit with anger.

Prakash, who was standing with the VIPs, moved a foot back.

A soft murmur rose from the crowds and then Gokulan moved to the front.

Clearing his throat, he said, "Let us all remain calm. We do not want to insult our visitors. Let us just stop for a moment. I know that we were all confused that we would be given jobs in the factory. However, the main work in the factory is for children, and if they are earning money, then isn't it the same as all of you earning money?"

Prabhu felt a rage building in his stomach. Quelling it, he asked, "What do you mean by that? Do you mean that our children should work and we should spend that money?"

"No Prabhu. I did not mean that and you know it. I meant that children will also bring home money and the elders can go back to working on the fields."

But Prabhu knew in his heart that for people like Deva, this would be a god sent opportunity. It would be children who would work and the elders would stay at home. But was there anything he could say? And even if he did, would it make a difference?

He looked at the ground. The sun had dried up the earth and most of the land had lost its look of fertility. The men would have a tough time getting the land ready for harvest again. He looked at the factory entrance. Chettiar was twisting and twirling his ring and a shaft of bright light shot off from whichever direction he turned the ring.

He looked at Prakash, who after his initial fear, had stepped to the front and stood next to Chettiar. He looked at the police officer who was watching the women.

For a moment, he was reminded of the accident he had seen in Madras. The same people with the same absorption in money and material things. The first seeds of corruption were now germinating in his village and the thought saddened him. Life would never be the same again. And then he realized with a pang that it had all started with Mariamma's death. Whoever had killed her was determined to wreak havoc, for his or her own personal gains.

Once again a disturbing thought occurred to him. He thought of Raju's tears, flowing so terribly. Raju would know the answers to most of these questions and whoever had started this course of destruction was also aware of that. That person then was taking solace from the fact that Raju was dumb.

Chettiar's voice was droning on about the wonders of village life and his factories. He talked about his 'little twenty-five-room house' in Madras as though it was an unwanted asset. None of the villagers interrupted him, or asked him questions. Prabhu moved away from this group and walked towards the lake.

His mind wandered around the tall water plants and seemed to belong to the nature around him. It was not his mind any more. With this detached feeling came a sense of well being he had not experienced in a long time. These tall trees, green grass, this silvery lake and blue sky would continue to exist timelessly. It was only foolish human beings who did not realize this. They fretted and wasted their time pursuing money when all that they wanted was already available here.

Sitting down on the dew-covered grass, he threw a pebble into the lake. It broke the surface of the water into a hundred ripples, before settling down at the bottom. He threw pebbles again and again and watched the ripples; fascinated by the patterns they formed in the water.

The next morning, Prabhu woke up to the sound of disturbance outside his house. Rubbing the sleep out of his eyes, he opened the door. It was a misty morning and it took him a second to make out the shape of men and women standing around.

He saw that all those workers who had deserted him without a fleeting thought for the land, were now back looking for work. He knew then that this would be a difficult moment in his life. In fact, it was the most difficult moment of his life.

The workers whom he had brought from the neighbouring village were waiting cautiously to see what Prabhu would do.

He breathed in the morning air, heavy with the scent of blossoms and shut his eyes to think for a moment. When he spoke, he could not keep away a little tremble in his voice. "So all of you are back. That is nice to see."

His workers looked at him fearfully.

"However," he paused, "I have brought all these brothers from the nearby village and it is because of them that the harvest is possible. Just like any of you, I too have eaten and grown up on the food that this land has provided me. I cannot become a traitor."

His voice rose in volume and he said, "They will continue to tend to this land. But this decision should not leave my own men jobless and I suggest that henceforth all of you look after the other cultivations in this land.

"The banana plantation, the roots plantation, the coconut groves – all this I can manage even if you go away, but this land with its paddy fields will not cope without attention. If I, believing that you all are back, send away these men, what happens if another Prakaas comes with another idea about one more factory? What guarantee do I have that you will not go away once again?"

He felt a strong emotion building up, a feeling of remorse that these innocent people led astray by the Prakashes of this world were now being punished. But it was not so much the idea of meting out punishment, as the caring for this precious land, which shaped his decision. Hence, he held his head high as he spoke.

"You have all lived on this land and you can continue to do so. Do not fear that I will send you away. But I beg you to please work and not stay at home depending on the money your children can earn.

"I have several plans for us, and over time, seeing how serious all of you are about work, I will share them with you. Some of these plans will definitely improve our living conditions without interfering with our other sources of occupation. But for now we will have to limit our cultivation to the existing paddy fields and the farms."

For the men who had returned, it meant a cut in wages because it was those who worked in the paddy fields who earned the most amount of money. The work was difficult but the rewards were good. But tending to a coconut grove was different. The tree just grew and grew and the rewards were seen later, much later. If the men felt saddened by Prabhu's decision, they did not say anything. It was not in them to question the words of men like Prabhu. They would do as told.

Prabhu divided the men into smaller groups and gave them instructions. He would not pay his workers in advance, like Prakash had done. They would get weekly wages and some of them would only get half of what they were getting when they were tending to the paddy fields.

One of the men, a little older than the rest, said softly, "Prabhu, you have a lot of land which has not been cultivated but will be good for paddy. Perhaps, some of us can start on that land?"

Prabhu paused for a moment and considered the added cost. He would have to dig a bore well and maybe invest in one more tractor. But even after that, he would still have money for the school building. This was a good idea.

"Yes. That is a very good idea. Whoever wishes to take on the difficult task of readying the land for paddy cultivation, can go ahead with that."

Now they smiled, the men who had felt that they were not useful anymore. And the sun too drifted out from behind the clouds. The sun's rays lit up the little village and with soft smiles on their faces, the men moved away in different directions.

How nice it would have been if Kuyili had been with him now. Together, they could have cooked something for all these people on their first day back at work. Turning around, he walked towards the door of his house, when he saw a little boy watching him.

An idea occurred and he said, "Go and bring Kuyili akka. Tell her that I am calling her."

The water in the well behind his house was cold and as he poured it on his head, the drops stung his skin. He rubbed a bar of soap on his hands and legs, and watched a few early morning birds pecking the ground for worms. The land this side looked green and a few mango trees lent their soft shade. He sat there on the stone and admired the land around him. How he loved this little village.

He briskly rubbed the soap on his face. As he felt around for the mug of water his hand touched nothing. As he frantically felt around, he felt her cool hands on his back. A small laugh escaped from her lips and she poured a mug of water on his head. The water flowed down his face washing the soap away. He felt her cool hands rub the rough soap on his back. He kept his eyes closed and focused on the feel of her hands on his back.

So many things had happened since Mariamma's death, which now seemed to have happened long ago. In another fortnight, it would be a year since she passed away.

He felt her hands on his lower back moving downwards and said, "Hey! Stop!"

He heard her muffled giggles and opening his eyes, turned

around. She moved quickly out of his reach and stood a little distance away.

He smiled at her and said, "Did you see the men outside?"

"Yes. Looks like some of them have learnt their lesson and have come back to you."

He got up from where he sat and wiped himself dry. Tiny diamonds of water sprang away from his hair and fell on the ground. As he stood there, his hair tousled, his skin shiny clean, a strange stirring assailed her. She turned her face away and watched the little mango blossoms falling steadily from the mango tree. Their perfume tickled her nostrils and she breathed in the fragrance.

He walked up to her and said softly, "Kuyili, I am worried about the children working in the factory. I don't know how to explain my worries but it somehow does not seem right."

She frowned and wondered if she would send her children to the factory. No! She wouldn't.

"What is worrying you?" she asked him seriously.

"That's exactly what I don't know. All I do know is, keeping children close to fireworks is not a good idea. And that Prakaas – he is horrible. I don't trust him one bit."

"I spat on his face the other day." She smiled at the memory.

"What?" he asked her, startled. "What do you mean you spat on him?"

"Don't you know that he is trying to hook one or the other of the village girls?"

He paused and reflected. Yes! Come to think of it, the fellow had almost hinted about this.

"So what did he do to you?" He felt a cold anger building within him. But his voice was soft and calm.

"He caught my hand and pulled me towards him."

"And?" he prompted her.

"And nothing. I pulled my hand free. Slapped him on his cheek, spat on his face and walked away. When I went down the road and turned, he was still standing there wiping his cheek."

The cold anger changed to another emotion he could not understand. There was something he remembered but refused to acknowledge, for acknowledging that would change his life. The glorious light-hearted feeling swept out of his body and was replaced with a sense of shame. A sense of shame, that he could not command his brain to think.

He entered his little house and walked to the cracked mirror hanging on the wall. Picking up a pair of scissors, he trimmed his mustache. Keeping his hands busy kept his mind turned away from thoughts too deep and too terrible to work out.

She knew that something she had said had set off a train of disturbing thoughts. She stared at his back, and then briskly walked to the firewood stove and piled dry logs onto the stove. As the firewood crackled and sprang into flames, she filled a saucepan with water and put it on the stove.

By the time she had finished this, he seemed calmer and ready to talk.

"Kuyili, can we cook something for the workers today?" he asked and added, "There are about thirty of them."

"Yes, of course. I can call Devayani, Radhamma and Lakshmi to help."

She opened the rice bag and saw that there was enough. She gave him a list of things she would need and he went out to call one of the workers to buy the stuff from the nearby town.

When he came back, the smell of coffee filled the little house with its aroma. He sat down and drank the coffee. A part of him, since he was a fair man, was bothered that he could not follow the train of thoughts. Another part of him consoled him. You are not ready to confront your thoughts as yet, it said.

As he sat on the small cane chair and sipped his coffee, he watched Kuyili, piling firewood on the stove. As she bent back and forth, he watched her shapely curves and felt a desire building within him. Suddenly, she turned around, caught the look on his face and blushed. Slowly she turned and looked at him again and he saw in her eyes a reflection of the same desire. They sat in either corner of the room, not touching each other, enjoying the agony of not giving in. Each waiting for the other to make the move. There was something so agonizing about it and yet neither of them wanted to spoil the moment.

A small knock on the door and Prabhu, biting his lower lip, turned towards the door. Vadivel, one of the workers stood outside with a bucket in his hand. The spell was broken, but Kuyili's heart felt different as she went about her work. Her heart thudded a little faster than normal. A hot flush continued to burn her cheeks.

That afternoon as the workers sat down to eat, and Kuyili served them hot rice and *sambhar*, on fresh banana leaves, the sun crept slowly behind a layer of dark clouds. The last few weeks had been hot and the rain could not have chosen a better time. The workers stopped eating and watched the clouds. There was no movement, no breeze. They all knew that a breeze would blow the clouds away and they would lose out. They turned their attention back to the food. They only had a few more minutes before the rain came tumbling down. Prabhu gave brisk instructions. They would suspend work till the rain stopped and then they would resume their work, ploughing the uncultivated land, while it was still wet and soft after the showers.

As they ate their lunch quickly, the first huge drops fell. Hurriedly gulping down their food, they got up and rolled up their leaves. Now the rain came pouring down. Some of them drifted towards their huts and several others walked away to a barn in the distance, where they would huddle together in a group, smoke *beedis* and relax in comfortable male bonding.

Kuyili sat inside the hut, watching the grey sky and the sheets of rain falling. Her emotions stirred and a feeling of unrest disturbed her thoughts as she absentmindedly ate the food. He came in then, and closed the door behind him, his white *khadi dhoti* and white shirt wet with the rain. He had ensured that all the men were far away. She saw him coming towards her and she got up.

As the rain pounded outside, they lay in each other's arms. They had already tasted each other's bodies and they knew what it felt like. What they experienced today was not the thirst to know the other's body, but a lust born from awareness. She knew the curve where his neck ended and his shoulder began and he knew where her stomach curved downwards and it was this that both of them wanted. As he looked at her lying in his arms, he knew that he would never get bored with her body. It had nothing to do with shapely curves or firm breasts. It had something to do with excitement. An excitement born out of the knowledge that both of them could survive without each other but that survival would be the most painful one. It was not dependency and insecurity that made them lust for each other. It was confidence that they could each stand up for and against each other. For a moment, he imagined how she must have spat on Prakash's face. No fear there. He felt a stirring building within him again.

Her eyes softly closed, she felt his firm arms holding her body. His hard thigh muscles, his firm stomach and chest. She loved this man.

It was late in the evening, when both of them walked out looking for the men. But it was not the men that Prabhu saw there. It was Gokulan, sitting outside on the small parapet wall. As Prabhu looked at Gokulan and saw him watching him, both were aware that the other knew.

Gokulan smiled softly at him and embarrassed, Prabhu rubbed his lips, trying to rub away the feel of her soft lips on his.

He waited for Gokulan to say something. A few stray drops fell down from leaves as the breeze shook their stems.

"It is a year since Mariamma passed away. Should you not be thinking about getting married?" Once again, there was a smile.

So this was Gokulan's way of discreetly warning him of the consequences of living with Kuyili without marrying her. That was fine with him. He did want to marry her.

Without waiting for his reply Gokulan continued, "I would like to take care of your marriage arrangements. Shall we fix it for the week after next?"

A small butterfly with golden wings fluttered in his heart. Now, she would be with him all the time.

"Yes." His response was a monosyllable and yet he packed a lifetime into that word.

"Well, in that case; I will send my wife to Kuyili's house to talk to her mother. By the way, it is Kuyili that you want to get married to, right?"

Prabhu looked up startled, only to see that Gokulan was grinning and looking at Kuyili who had just walked out of the house. Hearing her name, she stopped in her tracks and stared at them.

"Hey Kuyili, come here. Do you like your bridegroom?"

She turned her face and ran into the house, her heart thudding softly against its cage. So Gokulan had realized what was going on between her and Prabhu and was taking the initiative. Nothing could be better than this! She uttered a small prayer in her mind and sat down on the mat to calm herself.

Her eyes strayed to the little bed that had been their playground just a little time ago. She saw the crumpled pillow and a few sad jasmines, which had fallen from her hair. Her mind floated back and she sat there recalling the afternoon, a dreamy smile on her face.

TWELVE

Chapter

When the sun rose up in the sky in the second week of the month of August in the year 1978, Prabhu and Kuyili met in the little temple that stood in the outskirts of the village. Weddings were a simple affair in their village, which did not boast of a marriage hall. It was the temple with its huge platforms and sculptured pillars, which doubled up as a marriage hall. The land behind the temple was used to cook food in huge cauldrons and the front of the temple boasted rows of small fairyland bulbs and aromatic flower garlands. The entire village, and some people from neighbouring villages, gathered to watch Prabhu tie the *mangalsutra* around Kuyili's neck that morning. The village musicians had begun beating the drums and blowing their *nadhaswarams* early in the morning and an air of festivity hung over the village. For Prabhu, the temple with its ancient corridors and tall pillars took on a new significance as he walked around ensuring that everything was taken care of. Older men teased him and one woman with her ears pierced in five different places pinched him on his thigh.

He laughed, his heart light and happy.

He remembered that night a year ago when he had been so bored with life, with no definite aim or purpose. Of course, he knew even then that his life was in the village but now he knew it better than ever before. He also knew that he would be the *panchayat* head when Gokulan stepped down. As long as he was alive he would safeguard the villagers from the Prakashes of this world.

As the villagers stood around, dressed in their finery and colourful clothes, Kuyili waited for the *poojari* to finish his *mantras*. She watched the man who had stirred her in more ways than one. It was not just his body, which she loved, but the way he led his life, untouched by all those things that others fought and killed each other for. She knew his plans for improving the school building and she knew that it was lack of time that held him up. She would help out she told herself and turned her face to watch the statue inside the temple. Closing her eyes, she prayed for Prabhu and herself when she suddenly remembered Raju. She uttered a small prayer for him. As the drummers increased the tempo of the music, she felt his hands going around her neck. Her mother and the village women bullied him as they helped him to tie the *mangalsutra*. He was laughing and flirting mildly with them.

After the wedding ceremony, they sat in rows in the huge courtyard at the back of the temple. Men dressed in white folded up *dhotis*, heaped the green leaves with *laddus* and *pullav*. It was an exotic meal and Prabhu realised that Gokulan must have gone to a lot of trouble to organize this. Prabhu had given Gokulan a sum of money and it looked like Gokulan had ensured that the money was well spent. But then Gokulan was in his element at social events, be it a funeral offering, a *thiruvizha* or a marriage. He knew how to organize and get the best out of a function.

Gokulan's wife had helped Prabhu choose the wedding sari for Kuyili, which was the colour of freshly blossoming jasmines. The sari had a broad red border and was splashed liberally with gold threads woven into the silk. The effect was stunning and every time she moved her body, some of the gold caught the sun and splayed its rays around. He had never seen her so beautifully dressed. Her neck was swathed in gold chains and on her arms, white glass bangles borrowed glory from a set of gold bangles. On her forehead, rested a tiny pearl pendant like a frozen tear. In her ears hung huge gold earrings, which threatened to pull her earlobes out of shape. He saw all this and also all that her clothes hid.

When he was a little child and his mother would talk about a fair bride for him, he would scowl and frown.

"I will never get married and go away from you," he would say and she would hold him tightly and kiss him. Though her mouth would scold him, his young mind guessed that his words pleased her.

Today, she was not here to see his marriage to this dark bride with a strong mind. If she had been, her eyes would have filled with gladness and she would have blessed him. Many of his decisions in life had somehow left him with question marks.

For the first time, he knew for sure that this was a good decision.

He watched the villagers eat their food heartily. Some of them were cracking jokes at his expense and he played the role of the jubilant bridegroom, all the time his mind ticking away waiting for the moment when he would be alone with Kuyili, in their little house.

It was evening when he went back home. Sometime during the afternoon, the women had whisked Kuyili away from him and he had not seen her after that. Now, he headed back home wondering where she was.

As he reached his house, the first stars were appearing in the evening sky, casting a shiny glow on the ground. A crescent shaped moon hung low upon the sky and night creatures were waking up for their nocturnal activities. As he turned the knob, he heard muffled giggles inside. Pushing the door open, he saw his bride perched on his bed, which now looked different. It had garlands of fragrant jasmines, hanging from the roof and falling softly around the cot. On the bed were rose petals and more jasmines. All the flowers had combined to set off a heady perfume and his senses swam in the onslaught. A few young village belles giggled again and ran out of the door, even as he stood inside gaping.

She peeped at him and smiled. He walked across to the window and saw the girls walking away into the twilight. Their footsteps rang with excitement. That was the effect a wedding had in a little village.

Walking over, he sat down next to her. The smell of jasmines mingled with the smell of sandalwood and turmeric, which lent a golden glow to her skin. She was still dressed in the same sari and around her neck hung a jasmine garland. Picking up the garland, he put it around his neck so that both of them were bound together. She seemed so shy, her eyes averted from his face, which was an inch away from his. He picked up her tiny palm and held it in his hands.

"Kuyili," he said in a serious tone. "Kuyili, just like the garland which is holding us together, we will always be there for each other. Trust me."

Now she was not the shy bride anymore. This was what he loved about her – the ability to become mature and serious when the situation demanded and to be feminine and girlish when she chose to. She looked at him challengingly and taking the garland away from her neck she pulled back and said, "Even if we are separated by time and fate, you will still be with me, as a part of me."

He pulled her close to him and she handed him the glass of milk, which rested on a tray near the bed. They quickly played the motions of drinking milk from the same glass and eating a sweet together and then they were in each other's arms.

The night deepened and lost its darkness in the first rays of the morning. That was when they slept, exhausted.

Early the next morning he woke up and after hurriedly washing himself in the cold well outside, walked towards the town. Kuyili had not seen him leave. He smiled as he walked, recollecting the night before. In the distance, women were washing clothes in the lake and he thought he could see Kuyili there with the village belles. They would be teasing his wife and she would be answering them cheekily.

Once again he smiled and walked on determinedly.

Barely a year ago, he had no idea that he would fall in love and get married. Barely a year ago, he did know that he had such strong feelings in his heart for this beloved land and its people. It was like knowledge born anew and it was as though love for Kuyili had rekindled his love for the land.

A woman was also like the land – ready to give herself to others. She bore life and nurtured it like the beloved earth.

In the happiness surrounding the harvest and the marriage, he had allowed his fears about Mariamma's death and the factory to take a back seat. He knew now that he could not delay action any further. He needed to do something at least about Mariamma's death and then follow up on that with finding out who was the betrayer who lived amongst them quietly.

When he reached the town, the shopkeepers were just opening their shops. A few were polishing their wares with pieces of cloth. Others were sweeping the floors. A few hens clucked around peacefully.

He went to the shop where he knew he would find what he was looking for.

After buying it, and blushing slightly when the shopkeeper asked him about the night before, he rushed back homewards.

Just as the morning sky was reaching a little higher into the sky, he crossed the thorny path that would lead to his house.

She was standing outside and he knew that she was wondering where he had gone off. He went to her and standing inside the doorway he gave her the packet. Tearing open the paper, she found a kerosene stove inside. They spent the morning making the stove work and stealing moments to hold each other. When the stove was finally ready and burning, they placed a kettle with water on it and forgot all about it.

When the burning smell wafted towards them, Prabhu ran in time to save the stove that was just a few hours old. They laughed and drank the tea, which had a slightly burnt smell about it.

THIRTEEN

Chapter

The schoolmaster opened the door to wake up Raju who slept in the classroom. Since coming to the school, the boy had changed. He seldom cried. He seemed to enjoy doing some chores around the school and most importantly, he was slowly making friends with the boys. The day after Raju had joined him, the school headmaster had sent him away on an errand.

Summoning all the children he had said in a loud clear voice, "Children, we all love to make fun of creatures weaker than us. That is why we love to catch butterflies and squash ants and beetles. It makes us feel powerful. But have you ever thought how a dead ant's mother must feel when she sees her child's body? How do you think a dead butterfly's brother would feel seeing that he will have to fly alone?"

One of the boys was digging his nose and staring blankly.

The headmaster paused for a second before continuing, "It is possible for us to be cruel and it is difficult to be kind. I have a test for all of you. A test of kindness." He stopped again.

"We will henceforth have in our midst a boy whose mother and father are dead, who is believed to be mad. Who has not spoken a word for many years and is yet not dumb. He is like the hurt butterfly that tries to fly around with the help of one wing. You can help this butterfly get its other wing back by being kind to him."

He stopped again to wipe away the sweat that gathered on his forehead, wondering if these children could understand his words. The quiet stillness indicated nothing.

"If you cannot be kind, at least do not hurt him and make him lose his other wing." His voice sounded harsh, sending a shiver down the backs of the little children.

"That's all. You can all go back to your classrooms now." As they turned to go, he added softly, "The kindest child here will win a prize."

The word prize brought a reaction, and they whispered excitedly amongst themselves as they went back to their studies.

In the beginning, none of them had tried to be Raju's friend but the headmaster's words had helped. They did not throw stones or laugh at him, these same children who had not allowed Raju to come anywhere close to festivities and functions.

But even the thought of the prize could not bring them closer to a boy who looked so different from them with his thin face and shabby hair. The fact that he never spoke a word made them avoid his company. But very often, they saw him sitting in a corner watching them play. He especially liked to watch them when they played *kabaddi,* – a game of maneuvering and cunning.

His toes moved to the sound of their voices saying, '*Kabaddi, kabaddi, kabaddi*'.

On one such day, Anjali, the tiniest girl in the school had fallen down. Raju picked her up. The children had watched, scared that he would hurt her. Anjali herself was staring at him with petrified eyes. But he had carried her to the shade of a tree, and placing her gently on the grass, had wiped her knee from which the blood was flowing freely. He gently pressed a piece of cloth to stop the flow. Soon, her tears and the blood stopped and he handed her a banana.

Some of the children recognized the banana as the same one they got for lunch. He had parted with it so easily. When he got up to work, they saw that a piece of his shirt was missing – the piece he had torn off to wipe the child's bleeding knee.

After that, a few of them played closer to where he sat and sometimes, if the ball landed near him they would shout, "Raju, pick up the ball and throw it here."

He would willingly do so but never responded with a smile or a word.

When the master heard about the way Raju had helped little Anjali, he realized that somewhere within the boy's heart was a chink through which change could enter, something that would make the boy embrace the world and the people around him.

The school regularly celebrated India's Independence Day on August 15th. The same month when Prabhu and Kuyili's marriage happened this year, the school readied itself for the celebration. The festivities in the school were limited to the tall pole, which stood like a sentry in the centre of the compound. The tall pole boasted the Indian flag, with its mellow shades of orange and green. As preparation for the celebration, the evening before, the flag would be lowered and washed. This year the job was entrusted to Raju and he washed it tenderly. He knew about India's independence and its meaning to its people. He had learnt of it when he used to attend school and he handled the flag like a precious lamb. When the flag was washed and dried, he folded it neatly, till the sun's rays ironed out the creases.

The next morning, the day India celebrated her independence twenty-one years ago, Vadhiyar gave him the job of plucking some flowers and this he did with enthusiasm. He knew where the wildest and most fragrant flowers grew and he ran around the lake's shore, plucking them. In the early morning sun's rays, he bathed himself in the crystal clear lake and wearing his khaki pant and torn shirt, headed back to the school building.

Vadhiyar and he then plucked the petals from the flowers and a fistful of these was bundled in the flag, which was tied to the pole. When the flag would be hoisted up, the flower petals would flutter to the ground like coloured snow flakes.

The children knew the ritual, but to Raju it brought an excitement his childish mind had never experienced. Along with the little children he stood still as they sang the national anthem. Their voices rang loudly like the chime of temple bells and they sang with gusto. His toes moved slowly to the sound of the words and he held his head straight and high. And then with the flourish of a magician's wand, Vadhiyar hoisted the flag. The petals flew around them and the children clapped their hands with joy. Sweets were passed around and the children eagerly popped it into their mouths.

As they chatted and laughed, Vadhiyar clapped his hands and said loudly, "Silence. How many of you know that there were many brave people who fought for our country's independence?"

One squeaky voiced boy said softly, "Raja Ram Mohan Roy".

Another little boy said, "MGR". Vadhiyar smiled in spite of himself and said, "Little Ramu, you see too many films. MGR was a film actor."

"Do you know that bravery comes in different forms?" To this question the children kept quiet. How could bravery come in different forms?

Vadhiyar continued in a loud voice, "Bravery is not limited to fighting wars and battles. It is also something to do with fighting life's hardships and problems and coming out of the same wiser."

One boy was sucking his sweet noisily and another was pulling a little girl's plait.

"Silence! How many of you know what it is to be alone in the world?" He raised his voice.

One girl said softly, "My amma is alone when I come away to school."

Vadhiyar smiled and said, "But she can look after herself. How about a young boy? He has braved a childhood filled with pain and he came to find his roots amongst all of you; you who were never kind to him when he was sad and lonely."

Raju felt his heart beating faster. Was Vadhiyar talking about him? He moved slowly to the back of the crowd.

"Let us celebrate our independence day by awarding a brave boy."

With a pause which seemed to last an eternity, Vadhiyar said, "Raju come over here!"

Raju's feet moved forwards, but his mind urged him to run away. As he hovered in indecision, he heard a small clap. Little Anjali was clapping her hands and smiling at him. His own eyes clouded over and he slowly dragged himself to the front. He felt some hands patting him on his back and shoulder as he walked to the front and the clapping sound grew louder as more children brought their hands together. The thundering sound of hands beating, invoked a storm in his heart. He wished his heart would not swell the way it was doing. The swelling seemed to be pushing his head upwards and he wanted to keep it lowered to hide the tears that were flowing freely now. He reached the front and closed his eyes, when he felt Vadhiyar's warm hands hold him in a hug. The clapping continued in the sunny morning, like a freak thunderstorm and Raju felt a sense of god's loving arms holding him. Everything he had suffered, every indignity he had undergone, every pain he had encountered fell off like flakes of dried skin. He felt a white ray of love lighting up his heart and cleansing it. He was free from all his suffering. He smiled and to the watching children it reminded them of days when the sun broke through behind a screen of rain. They watched out for this, because soon after this, the sky would be dressed in an arc of colours.

Raju smiled and yet the tears flowed.

Vadhiyar raised his voice and said "Silence."

The children grew quiet and Vadhiyar said, "For a boy who tore off his shirt to dress a little child's wound, all of you have contributed some little money. With the collection, I have bought Raju this pant and shirt."

Sniffing loudly, like a little boy, Raju collected the clothes in his hand. Just for a second he wished he could talk. He willed his mind to say something and his mouth to form the words, but they were stuck inside. Instead, he held the clothes in his hand and watched the little children dumbly.

As they clapped their hands, he turned and hurriedly ran away.

A little later the festivities ended and Raju went to an empty classroom and wore his new clothes. The shirt was a shade of green like the green of the paddy and the pant was blue, like a twilight night. He combed his hair and stared at himself in the little broken mirror that hung in the classroom. He saw an image of a thin-faced boy, whose eyes sparkled. He wished that Prabhu could see him now.

He had not gone by to his little green house for a long time. The thought of going there brought with it a fear that made him break out in a cold sweat. But he would go today. As he walked on the lonely path to his house, Raju's mind grappled with memories too painful to let go. The memory of his father beating him and his mother. This brought in quick succession the sudden image of his mother's dead body, wasted and uncared for. He remembered the day his father had beaten his mother relentlessly.

He had been repeating the words, "Whose son is he, whore? Whose son is he?"

Those words had not made sense then, but now as he walked the path to his green house, in his new clothes, he wondered what his father had meant. He was his father's son, wasn't he? Whose son could he be? The memory brought a fear in his heart, but for the first time along with the fear came a feeling of resolution. He would not allow his sorrows to rape his mind. He would feel sad, but he would not drown. Lifting his head a little higher he shuffled slowly towards his house.

As he passed the village *Banyan* tree he saw Gokulan sitting with two men. He had never been comfortable with grownups and Gokulan, especially, scared him. He wondered if he should turn and run back when he saw that all of them were watching him. For a moment he thought of Vadhiyar and Prabhu. They would be ashamed of him if he ran away so he resolutely walked along.

"Hey Raju!" He heard the words but commanded his ears to prevent the words from making a difference.

The voice changed in tone and he heard Gokulan saying, "Hey mad boy, come here."

The words rang with a mocking laugh. Raju felt a slight ache in his heart, but he was used to this. The only thing was it was coming again after a long time. So long that he had forgotten that he was the village's mad person.

But he was mad, wasn't he? Why else could he not talk? Why could he not ask these people why they called him mad? He walked on, trying to drown out Gokulan's voice but he heard him say to the other person, "This mad fellow does not know who his father is. If he only knew."

The words were accompanied by a loud laughing sound and the sound beat the wind out of his step. He felt himself staggering along like a drunken man. Why were they all ridiculing him about his father? What had he done? Could he choose his own father? If he could, he would have chosen Prabhu. But he didn't have a choice. Why were they mocking him? As he walked along, he felt his heart beat change its rhythm. The sound seemed to mock his footsteps and it kept saying, 'You are running away, coward! Go talk to them.' He heard his mind respond, 'But I cannot talk, stupid. What can I say?'

'So who is stopping you from beating them?' The thumping of his heartbeat changed to a war drum. The message was clear and he turned back. As he walked back, he saw that Gokulan was idly chewing a piece of grass and still smiling.

As he looked at him, he saw Gokulan's eyes falling on him and with a surprised look he told the others, "The mad fellow is returning. I think my words hurt him."

His words only spurred him on and as he came closer, Gokulan suddenly seemed to realize that Raju was walking towards him. He looked at the two men with him. The last thing he wanted was to be slapped by the mad fellow. He would be the laughing stock of his village. Better to let him have it before he raised his hands. The thoughts passed quickly through his mind and rushing towards Raju he pushed him on the ground. Raising his hands he brought it down in a hard punch on the boy's face. Lifting his right leg, he kicked the boy and then spitting on him for added effect, he moved back. As the shocked men watched, he quickly walked away.

Raju lay on the ground, his face rubbing against the small stones, which poked his face. He saw a small tear in his new shirt and felt a silent rage in his heart. As he tried to get up he saw one of the men dusting his pant and the other said, "Don't tell Prabhu what happened. He will be very angry."

And then the first man said softly, "Why did he beat him? Everyone in the village knows that he is this boy's father."

"Shhhussh. Keep quiet you fool. Do you know what you are saying?"

But the words had already been said and Raju fell back on the ground, his face rubbing the hard pebbles and his mind crushed under the weight of the words he had just heard. So this was why Gokulan beat him. He was Gokulan's illegal son. If this was true, then why did Gokulan hate him so? Was it because he did not measure up to his expectations of how a son should be? Was he ashamed of him? His mind staggered under the enormity of the words he had heard.

Velu was saying, "You fool! Look what you have gone and done. This boy is not getting up. God knows he can hear well. If Prabhu knows what you have done he will murder you!"

So Prabhu also knew this! It was out of sympathy and pity that he looked after him. Not out of love. No one in the world loved him. The words were spinning a web around his mind trapping it in a sorrow, which was as deep as a black hole.

"Here, drink this water."

One of them was pressing some water into his hands. As he sipped it, he felt a hole burning in his stomach. They would not let him be. They would destroy him. He looked at the tear in his new shirt and that was what finally broke his heart. He cried loudly, the sobs sounding like the howling of a pack of wild dogs. The men shut their ears to block out the sound but it penetrated and touched the core of their being. At that moment, Vela the younger of the two, hated Gokulan with all his heart. Though he had never bothered about Raju, he sat down now, next to the boy and ran his fingers slowly through his hair.

"Don't cry. It's okay. You haven't done anything." The words were falling out of his mouth hurriedly and his fingers continued to stroke the boy. After a while, which seemed liked hours, the loud crying softened to a whimpering sound.

At the same time that Raju was crying, Prabhu, who was on his way to the temple, crossed the path and saw the three men. In the distance, his eyes made out Velu and Sambu but he couldn't make out whom the man sitting on the ground was. Was someone hurt? Breaking into a sprint he ran towards the three. A slight dust storm was starting and the dry grains flew around like brown clouds. Dust storms were uncommon and, more often than not, they indicated that the rains were close by. As he ran faster, Prabhu saw the man on the ground was Raju. Oh god! Why was he sitting there so pitiably? As his mind asked him questions, his feet moved faster and faster on the ground till he reached the group.

He saw a look of fear cross Sambu's and Velu's face and then he saw the bleeding wound on Raju's cheek, where Gokulan's ruby ring had torn the skin. His eyes took in the disheveled hair and the new clothes; dirty but still new. He felt a white-hot rage build up within him. The rage blinded him and he caught Velu's shirt with his hands. His grip was so tight that Velu felt the shirt tearing under his grasp.

"Wait, Prabhu saami! Wait! We didn't do anything to Raju." Sambu's words were tripping over each other in their hurry to be said.

For the first time Prabhu turned and looked at him. His eyes narrowing, he said softly, "Who did this to him?"

The words were said softly and the grip on Vela's shirt was loosening, but there was no doubt that both the men were a few seconds away from having their bodies broken.

Vela cleared his throat and said, "We don't know. We were passing by and saw him sitting on the ground. If you don't believe us, see – I offered him water too."

All through the talking, Raju continued to sit with his head hidden in his lap and his body rocking in the strange old fashion. Prabhu felt a cold despair replacing the anger. All the good work of Vadhiyar and the school had been lost by the thoughtless act of a demonic individual.

Moving back from the group, he lit a cigarette and blowing on it softly, said, "Velu, I am providing your family a place to stay in my land. If not for me, you would not have been able to take your child to the doctor in the village when she fell ill. If not for me she would have died."

He hated uttering these words and yet he said them. He felt, rather than saw, Velu cringing and he continued, "When your child is so important to you, how can you let another boy suffer so? Tell me who did this to Raju."

Hovering in indecision, Velu saw Sambu watching him. He knew that saying the name would begin a rift in the village between the headman and the richest man. The villagers would suffer by the rift. He knew that though Gokulan played the *panchayat* head, it was Prabhu who was there for all of them, helping them along.

What good would it do telling Prabhu the truth? He shifted his eyes downwards and looked at Raju. The boy was still sniffing, totally lost in his own world.

Quickly he said, "I only did it, saami. I kept calling him and he refused to come to me. He was walking like a big shot in his new clothes. I got angry and gave him one slap. I didn't mean to hit him like this."

Prabhu looked at him for a long moment and then spitting on the ground he said, "Velu I always believed you were one of the trustworthy young men in the village. But now, for some reason you are choosing to speak a lie. I will find out who did this to Raju."

With these words, he put his arms tenderly around Raju's shoulder and lifted him up.

As they walked back together, both lost in their own world of dark thoughts, the sand storm shifted into a harsh rainfall. The rain fell relentlessly like huge sheets of transparent glass and jabbed their faces as they walked on oblivious of the drops. It was only when they reached the school building, that Prabhu realized that Raju had stopped crying. But his eyes had lost their sparkle and the look in them sent a terrible shiver down Prabhu's back. Who had hurt the boy? He would go back and tackle Sambu. If Velu refused to tell the truth he would get it out of Sambu.

The children had left the school and the building had a forlorn look to it. The flag, which they had hoisted that morning, dripped water and hung on its pole like a pitiable rag. As they walked in, Raju's eyes watched the flag and his own body slouched like a shadow of the rag cloth. He didn't want to fight anymore. He would only be a mad man. He didn't want their kindness. He didn't want their mockery. He had a world within him, a world of silence to which if he turned; they would not be able to reach him. He had found solace so many times in that world. In that world no one talked, no one shouted, no one hurt another. He walked like a silent ghost and the entire world around him was a two dimensional figure. It was his world of silence, which was real. Not this world of noise and people, of mountains and lakes. These were the props people used to spread their kind around. And all of them were terrible. His mind had shut out Prabhu and Vadhiyar because in his world of silence, these were the people who were breaking down the gates and trying to enter. Though he walked beside Prabhu he had moved away, far away. So far that his mind could not even recognize Prabhu's face anymore.

He looked around him at the strange building they had entered. Somewhere in the distance, his mind said this was the school building. A voice whispered that he had experienced an unknown emotion called 'happiness' here but that was so long ago and so brief that its memory was already gone. He looked at the forlorn playground. This is where little children played but he was not one of them. He never had been. The life he had chosen for himself was one of sorrow. The brief moments of happiness were already submerged in the heavy cloak of despair. His mother had looked peaceful in death. Maybe death was the answer. He saw a body being carried in the distance. Four men held the body up and as they walked the rain fell on the body wetting it. He desperately wanted to run to the body and cover it. He couldn't bear seeing the body getting soaked in the rain. It was indecent. It was not right that because a person was dead, the rain could fall and wet the person and that too his own mother. But it was not his mother. He saw his own face, calm in death. The rain continued to fall on his face and he did not feel it as they carried him. Wait! A group of men were hurrying towards his body. He prayed in death that they would let him die in peace but that was not to be. They were disturbing the pallbearers and telling them to put his body down. Don't carry a mad man's body. No I am not dead. But I will be soon and then you can call me mad for all you are worth and I won't respond. But now, just for now let them carry my body to the pyre.

He tried to say the words but his mouth wouldn't open and all the time they were fighting – the pallbearers and the destroyers. He ran towards the lake. Once he reached the lake he could lie down on the pyre and they would then be forced to burn his body. In the distance he heard the rain but he could not feel it. He knew Prabhu was holding his hand and he could not feel that too. They were all paper dolls. They reminded him of a puppet show he had seen in the village once. The dolls danced and fought and hurt each other. It was amazing till he had seen the threads, which suspended them and moved them around. The threads were tied to a hand and it was the hand that controlled the puppets.

Prabhu! He snorted in his mind. He just felt sorry for this pitiable mad man! Suddenly he saw a huge black spider hanging from a tree. Its huge tentacles were reaching out to him. He shut his eyes and the spider became a million spiders, dark and eerie. They spread a terrible smell, which reminded him of his mother's dead body. One spider was now crawling onto his leg. Letting out a shrill, blood curdling scream, he flayed his arms and legs.

Prabhu stared at Raju, shocked out of his wits. What had happened to him? With a shriek of terror, Raju tore his hand free from Prabhu and ran away towards the distant lake.

Prabhu felt a burning sensation in his heart. He knew that he was losing the child to hopelessness. If he allowed Raju to go back to the same desperate stage then he had failed in life. He had failed in his duty as a human being and as a protector of the villagers. He might as well go away to Madras or some crowded dirty town and hide his face amongst the toddy drinkers.

Standing there under the pelting rain, Prabhu felt tears of frustration dropping from his eyes. Was god really there? A strong doubt crept into his mind. He had always assumed there was a god. He had never questioned this and yet today he wondered. He wondered at life itself and the cruelty that hid behind the faces of men.

Why was Raju behaving like this? What could have happened? How would he be able to save him? The thoughts rushed through his mind when he suddenly saw Vadhiyar coming out of one the classrooms.

"That sounded like Raju. What happened?" asked Vadhiyar, alarm ringing in his voice.

"I don't know!" Prabhu shrugged his shoulders frustratedly. "I saw him sitting in the middle of the road. Somebody had hurt him. Velu and Sambu were with him. I need to question them."

He searched in his pocket for a cigarette. The rain had seeped through his pocket but the packet was dry. Heaving a sigh of relief, he shielded the cigarette with his hands and lit it.

With a resigned look on his face he said softly, "I think we have lost him. If anything, he has become even worse than before."

"How could that be? Just this morning he was so happy! The children had collected money for a gift for him. I have never seen the boy more happy."

Yes, happiness. Raju had seen a moment of happiness and immediately the same had been snatched away from him.

FOURTEEN Chapter

He turned his face away from Vadhiyar and walked towards the lake. The rain had simmered to a soft drizzle and the grass made a wet squishing noise under his feet. A lone cow mooed mournfully. The sky still looked sullen and gray. What could he do? Should he go after Raju or should he tackle Velu? He wouldn't know how to deal with Raju till he understood what had happened earlier.

He turned into the lane that took him to the soft path where his land lay. The huge land his father had left for him to nurture and the lives he was meant to protect. What lives? He fed their stomachs but not their hearts and while they ate from the land, they destroyed another. He felt a bitterness sweep into his mind and a bitter taste flooded his mouth. He retched on the ground. His stomach heaved and pushed out the bile. Finally he rested against a tree. His head ached and when he touched his forehead it burned against his fingers. He was coming down with fever. His feet grew heavy and he dragged them on the ground towards Velu's house. And then he saw Gokulan standing outside his house talking to Kuyili. They were both laughing.

On legs growing unsteady with every step, he dragged himself to his house. Kuyili saw him first and came running towards him.

"You are soaking wet!"

Her fingers touched his hand and with an alarmed look on her face, she said, "You are not well! What possessed you to walk in this rain?"

Quickly she dragged him inside and with a towel rubbed his hair dry. He took off his shirt with clumsy fingers and threw his *dhoti* on the ground. Tying the dry *dhoti* she passed him, he lay down on the mat. His mouth felt dry and his throat hurt. She ran to a small sweet box where he had a stock of tablets. Pulling out two aspirins she forced it into his hand. He swallowed the tablets and lay down. Beads of sweat were breaking out on his forehead and with tired fingers he wiped them away. His mind was revolving around Raju and the happenings of the afternoon. Where was the boy now? Would he do anything rash like drowning himself? He tried to get up but Kuyili pushed him back on the bed.

"Enough! Stop it! What's bothering you?" she asked, anger masking the alarm in her voice.

Gokulan, who had been standing quietly in the corner, came in and sat down. "What happened Prabhu? Why did you go out when you were not feeling well?"

"I am fine. It is just a slight fever. But Raju?"

He wanted to add that Raju had lost his senses when he felt rather than saw a sly look cross Gokulan"s face. It was gone before he could actually see it.

He looked hard at Gokulan and said, "Did you say anything to him?"

Clearing his throat Gokulan said gruffly, "Why should I say anything to that mad fellow? He thinks he is a big shot in his new clothes. One tight slap, that's all it took to bring him down to earth." He laughed loudly and outside, a rumble of thunder followed a burst of lightening.

Hopelessly, Prabhu lay back on the mat. He shut his eyes to shut out the evil but he couldn't ignore it. Gokulan was mad. He was destroying his own son. But he wouldn't let that happen. Suddenly he didn't mind the fever any more. His throat stopped hurting and he sat up on the mat.

In a soft tone he said, "You are not hurting your son. You are hurting yourself. The price you will pay will be so terrible that you will beg for death to release you from the pain."

He said the words and would have continued if Kuyili, who was near the stove, had not dropped the dish in her hand on the ground and run towards him.

She put her hand on his mouth and said, "He is not well. Go away. Don't listen to him."

Gokulan got up from where he sat. His heart told him to kill Prabhu. After all, murder was not new to him. But Prabhu was rich. He needed Prabhu's land and the paddy, which grew on it. Smiling softly, he said, "Don't worry, Kuyili. I will not hurt

Prabhu. He is delirious because of the fever. Raju my son?" Guffawing loudly, he walked out of the little house.

Exhausted after the outburst Prabhu rested his head on the mat. The headache had reached a peak and he felt his temples throbbing with pain. If he shut his eyes for a little while the pain would go and then he would be ready to tackle the problem. He felt rather than saw Kuyili sitting beside him, her cool hands rubbing his head.

When she left the hut, it was night and Prabhu's soft snoring sound was the only noise. Outside, the night breeze blew the drops of rain around and the trees shook their branches in acknowledgement. Every little shake produced a small shower of raindrops and they fell on Kuyili as she raced like a little deer towards the lake. Darkness did not frighten her nor did the strange night sounds. But the words that Prabhu had uttered! Was Raju in trouble? If he were, where would he be? She ran to the lake and standing on the shore, shouted loudly, "Raju, where are you?"

A mocking owl let out an indignant hoot. A cricket answered and a couple of bats took off from a tall tree. Once again she shouted, "Raju, answer me."

A still silence filled the place with eeriness.

She stood under a tree and shouted, again and again. And then a flash of lightening filled the sky with an eerie brightness. Another burst of rainfall would follow any moment and with a shrug of exasperation she turned towards home. When she reached her doorway, she heard the rain dash down to the ground behind her. Shutting the door tight to keep out the rain, she lay down on a mat.

When morning came, the rain had devastated some of the newly cultivated paddy fields. They lay wasted and forlorn. Some of the tree branches had crashed on the electric wire and a passing cow had died, electrocuted.

The land had changed into brown slush and the sky still looked sullen and bleak. Prabhu woke up when the cock outside crowed loudly. With a curse he tried to sit up, but he felt weak and tired. His mouth tasted foul. He looked for Kuyili but she was nowhere to be seen.

Getting up slowly, he walked out of his house. It had been a real downpour and his eyes quickly assessed the damage. Luckily it was not unmanageable. Suddenly he remembered that Raju had run away. Without further ado, he washed his face and rinsed his mouth with water. Putting on his slippers he walked briskly towards the lake.

As he neared it he heard Kuyili's voice calling out, "Raju! Answer me."

What was Kuyili doing here? She saw him coming towards her and running to him she said, "What are you doing outside in this weather?"

"Where is Raju?" He barely heard what she had to say.

"I don't know. I went to the school. He hasn't returned there. Vadhiyar is also looking for him."

As the three of them roamed through the undergrowth calling

for Raju, the remaining clouds drifted away and the sun peeped out of a watery sky. The rains had passed and it would be a warm day.

They searched the whole day and the following day and still there was no sign of Raju. Word passed quickly around the village and all those people who had respected Gokulan suddenly wondered at the kind of person he was.

Only at the factory, life continued as normal. The fever that had struck Prabhu spread through the village and several men fell ill. The symptoms were the same, fever, vomiting and stomach cramps. As they searched, Prabhu would creep out of his house and walk a few feet only to lie down exhausted. Nightmares haunted his sleep and his waking hours and in all of them he saw Raju running and demons chasing him. A fierce sun shone down on their village as though to make up for the sudden softness of the rains. The heat sapped the energy of the men and they sat in groups too tired even to talk.

It was three days later that Raju was found, in a little cave in the outskirts of the village. It was by chance that a couple of men who were passing the cave heard his soft moaning voice and peeped into the dark cave.

He lay in a corner of the cave, delirious and semi conscious. They half carried, half dragged him back and the news of his arrival reached Prabhu where he lay under a tree. Uttering a small prayer of thanks, Prabhu rushed towards the road and waited. When he saw Raju, his heart stopped beating for a moment and then raced terribly. He looked more dead than alive. Running up to him, he took the boys head in his arms and pressed it close to his face. The dark curls on Raju's head tickled Prabhu's chin and it brought out hot burning tears in his eyes. He cried softly, holding the boy's unconscious face.

When Kuyili came with water in a jug, she saw her husband's tear soaked face. Swallowing her own tears, she poured a few drops into Raju's mouth by forcing it open. Some of the men ran to borrow one of Prakash's vehicles. It was evening and dusk was enveloping the village with its golden glow when Raju was driven to the town hospital. Delirious and unconscious, his face pale, Raju looked terrible. As they drove, Prabhu prayed and held Raju's hands in his own.

The doctor did not spend too much time on frivolities. Seeing Prabhu was enough to prod him to do the needful for the boy. Soon an I V was connected and dextrose pumped into his body. The doctor added doses of vitamins and antibiotics to the drip.

That night Prabhu slept in the ward and Kuyili watched over the two of them. They hardly talked. Words were not necessary. Silence broken only by the sounds of trolleys being pushed around, the loud cry of a baby, two women discussing a dying man, were the only sounds which reached the ward where both Prabhu and Raju lay asleep. Words were passing through their minds, but they were not words spoken by men. They were words spoken by strange creatures, which sometimes wore golden feathers and flew around like pollen dust and at other times grew long tails and breathed terrible fire. The creatures spoke words, which hurt both of them as they lay in silence sharing a strange communion of silence.

When Raju came back to his senses, it was another twenty-four hours later and his first thought was that he had died and gone to heaven. He saw Prabhu's face and Kuyili's face but the wall he had put up between himself and the world was still in place and he saw them from afar. None of these people could ever hurt him again.

Kuyili saw Raju's eyelids fluttering and she quickly called Prabhu. Both of them bent over the boy waiting for him to open his eyes and he did, softly, like a butterfly trying out its newly born wings. Prabhu watched over him till he opened his eyes and then smiled at him. The smile was one of thankfulness for giving him another chance. He held the boys hand like a precious gem in both his hands. Kuyili watched over them and in her heart and mind there was only one thought – if god took away something, he always gave something else in its place. Raju had lost his mother but he had found Prabhu. But looking at his face now, hidden by lines acquired too early in life, she saw that Raju had retreated to a place far away from all of them.

The three of them went back home two days later. During those two days, Kuyili spent most of her time in taking care of Raju, and Prabhu, who had still not recovered from his fever.

When they began their journey back to the village, Prabhu held Raju's limp hand in his own and said, "Raju, you are very important to me and Kuyili. Whoever hurt you will pay a price for it. I will see that the person doesn't hurt you again. If there are some who hurt you, there are people like me who get hurt just seeing your pain. For our sakes please be stronger."

His voice broke with sorrow as he said these words but they seemed to fall on deaf years. Raju was walking with his head bent like a stalk of paddy bent by the wind.

They reached the village and Prabhu took Raju back to the school. Vadhiyar's eyes behind his thick glasses were clouded but if Raju noticed it, there was no reaction whatsoever.

The weather had settled to a soft breeze and tender sunlight played with the leaves. In the late evening Kuyili and Prabhu returned home.

Life continued in a normal fashion for all except Raju who still lived in a world beyond the reach of human beings. He heard commands and reacted to them like an actor in a play, but stayed uninvolved with all happenings. He avoided the children and spent most of his time tending the little vegetable garden at the back of the school. Vadhiyar left him alone except to yell commands to him now and then.

As the days passed, the rains began again and this time the school building shook under the weight of the rains. If repairs were not conducted soon, the building itself would collapse, thought Vadhiyar, as he rushed around the place one night pushing tables and chairs out of the reach of the leaking roof.

In one classroom the leaking roof was allowing rainwater to seep onto the students' books and he climbed onto a chair to block the leak. As he stood poised on the chair, a rumble of thunder broke loose and just for a moment he lost balance. The next thing he knew the chair was shaking and along with it, he lost his foothold and fell on the ground. The black board, which was swinging slightly, was his only chance to break his fall and he gripped it. But the nails, which held the black board in place, were rusted and they gave way. The board came down with him and Vadhiyar landed heavily on the ground with the board on top of him.

He felt a terrible pain in his elbow and screamed. At that moment the electricity failed and the lights went off with a plopping sound.

"Help me," he shouted, the pain in his elbow making him feel faint. Softly he touched his hand and felt warm fluid flowing out. The nail from the board had pierced his arm near the elbow. Once again he shouted 'help' and then lost consciousness.

Raju was sitting in the backyard on a small step watching the rain pelting down on the trees. Its hard drops were shaking the leaves and the branches. Suddenly breaking through his thoughts he heard the sound of a loud crash and the yell of a man in pain. Raju sat silently, his mind begging him to return to his world of silence. And yet he had recognized the cry. He hovered there on the thin brink of indecision and then he heard the cry again. It was Vadhiyar and he was hurt. The same Vadhiyar who had hoisted the flag and pressed the new clothes into his hand. He shut his eyes, his tired mind begging him to retreat. But the change had happened. He had heard and even at the cost of pain more terrible than death, he had to respond to the cry. He broke into a run.

It was his body which first reacted to the sound. It was his legs that stood up and moved, first slowly and then rapidly, as he broke into a run. But the sound penetrated his body and he felt a sudden response in his heart. A response he did not want. It was a response of dread and of fear. Fear that someone he loved was hurt. But he did not love them, his mind begged his heart to stay quiet, but his heart was beating erratically and every beat whispered to him that he was hearing the voice of a person he loved. That voice spelt pain, which propelled his feet towards the room from where the sound had come.

As he ran, the huge wave of sadness enveloping him fell away. He had not lost. God had saved him at the same moment when he had almost questioned god's existence. He knew now that nothing would make him retreat to his world of despair. He was ready to fight life's battles. The thoughts flew through his mind and he slowed down till his eyes got used to the dark and then he ran towards the classroom from where the sound had come.

Reaching the door, he saw Vadhiyar sitting on the ground.

Tears of pain were flooding his eyes and he said softly, "Come Raju. I tried to stand on this chair to stop the leaking roof and I lost my foothold. I think I have hurt my hand."

Why do you have to do all this? Raju's eyes questioned him and at that moment of physical pain, Vadhiyar realized that Raju had returned from the brink. He would now never be lost. Gladdened in spite of the pain, Vadhiyar lay back on the ground.

The rest of the night was like a dumb charade as Raju ran to

Prabhu's house and knocked on the door. Inside the house, Prabhu had just finished his dinner when he heard the knocking sound. He opened the door and saw a totally drenched Raju standing outside, but it was his eyes that Prabhu noticed. They were not the dead eyes of a boy who had given up on life. These eyes spoke volumes. They told him that someone he loved was in pain, they told him that the rain could go to hell but Prabhu needed to come immediately. They talked about hope, anticipation and pain. They talked about all those emotions except hopelessness. Thrilled to the core of his being, Prabhu ran out unquestioningly. When Kuyili returned from the backyard, she saw the two of them sprinting away in the pouring rain.

The rest of the night continued in unspoken emotions as Vadhiyar was tended to and taken to the local hospital where his wound was stitched up. The activities continued into the wee hours of the morning, when Prabhu finally went back home and lay in his cot.

It was Raju who ensured that the school did not suffer from Vadhiyar's absence and it was Raju who took over the job of getting the school ready as he ran around, cleaning the building, sweeping and mopping the classrooms and finally when the clock struck nine, ringing the school bell with gusto.

The children went to their classrooms and studied as Prabhu bustled about in the backyard ensuring that the workers made lunch for the children. As he spent his time in the school, his wandering eyes continued to keep tabs on Raju. The boy had returned to them and he seemed to have come back with renewed enthusiasm. It was with a slight ache of happiness that Prabhu watched over Raju.

As they ran around taking care of the school, Prabhu strolled into Vadhiyar's room. His eyes roamed around and rested on the paintings on the wall. Suddenly he felt a small movement next to him and he turned his head and saw Raju standing next to him. A shy smile hovered on his lips.

Prabhu turned around and just as suddenly caught the boy in a hug. He felt the boy's thin shoulders with the bones sticking out and he also felt a soft shiver.

Hugging him close, he said softly, "Raju, trust me. I will never hurt you. I know who hurt you."

He felt the boy's body tightening in his arms and said softly, "It's okay. We cannot choose our parents but we can choose whom we want to love. It's okay to hate your parents and hate those who hurt you."

The body was tightening further in his arms and running his fingers through the boy's hair he said, "You are strong enough to hear me out. You are my son and I know that no son of mine can be a coward."

There! He had said those words. Words he had never planned on saying and yet, he knew that they were there, right there, within and without his being. Raju was his son. A son given to him by god. Maybe he was not the boy's actual father but then who decided on who could be a father? He felt the boy's body relaxing against his own and repeatedly ran his hands over his back, soothing away the pain in the tight muscles and thin bones. How much of suffering the boy had gone through so soon in life. He felt a fierce determination welling up in his body. Never again! Never again would he allow anyone to hurt Raju. The emotions they felt for each other took over speech and they stood close together. Outside, the bright sunshine was triggering the children to try new tricks in naughtiness and they ran around the ground pulling, fighting and laughing.

Kuyili spent her time in the classrooms with the children teaching them. It was during the process of writing a sum on the wall that she realized that she actually enjoyed teaching. Maybe she should continue to work in the school as a teacher. Her eyes danced around the classroom taking in its clumsy mess, the little scruffy children and the black board stained white. She looked especially at the little children, crossing out their names in her mind – Raghupathi, SkyLab, Dimple, Rishikapoor, Hema Malini, Shivaji.

It was evening when Vadhiyar was brought back from the hospital and by then one more school day had ended. It was the workers who updated Vadhiyar on the way Raju had taken charge. Vadhiyar felt his heart swelling with pride. So all their investment had not been wasted. It had helped bring back the boy from the verge of insanity. Insanity caused by the unkind acts of men.

As Vadhiyar went about his tasks that day, he knew that he had helped bring about a change in Raju's life. From now on, it would be a matter of time before Raju began talking again.

But the master knew that it was only with children that Raju was normal. With adults, he still seemed unable to manage and ran away every time he saw Gokulan or Prakash passing by. Come to think of it, he had noticed Prakash passing by several times.

In the month of October, the villagers went to the temple to pray for wealth and fortune. Raju had stayed back in the school, as was his habit, to avoid crowds. He spent this time sweeping out the classrooms and cleaning the black boards. When Prakash had stolen into the classroom he had not heard him, then Raju heard a muffled chuckle and turned around to see him standing near the doorway. Standing with the sun falling on his hair, he looked like a terrible creature, his glasses shining like two oval shaped discs.

Terrified, he had backed away against the far wall. Grinning a little more, Prakash moved closer.

All of a sudden, he heard a noise and turned around to see Vadhiyar entering the school gate. That second had been enough and Raju dashed out of the room, an inhuman wail escaping his throat. The sound was so harsh and terrible that it stopped Vadhiyar in his tracks. Shocked, he watched Raju speeding away into the bushes behind the school.

"Raju, Raju," he screamed, but if the boy heard him he did not turn around or stop. Instead, he ran as though a hundred wild dogs were chasing him.

Vadhiyar looked at the classroom from where Raju had run out and he saw Prakash walking out. What was this fellow doing here and why was Raju so frightened?

With a grim look on his face he said, "Why are you here?

What do you want?"

"Oh, ho! Where is your politeness Master? If you are not polite to your visitors, how do you expect your children to learn any manners?"

Swallowing an epithet, and cursing softly under his breath, Vadhiyar said, "You don't have to worry about my manners. What are you doing here and why is Raju so frightened?"

That brought a loud laugh in reply and wiping his mouth, Prakash said, "I am here to see how your school building is. I thought I could ask my factory manager to give you some money."

He stopped and watched Vadhiyar with a sly look on his face.

"Our building is fine now. We do not want your money. And before I complain to Prabhu, tell me what happened. Why is Raju so frightened?"

"Why don't you ask him? Oh of course, he cannot speak, right? That's too bad. If you so desperately want to know what happened, you need to ask him."

Laughing loudly once again, he walked away.

Worried at the way Raju had sped away, Vadhiyar went out, looking for the boy. But there was no sign of Raju.

As Vadhiyar slowly walked back towards the temple, he realized that it was providence that had made him come back to the school. Actually, he had almost reached the temple, when the idea occurred to him that Prabhu would love to own one of the school children's paintings. He had come back to pick it up and that was when he had seen that dreadful Prakash. Poor Raju. There was no doubt that Prakash had been up to no good. Why should Raju be so frightened of him? Don't ignore this incident, his heart whispered.

With a bad feeling about the incident, he looked around for the boy and then walked back towards the temple as the temple gong sounded loudly.

Maybe talking to Prabhu about this would be good but it would have to wait. At least for a few days till the festival was over.

Reconciling himself to the thought that Prabhu would be able to help, Vadhiyar joined the big crowd of villagers outside the temple.

[illegible] He had [illegible]

[illegible]

It was the doom that Hacker had been quite no good. The [illegible]

[illegible] at whose [illegible].

With a bad feeling [illegible] he [illegible] would [illegible] [illegible] walked back towards the temple [illegible] come sounded loudly.

Maybe talking to Prabhu about this would be [illegible] would have to wait. At least some few days till the [illegible]

[illegible] the thought that Prabhu [illegible] [illegible] [illegible] villagers out [illegible] the temple.

FIFTEEN

Chapter

As Prabhu walked around his land one morning, he suddenly remembered that he had not met Raju for a long time. He felt an urge to see him now and singing softly under his breath walked towards the school.

As he walked, he watched the soft fluffy clouds in the clear blue sky. The rains were either coming down too fast or staying away completely. But the months of September and October always brought rains with it and the villagers knew that it was these rains that filled the streams and enriched the lake.

Walking briskly, he reached the school just as the morning bell rang loudly. Along with the sound of the bell, was the sound of children's voices – some loud and others soft. He opened the gate and walked into Vadhiyar's office. Vadhiyar was not in his seat and he stopped to stare at the paintings on the wall. It was good of Vadhiyar to present him with one of these.

He saw a new painting had been added to the ones on the wall. As he stared at it, he felt his skin breaking out in goose pimples. The painting was of a single rose. Some of its petals were pearly white and others were red, soaked in blood, which flowed from a wounded bird that sat on a branch above the rose. This was a popular story, which all the villagers knew, of how a little bird fell in love with a white rose. The rose promised to return his love the day it turned a bright red colour. Months and days passed and yet the rose remained white in colour. One day, the bird pricked its body on a thorn and its blood flowed onto the rose, staining its white petals a bright red. As its life blood flowed out, it stared longingly at the flower, its eyes beseeching the flower to say 'I love you' .

Prabhu looked for the name of the boy but it was not there. He stared at the rose and the bird. So startlingly lifelike was the painting that he did not hear Vadhiyar enter the room.

"So you seem to like your ward's painting?"

Prabhu turned around startled and Vadhiyar said with a smile, "Vannakam mapillai. What are you doing here when you should be at home with your new bride?"

"I came to meet Raju and also to thank you for the painting. Who has done this one?" The tremble in his voice made his words sound like an earthquake was passing through them.

"Raju. It is beautiful, isn't it? The boy really has some talent. I am encouraging him to paint now."

Suddenly Vadhiyar's face changed and frowning, he said, "The boy is petrified of that horrible Prakash."

Prabhu felt a cold hand clasp his heart. He could not escape this any longer. He had to face the truth, however terrible it was.

What could the man have done to make the boy so scared? He needed to know. Nodding his head, he abruptly turned around and walked out of the school. As he crossed the road, he heard some of the children chanting *Vande Mataram*.

He walked purposefully, his eyes staring ahead. As he reached Prakash's factory, he saw that a lot of things had changed since the last time he had been here. For one, a couple of lorries stood outside the building and the villagers were busy loading cracker cartons onto the vehicles. The scene looked so different that it almost seemed like somebody had superimposed a picture onto the original one of a calm and serene village.

There seemed more noise too, with people talking loudly as they worked. He went to the door and stood for a moment, his eyes getting used to the darkness after the strong sunlight outside. And then he saw the little children, sitting in long rows, filling the crackers with explosive powder. Some of the little girls were rolling incense sticks, which would be used to trigger cracker bombs, and small boys were sticking pictures on the boxes.

He looked around and saw Prakash standing a little away. As he watched, he noticed something peculiar in the way Prakash stood, his body bent over the little boy. Maybe it was that which made him creep up softly behind Prakash. And then he saw!

He saw Prakash's hand in the boy's lap, fondling him. A blinding rage exploded, and he brought his hand in a sharp crack on the back of Prakash's head. With a howl Prakash turned around, a look of startled pain in his eyes. The boy in whose lap Prakash's hand had rested a moment ago, looked at Prabhu with a funny look in his eyes. If he could read the expression, Prabhu would say it was almost as if the child was thanking him for intervening.

Several of the children got up, and shouting loudly, ran out of the factory. This attracted the attention of the workers outside who rushed in.

A mindless white rage continued to blind him and he brought his fist down again and again, raining terrible blows on Prakash. He lifted his leg and kicked him in the groin. With a terrible moan Prakash fell down, just as the workers rushed in. For a moment they watched startled as Prabhu continued to beat Prakash and then a few of them came and tried to restrain Prabhu.

"Calm down, calm down, Prabhu," said an old man, wagging his stick.

But he could not stop. He could only remember Prakash's hands in the boy's lap. So this was what he had done to Raju. No wonder the boy had been so terrified. Thinking of Raju brought a fresh wave of anger, and he brought his fist down with a resounding blow on Prakash's nose. Prakash's face looked a bloody mess as he tried to crawl away, out of Prabhu's reach.

Prabhu tried to speak but words would not come out. Some of the men pulled Prakash away while others held Prabhu tightly.

Babbling, Prakash sat down on the floor, making pitiful noises. Some of his workers were torn, between loyalty for their employer and Prabhu whom they trusted and respected. A still silence descended on the place. Looking at the doorway, Prabhu saw all the small children standing in a group, watching what was happening inside.

Finally, the old man with the stick came closer to Prabhu and asked him loudly what had happened.

Prabhu spat on the ground, close to where Prakash sat whimpering and said, "This person likes to fondle little children."

A terrible silence fell again on the crowd. The men looked uncertainly at the children standing outside. They wondered whether any of their own had been abused. The stillness seemed like the calm before a terrible cyclone and Prakash, sensing the danger, got up on uncertain feet. He tried to hobble out when he felt a kick on his back. Yelping, he fell down and the men rained blows on his body, beating him senseless, taking law into their own hands as was the practice in a village where the nearest police station was five miles away. They were suddenly tribal, and they ran around the fallen man in circles. They stopped to kick him and beat him and then continued running around.

The children, who were watching from outside, felt a chill steal up their spines and yet they watched because it was important for every one of them that the man who did strange things to their bodies was murdered. It was an ancient law of punishment, practiced in jungles by wild animals and primitives and which continued to run in every man's blood. Living in an isolated village, the men only knew one thing. To beat and murder the man who had done something so terrible to their children.

If Prabhu, watching the shower of blows, did not feel his own anger seep out, Prakash would have died right there, in the middle of his fireworks factory. But watching the angry men, an innate fairness for life made him intervene.

Raising a hand he said, "Stop! Enough! Let us not dirty our hands by killing this scum."

The men moved back and Prabhu saw the unconscious Prakash lying on the floor, battered and bleeding.

Instructing the old man to be in charge, he went outside to call the lorry driver.

The lorry driver, who had been watching this scene from far away, walked in hesitantly. His mind warned him that his fate could be the same as his employer. But Prabhu nodded his head curtly and asked him to take Prakash away.

The lorry driver carried the unconscious Prakash out just as the first bolt of lightning tore the sky.

Rumbling thunder followed and huge drops of rain fell heavily on the earth. The children who were standing outside, moved in and they all sat around waiting for the rain to stop.

Prabhu felt terrible. He should have guessed that Prakash was doing something like this to Raju. Why had he not guessed?

As the crowds fell silent and the rain battered the building, Prabhu felt a strange longing for the factory to just disappear. Life had changed in the village. It could never be the same again. He saw the little children huddling together, talking in hushed tones. He saw the men who had sent their children to work in a factory that would soil their little hands. Hands that should have been putting pencil to paper.

As they sat there, they all wondered what would happen next. They did not have to wait long. The very next day, the sound of cars raking up the dust brought them out of their huts. The two cars stopped outside the factory. One of the men ran across and called Prabhu. Soon the workers, the children and Prabhu stood near the factory. The rains had made the mud soft and marshy and their feet sank in the brown mud, dirtying the hems of their *dhotis*. The man who had come for the inauguration stood facing the crowd. That day his face had been calm, today he looked stern.

Fixing his eyes on the crowd he said, "Prakash, wounded by all of you, is lying in hospital. He is very ill. The doctors say that he may not survive."

Prabhu swatted a mosquito, hovering close by.

When he looked up, he saw that the man was looking at him strangely. "If he dies, all of you will be imprisoned and one of you will be the condemned man. For your sake, I pray that does not happen and Prakash recovers. Prison life is very different from the life here where you have so much of open space. There you have to sit inside four walls."

Prabhu looked at his palms to see if he had swatted the mosquito.

The old man who had intervened yesterday, said respectfully, "Please tell us what is the purpose of your visit."

These words seemed to anger the man and he shouted, "What do you mean, what is the purpose of my visit? You think I am just going to stand by and accept the fact that my factory manager has been beaten almost to death?"

Prabhu said softly, "Why don't you ask us what he has done?"

"It doesn't matter to me what he has done. Whatever it is, don't you know that there are police to take care of such things? Did you have to beat him up?" he asked scornfully.

The old man turned and beckoned Prabhu to join him in the front. Prabhu walked deliberately, his feet sinking in the wet mud.

They waited for the man to continue. All of them were silent.

"This is your new manager."

For the first time, Prabhu noticed the inconspicuous man standing nervously in the background.

"Ananda, come and see these people."

A frightened Ananda moved to the front of the crowd. Prabhu felt a sudden urge to laugh. The fellow looked so nervous as though they were a bunch of barbarians.

Seeing his smile, the man said, "I see that all of you are amused, you brutes. But let me warn you very clearly. If anything happens to Ananda here, I will see that your village is removed from the face of this earth."

As they turned to walk away, Prabhu and the old man smoking a cigarette each, Prabhu realised that something was not quite right.

It was only when he was eating his food, later that day, that he realised what it was that was bothering him. Why had the man not brought the police with him to frighten the villagers?

SIXTEEN

Chapter

With the new manager, things fell into routine once again. Slowly, the villagers sent their little children to the factory. The new manager became a joke of sorts for the villagers, as he spent a lot of his time peering over his shoulder in the dark and was careful what he said to the children. The advantage of this was that the children were safe and happy.

The rains came and the villagers worked in the swampy mud, cultivating the land and planting the tender paddy saplings. If the rains continued, this would be the second time in succession that the harvest was a good one.

Along with the rains, came the festivals and the fellows who raced in the *jallikattu* the previous year were back again to win. Only this time, Prabhu watched with Kuyili next to him. As they sat and watched the battle between the bullocks and human beings, Prabhu felt a shiver pass through his body. Arjuna and another young man were walking side by side. As he stared at them, confused, he saw the slightly crooked jaw line of the man.

At the same instant, Arjuna turned his face and caught the look on Prabhu's and in that instant both realised that the other knew. So the night attacker had been none other than Arjuna and his friend! But why?

As his thoughts raced in confused disarray, Kuyili sitting beside him was blissfully unaware of his turmoil. She remembered the previous year when things had been so different. Now she herself felt like the land, enriched with the rains. Their nights were spent idyllically as they ate their dinner under the stars. He ate with relish the food she cooked and with every mouthful both of them waited in anticipation for what the night would unfold. Kuyili felt a soft blush break out on her cheeks. Prabhu was a tender and passionate lover.

As soon as the race was over and the prizes given away, Prabhu searched the crowd for Arjuna. Suddenly he spotted him dashing away, pulling his bullock along. He had lost the races and many of the people watching made way for him, presuming he was upset with his defeat. Prabhu jumped down from the stage and sprinted after him. In a few minutes he had caught up.

He felt an urge to catch Arjuna by his shirt collar, but instead, clenching his hands, he said, "So, who is that fellow who stabbed me? Why did you both do it?"

Tears sprung into the eyes of the youth and he looked around to see if he could escape. Not seeing a way out he said, "Prakash paid me money to harm you. But I had no intention of murdering you. We just wanted to hurt you. Please forgive me."

The tears were flowing freely now.

Prabhu stroked his chin thoughtfully. So it was Prakash's work. He should have guessed that one. So then was he the person who had murdered Mariamma, too? Had he crept into the village in the guise of a madman and killed her?

"I know what you are thinking. You think that I murdered that old woman, Mariamma, too. No! I didn't. Please believe me."

A sudden idea crossing his mind, Prabhu said, "I will let you off if you tell me who murdered her."

A look of fear crossed Arjuna's face. "If I tell you then he will murder me." He was sobbing loudly now and a few of the people passing by were staring at them.

"Then I will have to hand you over to the police."

"No! No! I will only tell you this much. It was someone from your own village."

Saying that, he tugged his hand out of Prabhu's and deserting his bullock, ran as fast as his feet could carry him.

Prabhu looked around. Who was the traitor who lived among them and yet had sold them to a snake like Prakash? He looked after the sprinting youth, who did not have the same charm he had noticed in his face the year before. He would stay on the clear path henceforth, that was one thing Prabhu was sure of. Suddenly, the thoughts he was avoiding rose up in front of his eyes like a picture. It had to be Gokulan! And then he realized that he had known all along. He had known the day he saw that the knife was missing from under his cot. Gokulan was the only one who knew it was there and yet he had not confronted him. Neither had he confronted Prakash though he should have guessed that it was Prakash who was adding to Raju's troubles. Why had he avoided confrontations?

If he had not happened to drop in, in the factory that day, Prakash may have continued abusing little children. No more could he push his problems to the back of his mind in the hope that they would disappear. Problems didn't disappear! Nor did situations really change. The time had come to trap Gokulan and make him admit that he had murdered Mariamma. Yes! That was the only thing left for him to do.

With a shock Prabhu realized that Gokulan was also changing. Prabhu seldom ran into him these days, and when he did, he noticed that Gokulan had seemed a bit different. Something had changed in him after Prakash's hospitalization. He appeared to stay away from the villagers as much as possible, occupying himself with the land around his hut.

How could he tackle the man? And then he realized that it would be absolutely easy. All he had to do was invite the man home. After all he had helped out a lot with Prabhu's wedding. On the pretext of thanking him, he would invite him home and tackle him quietly in the privacy of his house.

Kuyili cooked an elaborate meal for Gokulan and she took trouble to cook the rice till it was fluffy and soft like fresh jasmines. The *sambhar* smelt of drumsticks and onions. The fleshy potatoes, plucked from the garden, she fried with peas. As the three of them sat down to eat in their hut, with the 60-watt bulb swinging crazily from the ceiling, Kuyili watched the way Gokulan stole glances at both of them when they were not looking. Something was not right, she thought to herself.

Gokulan was quiet, eating his food slowly and steadily. Prabhu watched and waited for the right moment. How could he accuse the man of murder as he ate his food? He would tackle him after his dinner and so they ate – the three of them. Each preoccupied with their thoughts.

Would confronting him really solve the problem? What would he say to him? 'Hey Gokulan – you murdered Mariamma?' He could imagine Gokulan's guffaw. No! That wouldn't do. He would have to say something that would startle the man into betraying the truth. But what could he say?

Mentioning Raju wouldn't help. The man was in complete denial. Maybe he should mention the knife. As these thoughts ran through Prabhu's mind, Gokulan ate his food quietly.

Lately, the nightmares seemed to come on even during his waking hours. Even now as he ate, he felt he saw strange shadows watching him from corners. The shadows had dark bodies and a horrible smell hung over them. It was the smell of death. Death was all around him surrounding him and yet he wouldn't be able to die. He ate his food quickly. Maybe he would stop by at the temple on his way back home.

As Gokulan finished his dinner and Kuyili poured some water on his hands to wash it, Prabhu casually peeped under the cot. With a deliberate action he made a show of searching for something under the cot. He felt Gokulan's body stiffening.

Slowly and deliberately, he said, "Kuyili, have you taken the bundle which was under the bed?"

Kuyili, clearing the vessels, replied she hadn't.

He bent under the bed and looked for a few more minutes. When he came up, he noticed that Gokulan was watching him intently.

"What was in the bundle?" Kuyili asked.

Looking straight at Gokulan, he said, "It was the knife which was used to murder Mariamma."

The glass in Gokulan's hands fell down with a clatter. The noise seemed deafening to the three people in the hut.

He had betrayed himself, thought Prabhu triumphantly. Whatever little doubts he might have had vanished. It was absolutely clear that Gokulan was the murderer. He had murdered Mariamma for her property. If ever Raju became normal, then he would claim back the land and that was why Gokulan continued to hurt the boy! As he watched him, he saw Gokulan's eyes drop down towards the ground and as suddenly as he dropped the glass, he got up and with a quick word of thanks to Kuyili, rushed out into the night.

That night, as they lay in bed, Kuyili talked to Prabhu about

Gokulan's strange reaction and behaviour.

He nodded his head and said, "Yes. It appears that he knows a lot more about Mariamma's death than we thought he did. I wonder what he will do now."

The words were merely his thoughts spoken aloud, but shivering slightly, Kuyili moved closer to him. If Gokulan was a murderer then he wouldn't hesitate to murder again was the last thought on both their minds as they drifted into sleep.

It was a day later that Kuyili went to the school. The first sight that met her was of Raju squatting on the ground watching the children playing. She felt a slight tug in her heart. He was just a little older than the other children and he had suffered so! Impulsively, she walked up to him and put her hand on his head. He looked at her, guardedly.

"Have you had your lunch, Raju?" she asked softly.

He nodded. The nod was so hesitant that if she had not been watching, she would have missed it.

"Do you like this school?" she asked, and once again she saw the small nod.

"Vannakam, vannakam."

She turned around to see Vadhiyar standing behind her, smiling broadly.

"Vanakam Vadhiyar, she said, her eyes still on Raju.

"Can you see the change in our little friend? Isn't he looking a lot happier these days?"

She smiled at that.

"Do you know that he even goes back to his hut regularly?"

That was surprising.

She saw that Raju was playing with a little ant that was climbing on his hand. He neither hurt it nor pushed it away.

"Push it away or it will bite you," she said.

He shook his head and continued to play with the ant.

"Is there something I can do for you?" Vadhiyar asked her.

She watched Raju and the ant and an idea crossed her mind. Hesitantly, with a thudding sensation in her heart she said, "Vadhiyar, would you be looking for some help in teaching the children?"

If he was surprised by her question, he did not show it. Instead he said, "Thank you for coming by. You know that we can do with all the help available. One more teacher will really help."

Softly she said, "Only on one condition. Raju will have to sit in my class."

He looked up at her then. A strange look passed through his eyes and she saw all the hurt and pain in that fleeting moment. The look constricted her heart and she felt tears stinging her eyelids.

"Would you like that, Raju?" she asked softly.

He did not answer but his eyes, focused on her face, spoke a story all its own. It spoke of all the happiness, which was blurred by anxiety. It spoke of terrible fears and worries, of the times when happiness had come hand in hand with pain.

She caught his hand and clasped it tight.

They would be together, the three of them – Raju, Prabhu and herself. No power on earth could separate them.

SEVENTEEN

Chapter

The next few days saw a bright sun shining relentlessly on them. It scorched the tender leaves and baked the mud. It was not uncommon for such strong heat waves but they would indicate to the villagers that the rain would swiftly follow and every day they gazed at the sky waiting for the rains. Since harvest was over, the water from the bore wells would be used for the paddy fields but if the rain stayed away too long then the water in the wells would also diminish.

One afternoon, Raju went back to his little hut, where the green stalks shook with the slight wind and cooled his sweating brow. As he lay there, half asleep and half awake, he dreamt of a strange creature, which called his name. The creature was made of fire and every time it called his name, bellows of smoke rushed out of its mouth. He tried to answer it, but he couldn't open his mouth. When he opened, strange sounds came out and this made the creature very angry. The heat from its red mouth made his skin hot.

Suddenly, with a start he woke up, disoriented and confused.

He knew it was noon and that it was a hot day, but there was something different about this heat. Then he realised what it was that had woken him. It was the smoke permeating the little hut, which had invaded his nostrils and woken him up.

With a frightened feeling in his heart, Raju rushed out and looked around. All around, smoke billowed. The acrid smell of burning was suddenly split by a loud sound. Jumping in fright, he saw that a tiny cracker set off by the fire had burst. He looked around frantically. Everywhere around him he could see smoke as the dried grass caught fire. The burning grass was heading in a single-minded way towards the factory. Horrified, he watched the flames reach the building. In a second the first flame swept into the factory. He opened his mouth but no words would come out. He felt tears sliding down his cheeks. As he opened his mouth, trying to call out, inhuman noises emanated. It seemed to bring a few children to the factory door. He beckoned with both hands, waving frantically. He saw the horrified fear on the children's faces as they saw the flames. They started running out, just as the first box of crackers lying outside in the dried grass, caught a roving flame.

As they ran out, the bigger children trampled the small ones. Raju waited no more. Using both his hands he lifted the children and deposited them a little away from the fire. All of them needed to be out of the factory before the box caught fire completely. Once it did, it would burst, spreading its lethal sparks in all directions. Then there would be no stopping it.

As he stood near the door, pulling the children out, he saw

the faint shadow of some little children at the other end of the room. These children were coming from an inside room where the wrapping material was stored. As he stood a little away from the doorway, he saw a little box catch fire and the flame licked the boxes lying near by. A part of his brain wondered where that timid factory manager was. And then he remembered hearing the sound of the vehicle. He must have gone to Madras! As disarrayed thoughts sped around his brain, his eyes took in the scene in front of him.

Children were running around screaming loudly. Those closer to him were running out. But the terrible crackers had started their path of destruction. As he watched horrified, he saw a rocket landing on a little boy's head. He ran in, past the smoke and putting his hands on the boy's head, beat the fire off. The children ran out now, but many of them were treading on burning crackers and the whistling rockets had started burning holes in their clothes.

He waved, but they could not see him standing there, hidden by the smoke.

Frustrated and angry, he opened his mouth to yell but again only inhuman sounds emanated. He felt angry tears rushing down his face. And then suddenly, like the sound of a bird's wings when it first lifts its body against the wind, a word floated out – "Amma". Wafting like a billowing cloud, the word rolled down the corridor and hit the children standing there.

The children were staring at Raju in astonishment and it was also at that moment that Raju realized that he could speak.

"Amma, amma," he shouted, for all those times when he wanted to call her and she was not around. As he stood there near the factory door, he felt he saw his mother in the back of the factory with the children. Then he knew. He was seeing an image from another world. His mother had died and he had burnt her body. So this image standing at the back of the factory was his mother's spirit and those children would soon be there. No! Not if he could help it.

Unheeding the ominous sound of paper catching fire, as the first boxes burst into flame, he ran in. The smoke was swirling around and blinding his path. But he ran straight on, overturning tables and boxes. When he neared the group, he saw there were six children. The eldest would have been around eight years old. As he stood and stared at them, he heard a huge noise as the first cracker bomb burst. Its burning embers fell haphazardly around. Each little ember was beginning its own path of destruction. There was no time to waste. They could not go back by the entrance as that was blocked. He turned around and pulled the children into the little room from where they had come out. The room was a small rectangle shaped one with no exit door. He ran, with the children following, into another room and there stacked against the boxes, he saw the glimpse of a wooden door. Apparently, whoever had arranged the stocks had not realised that it might at some point of time be important to open the door. Pulling the children into the room, he closed the door. Outside, the din was deafening as rockets and bombs competed with each other. The smallest girl in the group seemed to understand what Raju had in mind and she helped him pull the boxes away from the door. They all worked, their little hands pulling and shoving and throwing when they saw the smoke creeping in. Raju paused to wipe his sweating brow. In a few more minutes they would all be dead, inhaling the lethal smoke. The children were already beginning to cough. Now he threw his hands onto the boxes, flinging them away from the door. He stamped some of them and kicked the others when he saw the latch.

A huge lock hung from it. A look of disbelief crossed his face. This could not be true. Standing in the dark room, with the smoke swirling in, he looked at the lock. Once again he saw his mother smiling and beckoning him. In his mind he said, take me if you want to, but let these children live. Closing his eyes, he felt the lock and he saw that it was not locked.

When Raju and the children ran out, the first thing they saw was the group of children standing far away crying. In the distance, the villagers were running towards the factory that was now a huge burning disaster. Raju and the little children, whose lives he had saved, ran towards the other group. Quickly smiling at them, he beckoned them away from the flames. They followed him trustingly. It was only when he had walked a distance away that he realized that the little girl who had helped him in the storage room was missing.

He saw his life moving in front of his eyes, all in a fleeting second. He saw his father beating his mother and he felt the stinging pain when burning *beedis* were put out on him. He remembered the lake and he remembered the Evil One – Prakash, who had not hesitated to kill whatever happiness he had left in his body.

As he walked back purposefully towards the now raging fire, he heard the little children shout his name. He heard his name. Not just his name – they were calling him 'anna' (brother). The word spurred him on. It was in the company of children that his wounds had finally started healing.

As he neared the building, the fiery burning heat pushed against him. Inside the building, silhouetted like a while light, stood his mother. She was waving her hands. To him it seemed like she too was beckoning him inside. The last thought that passed through his mind was of Prabhu and Kuyili. Memories of them flooded his heart and warmed it. He remembered Vadhiyar's kind face. Like a memory milestone he saw himself standing under the Indian flag collecting his medal from Vadhiyar. It was not a packet of clothes he had got, it was a medal for bravery. He was a brave warrior and a soldier. The heat from outside which had not warmed his chilled heart, now lit it like a glowing ember. He knew that they would be proud of what he was doing. As he walked into the fire his last thoughts were of Prabhu supporting his head on his chest and holding it proudly. He would prove that he was a worthy son to him.

The children watched Raju entering the burning building. Some of them shouted "anna, anna" loudly and a few were sniffing. The older children took charge of the smaller ones, hustling them away from the burning building.

Prabhu, who had been in his fields, had first seen the swirling smoke forming cloud mirages in a clear blue sky. In a second his mind calculated where the fire was and with a sickening feeling he realized that it was coming from the direction of the fireworks factory. He had run then, on legs that seemed to fly over the ground. Seeing him running, the villagers followed and soon a group of them – men, women and children, ran towards the fire. When he reached the building, the first thing he saw was the group of children standing a little away from the fire. Mothers ran towards their children, hugging and petting them and then he heard a single loud wail, "Anjali!"

With a terrible chilling feeling gripping his heart, he heard another man shout, "Ramesh!" One more woman was shouting, "Narayana!" And then he heard his own voice shouting, "Raju!"

It was a wail that rose from his throat and hit the trees and the fire. One of the little children pointed towards the building, which was now a raging cauldron. He felt his legs giving way under him and he fell on the ground. As he lay there unmoving, his heart paralyzed with fear, he knew that Raju was dead.

Behind him the group of men and women were watching the burning factory in horror.

The next day the clouds burst in a strong rainfall and a beautiful rainbow arched down from the sky. The fire and the factory were long gone. Nothing remained of both. But for the villagers it would live forever, a constant reminder of all the things that went wrong.

Three children succumbed to burns; sixteen of them had severe burns and would never be the same again. Between the bodies of the dead children, lay Raju's, singed black, except for his face that remained calm and serene in death.

Soon after the fire, life in the village changed dramatically. The factory owners never came back. Prabhu found a lawyer who filed a case against the factory owner. The lawyer demanded compensation for the burnt and dead children's families. But the parents of the children did not seem to want any money. They avoided the burnt factory and pretended that it did not exist. One man, whom Prabhu knew to be the father of one of the dead children, became sick. He spent his time murmuring incoherently as he walked around the village like a mad man. One of the women, the mother of a burnt child, wept so loudly that her tears became dark clouds. The rains, which had come down like a soft promise, soon changed into a torrential downpour.

The crops lay wasted. But nobody seemed to care. It was a time for reckoning.

Prabhu withdrew into a world of his own where his mind kept tormenting him 'you knew better. You should have put your foot down with these people', it said.

Only Kuyili seemed able to understand his torment and she spent her time assuring him that it was not his mistake. It was now a common occurrence to hear wailing voices in the middle of the night, reminding the others who tried to sleep, that in their ignorance, they had sinned against their children.

The wasted lands and the destroyed crops meant that food would be scarce, but it was for a time like this that Prabhu had kept a stock of rations in his warehouse. Each day, Kuyili and he opened sacks of rice and handed out enough for each family. The stock would last till the weather cleared up and they could begin their next harvest.

Before the rains swept into the factory and turned the dead bodies into a rotting end, their funeral had to be finished. In the midst of heavy rainfall, Deva wove his green mats – one for Raju, one for his own Anjali and two for the other two dead children. There was no song on his lips, only a mournful wail, which rose inside his heart but remained stuck in his throat. His fingers clumsily wove the mat when he felt a firm hand on his shoulder. Turning his head, through tear-blurred vision, he saw Prabhu watching him. Prabhu sat down next to him and silently helped. The rain fell on their backs as they wove the mats, which would carry the dead bodies.

When they finished, Prabhu realized that he and Deva had been crying together silently. He held Deva as the bodies of the four dead were transferred onto the mats. Supporting Deva on one arm, he lent his left shoulder to carry Raju's body. The sad procession wove their way through the bleak rain to the spot near the lake. No one danced or sang. None of the older women narrated stories. They moved silently. Because of the unceasing rainfall, the bodies would not be cremated. Instead they were placed in a row in shallow graves that had been dug earlier. All the bodies were covered with wet clothes and the faces were hidden. The rain fell on the bodies moulding the cloth to the little bodies.

The ceremony was quick. All that remained at the end was mounds of earth, to remind the villagers that those who lay within had paid a price for the mistakes of grownups.

And then, Gokulan fell ill. It had nothing to do with his body but the doctors could not decipher his symptoms. He talked incoherently and lay feverishly in a corner of his darkened cottage. His eyes stared at the wall with a horrified look, as if strange ghosts danced there on the wall. His wife and children stayed outside, confining themselves to the other rooms. He grew thinner and a white beard decorated his sallow face like bleached grass.

When Prabhu went to see him, he was shocked to see the change in Gokulan. He looked like the devil was eating into his soul. As he stood leaning against the wall, he saw Gokulan's eyes focusing on him for a second. In that second, he sensed recognition. Moving closer, he sat down on the bed. Slowly he lifted Gokulan's cold hand and held it. As he watched the man, he saw that his red eyes were watching him. He sat quietly next to him and then he heard Gokulan clearing his throat. He turned and watched the way his eyes darted around the room like a creature being ferreted out. When he spoke, his voice shook as if a hundred earthquakes were shaking the core of his being.

The words were tortured, "Prabhu, I am responsible for the death of the children. I am responsible for all those children who will never be the same again."

"No. It is not you alone. We all are."

The tears poured down Prabhu's face and he realized with a shock that he could cry easily now. Outside, thunder rumbled softly, and once again, the rains came down. Just as it had done for the last ten days.

"No, Prabhu. You are not to be blamed. You warned all of us, but I didn't listen to you. I was greedy for money. Prabhu, I have wronged."

Suddenly he laughed like a man gone insane. Just as suddenly, the laugh stopped and he said, "I killed Mariamma. But I guess you already know that?"

Slowly, Prabhu nodded his head.

"We were together for some time, she and I. But she was of no use to me. I wanted her land for the factory but she was fighting with me, saying that she wanted to leave it for Raju, my son."

He felt Gokulan's cold hand doing something to his fingers, but in the darkened room with the blood chilling sound of Gokulan's words, Prabhu did not pay attention to it.

Once again the terrible laugh, dry like a blade of hay.

"You hate me now, no? How could I destroy my own son? But I am paying the price now, Prabhu. The ghosts torment me day and night. They look terrible and they attack me whenever I close my eyes. They stand around my bed, with blood on their faces. Their teeth are stained red with blood and it is my blood, Prabhu."

Gokulan stared unseeingly at the wall in front. A sudden scream, which chilled Prabhu and scared the children outside, broke out of Gokulan's body.

"Prabhu, I am scared. I cannot close my eyes. If I do, they come back. Terrible burnt children with scarred faces, old women with hungry eyes and dogs."

"Dogs?"

"Yes, dogs. I never thought dogs could frighten me. But they are there. See, there is one standing near your leg. It is going to bite you." He cowered and pulled the blanket around his head.

When Prabhu left the little hut a while later, he knew that Gokulan would have to be sent to the mental hospital in Madras.

As Prabhu walked through the lashing rain, he remembered the events of the last few months. So many things had changed but some things wouldn't. When he reached his house, he saw Kuyili outlined against the door. She was waiting with a towel in her hands. He walked into the house, wiping the tears on his face, pretending that it was raindrops.

When he sat down on the bed, he saw a dirty plate lying in the corner. Raju must have come home for his lunch. But Raju was dead! Dead before he could save him. Once again, the tears poured down. He cried helplessly. She sat down next to him and held his cold hands.

Prabhu saw how, over the last two years, his life had gone through a circle of human seasons. The beginning of summer when he had been ready to meet every problem and she had entered his heart. The height of summer, when their love matured into a relationship. Also the time when he learnt that like all else in life, in his village too, things could change whenever and however. It was now the monsoons, a time to contemplate, a time to ponder, and a time to grieve. He saw her soft hand resting on his own and he knew that she would always bring back sunny memories. As they sat there, the two of them, with the wind lashing outside, Prabhu saw Raju come in. He smiled at them and sat down. He was not the boy with torn shorts and dirty hair. This Raju shone with a transparent light that warmed the room and spread out of the door into the village. Prabhu saw his tousled hair, wet with raindrops and the soft smile on his lips and he realized that for Raju, summer had come in another world.

He bent down and looked at his hand and saw the glittering gold ring, with the red ruby in its centre. The ring too had seen its seasons and was back where it belonged. He quickly pulled off the ring and placed it on the ground. Kuyili picked it up and put it next to the photo of Raju. When Prabhu turned around, Raju had disappeared.

She cried then, Kuyili his wife and lover, the woman he had seen crying so very few times. The tears flowed freely down her face as she stood looking at the photo of the boy with the tousled hair.

[illegible]

[illegible]

[illegible]

[illegible]

"Bend your right knee on the fourth count," Aryan suggested to his buddy.

"There's no fourth count in Salsa, dumbo," Mahi said.

These four together made a trapezoid quadrilateral (a quad having no side parallel). All of them in their own tangents. After all nature (Natasha) hadn't been very fair with them.

"How much do you weigh?" Ron asked his partner.

"Why are you asking that?" Sameera replied.

"I might have to lift you...you know part of Salsa moves."

"No such moves will be taught today...so don't worry."

"Still...I insist."

"Last month when I weighed myself I was..." she thought for a while, "But this month it came down to...hmmm...actually, it fluctuates."

What else he expected the answer to be?

After one hour

Around 06:00 pm

"All righdee...let's take a break," Natasha clapped twice.

An hour of toil.

Gyrating hips certainly deserved a break.

Girls went out of the room for a chit-chat along with granny. Boys decided to be in the room.

"I think, she likes me," Ron pulled out a comb from his pocket.

"You are hitting on Natasha! She's your teacher," Mrigank said and parked himself on the chair.

"I am a follower of Nelson Mandela," he employed the toothed strip on his tousled hair, "I am against discrimination. Be it of any form."

"She's a hard nut Ron. Forget about her," Aryan said.

"You don't know my past records," Ron pulled a chair and jump sat on it.

"Stop living off your past glories buddy...wake up and smell the coffee," Aryan provoked Mandela's fan. Aryan and Mrigank were fully aware of Ron's challenge-accepting nature. Especially if it concerned the fairer sex.

"Aryan what are you saying...you don't know what Ron can do," Mrigank set the booby trap. No pun intended. I swear!

"Aaaahh...he's all fart and no substance," Aryan winked back.

"Are you trying to provoke me?" Ron sniffed the set up.

"I am not trying...I aeeemmm," Aryan said.

"Ron it's a risky enterprise...don't listen to Aryan," Mrigank added some more fuel.

"Little risk never killed anybody, dude," he sprung up from the chair, "Watch me crack this nut," and moved toward the balcony where Natasha was checking out her CD wallet.

The spectators could not hear the conversation between the nut and the cracker since the door was shut and the transparent glass that separated the room from the balcony was sound proof.

Ron returned after a while. His gait had changed. His posture too. Chest out. Shoulders back. Chin up. He came back prouder. Pride that General Maximus (Russel Crowe in Gladiator) had when he was welcomed by Marcus Aurelius Ceaser (Richard Harris) after his victory in the northern sector, Germania.

"You are gutsy man. What did she say?" the inquisitive Mrigank asked.

"Nothing," Ron shrugged his proud shoulders.

"Stop feeling pricey now. Say na what happened?" Aryan asked. Ron raised his collar up, "So you guys agree I am the coolest dude."

"Super-duper cool, boss," Mrigank would have even agreed to call Ron, his dad. He was too excited to know what happened.

"She's agreed for a caffeine shot at CCD."

"Don't tell me."

"And what makes you think we would believe that," Aryan said.

"Girls normally don't give their cell number to strangers."

"You got her number!" Mrigank jumped.

"In fact, she told me to call her tonight...here it is," Ron displayed the contacts page of Nokia N-73. "But she's requested me to keep it to myself so..."

"How did you open the talk?" Mrigank asked.

"Nothing great, I jussss..."

Natasha's, "On the floor," broke the gossip.

"I'll tell you later," Ron told the two.

"I'll change your dance partners for the second half," Natasha announced.

The hearing faculties got super activated. At this moment, Aryan's imagination decided to take him to his school days. He could see Br. Fitzpatrick, his Mathematics teacher, framing a question on Venn diagrams. He connected the past with the present.

He visualized the room as a universal set. He could see two intersecting circles on the floor. And the six of them scattered as the elements inside both the circles. He saw Natasha as his math's teacher, putting him and Sameera in the overlapping region, an area common to both the circles.

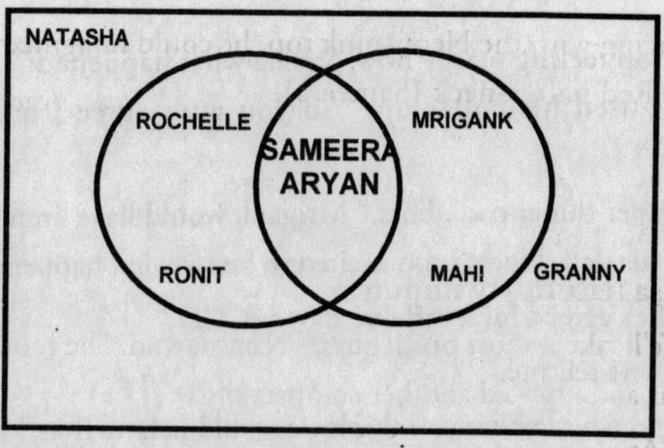

Natasha framed the question

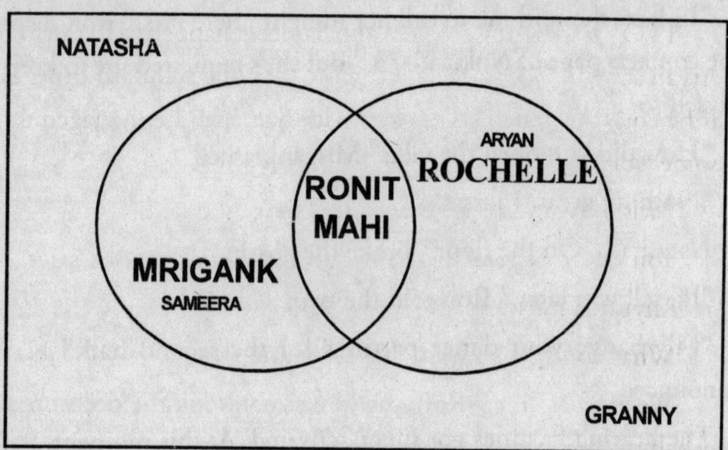

The 'two elements' were placed in two different circles. Far, far away from the overlapping region.

Lucky draw went on girl's favor. Each got their pick.

Lady luck somehow wasn't too happy with Aryan today.

Girls surprisingly started finding the same Salsa steps easier. Complex differential calculus turned into basic algebra.

Aryan too had learned to be friends with his destiny. Moreover, his imagination power had developed immensely. Though he was dancing with the Neon-pink top, he could imagine himself leading the Red halter-neck (Sameera).

Salsa (last thirty minutes)

"We'll take a short break guys," Natasha said. She took out the Moser Bear and inserted another compact disc.

"At last a song I know," Aryan said. The song was - Lady in red (sung by Chris De Burgh).

"You like this song?" Natasha asked.

"I LOVE this song," Aryan and Sameera happened to say in unison. Aryan smiled. His smile lasted more than the standard time. So what if he couldn't match Salsa steps with Sameera, he managed to match some words.

"I wish we could do Salsa on this song," he said.

"You really want to dance on this number?" Natasha said.

"Anytime," he replied.

"What about you guys?" she asked the group.

"We are all game," Ron, the spokesman took the decision on their behalf.

"Fine then...Salsa for today is over...I am going to teach you a self-stylized Ballroom Tango sequence."

"Wouuuuu." Aryan expressed his...his...something.

"What's Tango," Mrigank asked. Natasha walked up to the center of the floor, "If Salsa is flirting, Tango is Romance," she explained.

"Sounds cool," Rochelle said.

"We'll dance in close embrace...any girl has a problem with that?" Natasha asked.

"What's a close embrace?" Mahi said.

"It's a position where the lead and the follow are in constant connection with the body," Natasha replied.

"We are all adults...and after all it's an art," Rochelle, the spokeswoman said. Ron expressed his consent by nodding his head vehemently. I had never seen Ron agreeing to anything this passionately ever before. I know, those vehement nods were owing to the concept of close embrace and not because of any kind of respect for art.

"An art worth every penny," Natasha said and turned the music off.

"Hey, why you stopped the music?" Aryan cribbed.

"I want you people to learn the steps first," Natasha said.

She demonstrated the sequence. She set her body in motion across the floor through the flexing of her lower joints (hip, knee and ankle). Her body moved first and then the feet moved quickly to catch the body resulting in snatching and striking action. It took a little while for the students to catch on to the complex footwork.

"And now, I want the two admirers of this song to pair up and the other four can choose their own partners," Natasha said.

Aryan's imagination took another flight. He saw three people showering flowers on him.

Br. Fitzpatrick.

Lady Luck.

And Mother Nature.

The unshakable rock approached the calm stream.

He stood before her with an hour and a half of salsa seeping from him. She stood near him as fruity fresh as she was an hour and half back.

His 5' 11" against her 5'7".

The two.

Mano-a-mano with each other.

For the first time.

The blend of lotus and rosemary, further enhanced by fresh guava notes, teased his nasal cavity.

The vigorous, masculine, musky based sweat offered her olfactory receptors a nosey boost.

"Everybody...frame," Natasha instructed.

The command was followed in letter and spirit...and hands.

The Touch.

Delicate.

Delightful.

Little Cold.

But very soft.

Aryan's horizons broadened. A myth shattered. An education added. He now knew that much softer things exist. Softer than silk and velvet.

Her hands.

The touch did a little more. He felt his own hands. Like never before.

The Muscles.

The Tendons.

The Carpals.

The Metacarpals.

They always existed. But now they were...as if breathing. Heavily.

Nevertheless, the nervous hands bravely volunteered to introduce the rest of him to her. And in the bargain, be introduced too.

He felt a deep sense of gratitude.

Toward the person who created Tango, though he didn't know who was it. Toward Argentina for encouraging such form of dance style. Toward the person who brought Tango to India. Toward Mr. Ranvijay

Pathania who arranged it in Wilbur Woods. Toward Ms. Natasha, who presented him such opportunity. Such Uranium-encrusted opportunity.

Close position required the lead and the follow to be close.

Very close.

His 42 inches chest. Broad. Chiseled. Anxious. Met the softer counterpart.

Nose to nose.

All volcanoes occur at the edge of tectonic plates. Mrs. Simpson, my geography teacher used to say.

I doubt?

Aryan could precisely locate his blood-pumping organ, hidden behind the rib-cage. Hers too. It had never lubbd-dubbd like this before. For sure.

Several other first-time occurrences followed suit.

Funny shivers.

Moisture-free tongue.

Parched lips.

Twitches, all around.

And Giddy pleasures.

Soon, Chris De Burgh took over.

The song ruthlessly plundered their senses and the singer's succulent voice sluggishly swallowed them, deep in its intestine.

Music has its own way to get inside our skin and 'musicalize' its own space.

Never seen you looking so lovely as you are there tonight,

I've never seen you shine so bright….

...Lady in red is dancing with me, cheek to cheek,

It's nobody here, it's just you and me,... swear wanna be,

I hardly know, this beauty by my side,

I'll never forget, way you look tonight.

I never will forget, way you look tonight,

lady in red,... my lady in red... my lady in red.

Aryan had heard the song many a times before. Today it sounded different. The lyrics seemed scrumptiously meaningful and melody harmonically expressive.

A stupid power failure stifled Chris De Burgh's throat- ***Lady in reaiiiiiii........***

"Welcome to the capital," Natasha said and moved to the balcony, "Bhaiya, generator start karo," she shouted. Bhaiya was quick with his reactions, "Anyways, it's time we say adieus to each other," Natasha said seeing her wrist watch. "It was more than thrilling to be with you guys...hope you enjoyed Salsa...and Tango."

"Be in touch," Mahi said.

"Oh I forgot! I've given my number to Ron, take it from him. That's my office number, you can call me between 9 to 7, after that I switch it off," Natasha said wearing her summer jacket.

Mrigank started laughing hysterically.

"What happened to you?" Rochelle asked.

"Nothing," he continued laughing.

"Then why you laughing like this," Rochelle too started laughing seeing the cute teddy laugh.

"I remembered a joke that Ron had shared during the break," he said. Still giggling.

"What joke?" Mahi said.

"Ask the coolest dude he'll tell you."

"Ron, whaa...where's Ron?" Mahi looked around. Ron had fled.

"You guys enjoy your joke, I'll make a move," Natasha helped her granny get up from the chair.

Granny went up to Aryan, who had somehow survived the song though he hadn't come over the shock.

Deliciously dangerous shock.

She went near him and whispered, "Why don't you tell her?"

"Tell whom?" he whispered back.

"Your lady in red," she smiled and faded.

"What did she say?" Rochelle asked.

"She said I shouldn't dance in public places."

"And what did you tell her?"

"I thanked her for warning me."

After Salsa class

07:15 pm

Aryan had survived the song.

Had he?

Of course, he had!

So what, if the body part at the open end of his arms still wanted to reach out to their softer half. So what, if her fragrance still played mysterious nose with him. So what, if his chest had started emitting sparks which could produce electricity. Sufficient to take care of power cuts in Wilbur Woods. So what, if he could suffer a cardiac arrest anytime. So what, if the song bluntly refused to leave his skin and threatened him, that it would linger on for eternity.

"Hellouu! Everybody has left," Mrigank shook the survivor.

"Huh!"

"Boy! Boy!...look at you... you've been annihilated."

"You are right," Aryan started walking.

"Lady in red?" Mrigank followed him.

"Yeah man...Maggy, her hands... oh god!" Aryan exhaled an overdue breath, "They are so soft, so delicate, so...so clear."

"Clear?"

"Yeah clear...I felt I should have cotton-rubbed mine with Sternum, before touching them,"

"Aaaeyen...STERNUM?"

"Yeah! that chemical liquid that nurses rub on your arms with cotton before injecting...you know, to remove the germs," Aryan elucidated the aaaeyen.

"You mean a disinfectant,"

"That's right...a disinfectant,"

"That's Sterillium dumbo...Sternum is breast bone," Mrigank said.

"I said Sternum?" Aryan punished his head with a gentle tap, "How dumb of me."

Boys' pad

"So... Mr. Cooolest Duude, all set for a caffeine shot," Mrigank teased Ron as he and the Dumbo entered the room. "I am sure very soon you'll manage a Tequila shot too, the way you managed Natasha's number."

"Twenty four hours and she'll be having tequila shots with me...else I lose thousand bucks," Ron placed two light green, crispy laughing Gandhi on the table.

Mrigank admired the signature of RBI's Governor and very respectfully guided the Mahatma to his wallet.

"Your time starts..." Mrigank set his Fast track, "Now."

Aryan pulled Mrigank by the sleeve, "Maggy, did you also feel in the same way when you first touched Tiffany?"

"I didn't touch her...she did...I was too afraid to even come near her, but she made everything very comfy for me."

"Guys! Hold on. What's going on?"

Ron came in between the two, "Will somebody please educate me?"

"Ron this guy's gone senti after Sameera."

"Senty for panty haan."

"No man, he's big time into it," Maggy defended his client.

"It's LLLUST Maggy... it's the murky, hungry sinner...the ding-dong raising its ugly head," Ron attacked again.

"No Ron, it's not the reproductive organ," the client said, "It's her eyebrows. It's her eyelashes. It's her mascara…it alone can cultivate the thrill and the sensation that even the turquoise and the yellow together in the swimming pool couldn't." His smile conveyed more than what his words did.

"And now what?" Ron surrendered his case.

"I've no idea."

"Ask her out for coffee."

"Ask her!" Aryan laughed, "Ron, we haven't even exchanged a courtesy hi and hello till now. Moreover, I am afraid that she might deny."

"Fuck!...you call yourself a soldier...you are a sissy, man," Ron said.

"Ron, you are mixing things."

"No I'm not. You don't have any guts. Accept it."

"You asked for 24 hours for Natasha. I require not more than 24 minutes...and I bet 10 times your amount. But it's not about charming a lady."

"THEN?"

"There are greater things at stake."

"Like what?"

"Like I can't afford to lose this feeling," his voice grew tender, "It's a feeling that I've never experienced in the entire 92 seasons of my existence. I am afraid coz I don't wanna lose the hope...hope that probably one day she would look at me the way I do."

"But you gotta start some day," Ron's voice too turned convivial.

"I know that... but I don't want to hurry it up... and more

importantly, I don't want to FUCK IT UP. I want to know a lil bit about her before I..."

"Is it your first time with hooks and elastics?" Ron asked.

"As in?"

"As in, with bras and panties."

"You are funny Ron," Mrigank said.

"No, it's not like that. I have lot of friends who are girls but Sameera..." Aryan paused and said, "She's different, man," his eyes narrowed and his nose wrinkled.

"And why's she different," Ron imitated Aryan's expressions.

"Thousand and one tingling reasons."

"To name a few?"

"Her intelligence...the way she weaved her speech...power and energy in every word. Her voice. Her mannerisms. Her dressing sense. The sophistication in her simplicity. The sense of ease that surrounds her. Her sm..."

"Got it-got it...I've got it...I've understood," Ronit stopped the flow of thousand tingling reasons. "Are you on the Orkut?" he asked. Aryan shook his head in negation.

"No flashy mobile phone, no laptop, no Orkut, where you from? Mohen-jo-daro or the Indus valley," Ron said.

"I am a techno ignoramus...by choice...actually never felt the need therefore," Aryan shrugged his 3,000 BC shoulders.

"There's an internet café just two minutes away," Mrigank provided a 2010 AD information. The techno ignoramus took his left foot forward to measure one of the yardsticks of modern era civilization. ,Social networking sites.

Internet Café

08:00 pm

A solemn demeanor.

Fire in the belly.

Now or never.

Do or die.

I can do it...

...were some of the traits that every typing fingers shared in the browsing centre.

The twin-ponytail nibbled her nails and arranged a clandestine smile on her pimple-prone face as she relaxed back on her chair after she had formed her reply.

The scrawny, horn-rimmed spectacled, checkered shirt was managing eight Orkut scrapbooks and four Yahoo massanger chat boxes at one time.

One of the orkutoholics didn't even blink in the last 120 seconds. Same concentration with which he solved his Physics numerical.

Physics numericals ???

An uncleji who had recently been transferred from Nagpur to Delhi was chewing something. Not sure whether it was a gum or a tongue. He had typed Delhi + Female on the search slot.

From early savannahs of adolescence to late arid adulthood, all had but one aim. One clear and compelling aim- if not a date at least a phone number. Agreed, some were there for old friends, but it's the majority we are concentrating on.

"So... this is the before-n-after tuition classes gainful occupancy," Aryan said, admiring the missionary zeal of the gainfully occupied. Most of them were school going students.

He too joined the league of these extraordinary gentlemen...and ladies. Ron pressed the UPS button and switched on the LCD screen. A few seconds later, the famous Bill Gates' quadra-colored window opened up and covered the centre of the black screen. Just below it, three tiny blue squares appeared from the left side and disappeared to the right. This they did five to six times. Their timings matched Aryan's heartbeats.

Ron opened his Orkut account and tasked his search engine for:

Sameera Sanyal + Mica + Ahmedabad.

Hundred and ninety six Sameera Sanyals opened their Orkut window for Ron to peep in.

"One nine six...not bad, here I come Sameera," Aryan sleeved-up his shirt and held the mouse.

"One ninety six...lil too much, let me down size the list," Ron added:

+ St Steven's, Mumbai

Ron had extracted this information before the debate had commenced. He too was interested in Sameera. Once upon a time. The mighty army of 196 Sameera had reduced to a smoldering rubble. A mere eight. Ron then pulled himself a stool and started using the adjacent PC.

"There she is!" Aryan spotted out his lady in red in an easy pack of eight. His eyes shone with a small dose of joy. Pure...unadulterated dose of joy.

"*Bachche ki jaan legi ye*," Aryan said managing the tickling sensations that her potrait rendered.

"*Bachche ki jaan toh* already *le chuki hai ye*," Mrigank made the *bachcha* realize the reality.

Aryan greedily rubbed some blue ink on the available white paper. Her profile. Social. Professional. Personal. Her favourites. Her testimonials. Her communities. He copied them all. As if, he was to write a thesis on her.

"Look what I found...Sameera's 10-digit code!" Ron let out an exultant cry of eureka.

"Where?" Aryan left his paper-work.

Ron showed them both one of Sameera's scrapbook entry:

Hey bhai kaisa hai tu...apan bindaas yahaan...stood thrd in dbate...nt a vry good feelin ...this wz th best oprtunity 4 my scrpt 2 b included in th magzine...cud'v been a great help 4 my book...heard only frst two r bein included...everybody suspected rigging...th guy who stood frst didn't deserve it...second chap was an army guy...intelignt, witty and offnsive. Taken a new sim...9258012330...plz delete th scrap after you note it down...msg me yor new nmber... tc...

"It's a jackpot, man," Mrigank said. Aryan read the scrap. Four times. Though his IQ was above average. He was more deliberate on a specific part of the scrap- 'second chap...and offensive'. He mulled over each of these 10 words like it had some murder-mystery-cracking-clue.

The triumphant soldiers returned to their base. Their spirit soaring high. Their morale towering up.

Mission was accomplished.

The first phase of battle was won.

Hands down.

No casualty.

Wilbur Woods (Boy's pad)

09:00 pm

A small piece of untidily torn newspaper.

Ten neatly written digits on it.

Three thinking brains.

And two questions-

How should the ice be broken?...through text or through voice.

How will Sameera RSVP it?...with a yes or with a no.

"What you waiting for? Official blessings...call her man," Ron said, trimming his stubble.

"No Ron, I feel he should send a message first. It's safe coz you have more time to react plus she kind of already knows you a lil bit before you talk to her," Mrigank gulped half of the chicken burger in one bite. He had picked up ten such bites from KFC.

"Maggy you have a point there BUTTT the same rule doesn't apply to all the girls. I feel Sameera would appreciate a straight call," Ron countered, caressing his trimmed shrubbery.

"I'll call her," Aryan ended the debate.

"Listen Aryan if in case you feel she's dominating and you are short of words, pretend that you are not able to hear her and disconnect the phone. The first conversation is damn important. You've gotta strike it well," Ron said, punching on his own palm. Aryan typed Sameera's number, "I'll manage it."

"Wait!...have you planned the 'where did you get my number from' query?" Ron brought up the inevitable.

Aryan didn't answer that question. He just smiled. His smile had the confidence and the pride that Abhinav Bindra had while he stood on the victory dais with gold on his swelled chest seeing the world rise from their seat to the tune of- '*Jan gan man adhinayak jai hai, Bharat bhagya vidhata*'.

"Wish me luck guys."

"*Vijay bhaov, putra*!" Mrigank placed his right palm on Aryan's head.

"*Bhabhi lekar hee aana mere bhai*," Ron kissed his forehead.

Aryan pressed the green button of his 'non-flashy' Nokia-3110.

Aryan: 'Hello.'

Sameera: 'Yes.'

Aryan: 'Hello...could I speak to Sameera please.'

Sameera: 'Yes...Sameera speaking.'

Aryan: 'Hi Sameera...Aryan here.'

Sameera: 'Aryan?'

Aryan: 'Aryan Vyas...Lieutenant Aryan Vyas.'

Sameera: 'Oh!...Aryan Vyas...Hi Aryan...what's the matter?'

Aryan: 'Actually aa...(he paused)...hello..hello..hellou.' He disconnected the phone.

Manage? He did. A little quick though.

"Whuthappened?" Ron asked. Aryan shook his head laterally.

"Whuthappened?" Ron asked again.

"She didn't even ask where I got the number from...I thought I'll generate some conversation out of it."

"Take out the battery of the cell…hurry up," Ron panicked.

"Why?" Aryan said. Ron snatched the phone. "At least switch it off," Aryan complained.

"No switching it off," Ron took out the battery, "Now even if she calls you back, the Airtel babe would say- the Airtel number you are trying to reach is currently not reachable otherwise she would have said that it's switched off," Ron tutored the complaining child.

"Really!" Mrigank grinned. Mr. Thomas Alva Edison must have had a similar grin when the fine filament of his electric bulb glowed for the first time. Mrigank had learnt a new trick that he could use on Tiffany.

Ron nodded, "Two benefits: one, she'll think it's the poor connectivity and two, you've bought some time for yourself."

"What did she say, by the way?" Mrigank asked Aryan.

"Totally unpredictable...she didn't even bother to know where I managed her number from...she wasn't surprised AT ALL...she straightway said- Hi Aryan, what's the matter?...what was I supposed to say?"Aryan shared his pain.

"Was she polite?" Ron walked up to the billiards table and started arranging the balls. Billiard balls.

"Yes, she was...in fact very polite."

"Then you are JACKED," Ron used his fist to strike an equivalent gesture for the word- jacked.

"Why?"

"Coz I have a very strong feeling that she's one of those rare breed dames," Ron said with contemplative looks on his face. And cue in his hand.

"What you talking about?" Mrigank said.

"Out of all the types, this one is most lethal," Ron pointed at Aryan's cell. As if Sameera was inside the mobile. "These girls are very polite, very confident, very intelligent and very ambitious. They have an aura or say a sort of wall around them which disallows the ordinary to come near them."

"Ok," Aryan wanted to hear more. He went near the billiards table for a better reception.

"They know the psyche of the boys. They let you play the game, the way you want. They measure you on your standards. They enjoy the attention you shower on them without even letting you know. They are very focused and very clear with their life AND ...listen to this very carefully..."

Both the heads leaned ahead.

"They are the most unn...rrromantic persons coz they feel getting attracted toward somebody is a weakness... but they don't run away from it... they run towards it...and all the times, they beat the attraction," Ron winded up his thesis. And the first shot.

"All bloody hogwash," Mrigank wolfed down the eighth bite. Fourth jumbo-sized chicken burger had gone down the alimentary canal.

"Maggy, shut the fuck up and do humanity and yourself a favor. Aryan, you tell me, did you even once feel that Sameera is aware that you are interested in her?"

"Never...not even an iota."

"How come everybody else has noticed it and Sameera hasn't. You only told us that even Natasha's granny noticed it. Sameera knows everything. It's just that she cares no shit about it coz her priority is her career, her book and everything else... "

"How you so sure about all this?" Mrigank intervened.

"Had a good chat with her after the debate and also during Salsa practice."

"So."

"Ten years of experience dude...with almost all types of girls...I normally don't go wrong with girls," he picked up one ball in each hand and showed it to Mrigank.

"Ron, what you are saying might be true. Dealing with Sameera is more like kayaking in a notorious rapid but you know what," Aryan lowered his pitch, "Even if I get washed away, it's worth a shot."

The disassembled Nokia-3110 was brought back to life and deputized for the task. Once more.

"Are you sure?" the ten-years-experienced asked.

"I am just trusting my instincts here plus I have your experience and knowledge behind me," Aryan winked.

Aryan: 'Hi Sameera…Aryan once again.'

Sameera: 'Hi Aryan.'

Aryan: 'Sorry, the phone went phut...something wrong with the battery.'

Sameera: 'That's fine...you were saying something.'

Aryan: 'Yeah, I realized I was a little rude on the stage...so... I wanted to apologize for the same.'

Sameera: 'I appreciate your gesture but I feel it was part of the game...so no guilt feelings...it's all good.'

Aryan: 'Wow...I feel so light.'

Sameera: 'Well then...it was nice talking to you Aryan...'

Aryan: 'Oh I am sorry... I didn't even ask you if it was a convenient time to talk to you...it seems you were into something and I disturbed you.'

Sameera: 'Not exactly...I was about to go for my shower.'

Aryan: 'Oh then I am happy, I didn't drag you out from something important ...Sameera, I was wondering if I could ask you out for a small chit-chat over breakfast tomorrow morning...may be some freshly baked croissants layered with thick creamy cheese, hash browns, some farm-fresh eggs and some black grape juice.'

[Sameera was a breakfast person (reference Orkut).]

Sameera: 'Why would you wonder such a thing?'

Aryan: 'I am a Scorpio and I feel restless if my accounts are unsettled. I need to tally my debts and assets and zero them out on a regular basis. if you come I'll be convinced that our scores have been evened out.'

Sameera: 'I respect your sentiments regarding your zodiac sign and your daily balance sheet that you so diligently maintain...but believe me, the scores were always even...it was really sweet on your part to say something like that especially croissants with cheese and the black grape juice... it was tempting ...I am afraid I'll have to say no and I am sure you'll respect my decision. Won't you?'

Aryan: 'With all my heart and soul, lady.'

Sameera: 'Bye Aryan.'

No reply.

Sameera: 'Hellouu...are you there?'

It happens. Day in. Day out. All the time. Everywhere. A man is destined to suffer the pain and agony of a rejection. Some point of time in his life. Rejection in various forms. Basic necessity. Food for instance. A dinner, a lunch. In Aryan's case, a breakfast. Some time it's a beverage. A drink, a coffee. A lot of time it's entertainment. A movie, a dance. Even an information is denied. A phone number for example.

What the rejectionist fail to see is the efforts, feelings and courage behind the act. I wish if the Venusians could once undergo what Martians do on any such occasion. I remember I went under such pain once. It was as if you want to pee badly and when you finally find a suitable ,place your equipment gets stuck to your zip. It becomes a double 'blessing'. You can't pee in your trousers and at the same time the zip's sharp teeth are fondly nibbling the ultra sensitive equipment.

But for nature, men would've extinct. Nature has evolved a self healing mechanism, wherein the hurt diagnose himself.

"She said no!" Aryan spread himself on the bed.

"We heard that," Ron said.

I forgot to mention. Sameera was on loudspeaker. Ron wanted to analyze Sameera's reactions.

"You did a wonderful job Aryan," Mrigank consoled the denied.

"I think I hurried it up." Aryan banged his head against the pillow repetitively.

"No man...you were perfect...girls are like that...you never know what they want," Mrigank stated a fact. The fact.

"She must have had some commitment. Moreover breakfast wasn't the best idea," Aryan initiated the self-healing process.

"The hard fact is that she rejected you therefore accept it and move ahead. There are good-looking babes in the other group too. Let's explore them," Ron said, casually.

"Ron stop it ya," Mrigank looked at Ron in distaste. "Aryan what next?" he asked.

"I don't know," Aryan got up from the bed and opened the window, "I think fresh air will do some good," he inhaled and exhaled.

Aryan's phone rang.

By then he had inhaled and exhaled five times.

"Bloody hell! It's Sameera," Ron shouted.

"Sameera?" Aryan ditched the fresh air.

Ron did a "Ssssshhh", operated the two buttons- options and loudspeaker and handed over the set to Aryan.

Aryan: 'Hello.'

Sameera: 'Aryan I thought I hung up abruptly. You wanted to say something?'

"I told you na…see… she's running toward the attraction," Ron whispered.

"Hmmm…seems like," Mrigank whispered back.

Aryan took it as another chance that life presented him with. It was as if, what Aryan speaks next will decide his future with her.

Aryan: 'Sameera, whatever I said or whatever I'm gonna say was and IS just an excuse to be near you...I too, like other humans try to dodge sufferings and drift toward something that gives joy...Being near you gives me joy...I am just trying to chase my good time.'

For some moments, none spoke...

Sameera: 'Am I allowed to change my decision?'

Aryan repressed an exultant leap and pretended a cool and collected composure.

Aryan: 'Tomorrow morning, zero nine three zero hours, Ansal plaza.'

Sameera: 'I thought you'd pick me up.'

Aryan: 'Aah…I forgot you are my neighbor. Nine fifteen, outside your room.'

Sameera: 'Let's make it, ground floor center lobby."

Aryan: 'Roger.'

Sameera: 'See you tomorrow then…have a good sleep.'

Aryan: 'You too.'

What would have happened if East India Company itself surrendered the Indian sub continent to Bahadur Shah Jafar- the last Mughal emperor. Jafar Miya's body would've been speaking the language that, our dear Aryan babu's body was speaking.

Mouth open. Wider than normal.

Eyes open. Larger than normal.

Head. Oscillating horizontally. Non-stop.

All the expression-emoting representatives portraying a perfect- 'I know no fuck, how it happened?' posture.

"Hhhhhhowwww?" Mrigank asked.

The posture.

"Wwwwowwww!" Mrigank answered.

"Not bad," Ron said.

Night (01:00 am)

Aryan had already changed his sleeping posture six times. But all in vain.

Nervous system disagreed to be inactive.

The postural muscles were unwilling to get relaxed.

Consciousness denied suspension.

And eyes blatantly refused to close their shutters.

In short, none obeyed. Despite Sameera's instructions, "...have a good sleep."

Last that he felt like this was a night before his interview. He was equally anxious that night too. It was the final hurdle between him and the olive green uniform.

"Maggy, you've slept?" Aryan rolled about the seventh time. Few snorting and grunting sounds answered on Mrigank's behalf.

"Still dreaming about her," Ron's muzzy voice surprised Aryan.

"Ron, are you still awake?" Aryan said.

"Yeah…fantasizing about Mahi…feel like spanking her luscious tushhhh," the groggy Ron said.

"But you had the hots for Rochelle?" Asked the one-woman man.

"Yeahhh…I am fantasizing her bodacious boobies too," Ron answered.

Aryan laughed. Less in amusement and more in admiration. He admired the hunger of a semi-conscious Ron. An insatiable hunger for fairer and softer meat.

Saturday

It wasn't a usual dawn that occurs every day at this hour.

This one was special.

A special Delhi dawn.

A Delhi dawn that did doodlee-doodlee dum-dum in Aryan's *dil*. What is that suppose to mean? Sssssome...thing.

He had never felt so rejuvenated, though he'd haa just a paltry four hours sleep. Sleep loses its charm and importance in these moments, I guess. He greeted the cool breeze, which had wafted through the open-glazed window.

Never before did a rising sun change so many colours. Never before did the morning birds sing so many songs. Never before did he shout to his own self (this early in the morning...that too on a holiday), "Life's good...and mornings are great."

There must be something to these times. Thousands, can't go wrong.

The next few hours were constructively utilized.

Misbehaving nails were disciplined.

The flourishing savage garden under the armpits was trimmed.

Hair was twice shampooed and the face, thrice shaved.

An acne that had spread terror on the far end of the right cheek was also pinned down.

The hour prior to the H-hour, was reserved for tuning the finer aspects. The dress code, the accessories, the cologne etcetera. At around

08:30 am, an idea whizzed past Aryan's mind. He thought of SMS'ing a self authored text to Sameera. With two aims.

One, to create a sort of rapport before he actually meets her. Two, to ease out his own anxiety.

After a pensive thought he drafted the SMS but instead of sending it, he saved it. He had something better in mind. He then dialed her number.

Sameera: 'Hello'

Aryan: ————

Sameera: 'Hello...hello... Aryan, are you there.'

Aryan: ————. He disconnected the phone as planned and before Sameera could call him back, he send the drafted message:

They say, rise n shine wid d most soothing voice falling on yor eardrums ...i jst did tht... Thanx for makin my mrning...

Not a bad start, I must say.

Sameera's reply took one-tenth the time (somehow girls are good with their thumbs. I meant their SMS'ing speed.) and had ten times the effect.

Yor welcome officer.... *I hope you too will provide me with an opportunity to return the compliment (thanx 4 makin my mrning) aftr d b'fast... best of luck...*

Aryan wanted to ease out his anxiety. Ease out anxiety??

Did it backfire? Hell yess! It did. Did Aryan react? Oh yess! He did.

"Best of luck?...What does that mean?...Does that mean I'll be tested during breakfast?...How am I supposed to make her morning?" he bombarded himself with these questions. "Maggy...Ron," he shouted.

Maggy was still fast asleep. And the intensity with which he expelled air through his nose indicated that in the near future the status wouldn't change. Ron answered from inside the loo, "What happened lover boy?"

Aryan rattled off his misadventure.

"Seems like somebody's gonna get majorly fucked, today!" Ron opened the door, voiced his opinion and shut the door again.

Aryan banged the door, "Ron, I need you to un-fuck the whole scenario for me please."

"But why do you think Ron would do it?" Ron shouted back.

"Coz Ron's just won a Domino's pizza along with a coke and coz Ron is the only guy available in Delhi who can do it," Aryan gave Ron's ego a little polish. Ron opened the door, "You are a SMART son of a bitch,"

"No! I am a smart son of a gun," Aryan said, handing Ron his towel.

"Son of a gun?"

"I am an artillery officer…they call us gunners," Aryan said.

"Sssson of a ggggun…aahaaann…I like that…take a pen and a paper," Ron applied the after-shave on the face. The *shishya* promptly followed his *guru's command.*

"But before you write remember one thing...it becomes your moral responsibility to ensure that she enjoys every moment she's with you…coz it's you who's asked her for her time…so it's you, who'll make sure that she doesn't regret her decision."

"And how do I do it?"

"Think and plan out every minute that you intend to spend with her...like you were planning your dress code...are we ready?"

"Yupp," Aryan took a fresh page of the diary and wrote, (1).

"One… make her talk more and you talk less."

"How?"

"Ask her questions that she'll love to answer."

"Like?"

Fuckin' ass! You have her whole Orkut profile with you and you askin' me???...ask about her passions, her taste...her whatever...you should know it better."

"Okay... okay." He made notes without looking at the page. His eyes glued on his guru who was passing *gyan* while pacing like a caged panther.

"Next...do not praise her...rather look for some faults and tell her about them... shake her sense of self a lil bit," Ron shook his own torso to give impact.

"Whyyyy?"

"You've got to understand this girl...I feel since the time she rode her first menstruation cycle, she'd been hearing that she's beautiful and intelligent and this and that...but youuu..." Ron poked Aryan's chest with his index finger, "...will go deeper and come up with something that she herself isn't aware of...you get me?"

"Yeah...I see lot of new responsibilities on my shoulders."

"AND...when you get a hint that she's getting impressed...pack your bag."

"Didn't get this one?"

"It means leave her when she's enjoying your conversations most...and leave her with a shock."

"Shock?"

"Yeah...make the end abrupt...sudden...unexpected...and if everything goes tickee-tickee boo, she'll certainly think about it after you leave and that's what we want," Ron said snapping his fingers.

"Sounds quite..." Aryan exhaled some air, "tickee-tickee boo."

"And for demon's sake make a list of all the topics that you are planning to bring in during breakfast."

"Make a list?"

"So that you don't go there and start saying 'so... what else' after every two minutes and then when you don't find anything else you start discussing the universally surveyed and certified dullest subject-WEATHER. Please keep that list in your pocket... whenever you feel you are running short of small talk, which I am very sure you will, excuse yourself and pay a visit to loo," Ron fetched himself a glass of water from the 486-litre four-door Haier slide by slide red colored fridge.

"Wondrous words of wisdom," the illuminated *shishya* extolled.

"And keep this with you...It's my lucky charm," Ron tossed a packet.

"Ron... *mere baap*..." Aryan said paying obeisance with hands joined in reverence, "...I am going for breakfast...why you giving me a condom?"

"Coz... it's better safe than never."

"It was very thoughtful of you...but thank you...I don't require it," Aryan tossed it back.

"Oh, Lord! Aryan I hope it's not *that.*"

"It's not what?"

"That your *pappu* can't dance *sala*... Are you a Mr. Can't?" Ron laughed.

"No, I am not a Mr. Can't...I am a Mr. Won't."

"Don't feel shy...keep it man...for my selfless sake...comm-oonnn," Ron again tossed his lucky charm.

"Ron, I respect women, I respect Sameera...please don't talk like this," Aryan tossed it back. It appeared they were playing passing-passing.

"You mean all the husbands and fathers and uncles and grandfathers in this world don't respect women?"

"Faaiyn...give it...I'll keep...you are such a dickhead...I swear,"

Aryan took the lucky charm.

The dotted…vanilla flavoured…rubberized…lucky charm.

It was a springy affair. Pleasant sun and soft breeze. Winter had just left the city. Correction. It had been quite a while that winter had left the city. This I say coz the week before last, I had gone to the market and had seen girls wearing all those interesting garments, that come out of the wardrobes after winters. The ones that help you know more about them. The M-skirts and all.

Aryan's beige linen trousers and white cotton shirt gelled well with the cool, sunny spirit that morning held. His two, Lee Cooper donned feet choreographed their confident albeit anxious steps all the way to the ground floor centre lobby.

Two final checks were done at this place.

The concave-shaped right palm checked the freshness of the breath "hh-haa" and the puckered nose checked the strength of cologne. Both passed.

Sameera showed up. In time. Quite a feat for any Venusian. She wore a white dress with bursts of small brown floral prints and a dash of lemon yellow thrown in ungenerously. Each print on the dress seemed to be enjoying its nearness to Sameera. The puff-sleeved dress cinched at the waist before flowing down, accentuating the lethality of her curves. Her brown, down-to-earth slip-ons shared their colour with the arrogant Dolce n Gabbana handbag that she was carrying

Aryan couldn't do much than just watch the breeze enjoy the exclusivity of playing around with Sameera's neatly straightened hair. I suppose the early morning wind must have passed on a word to keep them open.

"So what you selling today lieutenant?" Sameera doled out the first punch as she alighted the last staircase.

Aryan was still absorbing her layout, which wasn't very easy on his eyes since the dress though knee-length, intermittently exposed some part of her well-toned thighs, while she came down the steps.

"...Hhmmm...nothing...nothing at all...in fact today I am here to make some purchases...I always fancied humor and intellect...and you seem to have abundance of both... so I thought I'll buy some from you," Aryan dodged the jab.

He was happy that he could gather his wits around him against the unapologetically charming beauty.

"Then I hope you are carrying enough cash," came the second one from the MICA girl.

"I thought it can't be bought with cash?" he ducked it again.

"So you plan to pay back in kind?" Sameera countered, gently nibbling her lower lip. The gesture drew Aryan's attention to the subtle hint of lip gloss that shimmered more after Sameera bit her lip.

"I wish I could. I wish I had something that you required. But...I think I can always..."

"You can always?"

"I can always...formally, thank Sameera Sanyal for this GREAT compliment of coming over."

"Her pleasure." She closed both her eyes together for a second.

"Shall we?" Aryan asked.

"Yeah...how we going?" Sameera surveyed the area, "...I don't see a car anywhere."

"We'll walk."

"Walk! ...all the way to the Ansal plaza...I guess it's a good eight kilometers."

"No...we'll walk till the gate...take a rickshaw from there, that'll drop us at the auto stand and then...we'll let Mr. Bajaj do the rest," Aryan submitted the rundown.

"Whatever the host proposes."

The journey began. Through the concrete-clay path and the lush green golf ground where a petrol-powered rotary lawn-mower was mowing the lawn.

"I wanted to ask something. No offences ok…it's just curiosity kicking up," Sameera plucked a leaf from one of the smartly trimmed hedges that stood on both the side of the path.

"None of them taken...feel free to ask."

"I was wondering, why would one choose rickshaw and auto when a Skoda oblique a Fiesta was available as chariots on call?"

Mr. Pathania had allocated a car each for all the finalists.

"If I may, I'd like to put this question in a wrapper….keep it aside very-very carefully…and open it only once we've reached the mall….till such time I'll request the lady to bear Ms. Curiosity's kicks," Aryan returned the, "Salaam saab" given by the gatekeeper.

"All right…I'll bear the pain… till then."

"Rickshaa," Aryan called a rickshaw wala.

Not every springy, soothingly sunny, Saturday morning you get a chance to take a rickshaw ride with your dream woman (elbow to elbow) and enjoy watch her manage her dress against the raunchy wind.

Opportunist wind.

This was her first ever rickshaw ride. She didn't speak anything during the rickshaw ride. Neither did he. Both were busy capitalizing on the rejuvenating freshness, the cool breeze provided. In between they did speak something. I believe it was "Sorry", said twice by Sameera and thrice by Aryan. That was when the rickshaw went through some bad patches on the road. Aryan liked this whole funda of bumping and saying sorry. He had no complaints against Delhi Municipal Corporation.

A plethora of yellow-green crafts surrounded the couple from all possible directions at the auto stand. Delhi autos give you that VIP-treatment.

"Ansal Plaza?" Aryan asked one of them.

"*Chalo*, two hundred," the auto wala said.

"Two hundred? It's hardly twenty minutes."

"*Saab petrowl kitna mahanga ho gaya hai…chalo boni ka time hai aap one ninety de dena…essey kam nahin hoga*," he said pushing a *paan* in his mouth. The smart Alec knew that Aryan wouldn't bargain much. After all no guy would want to tarnish his image in front of a girl for few bucks. Moreover they can differentiate the regular, stuck, committed -type from the nervous, independent, first-meeting types.

"*Chalna hai toh meter se chalo…nahi toh dusra* auto *kar lenge*," Aryan said and started walking to the other auto *walas*.

"*Baitho…jyada* difference *nahin hoga kahae de rahae hain*," auto wala said in irritation.

"South-ex *se* left *le lena*," Aryan said.

"You've been on this route before?" Sameera said as she settled in the auto.

"Negative."

"Then how come you are directing him the route?"

"All I know is that there's some place called South ex en route and that you gotta take a left from there to reach Ansal Plaza…I extracted that piece of knowledge from the rickshaa wala," Aryan smiled, "This fella must be thinking I know the whole way so now he wouldn't intentionally take a longer route," Aryan explained in subdued tone. Sameera smiled.

The auto *wala* adjusted the rear view mirror. He had divided the movement of his eyeballs in a manner that it remained focused at one place for around two to three seconds. Once on the road and once on Sameera.

Aryan noticed it and started smiling.

"Why you smiling so much?" Sameera asked. Smilingly. It's so funny but when we ask a person, why he or she is smiling, we ourselves start smiling.

"Nothing...just like that."

"Now you are making me conscious," Sameera pulled up one of those girlie stuff to extract things out.

Aryan got caught, "He's hoping that he'll get lucky."

"As in?"

"Sometimes they get to see some kissing scenes behind...you know that's why he's adjusted that rear view mirror," Aryan shared the secret.

He wasn't sure whether he should have told it to Sameera or not since Sameera didn't quite react. She just nodded her head. Aryan thought he'd screwed up the gig even before it had begun.

"South ex *aane mein kitna aur* time *lagega*?" Aryan deliberately started a conversation with the auto *wala* to ease out the awkwardness.

"Aaaakhhhggg- thooo," the auto wala spat the betel juice, "*Bus aane wala hai sahab.*"

Sameera turned her head toward Aryan, "Aryan, I believe you aren't hoping?"

"Hoping?"

"To get lucky," Sameera smiled.

Aryan's moderately fair cheeks assumed the least refracted color of the visible spectrum. And they say men don't blush. The traffic lights turned red. Delhi on wheels came to a halt. And the one on foot got active.

Aryan could see a gentleman across the road redefining democracy in his own special way. He did the very thing that the graffiti on the wall denied him - '*Yahan peshab karna mana hai.*'

Aryan didn't want Sameera to witness the streamlined sense of freedom. But...Murphy's law...

A Hero Honda Splendor, that wanted to be the first to see the red turn into green was maneuvering its way through the jam and in the process kissed a shining, classic white Mercedes Benz a little too hard. The two owners were soon face to face. Each was making tall claims about the other's sister and mother. I have always wondered how two complete strangers know so much about each other's family.

A very young girl, who was trying to sell hand towels was shooed away by a car driver. He too mouthed some raw information about her parents.

Mahatma's country. ???

It reminds me of Muzaffar Ali, who once wrote- *seene mein jalan aankhon mein toofan sa kyon hai? Iss sheher mein har shaqs pareshan sa kyon hai?*

Two buffaloes attached to a cart were also waiting for the green bulb. One of them started rubbing its neck against the auto.

Time pass.

Curious about the sudden movement in the auto, Aryan glanced outside. The buffalo sensed that somebody was ogling. It turned its head toward Aryan. With an attitude. Its big black eyes met Aryan's small light brown. Its mouth was busy munching something. Looked as if it was chewing a bubble gum. A story was on the making but a honking separated the two.

The lights had turned green. The machines roared again. The auto, the Merc, the motor cycle and the buffalo...all raced ahead. Till the next red light. Shoulder to shoulder. She doesn't mind a buffalo competing with a Merc on her tracks. She's large-hearted. The great

Indian road.

The auto soon reached its destination. The meter displayed its reading. It was sixty six rupees. The auto guy wasn't grossly out. Was he?

Ansal Plaza

10: 30 am

Every MAN who walked past the couple turned back. At least once. Under various pretexts. Aryan had never walked beside such scandalous glamour. And never before had people looked at him with such respect(some with jealousy too). He reciprocated it with a look that said, GUY'S IT'S MY HANDIWORK...I AM THE OWNER.

He wished, it was his home town Nainital where all his childhood friends and all the uncles and aunties could see him walking along with Sameera. He knew he could have been the talk of the town. For years to come.

He wished that his elder brother Kabeer was there to realize that Aryan was no little mileage. And that he too had a taste. Better than Kabeer.

He hoped that he met one of his NDA (National Defense Academy) or IMA (Indian Military Academy) course mates who always boasted about their girlfriends. He wanted to show them his standard.

And he wished he could never come out of the stardom he was luxuriating in.

"Aryan, I must thank you for both the rides and...I guess, my query can remain wrapped…forever," Sameera stopped outside the Tommy Hilfiger showroom. Aryan had actually forgotten about the question that he had kept aside very-very carefully in a wrapper.

"My pleasure," Aryan was still enjoying the heady drug of recognition that he was receiving from all the directions. "Nice shirt," she said looking at the mannequin in the show window. It was a short sleeves men's shirt. Aryan took a close view at the cardiac-inducing price tag, " It's really good...I gotta buy this one..as it is I had to buy a shirt."

"You want to buy it right away?" Sameera asked.

"No I'll buy it later," Aryan didn't want to take a chance with the budget he had planned for the date.

The two debaters sat face to face separated only by a table two feet in length. Aryan had never seen her this closely. He now fully realized why so many heads did what they did. He employed little ruses to ensure she doesn't catch him staring at her face and elsewhere. After studying her face for a good four to five minutes he concluded that her skin was approvingly edible. Though he was a little confused as to how her face threw light and warmth without any flames.

The restaurant staff curried favor which was too apparent. The four tables (an uncle ji and auntee ji with their little daughter, four college-bunking boys, three old ladies and another couple) that arrived earlier in the restaurant had long been waiting for the waiters, all of whom chose to make an appearance only before the incandescent face. But I presume the deed was justified. People with elegant physical proportions normally have an edge over us- the third-world lookers.

"Is it a fiction or a non-fiction that you are writing," Aryan rolled the ball.

"It's a fiction. It's about a girl who wants to know the reason of her being in this world. She shifts many gears to find a perfect job for herself. A job that provides meaning to her life. A job that helps her find her mission on earth."

Every word that issued forth from her well-trained tongue was worth preserving as a voice sample. Pronunciation, correct and crispy and annunciation, clear and distinct.

"So what was the reason of her existence and what job did she finally choose for herself?"

"For that you need to buy my words...wait a few months for them to get published," she said researching the menu card. She never missed a chance to mystify her persona.

Sameera wore a tiny crucified Christ in her pendant that kept monitoring Aryan's eyeballs whenever they attempted to roll down to the prohibited areas.

"I already know the idea...beware...I might sell it," he said. His eyes wandered innocently.

"Don't worry yourself. I've already registered my work."

"Oh so you are already on record."

"Yeah...It's safe to be on record...and it's a testament to your professionalism too."

The waiter laid their order on the table.

"By any miniscule chance is that girl in the story Sameera Sanyal?" Aryan poured her some water.

"Thank you!...Yes, a big part of her izzz...Sameera Sanyal," she unfolded the napkin and placed it on her lap.

"And when the girl finally reaches her destination, who's she celebrating her reason with. You know somebody in the journey...every story has a love element," Aryan subtly threw the dice.

"This one is different. There's no love element in it. Of course there are associates and friends...good friends...but no love."

"It's different," Aryan imagined a glass. Shattering. "Would you be including this Delhi trip in your book," he said.

"Haven't thought of as yet."

"You must. You know, then...whenever you feel like doing Salsa or taking a rickshaw ride or having a nourishing breakfast on a spring morning all you would need to do is turn to the pages of your book," Aryan sipped the pomegranate juice, "And tomorrow when you become an international bestseller author and you deny to recognize me when I come to ask for your autograph, I could also refer to the same pages."

"That was flattering," Sameera smiled. "I think I should write something about it...at least two pages." Her smile had a cataclysmic effect on Aryan. He realized that he could even take a beating of his life to get a single slice of that smile. He had even tried copying her smile in front of the mirror once, in an attempt to enhance his face value but soon understood the reason why Sameera never had to copyright her smile.

He couldn't help but notice the adjacent table where the uncle and auntee ji were having pizza with their pink frock clad, cute looking daughter. She must have been in fourth or fifth standard. While her right hand fed her the pizza slices, her left hand's index finger was busy digging the nose. She looked cuter with half of her index finger inside her nostril. The expressions on her face indicated that she was enjoying the act. As much as Aryan was enjoying Sameera's smile.

"Wow...I am almost dating a future best-seller novelist," Aryan said.

"No...you are dating a future business tycoon," Sameera took a bite of grilled-sandwich.

"How come business?" Aryan's lips curved upwards. He was

visualizing the future business tycoon, fifteen years ago. Grilled sandwich on the right hand and half her left index finger inside nostril.

"Writing is my passion therefore this book...but that's not all...I plan to go for a one year executive program after MICA. This book would cast my academic acumen in a good light and also help me enrich my resume...I'd like to be where guerilla wars of business are fought."

"Oh I see...which MBA school have you thought of?"

"London School of Business...but there are a few kinks that still need to be ironed out...but that's fine...everyone has an agenda that needs some pushing and kicking."

"Agendas like?"

"Like I need to score big time in GMAT." she replied

The diagonally opposite table, where the three old ladies were sitting got replaced by two suit-clad gentleman. One of them had stubble like Ron, a little neater though.

"What are you planning to specialize in?" Aryan asked.

"Entrepreneurship."

"You plan to start something of your own?"

"Sort of. In less than a year I'll be an MBA in creative communications from MICA plus a PhD program in entrepreneurship from LSB. I think I'll be equipped enough to set up my own media company."

"Not bad."

"I intend to launch a channel which features only the common mass. Common, unrecognized people who've made difference in society. We would pick and select these people and make them celebrities. I know it sounds far-fetched but I know I'll do it," Sameera sounded very determined.

"Noble and inspiring thoughts...my views have broadened...well beyond the usual. I completely agree, It's all about bringing a change in larger format, otherwise a business doesn't make any sense," Aryan tore a piece of freshly baked croissant and put it in his mouth.

"You are right," she said.

"How do you plan to fund your company?" Aryan asked chewing the croissant.

"I have a fffundoo idea in my mind," her lower lip brushed against her upper canine before she uttered the first syllable of fffundoo, "But I won't tell you...it's a secret," she whispered. As if she was leaking a confidential matter of national importance. Aryan enjoyed the undertone and her choice of word- *fundoo*. Like he had enjoyed the word- *bhandpanti* that Sameera had used for Aryan on the stage and *bindass* that she had written in her Orkut scrapbook. These words were unlike Sameera. A little out of character. But they always added to the charm.

"Ok!...tell me one thing...god forbid if your book fails," Aryan said showing his crossed fingers to Sameera, "You know no planning has ever survived the first contact with the enemy...destiny?"

"Aryan, part of growing up is making your own decisions and living with the consequences...so...be it!...Honestly, I would probably sleep on this whole issue of writing a book for a week or so but then when I get up I would walk up, give a tight slap on the face of destiny and start writing another book...a fail-proof book," her eyes reminded Aryan of *Mahishasur mardini, Shakti rupini Durga maa*.

It reminds me of Winston Churchill who once said, *'Twenty to twenty five! These are the years! Don't be content with things as they are. Don't take 'No' for an answer. Never submit to failure. You will make all kinds of mistakes; but as long as you are generous true and fierce, you cannot hurt the world or even seriously distress it.* **She (the world) was made to be wooed and won by youth.'**

"Aryan I am feeling as if you are interviewing me."

"No!...but then in a way yes!...and it's good...I am preparing you for the gaudy times ahead."

"Tell me something about your world...the bullets and the bunkers!" she rested her chin on her knuckles.

"Well..." he heaved a luxurious sigh, "I am in the business of saving and... taking lives...the core business being saving lives."Aryan replied.

"Aanhaan...Saving lives, the core business," she nodded her head, "So how does this business work?"

"It works on the concept of avoiding the metal from meeting the meat," Aryan threw a googlee. She waved her fork, "Metal meeting the meat...what's that?"

"Metal...enemy's bullets and meat...our flesh." he explained.

"Ohhhh!"

"So it all starts from training myself to save my own life and then I train my boys under my command to save theirs...and together we save yours."

"So you are a trainer too."

Aryan smiled, "To lead soldiers you've gotta be all in one...a coach who makes you sweat, a father who kicks your butt, a mother who cares, a brother who listens, a guide who crafts your career path, an income tax advisor who helps you save some dough...the duty of an officer goes well beyond the job description. You like to be where millions and billions are made. My stakes aren't that big... just a fine and fuzzy line between death and life." Aryan delivered his world of bullets and bunkers with a lot of style. He was all set to impress his lady in red.

Sameera signaled the waiter to get some water, "I feel you guys are severely low balled by government...I've heard the sixth pay commission ain't delivering the promises it made."

"The modest Army wages certainly demand significant attention. But we've stopped bothering ourselves with that now...we are satisfied souls...we are happy with our psychic income."

"Psychic income?"

"Yeah...the income that can't be neatly quantified by a rupee sign...honor, self-pride, opportunity to lead men in difficult times, bonding between the olive greens, rich traditions...basically the whole old-world charm gamut," he dabbed his chin with his hanky. Only if he had used the available napkin paper and not taken out his hand-kerchief from his pocket to dab his chin. Came along with Aryan's hand-kerchief...Ron's lucky charm, that fell bang on Aryan's plate. Face up.

"Kama Sutra...dotted...vanilla flavored...," Sameera read. Her eyeballs doing to and fro. Once at the charm and once at the charmer.

Sometimes shit gets fired at us at point blank range and we rarely if ever get time to duck.

The metal it seemed had torn apart the meat.

Destiny had put his core business on test. The savior was now supposed to save his own life. Actually grace.

It was just a fine and fuzzy line between 'goshhh he was a cheapo' and 'woww... he had a panache.'

A lot was at stake...honor, self pride, rich traditions...basically the whole old world charm gamut.

An insult that could't have been neatly quantified by slaps on face.

Aryan had worked hard to get this date. And he never wanted it to end in such an undignified manner. Rather he never wanted it to end. He was doing well till now. He knew he was rogered. He also knew that Ron's testicles would now be his personal property and that he'll misuse the property. Ruthlessly.

Aryan after a pensive thought hazarded his best attempt to diagnose the situation, "Sameera when I think of you, I do it with a sense of respect with which I think about my sister, Arushi or my mother Mrs. Vyas, so though it's here on my plate..." he picked up the **un**-lucky charm, "And it was there in my pocket...it's not me...there are always degrees of truth and things are not always what they seem...please don't think less of me."

Sameera took a while before she lent him her piece of mind, "Your eyes though a little small, spoke more eloquently and convinced me more than what your words did...Vanilla boy, I'd still like to go round two with you some day." Sameera smiled.

Aryan just nodded his nervous nut.

"Oh no!... Oh God!" Sameera's big brown eyes widened. Vanilla boy turned back to see Sameera's god.

"Don't look behind, pleazzzzz," Sameera elasticized the last word. She hid behind Aryan's broad frame. She looked like one of those cute, shy, afraid, hidden-beneath-a-sofa kinda puppy. Aryan saw her jawline, which was a little tense. Her expressions were strained, like when she was managing her dress against the wind during the rickshaw ride.

"Aryan can we please move out of this place?"

"Yeah of course...everything fine?" the broad frame asked.

"Can we please move out and then talk about it?" she sounded like Aryan's head mistress.

"Sure," the obedient student replied.

He resisted the temptation to see Sameera's god who had ended his date so abruptly. He hated that god. But on the other hand, he didn't mind it much. He desperately required a break after the lucky charm episode. The pouch that contained his pair of testicles had almost reached his throat, blocking the air passage. Some fresh air was certainly a boon.

"It was me who was supposed to make the end abrupt…Is it, that she did it before me?..no..no ..no…not possible…she doesn't have Ron to guide her…why didn't she let me see the person behind?…or is it about lucky charm…no…no… no…if that was the case why would she propose a round two?...what could it be?" - Aryan's mind ran all these queries, while he tapped the bill.

The two moved out.

"How much damage?" Sameera jigged about her Dolce n Gabbana.

"Damage?"

"The bill…I mean."

"Why would you want to know it?"

"Coz decency demands that a person pays for what she ate…there aren't any free breakfasts."

"With due respect, I agree with the philosophy…but…the fair lady was invited and protocol says that the invitee pays the bill."

"If the lady still insists."

"The gentleman then would humbly request the lady to pay the entire amount…"

"Ok," she said and started searching her bag for money.

"I had not finished…pay the entire amount, the next time…when she invites him." Aryan played smart.

"The gentleman wins," she stopped the search.

"Yes he does…a chance…to see the lady again."

"Aryan I apologize for all that."

"That's fine...Sameera, I know you don't owe me an explanation but in case if there's something that you would want to share...I'll be more than delighted to hear it," Aryan slowly slid the ball in her court. Aryan was actually dying to know about the villain god. But he didn't show it.

"Of course, I owe you an explanation...can we please go somewhere and sit?"

"How about that bench there," Aryan showed her the place.

Sameera sat while Aryan preferred standing.

"Aryan I was trying to avoid Gaurav," she unraveled the god's name.

"Ok," Aryan responded.

"Because he once walked out on me," Sameera's expressions changed.

"Huh?" Aryan didn't believe his ears.

"Yeah that's right...Gaurav dumped me," she reaffirmed.

Aryan didn't react with a "Ok" for this. He just blinked his eyes. He was cautious about his gestures. He knew that female homosapiens are very sensitive about their feelings and that utmost care is required to handle such situation. Army training had not equipped him for such eventualities. But he wasn't that nervous since he had a sister at home.

"I don't need to tell you all this but I think I'll feel better if I do. I thought my past would get a silent burial but...anyways...Gaurav was one year senior to me. We saw each other socially for around six months. Everybody in MICA knew about us. At his farewell party he publicly dumped me in front of the entire student body. He did this because his new girl friend, daughter of our head of department, wanted an assurance from him. He even insulted my physical attributes when I demanded a reason. I was plump then...not like Mrigank but still," she smiled.

Aryan reciprocated with a polite smile.

"Aryan, when I think about him my sense of pride shatters. I want to avoid his eyes because I see his victory in them…and I hate that," she grew melancholic, "I want to avoid him coz he's a nobody to me now."

Aryan responded with his eyes that said, 'I empathize.'

"Sameera, if you see objectively, you are letting a Nobody rule a part of you and this will continue for the rest of your life. Why don't you forgive him and finish it off…once and for all," Aryan said.

"Forgive him?" Sameera reacted. A little too strong. A passing old man, whose face had as many wrinkles as specs of doubts in Sameera's eyes turned back to see if everything was fine. "Forgive him?" she repeated, a little softer.

"Yeah…after you take your revenge," Aryan winked. He had some thing fishy cooking in his mind.

"Revenge?"

"Yes revenge…I have a plan." Aryan's face lit up. Like Ron's had, when he saw the girls in the swimming pool.

"No Aryan…we'll leave it."

"Sameera not everybody gets a chance to meet their ex-boyfriend or ex-girlfriend at a time when they are doing well in life. You know when I was in tenth standard, I had a major crush on one of my classmates who happened to be my neighbor too. Though I was always near her eyes, she never even noticed me because I was a low profile, shy, simple looking, average-built boy and because there were other smart, good-looking boys who knew how to talk to girls in my class. Today I wish I meet her somewhere, not because I want anything from her…not because I want her to like me...it's just coz today I am confident that I am doing pretty well in life…and this I say coz you said yes for the breakfast."

Sameera smiled.

"...And it's just coz I am confident that she won't miss noticing me this time...it's just a harmless, sweet revenge I want to take on her for not noticing me all those days ...Sameera you are at your best today...don't lose this chance...just go for it." Aryan motivated her for the plan.

"I am afraid."

"I'll be with you...but before that...just wait here," Aryan went back to the restaurant and took a wily peep inside the restaurant.

"Is he the same guy who's wearing a black shirt," he asked Sameera.

"Yes."

"There's a girl with him too."

"She's the same girl, Vaishali."

"Oh that's great...we'll be two on two."

"Aryan you are too decent for him...he's a shrewd and dominating kind of a guy plus he's so muscular...I don't want him to win again,"

"Point taken...give me two minutes," Aryan vanished.

He returned after two minutes.

"How about this?" Aryan posed in front of her.

Sameera pulled herself to the back rest of the bench, folded her legs, placed her left elbow on the arm rest and balanced her chin on her clinically taken-care-of fingers.

She repeatedly tapped her left cheek with one of her fingers. In between she even bit her lower lip once, with one of her canine. Her signature expression. The shamelessly sweet smile didn't move from her face even for a jiffy.

She was probably admiring the new short sleeves shirt that Aryan was wearing. The one that both liked in the Tommy Hilfiger show window. Perhaps she was amazed to see what always remained hidden beneath Aryan's full sleeves shirts.

Aryan's leisurely carved body.

She now learned why the back of the human upper arm was called triceps. Each of the three muscles that made Aryan's triceps was so distinctly visible.

While she wondered at his modeled chest, that unblushingly exposed itself through the top two unbuttoned buttons, she realized the quality a dedicated fitness regime can bring about to a human body.

She understood the power of his shoulders that cracked some pretty hard cement in the boxing ring.

She understood the beauty of each drop of his sweat that fell on the training ground.

She understood the magic of each moment when his muscles burned and veins pumped battery acid.

"Awesome for the occasion," she replied. Sameera's confidence had increased manifold.

"Are we ready?" Aryan preened his hair, that he had spiked and self-styled with water to give him a funky-chunky looks.

"What's your height," Sameera asked.

"5'11"...why?" Aryan wondered aloud at her ill-timed question.

"Great!...he's 5'10"," the kid inside Sameera jumped with joy.

Aryan almost laughed at Sameera's childishness. He rejoiced this new-found aspect of Sameera.

"The plan is very simple. We enter inside the restaurant, we meet them. Of course, you'll pretend...Oh wow! How come here," Aryan demonstrated. "You play a very cool girl as if nothing ever happened between the two of you. You then introduce him to me and after that I take over. I do my little act and then we leave…that's it…over …done…finito," the strategist gave out his plan.

"You said you'll take over and do a little act…what's that?…and what am I doing all this while?" the playmate asked the skipper.

"You are doing nothing," he said.

"Nothing?"

"Yeah…just let him see you once…and let him realize what he's missed,"

"And what are you doing there?"

"Oh me… I am not doing much," a glimmer of grin flashed across his face, "Just shaking his foundations a lil bit."

Gaurav's bad news walked inside the restaurant. In buddy pair.

"Hey Gaurav! What a pleasant surprise. Long time. How have you been?" Sameera opened the scene.

"Sameeeera?" Gaurav's teeth stopped munching, whatever they were munching.

A little shocked. No. Majorly shocked.

Two mammoth reasons.

Her coolness and her hotness.

"Hi Vaishali."

"Hi Sameera," Vaishali's eyes too began scanning Sameera's radiant beauty.

"Gaurav, meet Aryan," Sameera set the stage for Aryan.

"Hi dude," Gaurav brought forward his right arm for a courtesy handing. His eyes glued to Aryan's unmistakable biceps.

Aryan didn't reciprocate the courtesy, "I am amazed and appalled, Mr. Gaurav... I guess, Sameera just introduced me by my name… but you still called me DUDE…here's a basic concept you better start warming up to before we shake our hands...if you know my name, call me by my name…the name is…ARYAN," Aryan shook his hand. And also one of the pillars of his foundation.

"Aryan...Gaurav is also a MICA graduate. We were there together. He was my senior," Sameera nursed the blow.

"MICAAAA?…Gaurav?…if I am not wrong he's the same guy who you said had dumped you?"

"You heard that right…Mr. ...ARYAN," Gaurav's chest swelled an inch.

"HE dumped you?" Aryan faced Sameera, "Sammy, what had happened to your taste…look at him, gosh!…he looks like a guy who's already fathered four kids."

"What are you ssssss..."

"Gaurav, no disrespect intended," Aryan stopped him in between, "I am a bloody shameless son of a gun…but I am sure you'd agree with me on that."

"Gaurav don't mind…Aryan is little blunt and straightforward kinda guy," Sameera said. She was acting a perfect pacifier.

"Sammy, I believe you said he had good muscles and that he's a fitness freak..." Aryan took out his next hook. The tactic was to not give the opponent any time to react. He literally monopolized the conversation. "You've been bluffing me…he looks like a *pahalwaan.* Look at his paunch."

Vaishali eyed the subject. Surreptitiously.

"Gaurav, honestly speaking, since you are Sammy's friend you are now even my friend, so I am taking this liberty to tell you to please start doing something about your disproportionate stats…we've gotta go now …got someplace to be in," Aryan took a step back.

"Couple of commitments lined up. We apologize for leaving you guys in such a haste. We would have loved to have a cup of coffee together," Sameera cruised in.

"It was a pleasure meeting you Mr. Gaurav and you too Ms. Vaishali," Aryan held Sameera's hand, "Shall we...lady."

They came.

They met.

They did it.

They left.

"Wooouuu! That was a spectacular performance," Sameera let out a thunderous laughter. "Did you see that look on his face…he was zapped…completely shaken up…he didn't know what hit him," Sameera said overwhelming with joy. Her voice had changed. It was sharper. Like a kid's voice. Like that of cute pink frock who had a fascinating left index finger.

"Best thing was every time he parted his lips to say something, either of us came in the way…I bet, we'll haunt him in future now," Aryan chuckled.

"How I wish I could video record the scene," Sameera was still laughing. All her healthy, glossy Oral-B teeth joined the occasion.

"Aryan thanks for what you did in there…and thanks for making this morning ssssSOO wonderful…I'll leave now…gotta meet Mahi and Rochelle…we've planned some shopping,"

Just a dry thanks? At least a kiss. A hug. Otherwise a peck on the cheek. Something man. In movies they always do.

"I'll drop you till auto?" Aryan asked.

Poor chap!

"Thanks Aryan, I'll manage. You have a good day," she said.

"You too... have a great day."

Wilbur Woods (Boy's pad)

11:00 am

Ron's Nokia N-95 rang. It was some demon laughing. He picked up the phone.

Ron: "Yo!"

Tiffany: "Hello…may I know who's on the line please."

Ron: "No…you may not."

Tiffany: "Sorry?"

Ron: "Very funny...first commit the sin and then say sorry…anyways…don't repeat that again…now tell me who you are and what do you want from me."

If there was an award for insanity, Ron was sure to bag it.

Tiffany: "I wanted to…"

Ron: "Waitttt… if it's about a cup of coffee…I am not available for the next... say …hmmmm...one week."

Tiffany: "No, it's not about a cup of coffee…I just wanted to speak to Mrigank…I believe he's sharing room with you…I am his friend Tiffany."

Ron: "TIFFANY! Why didn't you tell me earlier."

Tiffany: "You didn't allow me, your highness."

Ron: "Just a sec. I'll get your dopu-popu baby on the line."

"Maggy baby, tiffy for you," Ron shouted.

"Commingggg," Mrigank shouted back from the loo.

Ron: "I am sure you would like to know the name of the person who's humoring you."

Tiffany: "I am dying to know."

Ron: "I am Ronit...but you can call me Ron...it's an honor that I am conferring upon you...live up to it...my l'il experience says you have a sister or a friend who's as gorgeous as you are and that you would pass me her number so that I tell her this on my own."

Tiffany: "As soon as I find such person I'll let you know...I already have your number, sir."

Ron: "Lo, your boring buddy has come."

Mrigank took the communicator, did a silent "Thank you," and moved out.

Mrigank: "Tiffy, I hope he din *pakao* you much."

Tiffany: "He didn't."

Mrigank: "Last evening he spoke to Tina (Mrigank's sister) for ten minutes before he got me on the line."

Tiffany: "Hhmm." she let out a faint murmur. Unlike her usual chirpy, Don't tell me! It surely indicated something. Something not very encouraging.

Mrigank: "Whud happened honey?"

After three and a half year of tele-romance, you kind of start catching even the subtlest of hints...the stresses, the pauses, the intonations, the monosyllables, the 'Hhmm's .

Tiffany: "Don't honey-baby me; I don't wanna talk to you."

Why the hell did she call then?

Mrigank: "My guchu-puchu baby is angry...I m sorry my bachcha...I'll get the sim today...in fact within an hour."

Tiffany: "You said that yester noon. I kept on waiting. You had all the time in the world. If you wanted you could've called me from your roomie's cell but you didn't. I believe your priorities have changed. Remember how you used to make things happen earlier. You aren't my same sweet Maggy anymore. You don't miss me anymore. You've changed."

Mrigank: "Hey! No! Of course I do miss you…and you know that...and I haven't changed...it's just that I missed out on it. I am saying I am sorry."

Tiffany: "In IIT you are always busy with your viva and projects...I thought you'll take some time out for me in Delhi but..."

Mrigank: "Sorry yaar...please na."

Tiffany: "Maggy tell me is there somebody else? For the last few days you've been constantly ignoring me."

Mrigank: "Tiffany what's wrong with you. Why you saying all these things?"

Tiffany: "What's wrong with me? What's wrong with youuu?"

Mrigank: "You called me to fight?"

Tiffany: "I called you to tell you that from now onwards don't bother to call me."

Mrigank: "What the fuck is wrong with you?"

Tiffany: "What did you say? Say that again."

Mrigank: "No I didn't say anything. I mean, I didn't mean it. Sorry for using that word."

Tiffany: "Why you doing this?"

Mrigank: "Doing what?"

Tiffany: "This whole business of ignoring me and then pretending as if nothing has happened. Why aren't you telling me if there's another woman that you are interested in."

Mrigank: "Tiffany I think you are in a very foul mood and I am not enjoying this conversation, so I better hang up."

Tiffany: "Ok."

Mrigank slammed open the door, "I swear women are bloody impossible creatures."

"Not if you know their psyche. Though a painstaking process, but if you put a right mix of effort it yields handsome dividends, my friend," Ron said. He was surfing TV channels. After browsing a few stations, he stopped at F TV. Tall, bony, malnourished, grim-faced girls in tattered clothes paraded back and forth on a raised narrow lane with people on either side clapping for them.

"No Ron, I think girls enjoy this melodrama. She has to have this session once in ten days, else her metabolic process starts rebelling. Sometimes you just want to be with yourself. But she never understands it," he punched in air. Ron pressed the mute button so that he could hear the complaining customer better. "Love stings, you see," he said.

"Actually! Love sucks sometimes! She complains that I don't give her the same attention that I used to, in our first few weeks? DAMMIT! Why doesn't she understand that when a relation is in its formative stage, we are curious and enthused to know most about the new person? It's human nature. It's like buying a new cell," he raised Ron's N-95 up in the air, "You want to know all the features therefore you devote a lot of time in the first few days."

"So, she's like a cellular phone for you huh?" Ron took back the cell.

"No, It's not that."

"I know you didn't mean that, I was just pulling your heavy leg. I'll tell you something. Pay all your attention to this, It might be one of the best lessons you ever got," Ron cleared his throat.

Maggy lent him all his attention. Ron had this knack of stealing the limelight and focusing it on himself.

"Let's talk about Mrigank as a person," Ron signaled him to sit down.

"Mrigank as in me?" he said sitting on the settee.

"Yeah. Mrigank as in you."

"Interesting."

"If you understand this, you'll understand yourself and Tiffany better, so listen carefully," the *guru* built the foreplay.

"I am all ears."

"Mrigank is a mix of THREE person put together," he said hoisting his index, middle and ring finger in the air. He wagged the raised fingers for effect. "ONE..." he shook his index finger, "...the actual Mrigank. How old are you?"

"Twenty three."

"One the 23- year- old Mrigank. TWO," he shook his middle finger, "the four-year-old Tiffany's Mrigank."

"Tiffany's Mrigank?"

"The actual Mrigank must have changed a lot in the last four year in order to fit in as Tiffany's lover," he explained, "I hope you are getting what I am saying."

"Yeah...kind of."

"And THREE," he smiled, "The Mrigank who is a MAN and men we know are from Mars. Therefore, if Tiffany has to understand why Mrigank does whatever he does or why he behaves in a certain way, she has to understand that he is three-in-one—the actual Mrigank, Tiffany's lover and the man. And the most confusing part is that when a situation is thrown in Mrigank's path he might behave in any of the three forms," he pulsated the three fingers again, "The same funda holds good for women. If you can understand this and if you can make your partner understand this, you guys'll be happier couple," the *guru* ended his sermon and went back to the fashion parade.

Mrigank grinned. He could sell this three-in-one concept to his lady and earn some Bownie points. And perhaps, some peace too.

11:30 am

Aryan entered the room.

"Maggy look who's come...the LOVER BOY," Ron announced.

"Dude, how did it go?...*chak diye phatte*," Maggy threw the novel that he was reading and got up from the bed.

Aryan presented a spoken account of his date. Act by act. Scene by scene.

"What's that in your hand?" Maggy pointed toward the sachet that Aryan was carrying.

"Nothing...just a perfume."

"Ohhh!...gift and all haan."

"Nouu, I bought it."

"Perfume!" Ron switched off the television, "I hope she didn't tick you off for bad smell?"

Mrigank opened the sachet, "Elle YSL!...this is supposed to be ladies perfume?"

"So the lover boy bought a gift for the MICA girl?" Ron teased.

"No, I bought it for myself."

"For YOURSELF!" Ron screamed, "Aryan, I hope your tendencies..."

"I don't want her fragrance to ever leave my senses, so I bought the perfume she uses," hc literally dropped on the chair, "Now, whenever I want her near me, all I need to do is spray a light pritzer from this bottle. At least her fragrance is mine...forever," he closed his eyes and sniffed the perfume.

"Crazy bugger," Ron said.

Now I understand what Bryan Adams meant when he sang-

When you love someone, you do anything,
you do all crazy things, that you can't explain.
You shoot the moon, put out the sun,
when you love someone.
You deny a truth, believe a lie,
every time that you believe that you can really fly.
Your lonely nights have just begun,
when you love someone.

"Ron lend me your cell. I need to call Tiffany right now," Mrigank extended his palm. Mrigank perhaps wanted a puff of Tiffany's voice.

"What happened?"

"I agree she gets unreasonable sometimes, but that's only because she loves me so much. I need to tell her how much I love her...love is divine, man."

"Crazy fuckers...both of you."

The crazy fucker went out with Ron's mobile to reason out with her sometimes unreasonable, divined love.

"Aryan how about meeting Sameera again?" Ron asked for Aryan's cell.

Aryan passed on his cell, "Anytime." Corner of his lips moved.

Ron dialed Mahi's number.

Ron: "Hey gorgeous,"

Mahi: "Yess!... gorgeous speaking."

Ron: "Gorgeous…It's handsome this end."

Mahi: "Rounnnnnn! So you managed my number haan."

Ron: "Yeah…Salsa classes…during break…you forgot your cell on the table. I am sure you left it for me."

Mahi: "You are one hell of an opportunist, Ron."

Ron: "Actually I called you to tell that I just conceived."

Mahi: "You conceived." She laughed.

Ron: "Yeah…I conceived a pregnant and an unhatched plan."

Mahi: "Wow that's news. When's the delivery."

Ron: "Today. Right now. All three of you are invited. Let's meet up. Tea, milk, coffee whatever you say, wherever you say."

Mahi: "But..."

Ron: "I know what you'll say. Look I don't mind you paying the bill. I don't believe in boys-only-to-pay funda."

Mahi: "I am with Rochelle and Sameera..."

Ron: "I know that. Just tell me the venue and time."

Mahi: "Hang on...lemme ask them."

"She's asking," Ron whispered to Aryan, who was impatiently trying to overhear the conversation.

Mahi: "Hello...Ron, we'll take another hour or so you guys come by around one-ish. Café Coffee Day, Connaught Place."

Ron: "We'll be there."

"Guys slide in your skirts and tops, we are going to CCD," Ron announced.

"Nowwww! Nouuu!" Maggy launched himself onto the bed.

"Yesssss! get up and move your heavy luggage," Ron smacked Mrigank's butt.

"Maggy just thirty-six hours left for this free fun and frolic time...Comm-mon."

"N-o-t r-i-g-h-t n-o-w," he strangled a deluxe yawn.

"Not even for our lover boy. Sameera's gonna be there. Moreover CCD, CP has good crowd, dude. Come on now, get ready."

Mrigank budged his baggage. Slightly.

"When I come back from the loo, I'd better be impressed," Ron snapped his fingers and went to the loo. Ron always had his way with others. His method of persuasion ranged from the democratic to the autocratic. Predominantly autocratic.

Café Coffee Day, CP

Around one-ish

"Where's the gang coming from?" Mrigank asked the girls; his mouth stuffed with Black Forest *gâteau*, theirs with ice cream. Each had a cone in their hand which they had picked up from the ice-cream shop bang opposite CCD.

"Went shopping, thought we should make our wardrobe look a little respectable ...how's this looking," Mahi struck a pose. She displayed the so-called newly bought jeans that she was wearing. The tailor it seemed had attempted some poetry on the jeans.

Some denim was missing on the knees and thighs. There were few orphaned pieces of thread hanging around aimlessly from those missing parts. The faded look narrated stories of merciless usage of the piece of cloth. At least, five years. It wasn't easy to believe that it was a recently purchased garment.

"Cool!...how much for?" Mrigank asked.

COOL??? Coz it allowed cool breeze to pass in?

"Fifteen grand," she said.

"FIFTEEN grrranddd!" Mrigank spilled the coffee on his corduroy trouser.

"Fifteen grand... Maggy must've spent on all the jeans he's bought in his entire life time till date... No, Maggy?" Ron quickly handed him some paper napkins.

"Even less!' Maggy quipped, furiously dabbing away the coffee that had made its way to his skin through the velvety ribs of the fabric. The mark wasn't visible since it was a dark shade.

"Mahi what does your dad do?" Aryan asked. Fifteen thousand Indian rupees on a pair of jeans which wasn't even complete (around a quarter of the cloth was missing) surely meant that Mr.Dad didn't hold money in very high regard.

"My mother owns four hotels and five nightclubs in Calcutta's prime locations ...and she loves me a lot...do you still wanna know what my father does?"

"Royal goose with rich feathers, haan," he said. While he spoke to Mahi his eyes strolled to a crumb of ice-cream that rested on the tip of Sameera's sharp nose. Aryan touched his own nose with his thumb to tell Sameera about the impudent ice-cream. She did a silent, "Oh!" and wiped it off.

"Mahi is that a question?" Ron pointed at Mahi's emerald green georgette top that had a big GUESS written on it.

"You are such a sicko, Ron" Rochelle said. Ron didn't mind her words. He was too busy admiring her plum red, dangerously low-necklined outfit. Rochelle's sense of dressing was relatively bold for the average Indian male's eyes. Luckier, actually!

"No Ron...It's the name of the brand. You guessed it wrong," the GUESS girl replied.

"I'd still like to know the answer."

Mahi answered in sign language. Middle Finger language.

The two-storeyed-café was largely occupied by young singles. Filtered violet décor light and warm red furnishing regulated the color scheme of the place.

"How's life in IIMB, Mahi?" Aryan asked. In the background he could see illuminated red square danglers with the Café Coffee Day insignia embossed in a white Slurry font.

"Oh it's pretty hectic...PUNISHING," she knit her brows. Her brows arched like the green stroke over 'e' of café on the hanging red squares.

"You aren't enjoying there it seems."

"My mother wanted me to be an IIM grad so I went for it. She's more than happy and that's what matters to me. Parents take care of you when you are a kid and then when you grow up you take care of them. That's how it goes," she shrugged her petite shoulders that were carrying the strappy GUESS top.

"Mahi, gone are the days when somebody drew a line and you had to walk on it," Sameera made her long fingers walk on the table, "Today you make your own space. When we try to fit ourselves into patterns to which we do not conform, we suffocate," she said. Aryan nodded his head in agreement. There was another reason why he was nodding his head. He had finally found out the exact shade of Sameera's eyes. He had even named the pair. Krazy kittens.

"And an even bigger quandary is the near impossibility of fooling what can't be fooled," Ron arranged his chair to come close to Mahi, "Look at the irony. You take pride in saying that you made your mom happy by doing what she told you to do but does your mom take equal pride in telling her friends that her daughter is genuinely happy doing what she's doing? If the answer is no, have you really taken care of her?"

Mahi too shifted her chair closer to Ron, "Ron, what matters is status and big bucks. The entirety of business wisdom is that business succeeds because of high revenue and falls because of low revenue. Cash flow is king. The same rule applies to our lives. An IIM stamp will ensure such flow in my life."

"Oh I am a big fan of money so don't give me that crap but you know what...I am a bigger fan of myself. I do things that I love to do or I don't do them at all," Ron said. He had subtly channelized the direction of the conversation to himself.

"That's because you are very SELFISH. You just think about your self."

"Paradoxically, the more I do what I love, the nearer I am to perfection. And the more perfect I am at what I do, the more helpful I am to others. Being selfish makes sense. Doesn't it?" he looked toward Rochelle and then toward Mahi. The same two, he was fantasizing about last night.

"Ron..."

"Moreover," he interrupted Mahi, "Article fifty one alpha...the forty second amendment...act nineteen seventy six of our constitution states that it shall be the duty of every citizen of India to strive towards excellence in all spheres of individual and collective activities."

"Fundamental duties?" Sameera prompted.

"That's right...the tenth fundamental duty. So you see I just do what a good citizen of this country should do. It's hardly being selfish," he cut a big piece of Black Forest with his spoon from Mrigank's plate.

Ron always had some recognized authority to back him up. Indian Penal Code, Reserve Bank of India... Election Commission. This time it was the Constitution. He had crammed dozen of such stuff to make him look knowledgeable.

"That's why you've changed three career options till now," Mahi sarcastically remarked. The whole conversation had taken on a new dimension. A bitter one. Ron had become the object of everyone's attention. But Ron always enjoyed this kind of attention. He enjoyed it when others around him waited for his answer. And he always took his own sweet time before replying. "I experiment with my life. I am on a hunt. I am finding myself every new day," he said, gobbling down the Black forest. His tone was still casual.

"George Bernard Shaw once said, 'It's not about finding yourself, it's about creating yourself'." The chat had become a debate. Each of the two wanted to win the point. Or let's say each wanted the other to shut up.

"Your George whatever Shaw didn't know that you gotta find yourself before you create yourself, else how would you know which was better? The one you created or the one you found," Ron released a roaring laughter.

Louder than his laughter was the sound of the wind that one of his body part (the south most member of the digestive system) emitted while he was laughing. It was loud enough for all six to hear. Though Ron felt accountable about the emission of the socially unacceptable sound, he feigned innocence. He knew that he was in a group and that anybody could have committed the act since all had the requisite equipment. He chose the benefit of doubt route to get himself out of a potentially embarrassing situation. He didn't let any peculiar expression stray across his face.

But...Murphy's law...

To his horror, Rochelle reacted, "*Chhieee*...who was that? Ron was it you?" Her hand passionately beating the air around her nose.

Five newly made friends.

Two of whom had started respecting Ron's theories about the opposite sex.

The other three, girls (all good looking). Plus a bright chance with one of them.

One small unintentional act.

And one big question- Ron was it you?

I, personally would never like to be in such a situation. Would you? I bet, you wouldn't.

"Noouuu!" came an obvious answer. Ron could have admitted to a murder but not this. Especially when he had just impressed the gang with his knowledge and rotated GB Shaw's philosophy upside down. "But why would it be only me?" he snarled.

"I am VERY sure it's you," Rochelle reaffirmed her faith. The others didn't say anything but it appeared as if they too knew who the culprit was.

They say if a daring act has got you into the trouble then only a more daring one can get you out of it. Ron followed the rule. He decided to play cool about the whole thing, "You are actually right…it was me. My stomach been playing pingie-pingie pong-pong round my ass since morning. It had to happen. Natural phenomenon you see." he said, grinning away to glory.

"Can't you exercise some control over your natural phenomenon…you are disgusting, I tell you…an uncivilized arsehole you are," Rochelle made the ugliest face that she was capable of. Even the ugliest of faces that good looking girls make can easily earn nine out of ten.

"I am or...I have?" he laughed. Mrigank and Aryan too burst with laughter.

"See...still no shame. You are such a shameless creature. Ron you better stick a tape or shove a cork there when you move out in public," she changed her seat to avoid the killing (smelling) zone.

"It was just a harmless audible gas. Why you making such a fuss, sweet heart?"

"Because it offended my delicate nasal passages, you piggo," Rochelle's over reaction was justified because she was sitting just beside Ron and as she'd bent sideways to pick her fallen hanky, Ron's natural phenomenon occurred.

Mahi slipped her arm around her waist, "Roche relax yaar."

"You are telling me to relax," the victim reacted.

"It was a biological mishap. It happens," Aryan tried to diffuse the situation.

"Why are we discussing all this guys, don't we have better things to talk about," Sameera said in irritation. Ron turned toward Sameera, "You only tell me, was there a need to make it public and embarrass me like this?"

"You've committed a crime and criminal should be exposed," the infuriated Rochelle retorted.

"What if I wouldn't have admitted? Would you've called Sherlock Holmes to find out?" he leered. Everybody laughed.

"Ron, leave her and look to your right," Maggy pulled his chin to show him a group of girls, who were sitting on the other flank.

In the mean time, the waiter came to take the order. Mahi placed the order on everybody's behalf except Ron's who chose to order for himself, "Can I have one of them on a bowl," Ron showed the waiter what Maggy had shown him.

"Sorry sir, they're not on the menu," the waiter smiled.

"Then, I'll manage with a traditional vanilla scoop with light strawberry drizzle and a heavy chocolate shower and...when you are done with it sprinkle the entire thing with lotsa titsy-bitsy dry nuts."

"In 10 minutes, sir," the waiter left.

"Guys I'll be back in a minute. I need to unload this dump somewhere," Ron got up from his chair and started massaging his tummy, "Rochelle, would you like to accompany me."

Few more college-going groups came in, so by the time Ron was back the place was packed with people whom Ron called good crowd.

"I am sure you missed me Rochelle," Ron made his entry.

"No not at all. Yeah…but Mahi was missing you," Rochelle teasingly said.

"*Arre*! why you dragging mmeeee into it?" Mahi slapped Rochelle's naked arm.

"Mahhhiiii…?"

Mahi blocked her ears with her fingers, "I can't hear anything."

"Ron did you see that new group?" Mrigank tugged at Ron's T-shirt.

"Which one?" Ron pulled out his chair and placed it between Mrigank and Aryan.

"The one behind you, on the left flank."

"Fuckin fuck," Ron's salivary gland leaked, "You see those watermelons on that chick? By Jove! They'll fall off any moment," Ron whispered in Mrigank's ear. He was talking about a large breasted girl in that group.

"They are enormous man," Maggy whispered back.

"Aryan did you see them?" Ron murmured, "They alone are enough to nourish your entire battalion."

"Ssssshhhh," Aryan pressed Ron's palm.

"That's fine we've already heard that," Mahi said nibbling the Chocó pie.

"I don't understand why all guys have such cheap mentality," Rochelle remarked.

"What cheap mentality?" Ron said.

"Whenever you people see a girl your criminal eyeballs aim at only two things- breasts and butt."

"That's because they are always covered. You stop wearing any thing on top of them, we'll stop staring at them," Ron high-fived Mrigank.

"Ha ha ha how funny."

"No," Mrigank voiced, "I feel it's because somehow the society has over-romanticized this whole issue and has fed us with the idea that it's wrong to see them and talk about them therefore the temptation to do the forbidden."

"There's another angle to it," Aryan said, meditatively.

"Oh...! So you also have a theory now?" Mahi remarked. Sameera imperceptibly shifted in her seat. Her body language conveyed that she was interested in knowing what Aryan had to say. Aryan noticed it.

"Do you agree, all of us feel at ease and have a sense of bonding with our homes. For that matter any place where we've stayed for a long time. Basically our personal four walls?" Aryan asked Rochelle. "Yeah we do…that's human but what..."

"Sssshhhhh! Hold on," Aryan shushed her, "Now tell me, which position you find most comfortable when you sleep?"

"Aaaa...hmmmm...when I am sleeping on one of my sides."

"That's by far the most common, the most familiar position to a human being. Most of us, when we are in pain, suffering or when we are thinking about some smile-inducing memory or simply when we want to draw comfort we fold our knees, close in our body and sleep on our sides—the foetal position basically. We are used to sleeping that way. We've stayed in that position for more or less nine months in our mother's womb."

"What's your point here?" Sameera asked, curiously.

"The point is that breasts feed us and hips bear us, so sub-consciously our eyeballs tend to get attracted to these places like we get attracted to our homes and the foetal position of sleeping. The point is that we sub consciously know these two parts so very well…perhaps, therefore the attraction."

"Wow! I feel so light today…" Ron started flapping both his arms, "...so guiltless. I always thought there was something wrong with me.

I used to feel like a sinner."

"You ARE a sinner," Rochelle said.

"Guys, I feel girls are feeling bad that we are staring at other girls," Ron said moving his neck like a duck.

"Oh please," Mahi said.

"You know what Ron it's very easy to stare from far and pass comments. Why don't you go and talk to her and offer her a cup of coffee," Rochelle winked at Mahi.

"That's no big deal."

"Right then, I'll give you a big deal. Do you see that girl beside your watermelons?" Mahi asked.

"The one in green."

"No, the one next to her."

"The blue *dupatta*."

"Yes, that cute kitten. You have to go, talk to her and get her phone number."

Ron started scratching his goatee.

"What happened, Mr. Confident? Calculating the numbers of sandals?" Rochelle said, aping his gestures. Ron bit one of his nails, "I am dreading that even if she wants to give her number, she might hesitate coz she's with her friends."

"Should I give you a smaller deal then?" Mahi said, teasingly.

"What are you saying Mahi? You don't know our Ron," Maggy too joined the ally.

"Ron don't listen to them. They are planning to set you up," Aryan threw his trap as well. None of them ever missed a chance to ambush Ron.

"What are the stakes?" the trapped prey mumbled.

"Whatever you say," Mahi, the challenger said.

"If I win, all of us go to Ecstasy (a lounge bar) tonight and each of you would have as many Tequila shots as the letters in my name. And Mahi you will pay the bill."

"That's a handsome bet...I am in."

Ron surveyed the situation, garnered all his little tricks in his mind and engineered a plan. He could see his target. The cute kitten in blue *dupatta* and her cellular phone.

"Guys gird your loins and girls strap yourselves tight. Sit back and watch me close this deal in few interesting minutes," Ron said and left for the mission.

"Dude, but how do you intend to get the number. Are you gonna rob her cell?" Maggy asked.

"Haven't really worked that part out yet," he turned back and winked.

It was a group of five girls. Ron concentrated his focus on the blue *dupatta* and the cellular phone that was kept on the table, though the Watermelons just beside her at times tempted him to go off on a different tangent.

"Girls, I hate to interrupt you like this but it's kind of important," Ron wriggled his space in the group, "May I talk to you for a minute please," he asked the cute kitten.

The girl immediately took on a defensive stance. The way a lot of girls do, when a stranger approaches them. Ron noticed her body movements which weren't very positive.

"Please don't mistake me for one of those road side Romeos. I am a married man," he issued a sweet smile, "Happily married...for the last four years now. Blessed with a son. I am here with my wife. She is sitting there on the last flank with her friends. The one in the green top," Ron pointed toward Mahi.

The defensive stance immediately underwent a change. It appeared more cordial.

Ron noted the change, "It might sound a little stupid but it's very important for me. My wife has an interview next month. In one of the five star hotels. She has applied for the post of a front desk manager and an attractive skin is a major criteria there. The problem is that she's not very confident about her skin. She's been admiring you for the last few minutes. She says that you have a skin to die for. She wanted to come herself but she's little shy kinda woman. Can you please help us out...just a few tips." Ronit made the most innocent face he could.

The rest of the girls started giggling and whispering among themselves.

"Thanks for the compliment but I'll suggest you consult one of the beauticians?" Blue *dupatta* said, smilingly.

"We tried but it doesn't seem to work. It'll just take you two minutes...please," he said.

"All this sounds so weird. I am no authority to..."

"Please."

"Okay! What kind of skin does she have? Oily, dry, normal or a combination type…" she threw the cushion on one of her friend who was making faces.

"Normal skin."

"That's good. Even I have normal skin. Tell her to use water with a little oil-type moisturizer, water-based cleanser and oil-free foundation and most importantly, she should keep her skin well-hydrated all the times."

While the girl was sharing her trade secrets, Ron casually slid his hand in the pocket of his trousers and gave a call from the cell that he had kept inside the pocket. The call was made on his other cell which he was carrying on his hand.

"Excuse me," Ron took his own call.

"Sure," the girl replied.

Ron started his act, "*Chacha ji namaskar…chacha ji can I call you after 5 minutes. I am in the mid of something important* …(some pause for effect)..*I'll note down the number later*…(pause again)…*Ok ok ok give it. Just one sec.*" he requested the girl, "Please note it down." The girl started searching her bag for a pen. Before she could react, Ron picked her cell from the table and signaled her to copy it on her mobile.

"*Haan chacha ji boliye...nine, eight, four, three, four, eight, zero, one, two, seven...three seven?...* It's not two seven it's three seven…the last two digits…*Thank you chacha ji...okay chacha ji.*"

Ron then took her cell and pretended to copy the number. In the interim he slyly pressed the call button on the girl's mobile. This number was his second mobile's number which he had kept on silence in his pocket. The one through which he made the call.

"Sorry, I pressed the wrong button. How do you delete the number?" Ron pretended while handing back her cell.

"No problem, I'll do it," she smiled.

Ron lingered on for some more time to make the scene look natural, "Thank you very much…sorry I didn't even ask your name."

"Vishakha."

"Thank You Vishakha…it was a pleasure meeting you…god bless you," Ron closed the deal.

Ron went back putting on a dejected expression. He quietly came and sat on the chair with his head down. "So Mr. Confident, how did the deal go?" Mahi assailed seeing the dispirited Ron. He slowly raised his head and very tenderly said, "The right question, honey, should have been where is Ecstasy and what time do we need to reach there? So I'll answer that first. It's in Greater Kailash-One. Be there by 9 o'clock and don't forget to bring enough cash."

"You got the number?" the confused Mahi asked.

"I just hate myself," Ron started his *nautanki*, "I don't wanna be presumptuous but there's this genius sitting inside this person I know...Ronit Kapoor. The guy is such a smooth operator. Imagine, he walks up to a bunch of girls...all strangers...speaks to them, charms them and in less than two minutes walks out with one of the girl's phone number and also her beauty secrets."

"Beauty secrets?" Rochelle said.

"Yeah things like what kind of skin she has and that she uses water-with-little-oil-type moisturizer, water-based cleanser and oil-free foundations. Actually Vishakha is very particular about keeping her skin well hydrated all the time...that's the reason she has such a clear and smooth skin."

"Her name is Vishakha?" Aryan said.

"That's right. Guys please ensure that media doesn't get a wind of this else it'll be on air. I hate being famous. I hate being on news."

"Where's the number?" Mahi asked.

"You guys can confirm whatever you need to," he said placing his cell in Mahi's palm, "Till then I'll go and take a lavish pee."

Later part of the Saturday afternoon was spent in R & R (rest and recoup). Mrigank engaged himself with a chick-lit novel he had picked up from Crossword. He also managed a SIM for himself and could finally speak to Tiffany from his own phone. They spoke for a good two hour. Mrigank was expressing himself so ardently on the corridor that Mahi literally had to shout from her room, "Guchi-puchi baby little softer, somebody is trying to sleep."

Aryan invested his time practicing Salsa. He had made up his mind to ask Sameera out to the dance at the Sunday gala night. Ron spent most of the time flirting with Vishakha (the blue dupatta in CCD) over the phone. Surprisingly, even after she came to know about the bet, she didn't react unfavorably. On the contrary she got impressed by Ron's courage and ingenuity. Blessed bugger!

Sameera spent her time on her Lenovo. She completed one of the chapters of her book. Mahi asked her rich mother to transfer some more money to her bank account. She then went with Sameera to draw some money from ATM booth for the evening's Tequila spree. Rochelle went to meet one of her aunts in Gurgaon and the rest of the evening, she spent on deciding what to wear.

Greater Kailash-1 (Ecstasy)
09:30 pm

Mahi dialed Ron's number.

Mahi: 'Hello.'

Ron: 'Just two more minutes.'

Mahi: 'Where the hell are you people? We've been waiting for more than half an hour now. Guys sometime show some chivalry.'

Ron: 'Whoa whoa whoa...my little fuming, furious rebellious girl calm down. Papa's almost reached. Got stuck in a choc-o-bloc jam. Some fuckin' bridge had collapsed. When did you guys reach?"

Mahi: 'If you guys aren't here in the next five minutes you can forget your Tequilas.'

Ron: 'You know how much I am aching to be there and see you beautiful. Just recite my name 50 times and we'll be there." Ron disconnected the phone.

Few facts need to be branded here before we move ahead.

Ron and his gang weren't stuck in any jam. They were with Natasha (remember their salsa instructor), in regards with the thousand bucks bet between Mrigank and Ron. Ron won.

Mahi and her gang hadn't been waiting for the time that Mahi had so vehemently claimed. They themselves were half an hour late but when they didn't find the boys around, they decided to exploit the situation.

Boys could still have reached in time but it was Ron's idea to make the girls wait for them. One of the laws propounded by Ron. No man should ever miss an opportunity to mount on a woman. Metaphorically.

And literally.

Ecstasy had a debauched sumptuousness about itself. The lounge bar housed two floors of rich red velvet tufted walls, double-sided leather chaise lounges, black glass chandeliers and subdued décor lighting. The accent was on personalized space. Little cocoon-shaped timber cubicles supplied privacy.

"Consiga la cerveza para la senorita," Sameera ordered Rochelle's drink.

"Maim?"

"Get beer for the lady," she transmuted it in a comprehensible tongue to the waiter. Her sparkling pearl-grey dress compensated for the muffled radiance inside the cubicle.

"Spanish! That's impressive," Mahi dolled up her newly done up wavy hair. Sameera smiled, "I am glad it's serving the purpose."

Classic lounge remixes and Indo-Western influenced vocals supplemented the already sinfully stimulating surrounding.

"Why is it that some people get everything they want in life without much effort and some though try real hard, get nothing?" Rochelle took a large draught from her Fosters pint. She had decided not to use beer glass.

"Who you talking about?" Sameera asked balancing her vodka as she leaned back on the bean bag.

"I am talking about myself and I am talking about Mahi. Look at Mahi. She's stinking rich, she's intelligent, she's got looks and she's in the IIMB, my dream school which she considers no big deal. Hhmnh…somebody ask me what a HUMONGOUS deal is IIM."

"Shall I freshen that up for you?" Mahi asked Rochelle.

"Sure, sweet heart," Rochelle said. Mahi asked the waiter to do the needful.

Three minutes for a pint was a good start.

"Sometimes, it's good to take a step back and see what you have,"

Sameera said munching cheese balls.

"Ok, here I go," Rochelle got up on her tottering feet. " I've taken a step back and now I can see what I have. You know what I see Sammy?...I see a BIG loser. A loser, who could hardly manage a 68% in boards so couldn't get an admission in a college of her choice. A loser, who failed almost all UPSC held exams and when she finally cleared one, she couldn't join coz her mother got seriously ill. A loser, who tried both CAT and GMAT, but could crack neither. Sammy all that I can see is a loser who's sick and tired of losing," she released herself back on the sofa.

"Coz I've studied history and it shows that if you persist long enough, something always happens...Winston Churchill. He wasn't wrong, Rochelle. Wheels of change are always in motion...something worthwhile always happens," Sameera comforted the self-pitying.

"Sammy is right, Rochelle. A sales slump is often followed by a sales boom. Something desirable always happens," the IIM girl raised her wine goblet.

"I know what'll happen. I'll lure a millionaire and marry him. Easy way out."

"What about Aryan? What about your impressing him with your multilingual skills...aamee tumake poshondo kori and all?" Mahi asked playfully.

"Arryannn! grow up, Mahi. He's just a crush. Time pass. Moreover, he's not interested in me."

"That's coz somebody else is busy mowing your lawn...no Sameera?" Mahi said narrowing her eyes.

"Why did you phrase it like that?" Sameera looped a strand of her hair around her ear. Even a simple gesture like pulling a strand of hair and placing it behind the ear can have such an appeasing effect. There's something about girls.

"You know that," Mahi said.

"It's not what you're thinking, Mahi. We had our reservations about each other about what we did on the stage and he wanted to make up for it...that's it."

"Mahi you are policing everybody around. What about you and Ron?" Rochelle threw a peanut on Mahi.

"Ron! I think I more than like him," she said ducking the projectile. The peanut missed Mahi and hit one of the staff. He was one of the five beefy Goliaths, who were scattered around the place to ensure that no eve teasing takes place. He was as black as his trousers and t-shirt. His biceps were bigger than Rochelle's thighs and it was difficult to tell, when his shoulders finished and neck began. Sameera called him a mobile mutton shop.

Rochelle offered a, "Oops...sorry," to the monster, who offered back a dull nod.

"Do you have any idea the degree of HELL Ron can bring down on you?" Sameera's open palms and stretched fingers supported the concern that her words carried.

"He's already done that, Sammy," Mahi spread her hands and dropped back her head on the bean bag.

"I have my serious reservations about him. He changes his mind every time the wind blows and a skirt flows past him."

"The kid gets brighter every time I see him. He's so spontaneous, so quick-witted, so smoooooth. I think I've found my rhythm."

"Ron's your rhythm! You are gloriously screwed, darling," Rochelle held Mahi's cheek and pulled it.

"Wow! Finally! I thought I'll die a virgin," Mahi laughed.

"Mahi, you seriously don't have any problem with other girls in his life?" Sameera asked.

"Problem with other girls! Sammy, she encourages him to pursue other girls. Didn't you see what she did in CCD? She provoked him to go for that blue dupatta," Rochelle spoke for Mahi.

"I feel all the women in his life have worked a lot on him. There's gone a lot of grooming into making him 'the Ron' that he is. So in a way I must thank them all," Mahi pulled two cushions from behind and put them on her lap. "I don't intend to change his playful nature. I like him that way. I believe that if you set your man free, his true self surfaces up and in the process if he comes out as a bastard he was always one and if he proves otherwise, you are a lucky woman," she winked.

"That means you yourself will show him an attractive girl and increase the chance of his getting spooked," Rochelle too pulled two cushions and wrapped her arms around them.

"I like to check out cute guys so why should I deprive him of this momentary pleasure. Remember Adam and the apple? Help him get the apple so that the temptation to get the forbidden fruit collapses."

"Revolutionary fundas," Rochelle vibrated her head, "I need another beer."

Boys joined in
10:00 pm

"Hey gang, whusz up? Chilling out with beer and all," Ron rapped his fist against Mahi's. Aryan too wanted to greet Sameera in a similar fashion but he contented himself with a boring, "Hi" from a distance.

"Whut happened to you? You look like a vandalized house," Mahi greeted Ron. Toussled hair, 48 hours-old shabby stubble, un-ironed tucked-out shirt, lousy slip-on and a loose cargo, kind of deserved that description and especially when it's put against Aryan's natty attire.

"Did you just throw a compliment at me?" Ron asked sweeping back his disheveled hair with his hand.

"Yeah! Why? Did I throw it hard? Did it hurt?"

"No! it's just that whenever I see you all I think of is BED and my appearance moulds itself accordingly. I think that's why the unmade bed looks or as you said the VANDALIZED house looks," Ron greeted her back.

"Guys Rochelle's getting hitched," Sameera butted in. She possibly perceived another of their regular squabble.

"Wow! Rochelle, you are getting married. A celebration in order then," Aryan tactically occupied a couch where from he could see Sameera without any hindrance.

"Who's the legend who accepted this martyrdom?" Ron asked taking a sip from Rochelle's pint. Mrigank giggled. Not even two days had passed since the group knew each other and Ron was brazenly sipping from Rochelle's glass without even a, "May I". And she didn't even mind it.

Some people have this quality to get inside our otherwise shielded private space and mess up the neat arrangement that we so haughtily boast about and the funny part is we let them do it.

"Hee hee hee hee...very funny." Rochelle pushed him to a side.

"No but seriously, who's he and what does he do?" Mrigank took a handful of cheese balls.

"Guys stop it. There's no body. Sameera was just teasing me."

"That's not fair. I thought we'll get to see a Christian wedding," Mrigank threw all the cheese balls inside his mouth. That was his way to show that he wasn't very happy with the news.

"Me too. I've never attended one. Just seen in movies," Aryan added.

"All white and fairytale like..." Mahi said.

"Yeah...lot of revelry, lot of wine flowing, dancing, the bride's maid, exchanging of vows, exchanging of rings..." Sameera said.

"Oh and that part where the bride throws the bouquet behind her." Mahi almost jumped with excitement. As if she was the one who was tasked to catch it.

"Rochelle by the way why is it done?" Mrigank's mouth all stuffed with cheese balls. Good that he kept his hand before his mouth while asking the question.

"It's believed that whoever catches the bouquet will be the next to get married."

"You know what's funny about the whole scene," Sameera turned her head toward Mrigank, "The same spinsters run in frenzy to catch the bouquet who just a couple of minutes ago professed marriage to be an outdated institution."

"That's true," Rochelle smiled.

While these nuptial specifics were being discussed, Aryan pampered himself with his regular abstract musing. This time it was a Christian wedding scene. Sameera's father was walking the bride down the aisle. Rochelle and Mahi were the bride's maids and Ron the best man. The priest, robed in a richly hued vestment was standing at the altar declaring- 'Do you Aryan Vyas take Sameera Sanyal to be your lawful wedded wife to have and to hold, to love and to cherish till death do you part? ('Yes I do'). With the power invested in me by the State of India, I now pronounce Aryan Vyas and Sameera Sanyal man and wife. Aryan you may now kiss the bride...'

"Aryan what'll you have?" Ron asked shaking the day-dreamer.

"Hhuhh?"

"What's your poison?"

"Vodka, lime cordial and onion pickle," the kiss deprived groom immediately expelled Ron from the position of best man. Couldn't he wait for few seconds. Worst man.

"Rochelle, what about Damien, no scene with him?" Mahi refilled her wine goblet.

"I broke up with him this morning."

"Whhhatt? He's the fourth guy in the row. I guess in the last eight months?"

"No! fifth guy in the last 6 months."

"Rochelle you are bad ya."

"It's not entirely my fault. They all appear so vibrant and interesting in the beginning and after some days they start boring you. Same PJ's, same compliments, same kinda gifts," Rochelle puckered her nose.

"Same faces," Ron prompted copying her expressions.

"Yeah...you can say that. Of late I've realized that men shouldn't be treated more than refundable delights."

Men, Refundable delights. Changing times!!!

Mrigank and Aryan just looked at each other. That's the best they could do. Probably they were intimidated by the crankiness with which Rochelle said those words.

"Break-ups are the in thing today. It's in fashion." Mahi said.

"But it's not the best thing to happen," Sameera's voice had an empathizing tone. Like one of those caring nurses, 'Don't worry baba ji, everything's gonna be all right.'

"But they still happen. I feel they are inevitable," Rochelle said.

"No! not at all," Mrigank shook his nut. "Not if two people are really in love with each other." Assertiveness in his tone.

"Not really, Maggy. I was in a relation for a good two years but we still broke up. You know why? Coz we couldn't handle each other's ego. Break-ups happen like that," Mahi snapped her fingers.

"Then it wouldn't have been love, probably just an admiration or a mere fondness OR…a strong infatuation," Maggy said. His head swayed with the music that had turned melodious.

"How can you say that Maggy? You don't even know what went on between them," Aryan butted in.

"I certainly don't know what went on between them but I know one thing for sure, which is that when two people are in love they don't break-up just like that," he imitated Mahi's action of snapping the fingers, "This I say coz I happen to complete four years myself with a hot-headed, egoistica, abusive but a fascinating person, Tiffany Samuel on twenty second March of the last month. We've fought, we've abused, we've attacked each other's ego but we didn't break up. You guys remember Archimedes' principle?"

"Hnnhhh?" Mahi was taken aback by the brusque mention of Archimedes amidst ego and break-ups. Rochelle sweetly lifted her hand, "I remember having read it in one of my physics classes in my school days. Something to do with the upthrust."

"I'll run it for you guys," the IIT'ian took a sip of water before giving a refresher class on Archimedes. "When a body is partially or wholly immersed in a fluid, it experiences an upthrust, which is equal to the weight of the fluid displaced by the object. Similarly, the upthrust that a 'reason for break-up' immersed in a relationship experiences is equal to the weight of the 'love between the two' displaced. In simpler terms, the reason for a break-up actually tells how much two people were in love with each other."

"Terrific correlation. It makes sense," Sameera endorsed the theory with raised eyebrows.

Though a little technical, Mrigank's analogy was approved by a round of applause. By all. He rewarded himself with another round of cheese balls.

Actually it made sense. Either you claim that you are in love or you don't, if you do, you better accommodate petty weaknesses of your partner. I'd like to borrow what Antonio Banderas said in one of his movies, 'No matter what the price is, you can't walk away from love.' I know, big words. But then, even love is not that small a deal.

Tequila binge
10:45 pm

"Ladies and gentlemen...boys and girls," Ron stood up, " I would demand all your scattered attention to these little jiggers laid down on the table before you," he pointed at the twelve tiny glasses (size of a peg measurer) that waiters had tidily arranged the table. "It offers me some tickling dollops and dudlums to present before you the legendary kick provider...None other than the Tequillla SHOT."

Dollops and dudlums?

What does that mean? God alone knows. I assume, even God wouldn't know it. Ron had the capacity to say anything just because it sounded nice and different.

None except Ron in the group had had Tequila before. He was aware of this fact.

"Before we devour this fluid, ladies and gentlemen, let's educate ourselves about it. Tequila is made from the sap of an agave, a plant that flowers only once in many years, so you see it's a rare commodity, quite like me. The name Tequila comes from a small town in Mexico where this plant is found..." An over curious Mrigank attempted to take a sip but was shooed away by a, "Put that glass down you over eager twin-legged dog."

"I was jusz..." growled the shunned dog.

"In order to fully appreciate this drink it's very important to follow the steps religiously."

"What steps?"

"The ones that'll be demonstrated to you now," Ron picked up a jigger, "Everybody please hold the jigger between your fore finger and thumb and the lime between your middle and ring finger and sprinkle a little salt on the back of your hand...perfect." He praised his apostles, who were religiously following the steps.

"And now, as I'll raise the toast, all of you lick the salt, pour the tequila down your throat and then quickly suck the lime...and then...just shut your eyes and allow the icy tang of this neat spirit cut you through and through in bits and pieces..." he shut his own for special effects.

They looked at each other with a mixed feeling of excitement and nervousness. Like that of a young boy who's about to steal money from his father's pocket. He's nervous that he might get caught and then get thrashed and at the same time excited that if he doesn't, what a treat it'll be. Cadbury and *Gol gappe* bonanza for the next few days.

"Now let's all of us thank the kind lord in heaven and not so kind Ronit on earth for the liquid merriment we are all about to have- Amen. For lust and thirst," Ron raised the toast and downed his first Tequila shot.

The lusty and thirsty shot was followed by other, a little reluctant and sober shots.

"Wwouuuu...it's pungent...but good," Mahi had another shot.

"Ron where the hell did you pick that knowledge about Tequila from. Read in some book or what?" the shaken up IIT'ian asked.

"I HATE books. Knowledge is caught not taught, dude. You've gotta move around, shake lot of hands, do a lot of dinners, meet interesting people, try new stuff."

"Yesss! he's right..." Aryan said recovering from the liquid kick, "Life is to be lived on the ground...in action...amidst people and not behind some papers and ink in solitude."

"I agree with most of what you said but books have their own charm. I just LLLLOVE books," Sameera said. Her tongue halted for a while before uttering the word 'love'.

"Me too. I can read and read and forget about everything in the world," Mrigank's chubby face lit up. "What sort of books do you read?" he asked Sameera.

"All kinds. Fiction, self help, leadership based, management based, autobiographies ...everything ya."

"What autobiographies have you read?"

"I've read Benjamin Franklin...I've read Herman Hesse, Adolph Hitler and Mahatma Gandhi," she smiled each time she named a luminary. As if they all were her own uncles. I believe, a smile invariably comes if one is answering something that one LLLLOVES.

"I just finished reading Gandhi, the story of my experiments with truth." Mrigank said.

"Guy had the guts, solid bloody guts," Aryan's displayed his fist, "Scrawny bugger but had the spunk."

"Yeah man," Mrigank shook his head in harmony.

"The grace with which he's confessed his own sins in his book is incredible," Sameera took a mouthful of *paneer tikka*, "In one of the chapters he mentions that even when his father was seriously ill and about to die he used to have sexual intercourse with his wife in spite of her being pregnant. Something that was against medical sciences, Hindu law and common sense."

"Don't tell me!" an amazed Rochelle said.

"She's right, Rochelle. He had the balls to pen it down in his autobiography knowing well that the entire nation looks up to him and almost worships him, " Mrigank contributed.

"I could have never admitted such a thing," she said.

"Guys let's dedicate this evening to Gandhi," Ron raised his glass.

"As in?"

"Let's experiment with truth. All of us have some dark secrets. Something that we fear to share. Something creepy, something immoral, something stupid. Let's get those gloomy suckers out of our closets and show them some light." Ron downed another shot.

"I am in," Mahi said.

Mrigank took his second Tequila shot, "Me too."

Alcohol gives you that kind of confidence, I tell you.

"But the rule is we don't judge each other after that," Rochelle said pouring the rare commodity down her oesophagus.

"Even if somebody does, hardly matters. We were strangers till yesterday and after some thirty odd hours we can again choose to continue being so." Aryan too downed another Mexican shot.

Two tequila shots and one Gandhi had done the magic.

"So I take it that everybody's game and everybody should take it that I shall be the show stopper. Let's begin anti-clockwise. Rochelle you first," Ron announced. Rochelle had to pay the price for being on the wrong side, sorry, right side of Ron.

A couch was selected (which they had named the 'confession- couch') for the assignment. They were to come one by one, sit on it and confess whatever they wished to.

The GT-instilled confidence brought the first sinner to the 'confession-couch' . (GT stands for Gandhi-Tequila). Five anxious lungs drew in and forced out, slow and deliberate breath in anticipation of what was to come from the sixth's vocal box.

"Guys I lied when I said I dumped all my boyfriends. Actually...they dumped me," the vocal box opened.

"Hhnnnhh?" Mahi reacted.

"But WHYYY?" a motherly Sameera voiced. Only a dumped person knows how another dumped feels.

"Coz I always turned them down when they wanted to sleep with me. I am one of those uncool girls who believe in love and commitment before getting into bed and they probably thought that just because I dress a little boldly and I fag and booze I might be getting laid left, right and center. Guys...I'm 25... and still a virgin."

"You're a VIRGIN?" Ron nearly yelled. Even the absolutely drunk and fat gentleman dancing on the other end of the floor heard it. He was as fat as Mr. Pathania's bank account and as fair as a firang. His trousers had failed to perform its duty since the LINE or shall I say the cleavage, that separated the left and the right of his buttocks could say, 'hi and hello' to the people around.

Ron always thought that Rochelle was an available, easy kinda girl. His 10 years proud experience with girls had fallen flat.

"I know it's hard to believe. People usually form an opinion about you based on the way you dress, the way you talk, the way you look but a person is much deeper and richer than just her physical appearances and most of the times we miss this fact. I like to celebrate my body. I love to look good. I am aware I have a figure many girls would die for. I know I look sexy when I wear short skirts and I know men drool and bang their heads on walls and pillars to have a second glimpse," Rochelle said.

Sameera smiled. It was a 'I agree' kinda smile.

"It's my life and I am happy to lead it this way and am not at all embarrassed that I am still a virgin," Rochelle concluded.

"Rochelle for me you are the coolest girl I've ever met. Guys, what do you say. Doesn't she deserve an ovation?" Mahi started clapping.

Others too put their hands together.

The revelation was no less than a kick in itself. And I surmise a harder one for Ron since he thought he could anytime raise his score.

Everything said and done, I didn't understand one thing. Why would a girl feel embarrassed to say that she's still a virgin? I thought it was a matter of pride.

Could be??? Changing times!!!

Second in line of fire was Sameera. More than anyone else Aryan was excited to hear Sameera's confession. He drew his head (since his sound perceiving organ was attached to it) near the confession-couch. He didn't want to miss out on anything.

Sameera looked around and then fastened her gaze at a particular point on the lacquered-finish carved center table. Not sure whether it was the chicken piece on the plate she was concentrating at or Mahi's Nokia N-95 or the fancy candle stand. While Sameera gathered her past, Aryan was thinking about the thoughts that were running in her mind. He always wanted to know what went on there.He wished there was a machine that could read Sameera's thoughts. Life could have been a lot better for him. Press the button, know what's in her mind and act correspondingly.

Her lips parted, ".Guys, please don't feel otherwise but there's nothing that is coming to my mind right now. Tequila effect, I guess," She displayed the empty jigger.

All that thinking and concentrating, just to say that nothing is coming to the mind. Not done.

"Sameera there must be something yaar. Even if it's stupid, nobody's gonna judge you for that," Mahi wheedled.

"Not that I can remember."

"That's not fair, Sameera," Mrigank cribbed.

"Come on, be a sport," Rochelle yanked her.

"Guys, stop pestering her. I feel it should be based on free will, else there's no fun," the knight came for his dame's rescue.

"Aryan is right. It should be based on free will," Ron, the creator of the concept put the stamp on Aryan's proposal.

All this time Aryan had been waiting for Sameera's turn. Two blissful reasons. One, of course the kinky thrill one gets, after knowing a secret about someone one is fond of. And two, he could directly stare at her face without bothering that he would get caught and without causing strain on his eyes as he had been for quite some time.

But the fact that he could help her, though in a very marginal way was a profitable bargain for him.

It was Aryan's turn next.

"Ammm...I've also...(he clears his throat) told a lie to all of you."

The respiratory organs again got dim-activated.

"Do you remember how the audience rose up from the seat, held and raised each other's hand and bowed before me during my speech. They made me look like a demi-god. Why do you think they did that?"

"They all were mesmerized by your extraordinary speech," Rochelle promptly replied.

"The content of the speech was too powerful for anybody to not be moved," Sameera added.

"Exactly...it was the content. The script basically, that got me to the second position and the same script supposedly is about to be published in Mr. Pathania's to be launched magazine. Guys, I lied when I said that the script is written by me. One of my seniors wrote it for me. I just styled it a lil bit and puked it out on the stage. I cheated on you people. Actually, I was enjoying the attention I was getting from all of you."

It was because of Aryan's enthralling speech that Sameera had probably agreed for the breakfast.

Aryan's confession was followed by a paranormal silence.

"Aryan I feel it's not just the script but the way one delivers it and everybody'll agree with me that you have an incredible way of putting across your views," Rochelle broke the silence.

"I just thought I'll feel better if I confess it."

Not everyone was convinced of what Rochelle said. Not at least, the third in merit, Sameera Sanyal. She looked reflective...pensive to be closer.

"Aryan I am impressed. I probably wouldn't have surrendered to such an attention seeking stuff," Mahi smiled.

"Aryan, but normally people who are good speakers are good writers too?" Mrigank said. His jaws busy chewing the goat. I mean the mutton.

"Not necessarily. I, for example can't write even a page for the love of anything. I can never imagine myself sitting down on a chair, thinking about a topic and seeing my thoughts crystallize into concrete words. That's not me. Ideas would never hit me if I make up my mind to write something. Even during my school days, Kabeer, my elder bro used to write essays for me. Yeah if you give me an extemporized topic and tell me to speak on it I might do a good job. I thrive on spontaneity and unpremeditated stuff."

"That means the message you sent me wasn't written by you?" Sameera said with a trace of contempt.

"Of course, it was written by him, Sameera. It took him half an hour to text that one bloody message. He literally racked his brains for that one." Ron replied on Aryan's behalf.

Mahi scratched her little cute nose as she colonized the hot seat, "Aryan if you remember, in CCD you had asked me what my father does and

I started bragging about my mother's wealth."

"Yeah."

"I actually didn't want you all to know who my father is," she paused for a moment and took a breath before she revealed, "My father is Mr. Ranvijay Pathania."

"Whhhhat?"

"Whhhhat?"

Five such "Whhhhats?" targeted Mr. Pathania's daughter.

"Yeah folks, the guy from Symbiosis who came first, Akshay Pathania is my brother. It's a long story. I'll cut it short. My parents were both classmates and toppers in a MBA school. Both from influential business families. After marriage, they decided to set up a new company. Both had different ideas and style to lead the company along with a massively puffed up ego. Soon their egos dominated their love and they decided to separate. With mutual agreement, Mr. Pathania decided to keep Akshay and I went to my mother. Today they are the biggest rivals in business and both of them are grooming their kids to continue their rivalry. That's why both of us are doing our MBA's. Akshay from Symbiosis and I from IIM."

That explained why Mahi considered her stay in IIMB as a duty and not a passion.

"Why don't you talk to Akshay and both of you together sort things out?" Aryan suggested.

"He is too arrogant and moreover he's shit scared of Mr. Pathania."

"Why don't you yourself do something?"

"I tried to talk to Mr. Pathania once and my mother found out. She created a big *tamasha*. She filed a false case against him. She fears that I also would leave her and go to him. After that incident I never tried anything."

natural death but till then let's pull together a lot of life in every moment of our times together. Lot of lives versus one death is a fair trade, ain't it? So we are busy doing that and have no time to bitch and bicker about it."

"Maggy, *tu toh sala apna bhi baap nikla*," Ron patted guchi-puchi baby's back.

"No doubt. You are one hell of a surprise, Maggy," Sameera said.

Rochelle was right to say that a person is much deeper and richer than just his physical appearances and that most of the time we miss this fact. Maggy and all this...I mean...totally unexpected! But I really liked that pulling together lot of life in every moment and lot of lives versus one death, a fair trade funda. It was thought provoking, man!

"Maggy, I've been thinking, in case if Ron marries Tiffany's daughter you'll be his father-in-law. *Baap* in a legal sense," Aryan said.

"This bastard will have to fight and kill me before reaching my daughter," the protective father challenged.

The showstopper modelled the ramp before taking the casting couch I mean, the confession-couch.

"I don't have many good friends and though it's just been two fuckin' days that I've known you buggers, I've kind of started liking you people and there's a fat possibility that some of you might become my best buddies. Therefore, I think you all should know that Ronit Kapoor, that's me..." he said, pointing all his fingers to the chest, "...is a BISEXUAL."

"Whoaaaat? You are kidding Ron?" Mahi furnished a hesitant smile.

"Fucker, you are trying to play garden ass with us," Aryan chucked a cushion at him.

"No I am not sweethearts," Ron said, grabbing the cushion. "But why are you both so stunned. Alexander the great was also a bisexual. He had a male lover named Haphaestion. Drew Barrymore, Calvin Klein, Angelina Jolie, Madonna, Marilyn Monroe, Lord Byron, David Bowie they all are bisexuals. Bisexuality is in the nature. Pygmy chimpanzee, Bottlenose dolphins, Humboldt penguins, gazelles, antelopes, bison, whiptail lizards they all are bisexuals. So what's so fuckin' astounding in me being one?" He sounded very convincing. Moreover they knew when he was joking and when he wasn't.

"You mean you've had sex with both men and women?" Mrigank's eyes didn't blink for some time.

"Just because you are bisexual doesn't necessarily mean you have to act on the attraction. Some have a preference of one gender over another, like I am more inclined towards women but yes, I've had sex with both the genders."

This disclosure had convincingly outran, outclassed, outshined and outstripped the rest of the confessions. Bisexual. Ron!!!

"That means you can get attracted towards me also," Mrigank teased.

"Never! I focus on appealing qualities of an individual, regardless of that person's gender and you have no appealing quality, fatso. Happy now. Yeah, if you talk about Aryan, I was attracted towards him; the way he talks, his wash- board belly, hairless back, chiseled thighs. But since his friendship was more dear to me, I repressed all my desires."

Two faces were worth seeing. Aryan's and Mahi's. Though for completely contradictory reasons.

"Aryan you are in danger buddy," Sameera said.

Indian Army had trained Aryan to fight and beat an assortment of dangers in different terrain and climatic conditions. This one didn't form part of the curriculum. He for once thought he wasn't adequately trained.

"Will you always be a bisexual?" Mahi investigated.

"I don't know. For some it's a temporary phase, for some a lifelong affair but bisexuals ARE capable of maintaining monogamous relationships."

"Your parents know about it?"

"No they don't and they don't need to."

"How many men have you had sex with?"

"Just one. He was a great sucker," Ron said.

"Ron nobody asked for details and Mahi please, stop probing his sex life." Sameera said.

"Is that man still in your life?" Mahi asked, ignoring Sameera. Mahi, never even in her silliest of dreams would have thought that she'll have to compete with a man to win another man.

"No! He left me coz he found me out with another woman. Anything else, anybody..... If there's nothing else let's get back to our evening and do what we came here to do. Don't forget you all have to have as many shots as letters in my name and we are still three counts behind," Ron called out for the waiter.

How could he be so cool after such a revelation?

Why shouldn't he? What's the big deal?

Sunday

Sunday morning
Wilbur Woods

A high-quality eleven hours powernap.

Some serious morning hangover following it . Well, quarter to twelve is not exactly morning.

And an even more serious realization of the yester night's Gandhi Tequila courage...

The confessions of the last night had changed the equations of the present morning in Wilbur Woods. Wow it rhymes! Confessions...equations.

The ease and comfort level among the gang had petered out. They moved around in the room scared of each other's judgmental eyes. A fear that somebody might squash their pressure points. Unknowingly. Or knowingly(Ron).

Aryan faced an added crisis. He felt awkward to move around bare-chested. And in his boxer shorts. Although Ron had clarified his intentions. Each avoided a direct eye contact with the other, until all gathered for brunch, where Aryan initiated the talk about the tainted equations. Thirty minutes of chat brought back the same crispness in their attitude. Talking it out, mostly helps. Furthermore, it helped bringing the group closer. There's a difference between sharing a secret under the influence of alcohol and sharing one without it.

One of the issues still managed to escape from the dining hall.

"Mahi, will you still...?" Sameera asked Mahi about Ron as they walked back to their room. Boys had already left for their den.

"I've been thinking 'bout it the whole morning," Mahi heaved a pending sigh, "I feel, I can't reject him outright for this one small...well, not small," she smiled,

"Whatever it is...I think...I'll give myself some time," she said nodding her head repetitively. It was as if, with every nod she was reassuring herself of the choice she had made.

"You sure about it?" Rochelle said. Mahi chucked a smile, "Why do I need to be sure and right all the time."

"Kudos for that...I'm with you Mahi," Sameera raised her thumb, "I remember when I was a kid I used to play doctor-doctor with my cousin sister. We had this plastic stethoscope with which we used to examine each other. I, most of the times wanted to be the patient. You know why?

"Why?"

"Because I used to love the feel of her hand and the instrument accidently brushing against my nipples. None of us are born knowing what's right or let's say 'accepted'. Innocence only knows pleasure and pleasure can come from any gender anything...animate or inanimate. I don't mean to say that Ron is innocent. NO WAY. What I mean is that none of us are born heterosexuals. All of us have some degree of homosexuality in us. In Ron's case it's little more. It's just a phase... that'll pass," she held Mahi's hand.

"I bet my left kidney on that. Shame on me if he gets attracted to any man now," the *Sati Savitri* in Mahi Banerjee voiced.

That kind of, resolved the escaped issue.

Boys' apartment

01:30 pm

"Guys do you realize it's our last day together. Tomorrow morning we'll be gone," Aryan said as he changed into his Calvin Klein shorts. Yes! You heard that right. Aryan had started wearing his shorts again. Among other things discussed during brunch, it was also decided (between Ron and Aryan) that Aryan should again start floating around bare chested and in shorts like he earlier used to.

"Oh gosh! same boring classes, books, labs, Mr. Kapadia...Mr. Kappaddiaa...nouuuuuu I don't want to gouuuuu ," Mrigank's face buried in the pillow and his hands and legs beating the mattress.

"Aryan you're bloody lucky; going on one month's leave," Ron said. Mrigank raised his heavy head from the crushed pillow, "One full month *ka chhutti*... Wow!...I miss my home."

"You aren't taking Sammy along with you," Ron said.

"I wish I could yaaarrr," Aryan hit his own chest, as if he was stabbing himself.

His phone beeped.

"Whoa! Talk of the angel and angel appears. Sameera's message," Aryan hopped.

Vanilla boy! how bout a round 2...

"GUYS, I am ON. She's called me for a round two...whoou!!"

"The magic is WORRR-kinggg," Mrigank said.

"No doubt...she'll become our *Bhabhi,*" Ron said.

after the first knock out round I decided not to take out my gloves...so anytime...

Haf n hour...centrl loby

roger!

"Aryan this time take her for a bike ride," Ron flung his limbs on the bean bag.

"Where would I get the bike from?"

"Will a Karizma do?"

"You have a Karizma?"

"No it's not mine. One of my friends has. But it's the first thing I'll buy as soon as I start earning."

"And wear your Gucci shades too. It looks really good on you," Mrigank picked up the sunglasses from the dressing table and ramp-walked wearing them.

"Take one of these," Ron pitched a packet toward Aryan.

"NOT AGAIN."

"No! it's not what you're thinking."

"Blank cards? What am I suppose to do with it?" Aryan asked. It was a packet of blank visiting cards.

"Write your name and permanent phone number in this card and while you're with her, secretly slip it inside her bag."

"Didn't get?"

"See Aryan, though you're doing pretty well with Sameera BUT in case if nothing works out between the two of you and tomorrow she forgets you. Then what?"

"Then what?"

"That's when this card will show it's magic. Imagine six months from now...things didn't work out, you are all sad and sulky and she's somewhere very far from you and THEN one fine day… while she's searching one of her misplaced papers or lip gloss or tampon, she accidently discovers this card with your name and number written on it. Her face will light up with a puzzled smile and to know all about it, she'll certainly call you and THERE (he clicked his fingers) will start your love story once again."

"Ron, that's too much of a coincidence." Mrigank said.

"Tell it to somebody else," Ron snapped, "It's a TRIED and TESTED tool, dude."

"I liked the idea," Aryan said cheerfully, "Coincidences do occur and there's no harm in preparing for something that…god forbid (Aryan crossed his fingers)…might happen. It's a fail-safe plan-B."

"What's a plan-B?" Mrigank asked.

"The main plan is called a plan-A and the alternative one is called a plan-B dumbo," Ron explained on Aryan's behalf.

"Hmmm…partially correct?" Aryan said.

"Why partially?"

"It's not plan-A and plan-B. There's a main plan and there's a plan-B. B is a short form for Bismarck…Otto Von Bismarck. He was a Prussian and a German statesman who always had a fool-proof alternate plan for every main plan."

"That's bloody news. I didn't know that," Ron said.

"I bet you wouldn't have."

A dash of blush…

A liberal layer of mascara…

And a figure-hugging, short, black Lycra dress that featured Sameera's arcs and bends quite flatteringly...

...was an agreeable combination that made Aryan's toughened muscles go malleable.

"*Arae dikhta nahin hai kya...andhe ho gaye ho... abhee abhee safai ki thi,*" the sweeper shouted out to Aryan, who had mistakenly messed up a part of the floor that was mopped by the sweeper.

"Sala, he's worried about the ground beneath my feet that he just swabbed. What about the one that just got swept?"

The molten-hot contours that were highlighted through her skin-embracing dress were actually to be blamed. The district magistrate should have issued orders for people to stay indoors; a sort of curfew should have been announced in order to avoid any other mishap.

"I thought it's better we meet right now," Sameera said. She was still five stairs far, "In the evening my mom and dad would be around so I'll be with them most of the time...won't be able to spend much time with you guys."

WITH YOU GUYS. '*Why does she have to add 'guys' when just 'with you' was fine?'*

"Auntee and uncle are coming. That's good news." he said.

Sameera sounded very excited to meet her parents. She was meeting them after six months. Aryan also wanted to meet these two people. He wanted to thank them for creating Sameera. For contributing the 46 chromosomes that constituted Sameera Sanyal. They had become the second most important mom and dad on the earth. And why not? Their one YES could assist him become the first emperor of the dynasty, that he wished to start (with the help of their daughter).

"So what ride today?" the shining teeth asked.

"Bicycle."

"BICYCLE?"

"A motor-driven bicycle," he said showing off the bike key chain. The sweeper while mopping the floor was trying to catch their conversation. AND a crafty glance at the black Lycra. He was a man after all.

"Aaahaan... hmmm... I like the idea though but... can we just go for a walk today? if that's ok with you... there's a park nearby." How could somebody deny a voice like that. Moreover, he realized that the dress that Sameera was wearing wasn't exactly a pillion-rider outfit so he kept Ron back in the pocket and strolled out for a walk with his lady in... black (today). He had hardly reached the door when he noticed that the sweeper had stopped scrubbing the floor and was literally following them. Actually following Sameera's buttocks. Gloriously globular buttocks. Aryan immediately changed his position and blocked the 'view', thought it was pretty difficult to block something so rounded with his rather leaner ones.

The smirk turned into a frown.

Aryan knew how to take revenge. Sweet revenge.

"Why you going that way?" Aryan asked.

"We are taking a short cut."

"Through the Golf Course?"

"Yes sir!"

"Lady, it's a Golf Course. They have RULES out there and moreover we are improperly dressed,"

"We won't go through the club house. We'll take a detour, through those screen of trees,"

"You mean..."

"Yyyesss!" Sameera blinked both her eyes, "Don't worry it's lunch hour and the teeing off time is three so nobody would be around." The idea of a screen of trees and nobody being around was far too tempting to decline. Circumnavigating the front gate they managed to enter the Golf Course without getting caught.

"Why are you taking off your shoes?" Aryan smiled in confusion.

"I can't resist this wet, soft putting green. I always wanted to walk bare foot on this grass. I remember I used to plead my dad but he never allowed me," Sameera said holding her long boots in one hand

and the Versace bag in the other. Seeing Sameera's bag, Aryan thought about Mr. Bismarck who was in his pocket dying to jump inside the bag. "Come, you can also take off your shoes." The expressions in her face, like that of the pink-frocked girl with the fascinating left index finger in the restaurant.

"No I am fine," the well groomed officer said. He knew about the sentiments that the owner shares with his grass in the putting green.

"You are remembered for the rules you break...one of your army generals once said," Sameera winked.

Aryan smiled and nodded, "American General...Douglas Mac Arthur."

Aryan had two reasons to take off his shoes.

The alluring wink of the lady in black.

And the verbal support of none other than the chief of staff of the American army, General Douglas himself.

The feel of a wet, well taken care, lush green grass on naked feet with a friendly sun on top was very much in competition with that of the rickshaw ride and the rejuvenating freshness that the cool breeze provided the other day. The wind though equally opportunist, couldn't avail much since the fabric of the dress was too stubborn to leave Sameera.

"So you read military leaders as well?" Aryan said. His jeans folded up till half his calf.

"I've read some of them," she replied, " Earlier I was big time into reading...I had this mini library sort of thing in my room but off late I am not able to devote much time so now I just read the selected ones, only the best sellers."

Aryan admired the two feet that walked beside his.

The feet.

So symmetrical.

So well treated.

So kissable.

After walking for some fifteen minutes, the four(feet) decided to take rest on a bench that was placed just beside the pathway.

"No boyfriends after Gaurav?" Aryan asked her offering a candy.

"Nou…not anymore. I think I've had a fair share of boyfriends," she put the candy in her mouth. Her cheeks and lips moved in and out as the candy travelled around inside her mouth, "Not that I've grown anti-men or something but I just feel that I've no inclination or will for any kinda relationship now. I guess, I've lost that feeling. Plus I'm too busy with my book and my MBA thing…How about you? You must be having lot of girlfriends," her voice though fuzzy with the moving object inside her mouth, sounded cute.

"Girlfriend! Never had even a single one…" Aryan smiled. *'And I think never will be able to have one.'*

"Can't believe it. You think I'm gonna buy that story." Her cheeks looked like a punctured bicycle tube, every time she sucked the candy.

"I swear I'm not ly..."

Sameera's phone rang.

"Excuse me…hey bro,…" she went away to take the call. Aryan taking advantage of the situation, quietly slipped the plan-B card inside the innermost pocket of Sameera's bag, that was lying on the bench along with her boots.

Sameera returned in a while, "Bro had called…he said that dad wanted to talk to me. Tried his number but it's not connecting… connectivity is a little poor out here. Shall we move on to the road," she said putting on her shoes.

"Yeah sure. There's a gate out there."

"Oops!" the strap of her wrist watch broke. The hinged pin in the buckle had come out. Aryan reacted briskly and mended the watch

Mending it was fine but the fun started when he tried to strap it back on her wrist. It was one of those fancy designer watches with sophisticated buckle systems. His army brain tried all possible permutations and combinations but it only spoiled the impression that he had created earlier by fixing the strap right.

"*Dhattt buddhu,* not like this," Sameera laughed. It was one of her characteristic, heartfelt laughs that used to cause one little depression on either cheek. Every time that he looked at the depression, he felt a bang in his gut. A nasty one.

Aryan didn't mind being called a *buddhu.* Anything for such laughter. And for those depressions.

"Still unreachable," Sameera said fidgeting with her cell. She had to raise her volume to beat the noise owing to the traffic.

"Try it once we reach the park…sometimes they have this problem."

"Just a sec. I'll message him." While she typed the text with her right hand, her left palm leaned against a movie poster that was pasted on the boundary wall of the Golf Course. It was one of those capital A in a circle type of movies- *mera tota teri maina.*

She was so engrossed with her cell that she didn't realize that she had placed her palm on the underpants (animal print type) of the semi-naked actor in the poster. In between she raised her eyes once when she noticed Aryan's sheepish grin.

"Wwhautt?" she asked.

"I didn't know you had a fancy for leopard print briefs?" the smiling Aryan signaled her with his eyebrows. She pulled back her hand at once. Her face grew pink.

"Well it brings out my animal instinct," the flushed face laughed.

Though it was a Sunday, the traffic was still bad.

"Why did you do that?" Sameera raised her brow.

"Do what?"

"You were walking on my left and you suddenly came onto my right side?"

"Lady is supposed to be on the safer side of the traffic," Aryan's eyes read a tailboard of a truck, *'jinhe jaldi thi... voh chale gaye.'*

"Hmmm...means and ways to impress a girl,"

"Not exactly," Aryan settled his Gucci shades.

"Not exactly. I've noticed, you always get vertical when girls walk in, you offer them a chair, you open doors for them. What do you call that?"

"Sameera, one of the established rules of a civilized society is that women deserve special consideration and that a man should do his teeny bit to make her comfortable. It's to tell her that you respect her and not to create some impression," Aryan's fiery temperament flared up.

"Hey chill...I was just pulling your leg...I like you because of these chivalrous gestures that you display. They are so hard to find these days."

'*Did she say I like you? I bet she did. Aryan, you are doing bloody good...keep the ball rolling...*'

Sameera's phone rang again.

"Oh! It's dad's...excuse me." She spoke to her dad for five-six minutes.

"Aryan, one little problem. I gotta leave right now."

'*Leave right now...why?...I had just started doing good...please don't go.*'

"Is everything fine?" Aryan asked.

"Yeah everything is fine. Dad require some phone numbers of our relatives so I'll have to go to the room; they are in my diary plus a few other important things he's asked me to coordinate. Actually he has a flight to catch in half an hour and it's very important for him to talk to them before he boards the plane. He's been trying my number for the past half an hour. Aryan, I am really sorry ya. I hate to do this."

'*I hate your dad.*'

"That's perfectly ok with me. First things first," Aryan smiled.

"Thanks for being so understanding."

"How you going back?"

"I'll take an auto," she called for an auto.

"I'll drop you."

"Thanks...I'll manage...It'll not take more than ten minutes. I'll catch you in the evening," she sat in the auto, "Oh I forgot, my dad wants to meet you. See you in the evening...*chalo bhaiya*," the auto left.

'*Her dad wants to meet me. Why?...Is it that he wants to check me out as a potential son-in-law?...so early, not possible...as it is, Sameera has no inclination or will for any kinda relationship...could be, he wants to warn me for coming near his daughter?...dads are like that...what could it be?*' the man on tenterhooks mulled.

Boys' apartment

05:00 pm

"*Khusaamdeed...Khusaamdeed...woh aaye hamari mehfil mein...hum kabhi unhe aur kabhi unke chehre ke tabassumae noor ko dekhte hain,*" Mrigank welcomed Aryan as he entered the room.

"*Wah wah! shubhaan allah! shubhaan allah!*" Aryan reciprocated the warm reception.

"*Zanabae aala*...three and a half hours...must have been a rocking-shocking date?"

"No ya, it wasn't even half an hour," Aryan puckered his brow and nose.

"Aaayen?" Maggy's face all distorted.

"Yeah! she had to leave. Some important thing came up. After she left, I went to meet Natasha."

"NATASHA?"

"For that dance thing."

"Oh! Yes, yes, yes I remember."

If you remember, just before the tequila bender, boys had gone to meet Natasha rregarding the thousand rupees bet. That's where Aryan persuaded Natasha for a two hours Salsa cum Tango session at her studio.

"Where's Ron?" Aryan looked around.

"Gone for a pee. He also just arrived. I thought you guys came together."

"No we didn't. Where had HE gone?"

"I believe, he'd gone to meet Vishakha."

"Vishakha! that CCD girl. She agreed to meet him?"

"Why do you doubt?" Ron said zipping himself.

"Hey buddy."

"Actually I wanted Upasana's number so I had to ask her for coffee."

"Who's Upasana now?" Aryan asked.

"Water Melons."

"Ffffuckkk," Mrigank pulled his own hair, "Ron, at least spare somebody ya."

"Byyyy ggggggod." Aryan swore.

"How was your date, lover boy?" Ron said nibbling on an apple.

Aryan narrated the half an hour. Minute by minute.

"Hmmm…interesting," Ron said scratching his stubble, "If her dad wants to meet you, it's because she must have projected you in a certain way. And it's obvious that the projection is a positive one. All you need to concentrate on right now is her dad. Your first encounter with him will decide about the rest of your encounters with Sameera, therefore start preparing yourself,"

"Preparing?"

"Everything...your handshake…your opening sentence…how you'll greet him…the questions he might ask you…if need be, check out Sameera's Orkut profile...might be you get something about her dad there."

"All this?"

"You have half an hour to prepare yourself. We meet after half an hour. Maggy, you'll act as Sameera's dad and I'll be observing you both to note down the inadequacies. Then we'll sit down to work on finer points. Are we clear."

"Crystal."

"Sparklingly."

'*Hello sir…no…good evening sir…no…good evening uncle…no…Namaste uncle…no…*,' A confused Indian male stood before the mirror.

Sunday gala night

08:30 pm

Mr. Pathania had spruced up Wilbur Woods from head to toe to meet and exceed the tastes and expectations of the invited guests. He had created a true carnival like atmosphere.

It was a perfect example of regal festivity.

Two life-size, black, stony Buddhas guarded the entrance of the grandiose foyer which boasted of shimmering salvers of crystals stacked from floor to ceiling.

A large pool with powdery white and sparkling blue tiles glittered with floating candles and sunflowers. Bordered by reflective translucent glass, the pool presented a brilliant focal point in the center of the lawn.

A majestic stage for live acts, a giant 360 degrees plasma screen on both the sides of the stage, little cubbyholes made of transparent drapery and leather settee, fortune tellers and tarot card readers; All catered for an uninhibited fun under the stars.

It was nothing short of a magical night.

Celebrities, editors, publishers, the insiders of the book world, big businessmen, the 12 finalists, their families and friends and a lot of other college going enthusiasts formed part of the dazzling evening.

"Did you see yourself in the mirror before you moved out?" Ron asked Rochelle. More than his words, his rotten expressions scared her.

"Yeah I did. Why? What happened?" Any girl would, for once get shaken up with a question like that and especially if one has taken two hours to deck oneself up.

Ron didn't even bother to answer her. He turned toward Aryan and Maggy and said, "I told you guys. See, I wasn't wrong." Both jiggled their head in agreement though they had no clue what he was talking about. They just knew he was up to something.

"Guys what's going on? Ron tell me what is it?" the puzzled and self-conscious Rochelle requested.

"That reminds me...have you made the payment?" Ron came up with the second one.

"What payment now?" Rochelle asked innocently.

"Payment for the mirror that cracked in your room when you stood before it."

Bbboooom!! The wacky blast of Ron's compliment!

Rochelle chuckled, "You are funny Ron…thank you...iffffff it was a compliment." Rochelle's daring yellow mini-skirt and equally courageous black vest had made its impact.

"That was wonderfully presented," Mahi clapped, " Especially, by a man who wears torn trousers for gala evenings." She had been watching the show and the showman's torn trousers for quite some time.

"TORN?" Ron inspected his trousers from all the approaches.

"See for yourself," Mahi showed him the grand mirror that was placed in the lobby.

"Oh fuck! When did this happen?" Ron said viewing himself in the mirror.

"Go and change fast," Maggy suggested.

"Balls! I am not going all the way back to the room now. As it is, it's not very noticeable. I don't know how come Mahi noticed it. Must be admiring my butt. No Mahi?"

"Your butt! Ron you are flat down there. What will I admire? The plateau," Mahi laughed. And so did others. Ron realized he created a big blunder. He convincingly didn't possess a butt that any girl would admire.

"Guys don't need big butt, ok. I can assure you that I'm more than generously endowed where I should be," Ron made a poor attempt to defend his meager ASSet.

"But what if somebody notices, Ron?" Maggy showed a genuine concern.

"I'll give that person the same reactions that I gave it to you guys. Oh fuck! when did this happen," Ron enacted, "Tell me did you guys come to know that I was acting?"

"What? You already knew that your trousers were torn. Why did you wear such trousers then," Rochelle gave a dazed look.

"No, they weren't torn. They got torn while we were coming down the stairs. A stupid nail kissed my butt," Ron explained.

"And you decided not to change them again," Rochelle said.

"That's right. I didn't want to go back to my room again and find another trouser that matches with my shirt."

"You are too much Ron?" Maggy said.

"Stop admiring yourself before the mirror now. Come let's move," Aryan said.

"Ron don't bother yourself too much. The objects won't appear larger than they actually are," Mahi cackled. Mahi was in full form.

"Mahi you are getting better and better. That was a slam dunk," Aryan said laughing loudly.

"Yeah! a perfect one," Mahi acknowledged.

08:45 pm

"Mahi, why's she taking so much time?" the anxious Aryan asked about Sameera.

"Offfficerrrr turn to your right," Mahi imitated a command.

Sameera's satin-silk red dress with golden polka dots, a Titanium bracelet on her right wrist and the Victorian pride in her smile did far more than just grabbing the eyeballs of all the men around.

It massacred some.

Aryan for once even thought of launching himself across the floor onto Sameera. He thought it would be better to embrace the enigmatic attraction and get butchered once and for all, than to die a slow death in anticipation.

"Save my soul, my lord!" Aryan's knees went weak, "She is...ooohhhh, I have no words," Aryan whispered to Maggy.

"No doubt she's looking gorgeous...but Aryan you too are looking great in this outfit. No way less striking than her," Maggy supported the weak knees.

"I thought so...until now." Aryan's gaze was fixed on the polka dots that were approaching him.

The slender silhouette provided by the soft, pastel lilac shirt with narrow lapel and tapered at the waist, Blackberry blazer was no way any less devastating than the captivating red-polka dress.

"Thank God we live in a country where looking this delectable is not a crime. I have never felt a human being so criminally pleasing to my senses," Aryan's vocal folds reacted involuntarily.

Polka effect.

His soulful look darkened with some unrecognizable emotion. Aryan had never been so upfront with Sameera, especially with everybody around. But there are times when you just can't control yourself.

"Oooohhhhhh!" Mahi burbled. All were stunned seeing the horrendously shy Aryan turn expressive. Aryan noticed the tell-tale warm color rushing up Sameera's neck. She swallowed hard before responding, "I'm usually very modest and humble dealing with compliments but with such a compliment and from such a person, I think I'd like to act a little snooty and snobbish today." Of course the bright smile went against her response somewhat.

"Ooooohhhhhh!" Mahi and Maggy burbled together.

Soon after the launch of the magazine and the prize distribution ceremony began the much awaited, high octane bash.

The lavish special effects of light, sound, smoke and neon mixed with vivid imagery hypnotized the audience. Dynamic images bounced from the surfaces of the swanky dance floor as the top-tier sound system pulsated the joint out.

A raised enclosed platform seemingly suspended over the dance floor housed a human looking creature with half of the face pierced. His hair was stiff straight pointing toward the stars challenging gravity in its own spiky fashion. People around called him DJ. Cooped up inside the raised booth, this savoy disc jockey made musical progressions through the evening from the riveting rock n roll mush-ups to funky lounge remixes to strongly accented reggae beats and to the chart-topping holly-bolly numbers.

09:30 pm

In the most unexpected manner the Master or shall I say the 'Mistress' of ceremony was brought onto the stage from somewhere high up, inside a hanging bird cage. Her entry along with perfectly coordinated fireworks gave every eye a dramatic airborne perspective. Dressed in a black chiffon evening gown coupled with exquisite diamond jewellery, she loaned her clairvoyant voice to the audience, "A very warm good evening ladies and gentlemen...It gives me, Kamini Kapoor, singular pleasure, double delight, triple honor and quadruple satisfaction to be here, on this platform and welcome all you wonderful people. Spring...they say is nature's best way of saying, let's party and spring...ladies and gentlemen is officially here. What better way to dedicate an ode to spring than to celebrate the launch of Mr. Ranvijay Pathania's new magazine- Spirit of Youth here at his own majestic club, Wilbur Woods. Ladies and gentlemen a rowdy round of applause once again for Mr. Ranvijay Pathania and SOY- the spirit of youth."

Kamini Kapoor's presence had suddenly raised the mercury level at Wilbur Woods. Not to mention the testosterone level.

After giving a quick rundown of the evening ahead she announced, "It'll be narcotic on my part, if I talk about spring and youth and miss LOVE and ROMANCE therefore...I would want some of the gentlemen to come up onstage...only the confident and the romantic ones...men, who believe in the magic of romance and power of love. All you have to do is answer a simple question. The answer that spreads maximum romance in the air walks away with a brand new Hero Honda Karizma. Now let me see how many such men we have among us. Can I see some hands in the air?"

The K-magic (K for Kamini and Karizma) was working. A plethora of hands answered the call.

"Now let me paint the scene for you guys. Imagine that you've just proposed to love of your life and she tells you that before she says YES she wants to hear 10 things that you'll do for her after you get married. What would they be? As simple as that. Guys, one personal piece of advice before you come onstage: Don't come up, if it's bike that is in your mind coz out of the five judges one is the audience itself. They'll catch you if you fake it. Beware. This is your chance to tell her how much you love her and who knows you might win your dream girl along with the bike...come and take her away...and in case if you've not yet found your dream girl just remember that Kamini... is stillllll...a bachchhhelorrretttte," she teased the crowd.

Her last line had evoked a lot of excitement and participation.

And some confusion too.

Confusion, because some of them seriously replaced their original dream girl with Kamini. They thought they might land up getting a better deal. One of them even devoted a two page poem to Kamini which was originally written for his girl friend. He lost both the birds. The one in the bush and the one...out of the bush.

"Ron why don't you give it a shot? Nice chance to impress the crowd and who knows Kamini might have a cute brother?" Mrigank winked.

"Bastard you are trying to play with your dad."

"No seriously Ron...show us your magic," Rochelle said.

"Sweetheart, she wants men who believe in the power of love. I am anti-love. Yeah, had it been the power of lust, I would have been the one to whoosh away with Karizma. Why don't you try Tiffany's dopu-popu baby? Love's your forte."

"I wish Tiffany was here. I would've surely gone," Mrigank pulled the skin near his Adam's apple.

"Aryan!" Ron, Maggy and Mahi shouted in harmony.

Ron held him by his arms and said, "Dude! this is your chance. Look around you. It's a perfect bloody evening. You are looking your best, awesome I must say. This whole place is oozing with fun and romance. A perfect fuckin' chance to show her how much you love her."

"Ron but..."

"No, nukko, nopes… I don't want to hear anything. Just go onstage and propose to her...fuck off now," Ron pushed him toward the stage.

"Hey, but where is Sameera?" Mahi asked.

"She would be somewhere around. Don't worry about that. When he gets on the stage she'll know it's for her," Ron replied.

Aryan turned back one last time to take the final approval from others.

"Conquer the world," Mrigank gave his approval. As if to Macedonian king Alexander was going on his world conquering trip. Mahi and Rochelle too endorsed it with their thumbs up.

"All right guys...we have another gentleman here. Please put your hands together for him," Kamini welcomed Aryan.

"Oh! you are the same guy who won the debate...Aryan Vyas...you are from the army right?" Kamini asked.

"That's right lady," Aryan replied.

"Wowww…Army and romance...sounds quite strange," she said.

"Strange?" Aryan said.

"Yeah!...you know when you think about the army all that comes to your mind is olive green uniform, drill, guns and bullets."

"And you miss the human inside the olive green...Kamini, I feel that they are the most romantic guys...they fall in love even with a small piece of land...a two by two feet post over some deserted, barren mountain to such an extent that they are willing to offer their lives for it. I guess, your perception requires a slight adjustment lady," Aryan smiled.

"Oh! you just adjusted it, lieutenant," she offered him a salute. Aryan smiled in reciprocation.

"Aryan, is your dream girl here this evening?" she asked.

"Yes, she is."

"So what are you waiting for...the stage is all yours," Kamini said and moved to a corner.

Aryan held the microphone with both hands and took a deep breath. The crowd facing him was a lot different than the one in the debate. Charged up and roused. He shut his eyes for a moment, took another breath and said, "I just wish, you realize that I am here on this stage for you." He paused for a while, took another deep breath. He hadn't taken these many, even before his Boxing finals, when his opponent was the 6' 4" feet tall hulk, Nigel Gibbs. Not even when he used to jump from the 55 feet high, diving board during his commando training.

Tough time I must say.

He then went down on to the floor of the stage on his knees. There's a difference between getting on your knees and dropping on your knees. Dropping is more exciting to watch. And more painful to do. It must have hurt him real bad. But I believe in these moments there's so much adrenaline rush that you hardly feel any pain.

He then in the most soft, tender and romantic voice verbalized, "I'll lift you and walk till home, change you into your nightie and tuck you into bed when you've had too many Tequila shots. I'll always be the first to inaugurate clapping whenever you do something good and be the last one to stop laughing at your silly jokes. Though I know I am not made for it, I'll learn Salsa to match your Salsa skills. By the way, today afternoon I devoted a good two hours with Natasha so that I could ask you for a dance this evening. When you talk, I'll listen and listen in the truest sense. I'll make your interests my passions. If we ever have an argument I'll be the first one to say sorry coz the sooner I say sorry, the sooner I'll see your smile and I know It's not good for my health to breathe for a long time without seeing you smile. I'll always train my body to be fit and strong so that when we get old and you have trouble climbing the stairs owing to your back and knee pain and there are no lifts around, I shall carry you in my arms and climb the stairs. I'll even learn how to drape saris and apply eyeliners so that you never get late for your office and for the parties. And this might sound a little creepy but I'll keep a track of your periods dates coz I know these days you undergo cramps and pain and feel a little irritated so I'll do no such thing which augments your agony...just the thought that you might say yes makes me a better and stronger person every day and every hour...help me achieving the best Aryan...and allow me to bring out the best in you...let's create us for eternity."

The whole process of the air being taken into the lungs and being expelled out from the lungs in Wilbur Woods slowed down for a moment. The exuberant whooping and clapping authenticated every single word that he spoke.

Aryan got so involved with the whole thing that he forgot that he was on the stage, on his knees. The cheering slogans made him realize that he owned a pair of knees and that the same pair was in pain.

Needless to mention that he won the bike.

"It's because of assholes like you that we men are subjected to such torturous inventory of demands by the opposite sex," Ron said, "And now the torture would only increase. Did you actually mean everything that you said, up there?"

"You have any doubts, Ron. Didn't you see the love in his eyes?" Mahi said and hugged Aryan.

"Brother, you were awwwwsssssom," Maggy hit Aryan's chest with his fist, "You should've seen the expressions of all the girls around. I am sure there'll be lot of fights tonight and lot of guys will have to learn how to drape saris and apply eyeliners," Maggy laughed.

"Sameera is really lucky to have you, Aryan," Rochelle too hugged Aryan.

"But where the hell is Sameera?...Oh! there she is," Mahi said.

Every step that Sameera took toward Aryan made his heart palpitate faster. He could feel a tug of war between his small and large intestine.

"Congrats Aryan. Two big prizes in a single evening," Sameera said.

"Congrats??? I thought she would...Either she's too great an actor and just pretending that she doesn't know anything or probably she wanted me to spell out her name...or it could be that she's too stupid to understand anything," Aryan's mind processed some quick assumptions.

The others were also perplexed by Sameera's reaction.

"You saw what he did on the stage na?" Mahi asked inquisitively.

"I missed it ya. I could just hear the last part...you know when MC was announcing winner's name.

"Youuu mmisssed it!" Ron almost shouted.

Maggy looked toward Aryan, who rendered a no-emotion expression.

"Yeaaahhhh! I would have loved to see Aryan on the stage," Sameera made a sad face.

"But where were you?" Maggy asked.

"My phone ran out of juice. I had to go back to the room to charge it. My folks are coming down. I was supposed to guide their way through the phone."

"Have they reached?"

"They are just ten minutes away. Dad said, he'll call me as reach the main gate. He said he has a surprise for me... leave all that....ell me what happened on the stage. God! I could hear the clapping and cheering. I am sure Aryan would have won the hearts of the crowd," Sameera said.

"Oh gosh! Sameera the way he dropped on his knees, the look in his eyes and the romance in his voice..." Mahi said.

"Mahi, will you please let me do the honor?" Aryan interrupted, "Sameera, Mahi's just exaggerating. It wasn't anything like that. The MC had painted a scene wherein the gentleman were to talk about 10 things that they are willing to do after they get married to their dream girl. I came up with some things. I don't even remember what I said. I think I just got a little lucky today."

Sameera's phone rang.

"Oh they've reached. Guys I'll just be back," Sameera said and left.

"Mahi I am really sorry to cut you like that. I just didn't want it to be a second hand thing. I value my feelings for her and I want to do it my way," Aryan said.

"I understand," Mahi held his hand.

"But I feel it's not my day today," Aryan lamented.

"What the hell is wrong with you. You are talking as if the world has come to an end. Cheer up dude," Ron said. Aryan constricted his brows as if some idea struck him, "In a way, you are right. The world would have come to an end. Ron do you have any idea what I did on the stage? I fuckin' proposed her. Thank god, she wasn't around. What if she had not liked it? It's just been three bloody days. How could I do it? What the hell went wrong with me? I could have lost her forever," Aryan reacted. Hyper-reacted.

"You're just over reacting. Nothing of that sort would have happened. She likes you and you know that. She called you herself today morning. And she even wants you to meet his dad. She didn't tell me or Maggy that," Ron said.

"She might be just fond of me, that doesn't mean she has something for me. Moreover she's too obsessed with her career and her book. Ron most of the relationsships die prematurely coz one of the two is in a hurry...and I am in no hurry," Aryan explained.

"Whatever you say bro," Ron smiled and wrapped his arm around his waist."

"Come guys let's have a drink," Rochelle pulled Aryan toward the bar.

Three silver-pebble stone bars housed under black and golden awnings offered a wide array of exotic libations. Personally selected wine, cognac, champagne and lady waitress intoxicated the guests. Trained bartenders amused the crowd with dazzling ice work, befuddling bottle work, rapid shelf shuffle and sophisticated cocktailing.

Mahi's phone beeped, "It's Sameera's message. She's called us near the dance floor."

"Ok let's go there first," Rochelle said.

"Guys hold on," Ron said, "I want your little cooperation. I want you guys to go first. Me and Aryan will come later."

"But why?" Maggy said.

"Guys timing matters. I don't want Aryan to be with the crowd. Aryan would enter after all your introductions are over. He should get that special, 'Oh! so you are Aryan. Heard a lot about you, young man'. Soon after Aryan has had his introduction and initial small talks you'll hear a song- Lady in red, courtesy Ron." Ron bowed down. "That is the time Maggy will ask Rochelle for a dance. After Maggy's done, Aryan like a true gentle man and an officer will approach Sameera's dad that is Aryan's dad-in-law and seek his permission before taking the lady in red on the dance floor."

Maggy giggled, "Dad-in-law."

"What am I doing when these guys are dancing ?" Mahi asked.

"Oh you!...you have an important role to play sweetheart. Your job is to tell Sameera's parents about how the crowd went mad when they heard Aryan's speech and that he also won a bike and etcetera etcetera...basically enhance Aryan's image. And this you have to do very diplomatically. I am sure I don't need to tell you how... Anybody any doubts...Well then ...the meeting is adjourned. Carry on." The team members left leaving the captain and the supposedly man of the match behind."

"Ron, are you sure about the dance part?" the hesitant would be man of the match asked.

"Well I should ask you. It's you who convinced Natasha to spare two hours to teach her, self stylized Tango sequences. And as far as I can remember you practiced for another two hours in the room," the captain replied.

Aryan bobbed his head in agreement, "Let's do it."

Aryan had arranged his position in a way that he could see all of them but they couldn't see him. Before making his entry he rehearsed his introduction one last time. He believed in the importance of first time impressions. He also believed that since Jurassic times, fathers-in-law have been important players in the game of relationships.

Toughest players.

Hurdle creating players.

He unified his confident self and moved on for the performance of his life. Performance for his life. He was just ten steps short of his entry when his feet froze. It was as if the barrel of an AK-47,...the- Avtomat-Kalashnikov model of 1947...has been placed on his forehead. AK-47, he would have still managed but this was a much more lethal and noxious knock. A surefire collapse. He saw Sameera's entire family laughing and clapping with joy and amidst all this celebration he saw

Sameera and some guy exchanging rings and kisses.

Sameera's Dad's surprise!!!

Varun Gupta, the 'some guy' was Sameera's father's friend's only son. Varun's father owned a publishing house and Sameera's father knew how important Sameera's book was to her. This was Varun's last evening in India since he was going to UK by the next morning flight to pursue his MBA from LSB (London school of business). If you remember, LSB was Sameera's dream school. Sameera had planned to join LSB next season after she finished her MBA from MICA. Both the fathers knew about Sameera's plan. It was Varun's father's idea to have an engagement ceremony before Varun left for UK. Sameera was totally unaware about the surprise engagement but she happily said yes to the engagement since she knew Varun from before plus the whole deal appeared very lucrative to her. Though she liked Aryan, when she weighed Varun and the offers attached with Varun against Aryan, Aryan proved very light.

Business tycoon she wanted to be. Business tycoon sure she would be. Her basics of business were very clear...very strong.

But then why she wanted Aryan to meet his dad?

Because Sameera's dad was also from the army. She wanted to surprise Aryan, therefore never told him about her dad's profession. Moreover, Sameera's dad Major General S.D Sanyal (retired) himself wanted to meet and congratulate the bright officer.

The team members by now had come back to the pavilion to be with their could-not-be man of the match. Nobody said anything. They just came and stood besides him. He was calm and serene. They watched him watching Sameera. They watched him smiling, seeing Sameera smile. In the mean time the DJ played the song Lady in red, as planned. The DJ couldn't have denied Ron.

Never seen you looking so lovely as you are there tonight,
I've never seen you shine so bright…………
…………Lady in red is dancing with me, cheek to cheek,
It's nobody here, it's just you and me,… swear wanna be,
I hardly know, this beauty by my side,
I'll never forget, way you look tonight.
I never will forget, way you look tonight,
lady in red,… my lady in red…my lady in red.

Songs have a mysterious power of taking us back to the good, old times. Aryan could recall his Salsa classes when he danced with Sameera in the same song. It was the first time he ever touched her. The only time he ever touched her.

He also recalled Natasha's Granny whispering in his ears, "Why don't you tell her?" He didn't want to return to the present where his lady in red was dancing with somebody else…cheek to cheek. His convincing Natasha to devote him two extra hours and the two hours practice after that went all in vain as the performance that he was to give was being given by somebody else.

Tiny…watery…warm…saline ambassadors of emotions started flowing…pouring…lavishly from Aryan's small, sad eyes. He didn't move. He didn't shake. He didn't wipe them. He let them go. And they kept on going.

The entire trip flashed before him. The unshakable rock and the calm stream. The after-debate snacks when he noticed her for the first time. The Salsa class. The ballroom Tango. The Orkuting. The phone call. The SMS. The first date. The white dress with bursts of small brown floral prints. The rickshaw and the auto ride. The buffalo. The Vanilla flavored unlucky charm. The body-hugging Lycra. The sweeper.

The lush green grass. The kissable feet. The wrist watch strap. Dhattt buddhu. The leopard print underwear. The rehearsal before the mirror...

Only two times had his tear ducts misbehaved like this before. One, when his grandfather died. He loved him the most. And HE, loved him the most. And two, when he left Oscar. His squadron (his home for three years) in National Defence Academy. You can't stop crying when you know that you might never meet some of your course mates from the other services,(in his case Air force and Navy) again in your life. Course mates with whom you've shared thousand ninety five days and NIGHTS of cold coffee, iron Maggie, jam sessions, seventh heaven and lot of stinking sweat.

"Whuthappened? Why you guys not on the floor. Aryan, why are...What happened to him? Why is he crying?" the confused Ron asked everybody. Mahi took him to a side and narrated the whole scene.

"What the fuckkk!" the angry Ron vented out, "How could she do it. Fuckin' whore."

Before anybody could even react Aryan turned around and released a punch on Ron's face. The power with which the punch was discharged made Ron and his two front teeth fall flat on the lawn. The unexpected whack left the wounded down for the count.

Aryan with no remorse of any form left the place. The panic after the action got muffled to a high degree owing to the high-pitched music in the background. Not many noticed it. For some who did, it was passed on as a mere accident.

Aryan went back to the room, packed his bag and left Wilbur Wood.

Twenty minutes later

"How are you feeling now?" Mahi fetched Ron some more water.

"Aaahhhhhhh," answered Ron.

"How was the punch by the way?" Maggy asked.

"Bassstarrrrrdd," Ron opened his eyes and massaged his jaw.

Maggy's cell phone beeped, "Must be Tiffany's message," Maggy said putting his hand in the pocket, "Aryan's message? Three of them."

Maggy read the SMS's loud:

Magy m sendin this txt to u coz I kno Ron won't b abl 2 read it, at least 4 nxt half n hour. Plz read it 2 him- Ron, I am not sory 4 what I did to u. U dezrvd it. But u r a grt guy. I like u very much. I luv u, man. Sum day try me out n u'll see what u mean 2 me. Don try me out 4 the nxt sum days. I myslf don kno wher I'll b. if u still hate me burn th bike n if you don, plz take it...it'll remind u of yor yunger brothr.

N th rst f th gang... I m sory guys...I hope u'll undrstnd. I m in pain yaar n it's killin me. I've had th bst time f my life wid u ppl n I'll alwyz relish evry moment spnt wid u guys.

One reqst, plz don tel Sameera bout anythin. She has big plans 4 her future n there's a noble cause attchd to it. She keeps her goals f life ahead thn her prsnl felins and I respect her 4 that. I want 2 trezr each momnt spnt wid her, plz don trnish it by tellin anythin 2 her. U guys kno where Sameera is concrnd I like things my way, so plz...

Magy I've left my Gucci shades on the table. They fit you better.

Take care f Tiffny th way she take cares f u...u r th luckiest, dude - goodbye...

Things were done the way Aryan wanted. Maggy took the shades. Ron didn't burn the bike. And Sameera was told some story about Aryan's abrupt departure. It's always easy to fabricate stories around olive greens.

The next morning, others too packed their bags, bid farewell to each other and left Wilbur Woods for their respective destinations. The short lived, unspoken, undelivered story of one sided love came to an end. All that remained in Wilbur Woods was...

...some bittersweet memories,

...a broken heart,

...and two broken teeth.

One Year Later

Four Indian seasons have passed since the Sunday gala evening. A great deal has changed all around. Black is the new White in United States...chocolate boy Aamir Khan turns mean and muscular...A slum dog becomes a millionaire and sweeps Oscars ...Mahi has changed her hair style...it's no longer a riot of curls but all shiny, sleek and straightened, sweeping across her face like a curtain. However, a few things have still not changed. For instance, the wind still manages to pass from the gap that Ron's two broken teeth had once created. He liked the look of the gap so much that he decided to live with it. Of course being Ron he told his friends that he had another reason for why he liked it so much...a much censored version...all I can say is that he claimed that the gap constantly gave his tongue the feel of resting in happier place.

Before I let slip the 'third reason' pertaining to the huge, circular, dark woody brown wall clock (I hope you remember), I must furnish you with the highlights of the times passed by. The hang-over of Wilbur Woods hung over the group for the first one week. You know that, "those were the good times man, you remember how we..." All except Aryan remained in contact with each other; through phone calls, messages and emails. Soon the call exchanges diminished as everybody got busy in their own little planet- studies, assignments, presentations, projects, interviews, jobs.

Mrigank landed up in Hewlett Packard. He's a software architect. Sounds nice. He's joined a gym but he still wears oversize t-shirts. And he still loves Tiffany and they still talk for hours over the phone...

...Tiffany: 'Bye honey. I'll catch you later.'

Mrigank: 'Bye, baby.'

Tiffany: 'I love you, bye.'

Mrigank: 'Me too, bye.'

Tiffany: 'Maggy, why do you always say, me too or same here? Why can't you say, I love you. I don't even remember when you last said those words.'

Mrigank: 'Me too or same here means I love you. It's one and the same thing.'

Tiffany: 'No it's not. Only when a person actually means it says it and I guess, since you don't say it, you don't love me anymore.'

Mrigank: 'That's not true and you know that.'

Tiffany: 'See, you could have still said it but you didn't.'

Mrigank: 'Tiffy please don't start off with it again.'

Tiffany: 'Start off with what?'

Mrigank: 'Whatever you are doing. Your weird love fundaes.'

Tiffany: 'Oh! weird haan.'

Mrigank: 'Look Tiffany, everybody has his own way to express emotions. I think I never finger with yours so it's only decency that you don't finger with mine.'

Tiffany: ' Maggy, that tone wasn't warranted. All I asked you was to say space. Was it too much?'

Mrigank: ' It doesn't happen that way.'

Tiffany: ' Sometimes you gotta do it your partner's way. It makes that person feel needed and wanted.'

Mrigank: 'I know that. I've heard that before.'

Tiffany: 'Yeah you know everything.'

Mrigank: 'I am getting late, bye.'

Tiffany: 'Ok, bye.' ...

And they still fight sometimes.

Rochelle got promoted to the position of asstt. manager. Her salary has increased by 25%. And the length of her skirts has decreased by 50%. Recently her new designer outfit, a royal blue denim skirt raised some hullabaloo in Carol's school (Carol is her younger sister). Rochelle had gone there to attend the school fete. She's still a virgin.

Mahi has done her MBA and joined her mother in business. She is taking care of her mother's dream project which her mother feels will surely muscle out Mr. Pathania's business.

Sameera's finished her MBA from MICA and has also scored well in GMAT. She has applied for London School of Business and is waiting for her interview call. Her book is about to be published.

Ron has successfully completed the Hotel Management course from PUSA. He is as polite and decent as ever. A true blue service industry man, ready to service anything with a smile.

Aryan is the only one who has decided to remain incognito. There's been no news from him. Everyone surmises that it's by design, for obvious reasons.

One of the interesting developments that took place in this time span was Mahi's engagement party. Sorry, I missed Ron.

Mahi and Ron's engagement party.

!!!!!

Woww! Howw!

The story is that Ron always knew that Mahi liked him. From day one. But, what difference did it make. Lot of girls liked him. Why only Mahi? Ron, though appeared to be confused between Mahi's luscious tush and Rochelle's bodacious boobies AND Natasha's oozing oomph and his other numerous girlfriends'(and boyfriend's) something-something, was always very clear in his head about what he wanted in his life partner. (Though it took him plentiful, vigorous self-journalizing sessions before proposing to Mahi).

One big reason that none of his past relationships ever worked was that all the girls who came in his life couldn't handle his flirtatious nature. They wanted to change him. Instantly. They wanted to domesticate him and in the process made him more wild.

Mahi on the other hand gave him what he loved most. His freedom. His space. And his uniqueness. She would herself provoke him to check out pretty girls (I wish all the girls were like that). Ron quoted this (not-commonly-found) quality in her as, 'sexy fuckin' confidence of a woman on his man and herself'. Furthermore, she could counter his wicked remarks with equal meanness. Not any Jeenat, Janet or Jaanu could do that either.

Ron was weird in many ways. He used to compliment Rochelle intentionally in front of Mahi, just to check out Mahi's reactions. And Mahi always handled the situation with grace. Even on the day of their departure from Wilbur Woods, he took everybody's contact number except Mahi's. He believed that if Mahi was the one for him then her absence should create a feeling of discomfort for him. And it did. Big time. Mega time.

After two months of telephonic conversations regime he proposed to Mahi to be his official girl friend.

Ron: 'Mahi I've been thinking a lot and I seriously feel that we both should agree to ruin each other's life...let's be a pain in the ass for each other...say tillllll the present government falls.

Mahi: 'Aaahhaan.'

Ron: 'And if we start enjoying the pain we'll renew the agreement till the next Olympics.'

After due thought...Mahi: 'No."

Ron: 'NO!'

Mahi: 'Not the Olympics...till the next Soccer world cup...it'll be safer since it's nearer.'

After graduating from PUSA he joined Mahi's mother and in three months became her blue eyed boy. The impressed mother deputed Ron to assist her daughter in her dream project. That's where the couple realized that they were enjoying the pain and decided to get engaged. Their engagement party and the inauguration of their dream project was celebrated on the same day. Mahi with help of Ron convinced her mother to invite Mr. Pathania for the occasion. Ron gave some bullshit about how psychological damage can be done to the rival by showing off the success of their dream project. Mahi's mother licked the bullshit. Ron knew that a vindictive mind can be manipulated more easily since it's vulnerable. Mr. Pathania agreed to attend the function. I guess an Indian father gets a little emotional when it comes to his daughter's marriage.

But the oldies weren't aware that the youngies had kept something in store for them. Mahi had secretively photostatted some pages of her mother's personal diary. Moments of her parents' love story, the courtship days and the love poems written by Ronnie rascal (well that's what Mahi's mother used to call Mr. Ranvijay Pathania. Rascal??? coz he was a nasty prankster).

Plan was to recreate the scenes, conversations and pranks that once existed between Mahi's parents. Poor Ron had to mug up Ronnie rascal's long poems, *"Bugger was one hell of a Romeo haan," Ron, reading the Xeroxed paper. Mahi: "Ronnie and Ron not much of a difference."* Rochelle was also given a role in the act. She was designated official designer for Mahi's Mom. She was the only one from the Wilbur Wood gang who attended the party. Mrigank couldn't make it because of job commitment and Sameera couldn't simply be traced. Rumours were that she had left for London.

Though the act was intelligently designed and brilliantly executed, it failed. The sharp business moguls saw through the plan. The set up was exposed but the gesture did its magic. Mr. Ranvijay Pathania, who had never celebrated his birthday for the last 20 years, out of the blue decided to celebrate it this year and invited Mahi's mother and family. Since then both the business tycoons spend most of their time arranging a chance meeting. Rumors are that they are planning a joint project.

Are the bitter halves turning into better halves?

Around a month after the engagement party, Ron received an email:

Bro, m aware that it's been ages since any news poured from this olive green brat... saying that I've been busy since... would certainly appear a gross understatement and knowing you, even if I tender a written apology, it won't do any good. But believe me, the nasty operational commitment of Armed Forces kept me preoccupied to such an extent that I got to see the civilization just the yester evening. Got lot to share and lot to hear (including your MC-BC)... tinkle me at-09904034839...

- Lt. Aryan Vyas.

The tinkle at- 09904034839 uncovered the eight months that Aryan so mysteriously hid from everyone. After Aryan left Wilbur Woods he went to one of his fellow officer's place. He didn't want to face his family members with dampened spirits. After staying there for four days he left for his hometown, Nainital.

Nainital

Aryan got off the Volvo bus, rubbing his eyes at the typically blinding brightness of the sun, which rose over his hometown. His eyes by now had grown used to travelling through the darkness of sleep and the dimness of the interiors of the shabby coach. There was a fresh, cold familiar smell in the air, which rose up and stung his nostrils. A smell that reminded him of his childhood. For a split second the scene that lay before him took away the dullness and heaviness of the heart-break. The cobblestone path along which he used to run to catch his bus was still the same. The emerald Naini lake lazing under the bright sun was still as breathtakingly magical. Its greenness still mesmerized him. As a child he used to stand by its side, staring into its fathomless depth for hours as if it was a wishing well, imagining that a genie would suddenly appear out of it and ask him his three wishes. He could never come to a conclusion about those three wishes. His list of achieving 'hundred and eleven things before he dies' always came in the way.

Gosh! if the genie only knew how sure he was today with his wish.

He crossed Dabbu's paan shop and saw that Dabbu's teeth were still as reddish brown as the *kattha* he puts in the paan. Sharma's Jalebi shop smelled as sweet as ever and Vickky's barber shop was as jam packed. He saw aunties and uncles wherever he turned. He belonged to all of them. They all were his extended family. He remembered the wonder he wanted to see in their eyes. His heart felt like lead again.

"*Abbe...tune bataya nahin tu aa raha hai,*" Kabeer opened the door, "Welcome home Lieutenant *sahib.* Debate-shebate, bike-shike...double double...*Mubarakan,*" he hugged Aryan and lifted him up in excitement. Kabeer, Aryan's elder brother was his opposite in every possible way. A self-acclaimed black sheep (actually bull) of the family, who never missed an opportunity of getting into trouble. He was always bashing up somebody and it was never his fault.

"Thanks bhai, but I didn't win the bike. There was a slight mix-up.

Initially my name was announced but later on the management clarified that it was Ron and not me...you remember Ron?"

Aryan said as he walked into the cool interiors of his sitting room. The room seemed to echo the character of his parents; the beauty of his mother against the strength of his father...long flowing white drapes against chestnut dark French window...feet-sinking white rugs against bee-waxed polished wooden floor... white ceramic urns against the intricately engraved teak table. In spite of the orderliness, the room had just the right amount of disarray to make it look lived in.

"Who? that Casanova...yeah I remember you told me about him over the phone. Anyways, hardly matters...small things...Leave all that...tell me about the big thing?" a wickedly inquisitive gleam flashed in his eyes.

"Big thing?" Aryan asked and turned over his dad's slipper that was upside down. It was an involuntary action. Result of years of his mother's superstitious belief that if slippers are upside down it means that there'll be a fight in the family.

"*Salaee*...don't pretend ok...*Baap hain hum tumhare*. I am talking about your lady in red...Sameera Sanyal prrrrroudly representing MICA. You promised me that you'll make me speak to her. Arre lemme also see who's the girl who stole my stud bro's heart. You've given her nine point nine out of ten. Our best till now was Reema...six point eight."

"Bhai battery is dead...and as it is she's gone back home. I don't have her home number. When she calls me next I'll make you talk to her," he let loose a smile. A dishonest smile. Only if Kabeer could understand what lay behind the fake smile. Only if Aryan could explain that his 9.9 has made him a zero.

"By mother khaa."

"Bhai, you know I don't swear for such small things. Where's maa?" he tried to divert Kabeer's attention.

"Soldiers word then?"

"I am feeling very hungry...first feed me something."

"Maa's gone with Gupta auntie to Swati didi's place to admire her cow's new born calf."

Admire a new born calf!!!

Now I know why the lives of people in small town is always so hectic.

So far Aryan's zeal for life never allowed him to look back. It was as if the one above us had shaped him out of rich alluvial. He was a model for living life to the fullest. He always had things to do, activities to keep him busy. And what his friends found most amazing is that everything he put his hand to, he ensured that he mastered it. Every new rise and shine brought with it the opportunities to work towards the fulfillment of his list of '111 things to do before I die'. Aryan lived life like a man on a mission. He often wondered at the philosophy of the motivational guru's that his well-read friends kept telling him about. He never told them but he found the entire idea ludicrous...read books for motivation...wasn't that something that came naturally?

So what had happened now? What was this strange feeling that made the colorful world he knew become a black and white print? He was fighting a dual battle. Aryan knew he loved Sameera enough to let her go, let her find her happiness in whatever or whoever she wished. But there was this thread of fear running through him that told him that his life would never be the same again.

The next few days at home were routine. It did help that his Dad was outstation for the next five days. He did everything that he usually did when at home, helped his mom with the gardening, went for long jogs alone, patiently faced all his enthusiastic aunties and uncles. The only thing that he avoided were situations with his brother where Sameera would come up.

It became little more difficult when his Dad returned. Aryan was determined that none of his family members should see through him. But his Dad knew him so well, how long was he going to be able to hide from those eyes. He started spending his evening taking dance classes so that he could avoid his Dad. This activity though nerve racking for him somehow kept him close to her and far from his Dad. But then there were still the weekends to deal with. One Sunday morning his father decided to join him for morning jog.

It was a clear and crisp April-morning. The sky was like an aquamarine canvas that had been airbrushed with wisps of white. A mild gentle wind with a touch of moisture from last night's dew accompanied the two track suits. The fresh smell of earth rose up to their nostrils but Aryan was like a man from the Arctic. None of the nature's warmth seemed to touch him.

While they walked briskly on the mall, Aryan thought about the uncharacteristic decision of his father, Mr. Subodh Vyas, who normally liked to laze around on Sundays.

He was a ruggedly tall man. He reminded Aryan of the Alps...high, mighty and never ending. His eyes were brown pools that reflected ideals and values. Pools that never entertained compromises and that mirrored great love. There must have been suffering too as it with all but I guess the other features in that reflection seemed to scare it away. Of course, Aryan didn't know that his father saw those same chocolaty pools on him too. What he knew for sure was that if he once looked into them his soul would be exposed. That's why from the time he had set his foot at home he had been furtively avoiding them. He remembered that when he was nine and wanted to fib about his English marks he would put on his little dark sunglasses thinking that it might help.

"That's a nice pair of glares you're wearing, Aryan."

"Papa, since yester evening something has been irritating my eyes, so I took Kabeer's glares," Aryan was playing his old childhood trick again today. He had Kabeer's glares firmly in place before facing his dad for the morning walk.

"Beta, you must be thinking how come papa decided to sacrifice his Sunday sleep today?"

Aryan nodded weakly.

"We don't get much time alone at home. You know your mother. How she's always glued onto you."

"Yeah," Aryan said escaping his father's burning gaze.

"Aryan actually I wanted to apologize to you," Aryan's father climbed a stone parapet. It was a breast-high brick wall with a broad top. Aryan remembered he used to climb the same parapet from one side and salute the passing Army vehicles; posing as a soldier with a gun, run over it and get down from the other end every day while going to school.

"Apologize? Why?" a confused smile in his face. Both the tracksuits now sat face to face on the parapet.

"I don't know why? You tell me," his father gently took out Aryan's glares from his eyes. This one move and Aryan felt as if he was... naked, "What do I...?"

"What mistake did I make that you've created such distance between us?"

"No! Why are you..."

"Beta it's been more three weeks and you still haven't asked for the car keys. You haven't troubled any of us with compulsory viewing of your favorite movies. You haven't demanded your *gajar ka halwa*. You haven't shared any funny incidents of your unit. There's something major going on inside you and you've decided to keep all of us away from it. I don't care about Kabeer and your mother but meeee... Aryan we are friends. You are the only one in the family who knows that I smoke. And it's not that you found out. I told you myself. We share that rapport with each other," a father cum friend prodded.

"Papa, I wanted to tell you everything. I wanted to surprise you with the news, but..." he paused for a while, "I assure you, I'll be back on the track. I'll come over it. It's a temporary thing. It'll go," he served a dry smile.

"It'll not go. It's not temporary. I know you beta. You are a very practical person. You don't let situations overpower you for this long...Aryan when you share your kinda stuff with me you make me feel young. And I love that. Hit me with it. Come on yaar," he held Aryan's hand.

A moment of needle falling silence...

And then there was this deep baritone voice. A voice that Aryan couldn't recognize as his own. Heavy with pain and anguish. Aryan couldn't deny the 'come on yaar'. It all started to come out. Tumbling out in gushes and gulps. The three days. From the time he saw her beautiful eyes shredding him to pieces to the time he saw them looking up into another pair.

"Papa, you must be thinking it's just been three days, how could I be so much into her. I don't even know it myself. She grows on me every day. I thought I'll be able to forget her but I just can't. Papa you know me I've never been into girls unlike Kabeer but Sameera is...and it's not just her beauty and intelligence, she understands me so well, for instance that condom episode. First meeting, any other girl would have blown her lid but she heard me patiently and understood the truth in my words. We just click. I would never for the love of anything go up onstage and do all that I did. I dropped on my knees in front of everybody and... I still can't believe I did all that...She gets the best out of me. Papa, she has all that I ever wanted in my Ms. Perfect and when you know it you don't want to lose it. You just want to hang onto it," he clasped both his palms.

"Aryan, you and I both know the laws of chemistry, you never feel attracted to a person unless there is some kind of reciprocation."

"Papa how do I work on 'some kind of reciprocation'."

"Good Lord, when has such a small thing become an issue for you. You command army my son. Go out there and tell her... the maximum she could do is say no. But at least you'll not live the rest of your life based on 'ifs'."

"Tell her what, papa? Tell her to break her engagement, leave Varun and come to me. *Aap bhee yaar*, you think it's that simple," the little boy was fighting with his papa.

"I don't even know what she thinks about me ...but I don't blame her for that. At the end of it, we were together just for three days and I didn't even tell her what I feel for her...I just wish...But Varun can't keep her happy. He doesn't even know how to hold a lady while dancing. I saw them dancing. You've gotta hold the lady like a man. And they didn't even look good together."

Mr. Subodh Vyas started smiling. Grinning.

"Why you smiling?"

"Not all fathers get to say this to their son," the grinning papa said, "I feel today I've learned something more...Aryan, I didn't love your mother with so much passion in our initial days like you've loved your woman. And I must say I am jealous of Sameera."

"Hhhnnn,"

"Most of us sleep everyday without loving anybody and without being loved by anybody. Some of us even die like that. You know while you were talking right now, I was just thinking if Sameera would have been here in my place, how would've she reacted? I don't know what she thinks about you and I don't know what she would've said but there's one thing that I certainly know. She would have felt very great about herself. She would have been in a different league altogether. Because I felt like that when I imagined myself to be Sameera for a while."

Aryan's expressions jazzed up.

"Sameera deserves to be in that league beta. She deserves to know what she's worth. No matter where she is and no matter WHO SHE IS WITH...make her proud and make her arrogant of your love. Let her brag and boast for the rest of her life. Let her carry in her smile, the pride of your love. Let her glow with your love. Let her know... what she means to you. Make her the richest lady on the planet."

Touching words.

Stirring thought.

Aryan's face underwent a change of color. Like that of the audience on the 28th of August, 1963 when Martin Luther King junior delivered his thundering speech, 'I have a dream' on the steps of Lincoln memorial, Washington D.C.

"Papa can I have the car keys?" an awakened smile asked.

"Right now!" a pleasant smile answered, giving away the keys. Aryan remembered his school days. The only time he used to get the car keys was when his father wanted him to wash the car.

"Gotta buy few movie dvd's and some *gajar,*" the smile winked.

Some people are lucky and some are Aryan. It was as if destiny held some hefty grudge against him. Hardly had the pain been nursed when he got a phone call from his regiment saying that his leave had been canceled and that he has to report back to the unit to proceed to Siachen Glacier.

Four reasons why Aryan shouldn't have felt his best:

One, leave was cancelled.

Two, leave got cancelled the very day Aryan started feeling better. He had to think about ways and means to make Sameera the richest lady on the planet.

Three, Siachen is a place not many look forward to going to.

Four, he couldn't eat his mother's *gajjar ka halwa* and couldn't even see the movie DVDs he'd brought.

The IL-76, military transport aircraft that took off from Chandigarh reached Thoise airbase, the nearest airlink to Siachen Glacier in two hours. This was Aryan's first ever plane ride...more like his first roller-coaster ride actually. At another time in his life the thought of boarding this air hawk would have made him incredibly excited. But now it was just a means to his destination. And to make bad matters worse, the weather was terrible. The aircraft kept plunging into air pockets at terrifying frequencies. The thought did pass through his mind that the pretty faces of some airhostess might have helped lighten up the atmosphere. But well, his thought process didn't align with that of the Indian Army.

Aryan spent the next thirty days in Snow Battle School. His mind and body was to be acclimatized and prepared for what was described to him as the toughest days of his life.

His climb up was far worse than what had been told to him. The first group set out from the base camp (an altitude of 12,000 feet) on a bone chillingly cold morning. Although the sun-goggles were firmly in place, the glare from the white world blinded him. The slope looked gentle and calm. It's only when they started did he realize the true meaning of the saying, 'still waters run deep'. One by one all the heavy equipment that they carried started finding its need. The rucksack, the radio set, the rope, the sling, the ice axe, the prober...one by one started becoming an extension of each of them. The knee-deep snow contributed to the fun. But they didn't grudge the heavy burden. In fact, they it carried protectively like a father carries his child on his back.

Somewhere deep down they knew if they lose it they probably lose themselves too.

They reached their next shelter looking like men from a concentration camp. Their bodies were covered with small nicks and cuts, their fingers numb through the thick thermals. There was only one thing that they longed for...as if they had been born with only this one need. The need for some heat...some warmth. Every morning they set out with only one thought in the minds, to reach the next level, to rest a while, to breathe evenly and get some heat. It took them twenty days of arduous climb before they finally reached their observation post at Siachen glacier.

Located in the eastern Karakoram range in the Himalayan mountains along the disputed India-Pak border, Siachen glacier, often referred to as the 'third pole' is the highest (up to an altitude of 25,000 feet) battleground on earth. Being the highest it offers the best:

Temperature that plunges down to minus fifty degree Celsius with no guilt whatsoever.

Air current that catch 150 nautical miles per hour speed in no time.

Snowstorm that starts but forgets to stop.

And the nippy, frosty, oxygen-robbed air that never seem to satisfy hungry human lungs.

Is this what heaven would look like? Aryan wondered standing at his observation post- 20,000 feet above the mean sea level. Untouched by the human hand, a pristine virginal beauty, a vastness that had no boundaries.

OR IS IT HELL? Holding millions of lives in its bowels. Crushing the breath out of their lungs. It's harshness only bringing destruction, suffering and sorrow.

A highly debatable topic between our soldiers and our poets.

"Sahab kya lagta hai aapko, zinda wapas ja payenge yahan se? Sau din kam nahin hote hai," Shiv Kumar (one of the two *jawans* who was part of the mission with Aryan) said. His skin had a pallor that separated him from the snow-clad mountains around him by just a few shade.

"Kya karega wapas jaake," Aryan smiled, wiping the snow-flakes from his face.

"Aisa mat bolo sahab jee, abhee tou shadi bhee nahin manai hai."

"Wapas ja payenge ya nahin, ye tou pata nahin magar haan etna jaroor kah sakta hoon ki kal ke din tere bachche school mein baaki bachcho ko teri bahaduri ke kisse suna-suna ke paka denge."

"Mere bachche?...Ohh terri!...ab samjha... Ye baat hooi na sahab. Bolo bharat mata ki jai...ki jai...ki jai."

Aryan was led to his room. It was a 12 by 12 feet igloo-shaped fiber glass hut, which he was to share with his two *jawans*. The room had humble accompaniments. A *Bukhari,* a kerosene-based heater, an oil-stove, a makeshift cot, a rickety study table and a chair. Images of. Mr. Albert Das showing the opulent 3,200 sq ft 3-bedroom suite in Wilbur Woods which he shared with Ron and Maggy flashed past his eyes. What a contrast in the same quarter of the year he thought.

His first day in the post made him realize far more than what he read in the books in the Snow Battle school. The rarified atmosphere made the daily chores of human survival heroic. Something as simple as tying a shoelace caused so much breathlessness as one feels after climbing fifty steps. It would take Aryan more than 12 minutes to cover 100 meters, a distance he used to cover in 12 seconds, flat. And to add to all these severe physical conditions and acute solitude was an all-pervading threat of the unexpected arrival of an enemy missile. In short, it was actually a fine and fuzzy line between life and death as told by him to Sameera on their first date.

From the time Aryan left Nainital for his unit to his stay at Snow Battle School and then to the climb to his observation post, not a single day passed when his life-force didn't resonate to his father's stirring words. He thought of ways and means to tell Sameera what she meant to him. He desperately waited for the day when he'd be back to civilization. He counted the days backward. He knew he had to do something. Something different. He just didn't know what and how...until one fine day...no...until one chilling Siachen night, "Yess! I've got it," Aryan bounced from his bed. He had finally figured out the answer for his WHAT and HOW. His euphoric hands located the torch in the dark and moved toward the switch on the solar lamp, nearly toppling it over in his eagerness. They then reached for the chewed-top Reynolds pen and the symbolic Artillery crest letter headed writing pad. He had something in mind that he wanted to pen down. After an hour of brain-racking session (at around midnight) he managed to write these lines:

Chapter 1

Friday

Brown...Dark brown...Dark woody brown.

Wall clock...Circular wall clock...

Huge, circular wall clock.The huge, circular, dark woody brown wall clock hanging on the shiny white wall of the Wilbur Woods auditorium showed a perfect noon. An exact 12.The tall and muscular minute-hand of the clock lay above the short and curvaceous hour-hand making a perfect Kama Sutra Missionary position.

For the world, it was 12. For them, they were one. They craved for this brief moment of being one. 60 seconds of blissful companionship after around 3,600 seconds of aching solitude...

Dear readers,

I did not address myself as Aryan in the book because I wasn't really comfortable narrating my own story. Moreover, I thought the book would gain more brownie points, if I reveal the fact that I am the author of the book at the end and thus increase the chances of it becoming a bestseller. Only if a book is a bestseller does Sameera read it. *(she had mentioned it on our second date- "Earlier I was big time into reading...I had this mini library sort of thing in my room but off late I am not able to devote much time so now I just read the selected ones, only the best sellers.").* And it's very important that she reads it. No matter where she is and who she is with, she deserves to know what she's worth. She deserves to feel great about herself like my father felt just by imagining himself to be Sameera for a while that morning. She deserves to brag and boast for the rest of her life.

With due respect to my emotions, I must also confess that writing this book wasn't an easy thing for me to do. I would repeat what I said on the Tequila night. I can't write even a page for the love of anything. I can never imagine myself sitting down on a chair, thinking about a topic and seeing my thoughts crystallize into concrete words. That's not me. Ideas would never hit me if I make up my mind to write something. Even during my school days, Kabeer used to write essays for me. There was another reason why it was such a big deal for me...Till date I haven't read a full novel. I tried a couple of times but could never go past page 10, so I actually had no idea how to structure a book and how to tell a story on paper. Putting a mike to mouth and putting a pen to paper are two TOTALLY bloody different things.

ASK ME ABOUT IT.

Apart from what I've already mentioned, there were three things that kept me motivated to write, despite the woozy bouts of headaches that the chilling, oxygen-denying air provided.

One, a hanger in which the red polka dotted dress was hung. A look-alike of the one Sameera had worn on the Sunday gala evening which I coincidentally came across in one of the showrooms in 17-sector, Chandigarh. The evening prior to the morning I boarded the IL-76. Satya and Shiv Kumar (my buddies in Siachen) did look at the hanger a little strangely and doubted my preference for clothes.

Two, a bottle of Elle YSL, her perfume that I had bought after our first date. One quick squirt before sleeping and one after getting up always did the trick.

Three, a portable Kachibo radio. I must thank Ameen Sayani and *Vividh Bharti* for their constant supply of melodies. Ameen's cheerful booming voice was my only connect with the civilization and a blessing especially on those days when Satya and Shiv Kumar were out at the base camp. I have to admit that on days like those it was easy to get discouraged and frustrated. The only sound that I could hear apart my own voice was the boom of an enemy shell or the rumbling of the rotor blades of the Cheetah helicopter dropping the food item or the howling of the icy winds.

After my successful tenure in Siachen, I moved back to my unit. That's when I sent the e-mail to Ron asking him to call me. And he did call me

....

....

Ron: 'Suckin suck...you are writing a BOOK? But WHY, what's wrong?'

WHAT'S WRONG? how was I supposed to answer such query?

Self: 'Hmmm...nothing wrong...actually…'

Ron: 'Aryan, if my memory serves me right... you used to hate writing.

Oh yes, you did. You had even confessed that."

Self: 'You are right dude. It's a long story. I'll tell you when I meet you.'

Ron: 'What are you writing about, by the way?'

Self: 'I am writing about those three days that I spent with you guys in Wilbur Woods. That's all I have with Sameera.'

Ron: 'SSSAMEERAAAA...MOTHER HELL!...you are still into her?"

Self: 'Deeper than before...but in a different sense.'

Ron: 'Soldier haan. Fuckin son of a gun. I like that! I really like that! Aryan, just hold on there's somebody knocking at the door...'

'Hey sexy, how did your presentation go?'

'It was good. Ron how loudly you speak man. I could hear you on the ground floor.'

'You know who's on the line.'

'Who?'

Aryan...and he's writing a book on me.'

'You mean ARYAN VYAS! Give me the phone.'

Mahi: 'Hey Aryan...Mahi here.'

Self: 'MAHI...Woww! what are you doing in Delhi?'

Mahi: 'How long have you been talking to Ron?'

Self: 'Ten minutes...Fifteen minutes. Why?"

Mahi: 'And I am sure he's not told you that we are engaged and that we both are in Delhi.'

Self: 'ENGAGED?...Ron and you?...you mean that marriage *wala* engaged? Oh god! What bloody news. I love you guys. When? Howww?'

Mahi, the gossip queen recited it all.

....

Mahi: 'You are writing a book for Sameera. God! That's so romantic...Aryan but how come...you *tou* couldn't even...'

Self: 'I know, I know ...I'm coming to Delhi next week. I'll meet you guys and tell you everything in detail.'

Mahi: 'All right done. See you next week. One sec, I'll give back the phone to Ron...I think he's gone to the loo. I'll tell him to call you back. *Chal* then we'll see you next week...ba-bye.'

I met them the coming week. They looked great together. We chatted for long hours over beer. I completed the first half of chapter 13 (the ONE YEAR LATER one) after I met them. Mahi shared all (almost all) the juicy gossip that went among girls. It helped me add those conversations where I wasn't present. They also helped me get one of the best literary agents for publication of my book. My book will soon be published.

There could have been better ways but writing a book is all that I could think of. I thought the best way to express myself before a budding novelist is through a book. I wanted to feel the same kind of feelings that she feels. It couldn't be love so I thought let it be a feeling generating from one of her passion. I've imagined her everyday sitting on her study table, wearing her reading glasses, thinking about her book and scribbling something. And I've done the same on my wobbly study table in the presence of the dark woody brown wall clock…

So what if the minute-hand might never reach the hour-hand.

So what if the 3600 seconds of aching solitude might always dally around...

...I'll live my blissful 60 seconds through the pages of this book, each day and each night...for eternity.

WHO SAYS YOU CAN'T FOOL THE DESTINY !!!!!

Six Months Later

CONCLUDING CHAPTER

Hang on!

I guess, we were done with the book??

Then why this concluding chapter??

Before we budge any further let's get some facts in order. The 14 chapters that you just read were written by Capt. Aryan Vyas (he's picked up his rank). Each and every word. This chapter that you are reading is written by me. Before I tell you who I am, I'd like to tell you why I am writing this chapter. Simply put, it's because I want to share with you all what happened AFTER Aryan's book got published.

You must be thinking if Aryan's book has already got published how this chapter could be a part of his book. Well, it wasn't meant to be a part of his book. It just happened.

Here's how it happened:

Aryan's book was published with much hype by Mr. Pathania's publishing house (courtesy Ron and Mahi). The book did a terrific business and became a bestseller.

Critics claimed that the success of the book was mainly because it was based on true incidents and because the book was different since was written in an inhospitable environment. Lots of e-mails started pouring in. The readers wanted to know what happened next. My own family members were one of them. I was also one of the readers therefore understood how curious each one of us would be to know that 'little more'.

"Aryan don't you agree you owe something to your readers? Shouldn't they know what happened after your book got published? I think you must write a sequel or some thing to your book." I said. I had called Aryan to my office. Well, I have the privilege to call him to my office since he's my junior. You would've got it by now. I am the same senior who wrote his script for the debate. Remember Aryan's confession on Tequila night.

Aryan smiled, "I share the concern sir...but I am no writer. Just got a little lucky. I might not do justice to my readers in my second book. Why don't you write? You know everything."

"No no no no no...something here and there is fine but not a book."

"Don't write a book, add another section to the existing one. Yes! Great idea... add another chapter. I'll speak to Mr. Pathania."

I thought for a while and said, "Why not. I think I can write one chapter...but I need you to help me with it."

See how things change. I am telling ARYAN to help me with writing.

"It'll be an honor sir."

I think I always wanted to be an author, perhaps therefore said yes to the offer or was it that I thought that if Aryan could, why can't I? Whatever it be...what matters is that I have got the opportunity to write. Therefore, with legal permission of Aryan and the publisher I am adding this chapter. I've tried my level best to copy Aryan's style to sustain my reader-friends' interest. I hope I am able to keep the same tone and tempo.

To tell you that 'little more' (which I believe is your book-right), let me take you to 'Vyas Villa' (Aryan's house) where Aryan's father had thrown a grand luncheon party. A party was justified since never before had any Vyas even tried to write a book, leave alone it getting so famous. Except of course, maharishi Ved Vyas, who authored the legendary, Mahabharata.

Vyas Villa, Nainital

This was my first ever visit to Aryan's house. It was a considerably large Villa, Need I mention the charm of an independent house? The feeling of having your own roof and your own lawn. I swear!

Vyas Villa was what can be called an imperial cornucopia of colors. Rich purple and deep crimson bougainvillea competed with the tender-green ivy that attempted to cover every bare patch of the warm honey-colored stone of the bungalow. Giant sized yellow, red and white dahlias lined the drive-in that was made of pebbles sunken into brown earth interspersed with buds of grass. To neutralize these bright shades were the burnt golds and dull greens of the crotons, which peeped coyly from in between their proud counterparts. The expanse of the lush lawn on one side of the Villa was covered with cane and rattan chairs and tables, which were shaded by gigantic billowing white umbrellas.

A red carnation mounted on a slender glass vase atop each table. On the other side of the lawn was a spluttering row of barbecues besides a long table of chafing dishes.

An appetizingly tempting aroma rising from that side of the lawn whetted my digestive juices. The ever-willing waiters in their starched white and black suits seemed to be intent on keeping the guests' glasses filled and hands full. Not anyone was complaining but I already noticed a slur in the speech and a bounce in the gait of many of the guests who were intent on the liquid diet.

At the far end of the lawn, I noticed a stage dressed up royally in blue. The tint it wore was a few shades darker than the tint of the sky that afternoon; besides it was a modest sound system with a cordless mike lying on top of one of the speakers. Aryan's father had told me that Kabeer was going to sing a song for the guests.

I'd specially like to highlight the attendees of this luncheon because it's they who made the party special. Apart from his family and friends (which almost covered half the town), Mr. Subodh Vyas had also invited all those people who were part of the book.

And to my surprise...all of them had come.

We hear stories of people who've achieved sensational success, all around us all the time but only when it happens to somebody among us, somebody we know so well, do we really start beleiving in the power of human spirit. I guess, the Wilbur Wood gang realized that, else why would they want to contribute their time and energies to come all the way to Nainital to the people they didn't know all that well. Of course, they knew that they were no less than mini-celebrities since Mr. Subodh Vyas while inviting them had told them that all his relatives and friends in Nainital had read the book and were looking forward to meeting them (especially Ron).

Looking at the Wilbur Wood gang huddled up in one corner with big smiles spanning the width of their faces it struck me that had it not been for this book they would've never have met as a group again. Then my glance passed over Aryan. Like me, his eyes also seemed to be scanning the guests intently... hoping to see that one person...the one who was the reason for the gathering.

"Aei Ron, come here," the dusky beautiful Bong called her errant fiancé who was as usual ambling over to a group of fairer sex.

"*Aaschi shona.*" If anything, Ron's engagement seemed to have given him the license to hunt far more vociferously.

"Dude, you seem to have lost your magic. The girls are more interested in the guy serving them than in you. Getting old huh," quipped Mrigank.

"Trust you, to get it all wrong. Who would be interested in those anorexic dames when I have THIS kind of flesh in front of me," pat came the answer from a never-lost-for-words Ron. His eyes deliberately lustful, while spanning the length of Mrigank's love, Tiffany.

Yes guys, Tiffany was there too. No matter how hard they tried to mask it, everybody in the group was ogling at the cream and peaches complexioned beauty with wonder in their eyes. Not one of them would have believed that she was way beyond her twenties, leave alone the mother of one in her twenties, had Maggy not confessed it on the Tequila night.

"Will he ever change Mahi?" Rochelle said. Rochelle was just back from a short break in Goa and her complexion had taken on the look of rich melted chocolate, which was alluringly displayed underneathe the hot pants that she had sported. If anything, she had grown more voluptuous and bolder over the months. Well, I don't know whether to attribute this to the time or to the fact that she was no longer a VIRGIN ...courtesy Mr. Akshay Pathania (Mahi's brother)!

Well, it all started with trading of phone numbers at Ron and Mahi's engagement ceremony. Since then the two have been seen together everywhere. Likewise Mr. Pathania and Mrs. (if I may say so) Pathania though officially still a separated couple never lose an opportunity to spend time with each other, obviously always giving it the impression of an official meeting. This match is being so closely played by the respective couples that at times, coincidentally, Akshay and Rochelle are occupying the chairs barely vacated by Mr. & Mrs. Pathania in the clubs and restaurants, which have become their common rendezvous. Everyone is hoping for a reunion between the couple. The older couple.

"I wish I had come for your engagement Ron," Maggy smiled nostalgically. "It's so great to be with you guys again. I think had I tried hard enough I would have probably made it. It's just that I let life and its events overrun me, forgetting what we shared together." He looked at Tiffany with eyes filled with remorse.

"It's ok love," her light blue eyes filled with love and pride, which was the usual case whenever she looked at Maggy, "What's important is that life has given you all an excuse to meet again and you guys should now often create such excuses."

Oh! did I tell you?...Tiffany is one month pregnant. Maggy and Tiffany decided to have a baby. After 3 years of her relationship with Maggy and a lot of thought, Tiffany had concluded that she was not doing any justice to herself or to her now ex-husband by just living their relationship for namesake therefore filed for divorce. She knew that Maggy's family would never allow them to be together and Maggy wouldn't go against them and also that parting ways with Maggy wouldn't be an easy thing for her. So she decided to have a part of him with her...for always. A part of him that would be purely hers.

And she even has her daughters' full support, "Ma, god forbid if something happens to you, I'll take care of the baby...so please do it." It had of course taken a lot of convincing where Maggy was concerned to concede to her wishes but looking at him now one would not believe that. He was beaming from ear to ear like a pregnant daddy.

"Aryan, you celebrity bugger, get your carcass over here," Ron shouted.

"Guys, guys, I hope you'll are taking care of yourselves. You know you'll are family so I'm not exactly behaving like an enthusiastic host," Aryan said with a smile that was a little strained and out of character because it somehow didn't reach his eyes.

"Aryan come here buddy, let me hug you. I am so proud that I am part of this gang and part of your book," Maggy stepped ahead with open arms.

"Aryan be careful not to crush his boobies," Ron grinned.

Maggy somehow feels that Aryan's story inspired him to agree for a baby with Tiffany. Well it's not just him; Rochelle started preparing for GMAT again. Mahi went up to her mother to ask her that she would like to be a VJ, something she always fancied but never dared to ask. Though Aryan's book didn't achieve its aim of touching Sameera, it had still done a lot of beautiful things to lot of people in various ways. I guess all of us need some push to do that extra and his book just did that.

Gave the push.

"You guys are *pundits*, right?" Mahi asked Aryan.

"Yeah, why?"

"I saw that telephone on the verandah. It had a big red *tikka* on it."

"No it's got nothing to do with our being *pundits*. That's Maa and her fantastic beliefs. Since the day papa narrated the book to her, she feels that Sameera will call me on that number some day. Remember, plan Bismarck and the small card I had slipped into her bag with my landline number on it. Maa firmly believes that one day that phone is going to ring with Sameera on the other side. So every morning after her prayers she puts a *tikka* on it."

"That's so sweet," Tiffany said with tears glazing her eyes.

"Yeah," echoed Rochelle and Mahi in equally choked voice.

"My father is a happy man since then. He doesn't have to get up to pick up any phone calls."

"May I please have your attention ladies and gentleman," Mr. Subodh Vyas climbed on the stage holding a cordless mike, "I thought before Kabeer changes his mind let me cash on the opportunity to call him on the stage for a song...ladies and gentleman, please welcome Kabeer."

"Hello...check, one two three," Kabeer tapped the head of the mike and tuned his guitar. As he cleared his throat to sing..trin-trin rang the

MTNL box. All the skulls; small, big; young, old; smiling, not smiling; talking, not talking; good looking, not that good looking turned toward the shrill sound. Aryan's mother went ahead to stifle the sound, "Hello."

"Hello...Auntie *Namaste,* may I talk to Aryan please?"

"*Beta aap kaun?*"

"Auntie *mein* Aryan *ki dost* Sameera,"

"SAMEERA...*beta...*"

"Hello Auntie...Auntie...Hello,"

"*Beta ek* minute, "she kept the receiver on the table fearing she might just burst out, "Aaruu... Sameera," her tears tagged along with her smile. She had planned to say so much...but...It happens.

"Sameera!" Mahi shouted. The word 'Sameera' had created an uproar in the crowd. Before Aryan could wrestle through the crowd, Mahi reached the phone, "Hey Sameera how're you yaar...shit it's been ages. You know we're all at Aryan's place, Ron, Maggy, Roch, and even Tiffany. You know Tiffany, Mags girlfrien... (whispering conspiratorially). Sammy you know Roch is going around with my bro Akshay." Ron looked at Mahi exasperatedly. However, the tirade went on, "We're having so much fun... where are you yaar, we're missing you and...hello, hello, helloooow, shit it got disconnected." Mahi gave an 'I-didn't-do-anything' looks to the crowd, which was glaring right at her.

The phone rang again.

"Ssshhh," Aryan's father sushed the audience, put Aryan on phone and the phone on loudspeaker. Somebody in the crowd gave the idea to put the mike before the phone so that everybody could hear the conversation. Kabeer had an amused smile playing around his lips as he handed over the mike; somewhere deep down he realized his first and maybe only attempt to become a celebrity had been politely snatched.

Every pair of eyes seemed to be boring holes into Aryan's back as he approached the receiver. Aryan hazily took in the keyed up faces of the crowd looking at him. 'Guys, for godsake don't stare like this, I am feeling so akward,' Aryan must have muttered these words in his heart. There was pin drop silence. Even his over-energetic dog Goofy and the nightingale, which diligently woke him up with its shrill kooeiing every morning during his holidays realized the magnitude of the moment.

"Hello," a voice disturbed his body mechanics. A voice that was like a caress to his bruised soul. A voice so familiar that it felt like he had never lived without it.

"Hello," was the best Aryan could afford to return huskily.

"Hi Aryan."

"Hi Sameera."

"How are you?"

"I am good. How are you?"

"I am doing great."

"It's been a long time."

"Yeah, 18 months."

"Ask her about the book," Ron whispered.

Aryan waggled his head for a 'no'.

"Howz your army thing going on?"

"Good…it's good."

"At least ask where she is?" Ron again butted in.

"So…where are you these days?"

"I am in UK."

"Nouuuuhhh," came a simultaneous utterance by the audience. Everybody in the crowd was hoping that she'd be in India. Including Aryan.

"What was that?"

"No nothing..." Aryan managed a, "How's the climate there."

"Lovely, I just love this place."

"And how's life in London School of Business."

"I haven't joined the school yet."

"Oh! so you are just chilling out in london these days."

"London? I am not in London?"

"You said you were in UK, I thought you must be...which city are you in then."

"By UK I meant Uttarakhand, buddhu."

"Did you say U-T-T-A-R-A-K-H-A-N-D?" Aryan repeated foolishly.

"Yeah man she did," somebody from behind, shouted.

"Yes, I am in summer capital of Uttarakhand."

"You are in NAINITAL. Where?"

"Outside this big, sturdy black gate...there's a small marble slab built into one of the impressive pillars of the gate. It has something written on it. Just one sec, let me see more closely what it reads. It says, V...Y...A...S oh! It reads Vyas Villa. Would you know where this leads?"

[Sameera's phone call was not a coincidence. It was a planned thing. She had actually called a week back at this number and Aryan's father had picked up the phone. Aryan's mother somehow missed the opportunity to be the first to talk to Sameera. She had gone with Gupta auntie to Swati didi's place. No, this time it wasn't to admire the new born calf. It was something more important. Taste the newly made mango pickle. She is a busy person, I tell you.

The luncheon party was actually a brainchild of Sameera. She had searched all the addresses and phone numbers of the people who were part of the book and had given them to Mr. Subodh Vyas. She wanted it to be grand and theatrical. Like how Aryan would do. It was Mr.

Subodh's idea to use Kabeer's latent talent as a lure to get the gathering's attention. Once Kabeer got the attention of the crowd, Mr. Vyas surreptiously called up Sameera and gave her the go-ahead for the prank that she had planned. Poor Kabir (guniea pig) was demoted to humbler grounds (which was basically below the stage).

Sameera had always liked Aryan but being the kind of person she was, she never understood the intensity of her feelings for him. Somewhere deep down she was afraid to love and give him all. She always liked to be in control of situations and was secretly afraid of losing her focus in life by anything that could cause her to feel too much of joy, or too much of sorrow. That was one of the reasons why Sameera never emoted too much and never allowed herself to get too moved by any situation. This could have been partly owing to the disciplined way in which she had been brought up and reiterated by the painful experience that she had with her ex-boyfriend. Whatever the reasons, Sameera had so far shut herself up in a little fortress hoping that she would rule the world from there.

In spite of smelling danger when she met Aryan, Sameera was unable to keep herself completely away. Even after she made her decisions about Varun and her career, she couldn't exactly get Aryan out of the mind. She even tried to contact him but somehow couldn't reach him. She went as far as enquiring about him from the rest of the gang, but nobody knew his whereabouts. Of course, she never admitted to herself that she thought about him and used his disappearance to strengthen her resolve to succeed in life.

She mule-headedly believed that to do something larger than life, one has to sacrifice all those feelings that can sidetrack one's focus and that her career would never go places if she mixes emotions with it. Therefore she took what she thought was a wiser and business like decision of planning her life with Varun, who was from an influential family and could thus take her aspirations forward. She dedicated a chapter in her book to the Delhi trip hoping that with this contribution she could relegate Aryan to the archives.

And then...one fine day she came across Aryan's book. Each page unfolded a new meaning to her life; challenged her belief; glorified her beauty; reveled in her power. She smiled with it, laughed with it, and cried with it. She must have read the part about his proposal on stage at least a dozen times. It touched her in hidden places, made her a narcissist. She started loving her edible skin that threw light and warmth without flames; her symmetrical, well-treated, kissable feet; her flattering arcs and bends and the Victorian pride in her smile. It made her feel alive; it made her want to experience things that she was shit scared of and for the first time in her life she realized that she loved being shit scared. Aryan's tribute became Sameera's Bible

She upturned all her old handbags and finally found it. The little plan-B card with the bold scribble...Vanilla boy- 05942238576.

"Maa, I am into journalism, writing is my passion, my forté I worked for almost one and a half year to write my book and I could barely manage a nomination in the Amazon breakthrough novel award. Whearas Aryan, who has no credentials to write a book, wrote a book in just four months on the three days that he spent with me and won the award. How would you explain that?" Apparently, Sameera's mom and dad had also read the book.

"I know it's hard to explain. I believe he's taken his sweet revenge for not noticing him. It's his way to tell you that he's the best thing that can ever happen to you and I agree with him."

"Dad I'm sending a copy of Aryan's book to Varun along with a letter. I am sure Varun will understand what's right for three of us. I want my blissful 60 seconds to start as soon as possible."]

'VYAS VILLA...*Oye bahadur* gate khol,' shouted a suddenly galvanized Aryan.

The big, sturdy black gate opened.

A little mascara...some lip-gloss...and a lot of mysterious sensuality in a figure-hugging red polka dotted dress stood at the entrance gate of Vyas Villa. Aryan's eyes lit up with a smile that aimed straight at her heart. The smile was akin to the one my face throws in the first two minutes, when I show myself to the January Sun after a chilling cold bath.

"Bhai pakka 9.9 hai," Kabeer's lascivious look communicated the sentiments of the crowd.

As she approached him, Aryan recalled every king sized minute detail of their moments together. The typical cool looks and those uncharacteristic sudden warm rushes of colour that said more about her than she wanted to reveal. The way her eyes would softly light up when they spotted him. The rhythmic sway of her hips when she would walk towards him. Those slender well-groomed fingers that he had longed to feel. That gentle curve of waist that he longed to hold. Every day he had touched each of them wondrously. Every night he re-lived each moment. It was his lullaby, his mantra, which offered him few hours of bliss.

So mesmerized was Aryan that only when she breezed past him did he realize that she was angling for the small stage and not him. With a determined gleam in her eyes Sameera picked up the mike, held it with both her hands, looked straight into Aryan's eyes and dropped her upper body on to the floor of the stage on her knees. Exactly like how Aryan had done. The act left the audience shocked. If I am not wrong, Aryan had his trousers on; moreoever his *fauji* knees were conditioned for such impact.

Bated breaths were anxious for what was to come.

She shut her eyes for a moment, took a deep breath and in a voice that could make any man go weak in the knees verbalized, "Even if I've not had one too many tequila shots I'll pretend to be drunk so that I feel your arms around me while you carry me home, change me into my nightclothes and tuck me into bed and then just when you think I'm fast asleep I'll reach out for you and hold on to you like I'm never going to let you go. I too will make your interests my passion, even if it means I'm bored to death," she smiled. "Infact I've already started watching Soccer matches...the English premier league. I think we can have far more interesting matches between us. After we've had an argument and you've apologised, I'll instantly smile coz I know when I smile your chinki eyes too smile and I LLLOVE the way they crinkle up at the corners...they provoked me to message you for our second date by the way. I'll also exercise and keep myself fit and light so that when I become old and weak and have trouble in climbing the steps owing to my backaches you can still easily swing me up into your arms and carry me up. I'll learn pole dancing for you and entertain you with some whacky moves in the evenings after you are back from office. Don't blush now...I know you like exotic dancestyles, I checked out your orkut profile. I'll make you brush eyeliner on to my eyelids even when I'm not getting late for office coz when you look into my eyes you put me on to a different league altogether. League of proud and arrogant ladies...Dear Vanilla boy...I was wondering if I could ask you out for a small chit-chat over breakfast tomorrow morning...may be some freshly baked croissants layered with thick creamy cheese, hash browns, farm-fresh eggs and some black grape juice." she winked brashly like a teenage boy.

The crowd broke out into a cacophony of hooting, cheering and whistling. And why not? There are only few opportunities that life presents us with, to experience joy in its truest and most undiluted form...and this certainly was one of those.

"Mahi, make sure you too learn pole dancing lessons with Sameera. I also want some sizzling entertainment in the evenings." Ron said.

"Ssshhh...look there."

The Unshakable Rock and the Calm Stream started walking toward each other, as if in a trance. Their eyes locked in a gaze that almost seemed as if they were already caressing each other; effortlessly brushing through the crowd, not realizing for a minute that there was a lot of jostling and jolting amongst the audience to clear the path. It took forever for them to cross those few yards, far longer than the one and a half year that had passed without them seeing each other. All sorts of implausible and impracticable thoughts started flashing through my mind. What if something happens now to prevent them from reaching each other? I realized I was desperately sending up a fervent prayer to God to let nothing happen now. Crazy thoughts from a crazy mind but somehow I felt that each one of us standing there was sending up the same wonderfully mad prayer......No God, nothing now, nothing to prevent them from meeting, touching and loving each other.

They just stood in front of each other for what appeared like a long while. Eyes overfilled with moist emotions. Aryan reached out to her gently, bundling her into his chest. The broad frame that she had longed to be engulfed in for months draped itself around her. They stood wrapped in each other, seemingly comforted just by feeling the other. She ran her hands over his broad chest, sinewy arms, tanned neck and then progressed upwards; tracing lines over his brows, caressing his fanning lashes, and gently running down his nose. It appeared as if she was using her fingers to taste him.

He moved his hands away from her and she moaned at this meanness but soon realized that they had left her so that they could bring some life elsewhere too. They gently kneaded her arms, rounded her elbows and then moved down to the throbbing transparent skin covering the veins on her wrists. Aryan was touching her as if she was a wax doll, cautious to exert any pressure lest it gets spoiled.

Sameera looked at him and smiled as if she had guessed his thoughts. That smile was his undoing. Those pearly teeth peeping through the soft pouty mound was actually his death. Everybody and everything melted into nothingness. His parents, his family, his friends didn't seem to inhabit the space that surrounded them. The space went only as far as Sameera. Coming from the kind of background, I am sure his next few moments would not have progressed thus, had it not been for the mirage that only a lover's mind can create. He gathered her up in his arms and pressed her against his length. It was as if his body was trying to swallow her up. Like a devotee placing his lips on the ground of his worship place, Aryan reverently bent down on Sameera.

Another myth shattered.

Another education added.

He now knew that much softer things exist. Softer than silk, velvet...and her hands. Her lips.

Sameera was now beyond all bounds of reality. She impatiently stood on her tiptoes to make up for the 4 inches of height. She pulled his head closer to her and started nibbling each lip like how a hungry puppy feeds itself on its mother's milk.

Their tears became one flow, their bodies fitted into each other like a clever jigsaw puzzle. For once, their mind was thinking similar thoughts...could anything in this world be more real, more beautiful or more worth living for.

"I am sure if Aryan records himself on Guiness book of record he'll win an award,"

Ron announced.

"What award?" Mahi crumpled her cute nose.

"Award for the most deserving kiss."

There are only two breeds of people...one who've experienced the magic and one who're yet to experience, coz things fuckin' happen...you just gotta ask for it...loudly...madly... passionately...ARYANLY!!

